BEACHES

Iris Rainer Dart

BANTAM BOOKS

TORONTO • NEW YORK • LONDON • SYDNEY • AUCKLAND

BEACHES

A Bantam Book

Bantam hardcover edition / June 1985

Bantam paperback edition / July 1986
9 printings through December 1988

ACKNOWLEDGMENTS

"Toot, Toot, Tootsie! (Good-Bye)" by Gus Kahn, Ernie Erdman, Ted Fiorito © 1922, Renewed 1950, Leo Feist, Inc. Rights assigned to CBS Catalogue Partnership. All rights controlled and administered by CBS Feist Catalogue Inc. All rights reserved. International Copyright Secured. Used by permission.

"You've Got to See Mama Ev'ry Night" by Billy Rose and Con Conrad © 1922, 1923 Renewed 1950, 1951 Leo Feist, Inc. Rights assigned to CBS Catalogue Partnership. All rights controlled and administered by CBS Feist Catalogue Inc. All rights reserved. International Copyright Secured. Used by permission.

"I'll Build a Stairway to Paradise" by George and Ira Gershwin and B. G. DeSylva © 1922 (Renewed) New World Music Corporation. All rights reserved. Used by permission.

"This Was a Real Nice Clam Bake" by Richard Rodgers and Oscar Hammerstein II © 1945 Williamson Music Inc. Copyright renewed. Sole Selling Agent—T. B. Harms Company (c/o The Welk Music Group, Santa Monica, CA 90401). International Copyright Secured. All rights reserved. Used by permission.

"You'll Never Walk Alone" by Richard Rodgers and Oscar Hammerstein II © 1945 Williamson Music Inc. Copyright renewed. Sole Selling Agent—T. B. Harms Company (c/o The Welk Music Group, Santa Monica, CA 90401). International Copyright Secured. All rights reserved. Used by permission.

"Poor Butterfly" by John Golden and Raymond Hubbel © 1916 (Renewed) Warner Bros. Inc. All rights reserved. Used by permission.

"Cecilia" by Herman Ruby and Dave Dyer © 1925 by Bourne Co. Copyright renewed. Used by permission.

"Ballin' the Jack" by Chris Smith and Jim Burris © 1913 by Jerry Vogel Music Co. Inc. E. B. Marks Music Company. Renewed 1980 Jerry Vogel Music and Christie-Max Music. Used by permission.

ISBN 0-553-27746-4

Published simultaneously in the United States and Canada

Bantam Books are published by Bantam Books, a division of Bantam Doubleday Dell Publishing Group, Inc. Its trademark, consisting of the words "Bantam Books" and the portrayal of a rooster, is Registered in the United States Patent and Trademark Office and in other countries. Marca Registrada. Bantam Books, 666 Fifth Avenue, New York, New York 10103.

PRINTED IN THE UNITED STATES OF AMERICA

O   18   17   16   15   14   13   12   11   10

Cee Cee got up casually and walked toward the piano. She was wearing white pants and a blue print Hawaiian shirt tied up, so her newly-thin-from-the-water-diet midriff showed.

Bertie watched her with awe. Bertie couldn't stand up in a strange restaurant and have everyone look at her, even to tell them the place was on fire, and now Cee Cee was going to stand there and sing with some piano player she'd never met before.

Cee sang her hit "I Wish You Love." After the first two bars, all the people who were eating stopped to listen. She was wonderful. To put such feeling into a soapy ballad. When the song was over the audience burst into applause, stomping and yelling for more.

Cee Cee had a look on her face Bertie could only describe as regal. She walked slowly back to the table with her head held high, and when some people shouted "More! More!" she finally smiled a little smile, shook her head no and sat down.

"You were great, Cee," Bertie told her best friend from childhood. Cee Cee, deadpan, downed the rest of her sake.

BEACHES

"*Beaches* is a carefully crafted novel that captures the essence of the need embodied in all human relationships. Its stunning conclusion is testimony to the meaning of every 'I'll be there' promised in friendship."

—*The Pittsburgh Press*

"Dart's writing is full of humor, vitality and an appealing sensitivity to the vagaries of human nature."

—*Los Angeles Magazine*

For STEPHEN DART
because his wisdom,
integrity, and fire inspire everything I do.

. . . if your love were a grain of sand,
mine would be a universe of beaches.

William Goldman,
The Princess Bride

AND

For GREGORY MICHAEL WOLF because his
sensitivity, warmth, and maturity are a loving lesson
to everyone who knows him.

Special Thank-Yous

SANDY MALAMUD—For the beaches we walked together and for your unconditional support.

MARY BLANN

ELAINE MARKSON

GEORGE ECKSTEIN

ALFRED PASTERNAK, M.D.

JEANNE BERNKOPF

PENNY LIEBERMAN

ELLIE TURK BARMEN

Los Angeles, California, 1983

The dancers were holding Cee Cee above their heads. "And now," she said, "as I lie in the arms of four promiscuous homosexuals from West Hollywood, my tits pointed towards the heavens like an offering to the gods, I slowly turn my head, look out at America and ask the musical question . . ."

Everyone was laughing. The dancers were laughing so hard they made Cee Cee bounce up and down. Then Hal played the arpeggio and Cee Cee sang,

> Toot, toot, tootsie good-bye!
> Toot, toot, tootsie don't cry,

with the slow soulful rhythm of a torch song. Then the dancers turned front, and Cee Cee slithered down their shoulders and their backs until she stood on the floor with the four handsome boys swaying behind her.

The little red light on the phone had been lighting up for a long time. The stage manager grabbed the receiver, put it up to his left ear and put his finger in his right ear so he could hear above the din of the music.

"Yeah?" he whispered into the phone. It was someone for Cee Cee.

"She's workin'," he said softly. "Huh?"

The caller was a woman and she wouldn't take no. The stage manager shrugged, told her to hold on, and then put the receiver down on the long table next to some scripts. Hey, Cee Cee Bloom was singing. As far as he was concerned the whole world could hold on.

> *The choo choo train that takes me,*
> *Away from you no words can*
> *tell how sad it makes me.*

Now the music went into the up tempo, and the boy dancers began to tap-dance and Cee Cee was tapping, too, keeping up with them. Her skill was remarkable. She hadn't tapped in years and it was hard, but she'd been knocking herself out for the last few weeks working on it, trying to get it back.

"Hey!" Cee Cee yelled as she came out of a turn. "These bozos are twenty-two years old and I'm thirty-six. So applaud, for chrissake."

Everyone laughed and applauded. The crew and the guest stars and the director and the guy from the network. Somebody even cheered bravo, and now Cee Cee whirled around the room looking just as skilled as the boy dancers. Someone, maybe it was one of the writers, whistled one of those whistles that people whistle for taxis in New York, and Cee Cee cracked a smile.

"All right," she hollered, "could I get you to fall for thirty-nine?" Everyone laughed, applauded, and cheered again.

Toot, toot tootsie don't cry
Toot, toot, tootsie good-bye!

Suddenly, the dancers lifted her onto their shoulders and twirled around. She raised her arms in the air. The crowd was applauding and stomping and cheering as the song ended, and Cee Cee was helped to the floor. The choreographer, elated with his own success, hugged her, and the director hugged her, and all the boy dancers hugged her.

"You did great on the hard parts," Lester, the curly-haired dancer said.

"Are you kidding?" Cee Cee answered. "Everybody knows hard parts are my specialty." The dancers laughed.

"Who's on the phone?" the wardrobe mistress asked.

"No one," the director said. "Hang it up."

The wardrobe mistress picked up the telephone receiver and held it to her ear.

"Hello?" She listened. "Just a second. Cee Cee," the wardrobe mistress called.

"Later," Cee Cee told her. "I'll have to call 'em back."

The wardrobe mistress held the phone receiver out to Cee Cee. She had a helpless look on her face.

"Roberta Barron," she said. She hoped Cee Cee would shrug noncommittally; then the phone could go back in its cradle and disconnect, and the wardrobe mistress could call her boyfriend and ask him what he wanted for dinner.

"Who?"

Good, it was no one important. The wardrobe mistress could hang up.

"Barron. Roberta."

Cee Cee ran to the phone and grabbed it out of the wardrobe mistress's hand.

"Lunch, people. One hour," the director said. Everyone was milling and talking and getting their things together.

Cee Cee spoke into the phone in a voice that didn't sound like her usual voice because it was almost timid.

"Bert, is it you?"

Her face was scrunched up as if that would help her to hear better over all the noise.

"Huh?" she said, working at listening. "Talk louder, Bert—I'm in a room full of people."

Later, when the others were trying frantically to locate her, someone who had been standing nearby remembered that what Cee Cee had said next was, "Hey, I get it. I'll *be* there." Then she had ripped part of an inside page out of a script that was on the table, scribbled something on it, and put it in her purse. After that, she hung up the phone and walked quickly out of the rehearsal hall. Everyone thought she was going to lunch. But they were wrong.

Atlantic City, New Jersey, 1951

Bertie White was lost. Not the kind of lost where you think you might know where you are. She was really, honest-to-God lost. She'd been digging with her bucket and shovel near the shoreline just down from where her mom was sitting when she spotted a great big seashell a few feet away, and then another one. Her bucket was getting all filled up with the pretty shells, so she just kept walking. But when she stopped to look around, she didn't see anyone she knew. Not her mom or her Aunt Neetie or anyone from Pittsburgh.

Bertie contemplated the busy, crowded boardwalk.

Well, there's the Traymore Hotel, she thought, reading the sign. Were we sitting near that beach . . . or was it—?

A chill came over Bertie. What if she couldn't find her mom? What if her mom couldn't find *her*?

Maybe the beach was too crowded and she'd be better off walking along the boardwalk and looking down. She could spot her mom and Aunt Neetie from up there.

Bertie ran up the beach toward the boardwalk. She got to the big wooden steps and turned to look back at the beach. So many people! And where were her bucket and shovel? Bertie's lower lip trembled and her face collapsed into a mask of sadness. The tears came and she sobbed aloud for her mom, who was responsible for this, anyway.

Sitting on the beach all day with Aunt Neetie yakking and smoking cigarettes and putting oil all over Bertie with sandy hands. Bertie hated sandy hands. And she hated her mom and Aunt Neetie for letting her get lost like this.

"Awwwww," she sobbed. "Awwww, noooooo."

"Hey, fa chrissake. Would ya mind shuttin' up ovah there?"

Bertie turned. The voice was coming from under the boardwalk.

"I mean, Jesus. I knock myself out workin' and I just wanna get a nap. Ya know?"

"I'm lost," Bertie sobbed to the voice. "I'm lost and I'm scared."

"Ah, fa chrissake. What *are* you? Some kinda baby or somethin'?" The voice was getting closer.

Bertie bit her lip. She was certainly not any kind of baby. She was only in second grade, but her teacher said her reading was on a fifth-grade level. And that was no baby.

"When I was your age, I was already in the business," said the voice, and out of the darkness stepped a little girl of ten.

Bertie looked at her. Cee Cee was skinny with very curly red hair. She was wearing a plaid cotton one-piece bathing suit with a little skirt attached. And nail polish. Red! On every finger and toe.

"Boy, I was dead to the world under there, kiddo," Cee Cee said. "I was up till two in the morning. We had to put on an extra show."

"I'm lost," said Bertie.

"Relax, kid," Cee Cee said. "You're not lost anymore. *I* found you! I'm Cee Cee Bloom. Recognize me?"

"Huh?" Bertie answered.

"Maybe out of sequins I look different. I do the 'Mama' number."

"Huh?" Bertie repeated.

"At Jerry Grey's. You been there?"

Bertie shook her head.

"Never been there? Jeez, whaddya been doin', for chrissake? Every kid on vacation in Atlantic City comes to Jerry Grey's Kiddie Show down at the Steel Pier. It's the greatest."

Bertie felt bad. She considered crying again.

"I do the 'Mama' number."

> *You've got to see mama ev'ry night,*
> *Or you can't see mama at all,*

Cee Cee sang.

Bertie listened. That voice. It sounded like a real person's voice. Not a kid's, but a lady's.

> *You've got to kiss mama, treat her right,*
> *Or she won't be home when you call.*

Cee Cee was starting to get into the song. Her little lips did funny things when she sang. Even when her voice had finished a word in the song, her lips kept moving. Her hands with the polished nails did what Bertie's mom called "the motions." Bertie's mom used to sing sometimes in front of the mirror, and she once told Bertie, "You can't sing a song without the motions."

> *If you want my company,*
> *You can't fifty-fifty me. . . .*

Bertie blushed. One of the motions Cee Cee did was
to put her hands right on her own bust, or rather, where
her bust would have been if she had one. If there was one
thing Bertie knew for sure, it was that you didn't ever
touch your bust in public, whether you had one or not.

> *You've got to see mama every night,*
> *Or you can't see mama at all.*

"Then I do a real hot tap," Cee Cee said. "But I can't
do it here. I haven't got the right shoes. And then I come
back to the last two lines and I really sell it. It's a show-
stopper. Ya know what I mean?"

"I'm lost," said Bertie. The words had little meaning
now, but she didn't know what else to say.

"Fa chrissake. Is that all you can say?"

"Will you help me find my mom and Aunt Neetie?"
Bertie asked.

"How old are you, kid?"

"Seven."

"Seven? Jeez. I'm ten. Practically old enough to nurse
you."

"My mom was sitting on the beach and I . . ."

"You sure are serious about finding your mom," Cee
Cee said. "I spend half my time trying to *lose* mine."

"Oh, you do, huh, you little shtoonk. I'll beat you
black and blue when I get my hands on you," came a voice
from up on the boardwalk. The two girls looked up.

"Aww, crap," muttered Cee Cee.

Rumbling down the steps came the fattest woman
Bertie had ever seen. She wore a giant yellow beach hat
and a dress that showed legs that looked as though she had
borrowed them from a hippo. Each of the old wooden
steps from the boardwalk sank as her weight fell on them.
Bertie couldn't understand why the woman looked familiar
until she took a side glance at Cee Cee, and then realized
that if someone took one of those air pumps that they used

to blow up Mickey Mouse for the Macy's parade and blew up Cee Cee, she would look exactly like this woman.

"Oh, Leona, take it easy," Cee Cee said as the woman fell on her in tears.

"I woke up and you was gone, ya little brat. What was I gonna think, fa chrissake?" Leona sobbed. "And then Mistah Grey called. He said he's got somethin' big ta tell us. I sweah to God, Cee, I almost called the cops."

"Leona, you're a real jerk!" Cee Cee said.

Bertie thought it was amazing that Leona hadn't even noticed that her daughter had said something terrible to her. She just wiped her eyes.

"Is this kid in the show?" Leona asked, pointing to Bertie.

"Nah."

"Well, let's go. Over to the pier. Come on," Leona said, reaching for Cee Cee's arm. Cee Cee took a deliberate step away so Leona couldn't touch her.

"I'm comin'! I'm comin'!" she said.

Leona turned and started back toward the steps to the boardwalk. Cee Cee walked a few feet behind her, slowly, looking down, watching the impressions her red-polished toes made in the sand. Cee Cee was on the bottom step when Bertie spoke in a tiny voice.

"I'm lost."

There were lots of noisy people on the beach, and the roar of the surf was very loud, but still Cee Cee heard Bertie's voice and turned back.

"What's your name?" Cee Cee asked her.

"Bertie."

"Ya mean like the kind that sing in the trees?"

"Nope. Short for Roberta."

"Ah. Cute," said Cee Cee. "Well, whaddya waitin' for?" she asked, and moved her head in a way that meant come with us.

Bertie had no idea where they were going, but she

knew that she didn't ever want Cee Cee to be out of her sight again, so she went.

Jerry Grey's office was at the back of the Steel Pier. To get there, they walked by the Auto Show where Bertie had passed before with her mom and Aunt .Neetie in the straw carriage pushed by the colored man. Then through the building and up a long staircase. Bertie must have gotten a sunburn while she was looking for shells, because now in the cool of the building her bathing suit straps were hurting. Leona trailed behind the two girls, panting as she walked up the steps.

"Be polite," she yelled ahead to Cee Cee, who was already at the top; Bertie was between them. "No swearin'."

Cee Cee waited at the top for Bertie and Leona, and the three of them walked to an open door at the end of the hallway.

Jerry Grey was a little fat man. Not as fat as Leona, but his belt buckled under his large stomach.

"Kid," he shouted, coming around from the back of the desk, arms open to give Cee Cee a hug.

"Whaddya say, Jerry," said Cee Cee, extending her hand to avoid the hug.

"Kid, I got great news. Sit down."

There were two wooden chairs next to the desk. Bertie sat in one and Cee Cee in the other. Leona stood, fanning herself with the big yellow straw hat.

"Last night, kid," said Jerry directly to Cee Cee, "unbeknownst to even me, there was a guy from Hollywood in the audience."

"Hollywood," Leona screamed out, so loud it made Bertie jump. "Oh, my God!"

"Seems the guy couldn't sleep, so he was walking on the boardwalk and stopped in for our twelve o'clock show. See? And all the mothers thought I was a slave driver making you kids do three shows last night. Well, God moves in mysterious ways."

Cee Cee sat silently.

"Well, he liked Lewandowski a lot. A whole lot. Thought her handwalk on the lighted staircase was great."

"Yeah, yeah," said Leona impatiently, starting to pant again.

Jerry didn't look at her. "But he loved you, kid! He called me this morning and that's all he could talk about. Besides mentioning Lewandowski, that is. The kid that did the Mama number. The son of a gun couldn't believe that was really you singing. Said you must have been pantomiming a record."

Bertie looked at Cee Cee for a hint at the excitement she must be feeling.

Cee Cee's face was a blank. "So?" she asked.

"So?" Grey said excitedly. "So? So he wants you to have a screen test."

Leona let out a wail and waddled over to Bertie's chair.

"Oh, my God. I gotta sit down," she said, tapping Bertie hard on the arm. Bertie jumped up, and Leona's big body fell into the chair.

"Oh, my God. A screen test."

"When?" Cee Cee asked.

"Well, he wants to see you again. Today. I'll call him now. I'll have him here right away. At three o'clock. Hollywood," said Jerry Grey.

Bertie wasn't sure, but she thought his eyes filled with tears.

"Some of my kids have been on Broadway . . . but Hollywood." He put his head in his hands and just sat there.

Bertie, Cee Cee, and Leona walked down the stairs and through the building.

"You start getting ready," Leona said. "I'll go get some sandwiches."

"C'mon, kid," Cee Cee said, taking Bertie's hand. Leona walked out of the building, and Cee Cee walked with Bertie to a big brown door marked 'Backstage.' She pushed the door open, and cool darkness surrounded them as they walked inside.

Bertie looked up at the enormous fly gallery and the massive area beyond it that she figured must be the stage. She couldn't move. She had never seen anything like it before.

"Move it, kid," Cee Cee said, pulling Bertie's arm. "I gotta be in full dress, fa chrissake." They walked past the various colored flats and behind the vast black curtains to the dressing room. A small room with six mirrors, each surrounded by six bare light bulbs.

Cee Cee plopped herself down in a chair. There was a telegram stuck in the corner of her mirror. YOU MAY SING ABOUT YOUR MAMA BUT YOU'RE STILL MY GIRL—LOVE DADDY. Cee Cee opened what looked like a blue metal toolbox. It was filled with makeup. Bertie peeked inside. She gazed at the little round metal containers. Some had names on them. Clown white. Lip rouge. Some of them had only numbers.

Cee Cee pulled out a parrot green tube with a black cap and removed the cap. She turned on the mirror light and squeezed some of the contents of the tube onto her finger. A little blob on her forehead, one on each cheek, and one on her chin. Quickly she smoothed them out across her face until it was a creamy suntan color.

Bertie watched the way Cee Cee's tiny red-tipped hands dug into the blue metal chest, taking out first one little container and then another. Blue for her eyelids, red for her cheeks, a little white under the eyebrows, a different red for her lips, some black stuff in a tiny red box marked Maybelline that she applied to her eyelashes with an itty-bitty brush.

Bertie couldn't believe it. Cee Cee looked like a movie star.

The door opened and Leona came in carrying a paper bag.

"Anybody hungry? I'm starving," Leona said, rummaging through the bag, peeking in the waxed paper for her own sandwich.

Cee Cee didn't answer. Bertie wasn't hungry. Leona started eating.

"What time is it?" Cee Cee asked, getting up.

"Ten to three," Leona told her.

"Is Harry gonna be here?" Cee Cee asked. "Is he playin' for me?"

"I guess so," Leona said, getting up. "I'm sure Jerry'll get him over here." She wiped her hands off on a napkin and started going through the rack of clothes that hung near the wall.

"Which one?" she asked.

"The red," Cee Cee said positively.

"Why the red?"

"It's what I wore last night. Sit down and eat, Leona. Bertie will help me."

"No, it's okay. I'll eat later!"

"Leona!"

"Okay."

Cee Cee had removed her bathing suit and now stood naked. She pulled out a pair of red mesh stockings and put them on. Here and there in the mesh was a tiny rhinestone. Her grown-up, made-up face looked weird with her little-girl body. She took down a hanger with something red and sparkly on it and handed it to Bertie.

"You hold it while I step into it," she said.

Bertie wasn't sure she was holding it right, but she held it anyway. It didn't seem to have any recognizable form, no arms or legs or a label on the back so you could tell where the front was. Cee Cee seemed to know what she was doing, though. With great agility, she stepped into two holes, put her arms through two others, did a little shimmy to pull it up, and there she was, resplendent in a tiny red-sequined suit that clung to her child's body in a way that made it look almost curvy. Out of a little

cardboard box she pulled a sparkly red pair of shoes with
taps on them and sat down on the floor to put them on.

"I'm ready," she said.

"Tune up," said Leona.

"No."

Cee Cee took Bertie's hand and they walked back
toward the backstage area. Cee Cee's taps clicked on the
hard floor.

"Sometimes I puke before I go on," she told Bertie,
"but this is just an audition." As they approached the area
next to the stage, a tall man wearing a bright purple
long-sleeved shirt and a matching scarf around his neck
came running toward Leona.

"Oh, my God," he said, "can you believe this?"

"You got the music?" Leona asked.

"Oh, sweetie, do I ever," the man named Harry said.
"And when the kid's a star, honey, just remember who
never played a wrong note for her, even saved her ass a
few times on the high notes. You know?"

Cee Cee had wandered over to the stage. She took
the edge of the large curtain in her hand and pulled it
back ever so slightly and peeked out at the auditorium.

"They're coming in," she said, turning quickly to
Harry, Leona, and Bertie. It was the first trace of true
excitement Bertie had seen from her.

"Harry, hurry up."

"Whaddya mean?"

"Get to that piano," Cee Cee said, her teeth clenched.

"I'm not moving until Jerry tells me to," Harry said
haughtily. "He's my boss, little Miss Movie Star, not
you."

"Aw, go on, Harry," Leona pleaded. "Warm them up
a little. Play a few tunes."

"Absolutely not," Harry said.

"Fine, Harry," Cee Cee said. "You're right. Wait till
Jerry Grey, the king of the kiddie shows, tells you what to
do."

"But it would be such a good warm-up," Leona began.

"Say, Ma," Cee Cee said sweetly. It was the first time Bertie had heard her call Leona anything but Leona. "What's Charlie doin' these days? The crippled kid who used to play for my recitals? I'll bet he'd love Hollywood."

Harry pouted and walked across the stage and down the steps to the piano. Bertie could see him from where she was standing, even though the piano was in the orchestra pit. He spread all the music out on the piano and then he waved to Jerry Grey and said something that sounded to Bertie like, "Any requests?" Then he laughed and dusted off the piano stool and twisted it around a few times to make it just the right height, and unbuttoned his cuffs and shuffled through the music a few times and smiled out to where Jerry Grey was sitting and brushed back his hair, and buttoned his cuffs, until Jerry Grey finally yelled, "Hey, Harry. Get on with it. Bring out the kid."

Bertie was nervous. All of a sudden, she had a strange feeling that she was the one who was supposed to go out there. It was as though any second, by mistake, somebody might give her a big push and she'd find herself standing on the stage wearing the mesh stockings that had a rhinestone here and there, and that red-sequined thing, singing that song of Cee Cee's. Bertie came out of her reverie. Cee Cee was already on stage. And that voice. That great big grown-up voice was a hundred times bigger, a hundred times better than it had been when they were standing near the boardwalk earlier. Bertie moved closer to the stage. It was difficult seeing past Leona who stood clinging to the curtain's edge, moaning ever so slightly.

Now Cee Cee was doing what Bertie figured must be the part Cee Cee had described as the "hot tap." Harry pounded a few chords on the piano and then he stopped. The only sound in the place was Cee Cee's taps on the wooden floor. Then Harry played a few more chords and Cee Cee moved those bright red shoes and made her feet fly all around. Harry began to play the regular music again, and Cee Cee whirled in a giant circle around the stage until she was almost near the center. Then suddenly, as if she'd just thought of it, she did a perfect cartwheel and stood up. Without a gasp, in perfect control, the voice came, belting out the last two lines.

> *You've got to see mama ev'ry night,*
> *Or you can't . . .*
> *No, you can't . . .*

Harry pounded the piano dramatically.

> *See mama . . .*
> *At all!!!!*

Cee Cee's arms stretched to the sky until her last note was completed, and when it was, she leaned forward at the waist in a deep, deep bow.

Bertie and Leona jumped up and down with excitement. Leona was crying and laughing, and without warning, she picked a surprised Bertie up into her big flabby arms and swung her happily in a circle.

Harry was still playing as Cee Cee ran off the stage in the other direction and then ran back on, blowing kisses.

She ran offstage for the last time and the music stopped. There had been some applause during the playoff, but now there wasn't a sound. Bertie and Leona stood looking across to the other side of the wings at Cee Cee who just stood there as though she was in shock.

Everyone, including Harry, was frozen to the spots they were in when the song ended. The silence seemed to go on forever.

Jerry Grey's voice broke the stillness. "Kid," he yelled, "kid, c'mon out."

Cee Cee took a deep breath and walked slowly to the edge of the stage.

"This is Joe Melman," Jerry said, "and his wife, Irene. Mr. Melman is a casting director in Hollywood and he saw you in the show last night," he continued, as if all of them didn't know what they were doing there.

Bertie got brave and nudged Leona out of the way so she could peek out. Melman was a handsome man. He was tall, with dark hair and glasses, and he wore a shirt and a tie and a seersucker jacket. His wife was pretty enough to be a movie star.

"How do you do," Cee Cee said in a voice that was so polite, it sounded to Bertie like a foreign accent. "I'd like you to meet Harry Chalmers, my accompanist," she continued, "and my mother, who is here as well. Perhaps you'd like to meet her."

Melman nodded.

Leona adjusted her dress and walked out onto the stage, timidly. Bertie followed a few feet behind.

"My mother, Leona Bloom. This is Mr. Melman and his wife, Irene," Cee Cee said. "Oh, and this is Bertie, my younger sister."

Bertie flushed. Her sister. Wouldn't it be something to have a sister like Cee Cee Bloom.

"You're very talented, Cee Cee," Melman said. "And I'd like to arrange for you to come out to California and test for a—"

Suddenly, there was a loud rumbling noise from the back of the theater and some shouting. Everyone turned to look.

"Let me in there, Grey, you son of a bitch," screamed a voice. "Open these lousy doors or I'll kill somebody, Grey, you bastard." Just then, one of the doors in the back of the theater crashed open. A skinny, dark-haired woman stood there wild-eyed, surveying the scene at the edge of the stage. Then she charged down the aisle toward the assembled group.

"You got some guy here from Hollywood, huh, Grey, you no-good? What's the matter? My Karen's no good for

Hollywood? Three summers you been making her stay up till two in the goddamned morning. Since she was a baby. I ought to report you to the child labor people."

"Mrs. Lewandowski," Jerry Grey said nervously, "this man, Mr. Melman, he asked for Cee Cee."

"Cee Cee, my ass. I know he liked my Karen. Handwalks she does. On a lighted staircase. She sings, too. 'Stairway to Paradise.' Been doing the act for that ungrateful son of a bitch, three years," she said, pointing to Grey. "Three shows on the weekend. Then Hollywood comes, and does he give my Karen a chance? Hell, no! Listen, Mr. Melman from Hollywood. What's the sense of just seeing one kid? You know what I mean? While you're in the neighborhood, see two kids."

No one had moved since Mrs. Lewandowski burst in. Melman adjusted his tie uncomfortably. Harry's mouth was open in surprise. Leona's breathing was loud enough for Bertie to hear several feet away.

"Well, I don't mind, Jerry. Do you?" Melman asked diplomatically.

Jerry Grey collected himself. "No. No, Joe. Please. I mean, it's nice of you. How about your lovely wife. Does she mind?"

The lovely wife just smiled.

No one asked Cee Cee if she minded.

"How long will it take Karen to get ready?" Grey asked.

"She's ready now," Mrs. Lewandowski said.

All heads turned toward the wings, and there, in a bright yellow sequined leotard, stood tiny Karen Lewandowski. Six. Next to her was a little staircase, which she leaned on expectantly.

"Hello, Karen," said Jerry, in a tone completely different from the one he used with Cee Cee. "Come on out, honey," he said.

"Hi, Mister Grey," Karen said in a sweet, baby-girl voice.

Bertie stared. Karen Lewandowski was the most beautiful child God ever made. Long blond braids, bangs that were perfectly even, big blue eyes, a perfect face, and a tiny athletic-looking body.

"Need any help, Karen?" Jerry asked.

"No, sir," she responded, and gently wheeled her little staircase onto the stage.

"Hello, Harry," Karen said, looking into the orchestra pit and waving warmly.

Harry melted. "Hi, Karen, precious," he said. "I have your song right on top."

"Thank you, Harry," Karen said. "And thank you, Mister Grey, for giving me the opportunity to present my act before your guests."

Bertie looked at Mrs. Lewandowski. She had sat down in the front row when Karen came onstage, and her eyes watched her daughter, knowingly.

"Clear the stage," yelled Jerry Grey. He was talking to Bertie, Leona, and Cee Cee.

Led by Cee Cee, they walked down the steps and sat in the front row. They were lined up now. Mrs. Lewandowski, Bertie, Leona, Cee Cee, Jerry Grey, Melman, and Irene.

Harry played a few bars of music and Karen walked around to the back of the staircase and turned a switch and the stairs lighted up. Then Karen walked to the top of the staircase and sat down. She put her sweet little face into one of her hands and cocked her head to the side.

> *I'll build a stairway to paradise,*
> *With a new step every day . . .*

Bertie peeked out of the corner of her eye at Mrs. Lewandowski, who mouthed each word as her daughter sang.

When the song was finished, Karen jumped daintily to the stage floor and then, just as daintily, turned upside down and stood on her hands. In this position, she began walking on her hands around the staircase. When she had circled once, she paused for a moment at the bottom of the steps and then, on her hands, walked up the steps. It was something to see.

Irene Melman applauded. The others sat quietly. When Karen reached the platform at the top of the staircase on her hands, Harry stopped playing. Slowly, Karen brought her feet over her head until she was standing and then she leaned forward onto her hands, lifting her feet over, and then turning over again and again on the platform, until her little body was making such rapid head-over-heels circles that Bertie was reminded of the story of Little Black Sambo. And as the yellow sequins flashed by, Bertie wondered if Karen would turn into a pool of butter. The music peaked and Karen stopped and stood for a moment at the top of the staircase, her face flushed, looking more beautiful than ever. She sang,

> *I'll build a stairway to paradise,*
> *With a new step . . .*

She twirled around.

> *I said a new step . . .*

She twirled again.

> *That's right, a new step e-ve-ry day!*

At that, Karen leaped into the air, her tiny legs spread, her toes pointed, and landed on the platform in a perfect split.

Mrs. Lewandowski applauded. Jerry Grey cheered; Melman and Irene rose to their feet, applauding. Cee Cee, Leona, and Bertie just sat there.

Karen smiled sweetly. "Thank you. Thank all of you,"

she said as she alighted from the staircase, turned off the switch, and pushed the staircase offstage. Mrs. Lewandowski ran up on the stage to help.

"Why don't you girls change clothes and come back," Jerry Grey said to the air.

Cee Cee got up and walked across the stage. Bertie and Leona followed.

In the dressing room, Cee Cee changed silently back into her plaid bathing suit. Leona ate the remainder of the sandwiches, and Bertie closed all of the make-up containers and put them neatly into the tool kit. Bertie wanted to tell Cee Cee how wonderful she had been, how she was the best one, and how Mrs. Lewandowski had had some nerve with that big mouth to come in there and push her way into Cee Cee's audition. But she was afraid to say it, in case maybe it would make Cee Cee feel bad instead of cheering her up.

Leona hung the red costume on the rack, and the three of them headed back toward the stage.

Mrs. Lewandowski and Karen were already there. Karen had changed into a white piqué pinafore. They sat in the front row talking to Jerry, Melman, and Irene. Harry was gone. When they saw Cee Cee, they were quiet.

Cee Cee, Leona, and Bertie sat in the front row, too.

When they were seated, Joe Melman got up on the stage and walked back and forth as if he was in a play. Then he stopped and looked out at all of them. "Well, now," he said. "Well. This was certainly a lucky break for Joe Melman. Yes, it was. Indeed. Visiting here in Atlantic City with my wife, Irene, after a brief business trip to New York, and what do I find? Yep. What do I find? Well, now. After conducting a long and arduous search on the Coast for a child to star in a picture I'm casting, as luck would have it, I happen upon the Jerry Grey Kiddie Show. And . . . what a wonderful surprise I get when not *one* child in the show is a great little star . . . but two.

There are two of them. Well, needless to say, I said to myself, 'Joe, perhaps, now just perhaps, instead of there being just one little girl in the film, perhaps I could have them rewrite the film and have there be two. Two little girls.' After all, I mean, after all. Here are two wonderful, and I mean that—" Bertie saw him look right at Cee Cee—"both equally wonderful, uh . . . little actresses. Right?" Melman smiled.

"But then I thought about it and I said to myself, 'Joe. Joe Melman. You have been a casting director for quite a few years, despite your tender age.' " Mr. Melman laughed at his own joke. Jerry Grey laughed. Irene Melman smiled. Cee Cee, Bertie, and Leona didn't react.

" 'And you know better than that. In spite of the fact that that's the way you would like to handle this, because they're both little stars, and they are both great little stars, that's just not the way it's done.' So I'm afraid that one of you is going to have to be disappointed." Bertie started to sweat. "And, Cee Cee, I'm afraid it will have to be you."

Without another word, as if on cue, everyone stood up. Karen stayed very close to her mother, holding on to her skirt. She didn't look at Cee Cee at all. Jerry Grey walked over and patted Cee Cee on the head, then walked back to Irene, Mrs. Lewandowski, and Karen. Joe Melman joined them, and they walked up the aisle and out of the theater.

Cee Cee sat down quietly in the center seat in the front row and stared at the stage. Bertie and Leona looked at her silently. The moment the back door of the theater closed, Cee Cee put her head in her hands. Then her tiny red curls began to shake and then to heave and then she let out a giant gasp and then another. When she lifted her head, her made-up face was covered with long, black tracks of mascara, and tears poured from her eyes.

Leona started to go to her, but stopped when Cee Cee emitted a piercing cry. "My life. My whole life. Oh, God. It's over," she sobbed.

"Cee," Leona cried out, "it ain't ovah. Ye'r a kid."
Leona moved toward her.

"No!" Cee Cee screamed. "No!" and she jumped to
her feet and she ran, into the orchestra pit, fists in the air.
When she got to the piano, she stopped and began punch-
ing the piano wildly, banging out an eerie, violent tune on
the keys. She grabbed her head in her hands for a moment and then pushed her way through the orchestra pit,
knocking over folding chairs and music stands as she went,
still screaming.

"My life. Oh, God. Oh, no."

She jumped up on the stage, still screaming, took one
last, long breath and then collapsed in a heap on the stage,
where she sat sobbing quietly.

Bertie and Leona walked to the stage. "Cee?" Leona
said.

Cee Cee looked up at her mother, her eyes burning,
her entire face swollen. "How," she asked. "How did she
know, Leona? How did Lewandowski find out?" Then,
screaming, "How, fa chrissake?"

Bertie looked at Leona. Leona had gone very pale.

"Look . . . um . . . kids. How 'bout a bite? I'll treat
yiz both, you and the kid, to a big meal somewheres."

"Leona," shouted Cee Cee, standing up. "How did
she know? How?"

Leona looked helplessly at Bertie as though Bertie
would have some magic answer. When Bertie's look was
equally helpless, Leona turned back to Cee Cee and replied timidly, "Well, um . . . I did happen to run into her
when I was gettin' the sandwiches and—"

"Leona," Cee Cee said quietly. "You told her. It was
you. You saw Lewandowski and told her. You were braggin'
to her, weren't you?"

"Well, I mentioned—"

"Leona," Cee Cee screamed. "Leona!" And with that,
the small girl thrust her entire body at her mother, the
way football players thrust themselves at the practice bag,

and then pulled away and thrust herself at her mother again and again. With each thrust of her body, she cried out like an animal.

Leona stood there as though the child was making a gesture of love. Tirelessly, Cee Cee fell on Leona until at last she slid to the floor at her mother's feet. Leona stooped down on her haunches next to the girl and caressed her baby's hair, and the mother and daughter sobbed together for a long time.

Bertie turned quietly and walked into the wings to the brown wooden door marked EXIT and left. Standing on the boardwalk, all the directions seemed clear to her for the first time and, unafraid, she walked on the boardwalk toward the place where she knew her mother and Aunt Neetie would be, and down the steps to the beach.

Neetie was asleep, and Bertie's mom was under an umbrella reading *Reader's Digest* and smoking a cigarette. When Bertie stood next to the umbrella, her mom looked up.

"Oh, Bert. Hi, honey," she said. "Ready to go up? It's getting late, angel. I'll bet you're hungry."

"Yeah," Bertie said.

"Neetie," Bertie's mom said, poking Aunt Neetie. "Wake up. It's almost five o'clock, and your back looks like a lobster."

Bertie's mom put out her cigarette and began gathering the towels, magazines and suntan lotion.

"Have a nice day, Puss?" she asked.

"Mmmm-hmmm."

"Where's your bucket and shovel?"

"Don't know."

"Lost? Well, we'll get another one tomorrow."

Aunt Neetie, Bertie's mom, and Bertie each carried some of the beach stuff and headed for their hotel room. They had just enough time to take a shower and dress and stop for an early dinner before the dinner crowd got there.

*   *   *

Bertie decided that the new bucket and shovel set was better than the old one. To begin with, the shovel said "Atlantic City" on the handle, so when she took it back to Pittsburgh, she could show the other kids where she got it, and the new bucket was deeper than the old one, so when she filled it with wet sand and then turned it over, the bucket-shaped piles it made were very impressive.

"Hiya, kid," said a voice.

Bertie looked up. It was Cee Cee Bloom. She was wearing white pedal pushers and a pink printed shirt. Her eyes were a little puffy, but her smile was big and warm.

"Been lookin' all over for ya. Me and Leona are goin' home today. I miss my dad . . . so I quit the show. Leona says after we get home, maybe I could go to summer camp for a few weeks. You know, like the real kids. So here's my address in the Bronx," she said, handing Bertie a little white piece of paper. "Maybe we'll be pen pals or somethin'."

"Thanks, Cee," Bertie said, then hoped the familiarity was okay.

"Thank *you*, kid," Cee Cee said as she turned to walk up the beach. Bertie watched her go.

When she reached the steps, before she walked up to the boardwalk, Cee Cee turned back to where she knew Bertie was watching, and she smiled and blew Bertie a kiss. Bertie recognized the gesture. It was the kind of kiss Cee Cee blew to the audience when the show was over and she was taking her bows. Bertie held the little white piece of paper tightly in her hand.

DEAR CEE CEE,

I KNOW THAT YOU CANNOT COME TO MY PARTY BUT I THOUGHT YOU WOULD LIKE TO SEE MY INVITATIONS ANYWAY.

RAGGEDY ANN AND RAGGEDY ANDY ARE JOINING US FOR CAKE AND CANDY. HOPE THAT YOU WILL COME TO SAY HAPPY TIMES ON MY BIRTHDAY.

BERTIE WHITE

REMEMBER ME FROM A.C.?

DEAR BERTIE,

IN SCHOOL WE ARE WRITING LETTERS TO PEN PALS. SO WILL YOU BE MINE, OKAY? THE BEST NEWS IS THAT MY MOM'S GOING TO GET ME A BRA. IT HAS ELASTIC SO IT COULD FIT AND I WON'T NEED AN UNDER-SHIRT ANYMORE.

LOVE,

CECILIA BLOOM

DEAR CEE CEE,

MY MOM SAID I SHOULD SEND YOU A COPY OF THIS DUMB PICTURE. EVEN THOUGH I HATE IT. YESTERDAY WHEN WE GOT THEM SHARON WHITMAN WHO SITS NEXT TO ME AND GOT MINE BY MISTAKE SAID I AM SO SKINNY I LOOK LIKE OLIVE OYL WHICH IS THE SKINNY GIRL IN POPEYE AND I CRIED.

MY MOM SAYS SHARON WHITMAN IS ONLY JEALOUS AND SHE SAID THAT POPEYE AND THE MEAN GUY WHO HAS THE BEARD BOTH LOVE OLIVE OYL SO SHE MUST BE PRETTY GOOD EVEN IF SHE'S SKINNY.

MOM HAS PUT THIS PICTURE INTO A FRAME AND EVERY TIME I COME HOME FROM SCHOOL I TURN THE FRAME TO THE WALL AND SHE GETS MAD. HA HA.

DO YOU HAVE ANY PICTURES?

BERTIE W. XX OO

P.S. SEND ME ONE.

DEAR BERTIE,

I NEVER ASKED YOU IF YOU HAVE ANY BROTHERS AND SISTERS. I DON'T. DO YOU?

SOMETIMES I PRETEND I DO AND I LEAVE ROOM FOR HER IN MY BED AND SLEEP ALL THE WAY OVER ON ONE SIDE.

HERE'S A PHOTO OF ME AT SCHOOL. IT IS YUCKY BUT LEONA TRIED TO IRON MY HAIR LIKE A TABLECLOTH AND I LOOK REALLY DRIPPY. ANYWAY, I AM FINE. ARE YOU? MY MOM TAKES ME TO DANCING SCHOOL EVERY DAY. OTHERWISE I WOULD HAVE MORE TIME TO WRITE YOU.

CEE CEE

P.S. I AM SAVING YOUR LETTERS IN A SHOEBOX. THEY ARE THE FIRST REAL MAIL THAT EVER CAME TO ME.

DEAR CEE,

GOT YOUR LAST LETTER ON FRIDAY AND IT WAS ALSO A SPECIAL DAY FOR ANOTHER REASON BECAUSE I HAD MY FIRST REAL DATE!!

IT WAS SORT OF DUMB BECAUSE HIS FATHER DROVE US TO THE MOVIES AND THEN WE WALKED TO WEINSTEIN'S (A DELICATESSEN) FOR A SANDWICH AND THEN HE CALLED HIS FATHER AND WE WAITED OUTSIDE OF WEINSTEIN'S FOR HIM TO PICK US UP, BUT, BOY, DID I HAVE FUN!!! HE PUT HIS ARM AROUND ME AND EVERYTHING. (MY MOTHER WILL KILL ME IF SHE FINDS THIS!!!!)

MY MOTHER SAYS THIRTEEN IS TOO YOUNG TO HAVE DATES BUT IF WE DIDN'T GO ON HAYRIDES OR ANYTHING, ONLY MOVIES, THEN IT'S OKAY.

OH! THIS BOY'S NAME IS SANFORD GLASS. HE HAS RED HAIR. BUT I DON'T LOVE HIM. (YET!!!)

LOVE,

BERTIE

Dear Bert,

 I am so relieved. Today my dad agreed with Leona that I don't have to go to college. It would be a waste of time and money for me since I'm going to be a star and that's something you can't learn about in school. Right?

 Anyhow, I hate school. I am a moron in math. I got a D in algebra, and that was just lucky. In English I'm better, because I like reading the stuff we have to read there, but I can't write good papers. The only time I like to write is these letters to you because I know you better than some kids in New York. I mean, I know more about you. Maybe it's because when someone writes things down, they don't have to look you in the eye, or have you look them in the eye or something.

 I am so glad I'm almost graduating. Not just because I won't have any more homework ever again in my life (YAY), but because I don't like the kids in my school very much. The girls are all snobs and think they're real big if they're pretty or if their dads have money or nice cars. I don't care about them. In fact, I hate them, so it will be nice to never have to see their snobby faces again.

 Leona bought me this dumb stationery with ballerinas on it for my birthday. I think it's kind of jerky. Do you? Oh yeah. Thanks for that key ring you sent me for my birthday. How did you know I like Elvis? I guess I told you one time. Some of the girls in my school think he's filthy, but I think he's soooo gorgeous, and even though

I don't drive a car I put my key to the apartment on it and get to look at Elvis every day when I get home and take my key out of my purse.

Anyway, it's really late at night, and if Leona comes out to go to the bathroom and sees my light on, she'll brain me 'cause I have an audition tomorrow for some children's show in Greenwich Village, so I'm going to put this in an envelope and go to sleep.

WRITE MORE, I LOVE YOUR LETTERS.

C.C. BLOOM

    CECILIA BLOOM

    CEE CEE BLOOM

    SEE SEE BLOOM

    SI SI BLUE M.

Los Angeles, California, 1983

Within an hour, Cee Cee was getting out of the car at LAX. She'd asked Jake, the limo driver who usually drove her to an exercise teacher's studio at lunchtime, to drive her home instead. While he waited, she packed and called the airlines. Shit. There were no seats available to Monterey. Not that afternoon, or that evening.

"How 'bout outta Burbank?" she asked.

Why had she let her lousy secretary take the day off to go see her goddamned parents in San Diego? And there was no way she could call her pain-in-the-ass business manager to try and get the airlines to bump somebody and give the seat to her. Because then her business manager would know she was leaving town, and he'd try to stop her. She had to get on a plane. Had to. Now. She'd never tried this before, but maybe it would work.

"Hey, this is Cee Cee Bloom, for chrissake," she yelled into the telephone, "and I gotta get to Monterey. Today. Now."

"Sorry, Miss Blue," the dumb bimbo on the other

end of the line said. Blue. The vacuum head didn't even get who Cee Cee was.

"But sometimes people change their plans and don't show up, so you could come to the airport and stand by, or—"

"The name's Bloom, you stupid dipshit. Bloom," Cee Cee said, and slammed down the receiver. A cigarette. She lit a cigarette and paced. What could she do? Connections. She needed connections. Who were her connections? Cee Cee dialed the number at Burbank Studios.

"Burbank Studios."

"Ray Stark," Cee Cee said.

"Ray Stark's office."

"This is Cee Cee Bloom."

"He's in Europe, Miss Bloom."

"I need to borrow his airplane."

"Why don't I have him call you when I hear from him?"

"When will that be?"

"Tonight. Tomorrow morning at the latest."

"Thanks anyway." Cee Cee slammed the phone down. Jesus Christ. She started to shuffle through her address book for more ideas, but finally slapped it shut in frustration. "Ahh, why not," she thought and grabbed the small overnight suitcase she'd packed and ran down the steps.

"Hey, Jakee," she hollered out to the limo driver. "Let's hit the road, pal. I'm gonna pretend I'm a real person and fly standby."

Jake, he was okay. She'd make him swear he'd never seen her leave CBS. Say that she'd gone out a back door and that he didn't know where she was.

"There's five hundred bucks in it for you, Jake-o," she said just as they were driving onto the San Diego Freeway going south. "Buy somethin' for your kid."

"Fuck you, Cee Cee," Jake said. "You think you have to buy my loyalty? I never saw you since I drove you in this morning at eight, even if they cut my balls off."

Cee Cee's eyes filled with tears of embarrassment. Why were people so nice to her even if she was such an asshole? How could she be so stupid to offer Jake money? God, she was a klutz.

"I'm sorry," Cee Cee said, and she was silent for the rest of the ride. Thinking about how dumb she was. So friggin' dumb and crass, and all the money and clothes and chauffeurs in the world couldn't take that away.

It took her till she was twenty-one, for chrissake, before she figured out why, when you ate in a restaurant, they put all those forks next to your plate. Who needed more than one fork? She always figured the forks were there to give you a choice of what size you liked the best. God knows Leona never taught her stuff about forks, and J.P., well he didn't know much more than Cee Cee did. Even though he always pretended he did, the phony.

And tipping. Christ, she never knew anything about tipping. She always gave too much or not enough, or gave it to the wrong people. Once she got off an elevator. She was with Bertie that time—where the hell were they? maybe in Hawaii—and when they stepped off the elevator, Cee Cee handed the elevator girl a quarter. When the elevator door closed, Bertie said, "I must be going crazy. I could have sworn I saw you tip the elevator girl." And Cee Cee said, "You mean you're not supposed to?" And Bertie laughed so hard at that she had to lean against the wall in the hallway just to laugh. Of course, Cee Cee laughed with her, pretending it was a joke, pretending she'd never done that before, but the truth was she really didn't know one thing about manners or politeness, especially when it came to money.

Well, who was gonna teach her? Nathan didn't know and Leona sure as hell didn't know, and once when her business manager was telling Cee Cee about payment for a certain club date he told her she was gonna be paid in increments, and before she looked it up and found out that increments were a series of payments, she thought they were little gold coins or something like that.

Anyhow, even now, even though she had a secretary and a maid and a business manager and a driver and a cook and a gardener, when it came to knowing rules about life, she was a lox. Like her mother. Leona, the poor cow. Cee Cee felt like laughing and crying at the same time when she thought about it.

"Chawmed I'm shuwah," Leona used to say to some dopey shoe salesman wearing a bad rug when he told Leona what attractive feet she had so she'd buy the patent leather pumps from him. Cee Cee would die of humiliation. Wish for one day, even one hour, she could have a pretty mother, a thin mother, a mother who didn't look at television and eat popcorn and laugh so loud with her mouth open that pieces of chewed popcorn flew across the room.

But you couldn't pick your mother, and Cee Cee was stuck with Leona saying, "Chawmed I'm shuwah," and elbowing people out of the way to be the first on line wherever she went. That was Cee Cee's teacher about life. Leona.

"Thanks a lot," she said as Jake opened the door for her at the curbside check-in. She was embarrassed to look at him. "I just have this one little bag, so I'll carry it on and—"

Jake took her gently by the arm. "I'll walk you up, Cee Cee," he said.

She knew he must think she looked silly, because she was wearing that dumb outfit she always wore when she didn't want to be recognized by anybody, and every time she wore it everybody recognized her anyway. Even with the hat, the scarf, and those dumb sunglasses.

"I'll walk you up 'cause you'll be less noticeable with me," Jake offered. Cee Cee bought it.

"S'go," she said.

The PSA flight was leaving for Monterey in fifteen minutes.

The check-in area was filled with people. Everyone was so busy with their crying children or saying good-by to loved ones or reading *Newsweek* that no one even looked at Cee Cee, who sat on a bench while Jake went to get her a standby number.

"Think I'll make it?" she asked Jake when he got back.

"You're on," he said.

"No other standbys?"

Jake patted her on the back.

"You're on," he said again, with a look that meant he had somehow used influence to push her through.

"Thanks, Jake," she said, more embarrassed than ever about offering him the five hundred dollars.

The stewardess recognized her right away. Cee Cee could always see it in people's eyes. Even though the person was trying to act like Cee Cee was just some regular woman from off the street, their eyes gave it away, got fogged up or something in that way that Cee Cee had once described to Bertie, "As if I'm the Pope and they're an Italian shoemaker. Ya know?" Bertie had cracked up at that. Cee Cee was always cracking Bertie up. They were the cracker and the crackee. Titles that Bertie made up, and when she told them to Cee Cee she cracked Cee Cee up and Bertie said, "Thank God. For once *I* made *you* laugh."

"Did you want anything to drink?" the stewardess asked.

That's when Cee Cee realized she was hungry. But shit, this was a goddamned forty-five-minute flight and there wasn't any food.

"Just a Coca-Cola . . . and . . . could I have some extra peanuts?"

The stewardess smiled. "Sure. If you give me your

autograph for my daughter. Right on the napkin would be okay. Her name's Sharon."

Cee Cee nodded. "Right." The stewardess handed her a pen. To Sharon, Love, Cee Cee Bloom. That signature. She'd spent years practicing it, and it still looked stupid. Childish.

"Thank you. She'll be thrilled," the stewardess said as she put three packs of peanuts on Cee Cee's tray.

Three packs of peanuts. A Cee Cee Bloom autograph on the open market was worth three packs of peanuts.

The plane dipped and Cee Cee clutched the armrest. Fuck. This had to be a joke. Some sort of gag. Bertie calling. Telling her it was urgent or pressing or some other Bertie word with exclamation points. Anyhow, whatever it was, it worked. It got Softie the Schmuck to walk out of her own rehearsal.

In fact, Cee Cee remembered, maybe Bertie had even been crying a little on the phone. Of course with all those loud mouths in the rehearsal hall yakkin' so loud it was hard to tell for sure. But right after she told her to hurry up and get to Carmel, it seemed like Bertie's voice got real weird and mysterious and then she said, "Cee, you have to come because I'm dying to see you."

Maybe Cee Cee should have asked Bertie more questions. Maybe she should have called her back from a quieter room. Maybe even from home. Because now she was confused and afraid and wondering if what she thought she'd heard wasn't what Bertie had said at all.

Beach Haven, New Jersey, 1960

The pictures of the singers were already up on the bulletin board. The dancers' pictures would go up today. That's the way John Perry hired them. Singers and dancers. Then he hoped they could act. Actually, it didn't matter much; the tourists loved them, no matter what. Picked out their favorites, not by talent, but by personality and looks, or sometimes just because they resembled someone familiar. A grandchild, a child, whatever.

This year would be Perry's best season. That's what he told Marilyn Loughlin, his assistant, and the choreographer. That's what he told her every year. But this year he had that young boy dancer, Richie Day, and that crazy loud-mouthed girl singer, Cee Cee Bloom. She got to him. Even at the audition in New York, she got to him. She stood out in that room full of nervous girls with a don't-give-a-shit attitude he admired, even though her fat mother was sitting there the whole time eating a stinking lunch, which two of the girls had complained privately to him, made them nauseous.

Then the girl sang, and it was all he could do to contain himself. Christ, if she knew how good she was, she'd ask for money. He even liked her choices of songs. First she sang "I'm Going Back" from *Bells Are Ringing*—and he believed her.

One minute before, she'd come clomping in in those big ugly shoes, wearing that brown Dynel coat that was ripped up near the shoulder, looking like some whacko off the street. Then she'd handed her music to Jay Miller, sat down on the stool, and in just the time it took for Miller to play the arpeggio, somehow, magically, she'd become the girl from the answering service, in love, and rejected.

The second song was even better. The choice was perfect. That sexy oldie, "Daddy." A totally new character. Slinky, sexy, dynamic. Mother of God. The girl was only nineteen. But when he watched her work, John Perry was gone. He had to hire her for his stock company before anyone else heard her.

He'd never hired anyone on the spot like that. Summer kids were a dime a dozen. He tried to seem casual, but his heart was pounding as he laid it all out for her. Non-Equity, tiny salary, room, board, transportation, and laundry. Some weeks leads, some chorus. Maybe she could play Annie in *Annie Get Your Gun*. Maybe Adelaide in *Guys and Dolls*—did she dance? Yes, great. No, he didn't need to see that. Accommodations were small. Ten or eleven girls in two rooms. No scenery to build; he had apprentices to do that.

She'd go get her mother and ask. That mother. The kid would probably take the job just to be away from her. Leona—she called her by her first name—was still sitting in the reception room with the girl singers. Now she was reading a movie magazine she must have been keeping in that Saks Fifth Avenue shopping bag. When had she ever shopped in Saks Fifth Avenue? The girl took her mother into the corridor outside the reception room, and John closed the door to the rehearsal hall, turning to look at Marilyn and Jay.

"Jesus Christ," Marilyn said. "Where'd she come from? Think we'll get her?"

"Honey, I'd go down on Godzilla if we could have that one," Perry exclaimed.

Jay Miller laughed and wiped his eyes. He loved John Perry. The little scamp was only thirty-one years old and the owner of the most successful nonunion summer stock theater in the East. During the year, he directed and produced industrial shows, not yet able to make it in the real mainstream of show business. But in the summer, John Perry was a star. On the little island forty miles north of Atlantic City, in the town of Beach Haven, New Jersey, the locals idolized his flamboyant lifestyle and the tourists fell in love with his theatrical charm. At the Sunshine Summer Theater, his baby, he introduced the shows, directed the shows, and somehow managed to convert an unruly, moderately talented group of stagestruck young kids into a functioning repertory company that delivered a different musical comedy every week.

The door opened slowly. It was Leona; Cee Cee stood behind her, almost timidly. John led them into the room. No one said a word as Leona sat down on the rickety folding chair that creaked in protest against her enormous weight.

"When does she start?" Leona asked.

Perry tried to conceal his excitement. "June fifteenth."

And now she was here. In the house on Ohio Avenue with the rest of his summer kids, each of whom would pale in comparison to Cee Cee Bloom. Of course, they all had something to offer, Perry thought. Two of the dancers, Annie and Kaye, had separately confided to Marilyn that they'd never played leads and would do anything to play Louise in *Gypsy*. One of them would inevitably approach him. She'd wait until the others were asleep, walk over to his house on the beach complaining of insomnia,

pleased to find him receptive to her visit. Then it would
be a glass of wine, a walk on the beach and some sidelong
looks, and he would have her. John loved making love to
pretty little dancers; their tummies were so flat. And even
though they were all small-breasted, they made up for
that by being limber. God, were they limber; as they
climbed all over him—not telling him what they wanted
until he had come and was stroking their long straight
hair.

"A dancer could play the part in *Gypsy*," they would
say as though they weren't campaigning for themselves,
but for the entire dance community at large. "There's
really only one song and it's pretty easy."

It was odd, Perry thought. Because it was usually the
girl he would have given the part to, anyway, even if she
hadn't lured him to bed. But performers were so insecure.

Cee Cee took her time unpacking. In fact, she folded
everything so neatly, she was sure Leona would have
laughed her ass off and asked her who she was trying to
impress. The room looked like a goddamned reformatory
with those five metal beds stuck into corners, each next to
some crummy unpainted dresser and a rod for hanging
clothes instead of a closet. Chintzy.

Cee Cee was the last of the company to arrive on "the
island," as they called it. The others were already un-
packed, organized, and downstairs giggling and getting to
know each other, and she was nervous. If only there was
one familiar face. One person she knew from home, even
someone she didn't like, she would feel better. Instead,
there was a blur of new people she couldn't sort out. A
few girl dancers with big calves and straight hair, a tall
skinny boy dancer, an older guy (very faggy), Peggy somebody or other, who was vocalizing in the bathroom when
Cee Cee first arrived—or at least that's what she said she
was doing, even though Cee Cee knew she was just showing off her high notes—and some others she couldn't

remember. She hadn't seen John Perry yet, and maybe
seeing him would make her feel better. He'd adored her
audition in New York. She could tell, even though he
tried to be real calm about it. She knew he would make a
big fuss over her this afternoon when they all went down
to have their first look at the theater.

"The theayter," as Leona would call it. Leona. Poor
Leona. Jeez, she was a wreck at the Port Authority. You'd
think she was the one who was going away. She must have
gone into the ladies' room six times while they were
waiting for the bus. And when the voice finally came over
the loudspeaker announcing departures, she started fanning herself and taking real deep breaths as if she was
maybe going to faint. Acting as if Cee Cee was running
away from home, like it wasn't her own idea to begin with.

Subscribing to *Backstage*, and every time it came,
sitting at the kitchen table with her half-glasses that Cee
Cee's dad said made her look like she was Benjamin
Franklin's mother; and then he had to apologize because
Leona got pissed off at him (for a change). Always Leona
turned to the page where it said "Casting" at the top, and
read it very carefully and slowly, going through the break-
downs, sometimes reading a few words out loud so Cee
Cee could hear, while she was eating her breakfast.
"Woman, early twenties—young Jean Harlow . . . no,"
she'd say, moving her chubby finger down the page as
Cee Cee hoped there would be nothing that sounded right
for her to try for, again, and be disappointed, again. And
mainly disappoint Leona again.

Eventually, something would be right, and Leona
would make Cee Cee call in sick to her receptionist's job,
which she liked a lot, at her cousin Myra's father-in-law's
dentist's office. Even though the others at the office always knew the truth, which was that Cee Cee and Leona
were going to schlep into Manhattan so Cee Cee could
audition for another Broadway musical, they always said,
"Okay, Cee. Hope you feel better," before they hung up.

And it was the same every time. Without an Equity card, Cee Cee could only go to cattle calls. She would stand in the cold waiting rooms, waiting to go into a rehearsal hall or onto a work-lit stage, clutching her music and shivering, trying to look grown-up even though her mother was with her, wondering why all the other girls in slinky outfits weren't cold enough to wear their coats or jerky enough to bring their mothers along. At least, it had been the same until now. She had to get it into her head that she really had the job. And she was excited. She loved telling her cousin Myra (with the three kids in Riverdale) she'd have to leave the phones at Dr. Jacoby's office to someone else because she was off to do summer stock. She even wrote it in a letter to her friend in Pittsburgh, Bertie White.

Bertie had been excited for Cee Cee. Bertie was always excited. At least, she used a lot of exclamation points in her letters, which made her seem excited. She told Cee Cee she was proud of her, which nobody had ever told Cee Cee before, except maybe her dad once when she got a strike, by accident, when he took her bowling. Bertie also said she loved Beach Haven and maybe, only maybe, she might be there herself sometime this summer!! Her Uncle Herbie, who was a bookie, had walked out on her Aunt Anita (Bertie called her Neetie) for a younger woman, and this Neetie was talking about going to the beach at Ship Bottom, one town away from Beach Haven, probably to cry her eyes out, and maybe she would bring Bertie along!!!!

Christ, it would be weird to see Bertie, after all those years of just looking at those dumb school pictures she sent in her letters, with her hair in that God-awful ponytail.

A voice downstairs yelled, "Car leaving for the theater."

Cee Cee tried to relax. She wouldn't be afraid. She'd act real strong. John Perry would like that. He'd probably tell the others how great her audition had been and give her a starring part right away. She folded her yellow

leotard, placed it neatly into the drawer, and headed for
the stairs.

The cars pulled up outside the theater at noon and
John Perry smiled to himself. It was like watching children on their first day of school. Everyone nervously
looking everyone else over, checking out the group to see
how he or she fit in. The doors opened and the new
company piled out and filed past him.

"Hiya, Mr. Perry."

"Wow, look at this place."

As each one walked into the theater, Perry remembered their respective auditions. The wrong notes, the
trembling, the falls in the middle of difficult combinations,
the ecstasy when he had told them they'd been chosen.
His eyes followed the two little dancers, Annie and Kaye,
as they walked together, already friends, and both avoided
his look. Richie Day, the boy dancer, had been befriended
by Moro Rollins, that old queen singer. Rollins had a good
voice and had worked for Perry in two industrials. He
could easily handle the Ezio Pinza role if they did *South
Pacific*. Perry would overlook the way Rollins seduced the
boys unless Rollins tried touching the boys at the company
parties. The locals were always at those parties, and they
would never understand.

"Hiya, Mr. Perry."

It was Cee Cee Bloom.

"Place looks like a goddamned airplane hangar," she
said.

Perry had to laugh. The theater actually had been a
warehouse before he bought it; the curved metal roof that
held the heat and drove the dancers rehearsing in the
afternoon to take salt pills made it look exactly like an
airplane hangar.

"Welcome, Cee Cee," he said. "Did you get all settled at the house?" Why hadn't he noticed her body at the
audition? Maybe because when she sang she was all face

and hands, with those long red fingernails. But now, in
that burgundy leotard with the wrap skirt and mesh stockings . . .

"Yeah. What a dive!" she said, grinning. "You got
some nerve packin' ten of us in those two attic cells. Boy,
if I didn't need to sing so bad, I'd tell you to shove it, pal."

The audacity! He loved her. The others would never
have had the balls.

"Let's go inside."

The theater was cool, and the house lights were on.
Cee Cee sat in the last row away from the others and lit a
cigarette despite the four rather large NO SMOKING
signs, one of which was hanging right next to where she
sat. Perry took a folding chair and sat in the center of the
small three-quarter thrust stage. He had given this speech
so often that it bored him, but . . .

"Welcome to the Sunshine. I hope you're all settled
in your accommodations at the house. For those of you
who haven't forgotten, I'm John Perry. For those of you
who have forgotten, you're fired." Beat. Laugh. "I own
and operate this place. I produce and direct the shows. I
make the policy here and I decide on the casting. If you
have any problems, come to me. Don't bitch and moan
among yourselves.

"This is a repertory company. That means one week
you may have a lead in a show and the next week you may
have a lowly chorus part, but I expect the same enthusi-
asm, punctuality, and professionalism from you no matter
what your standing in the cast is.

"Marilyn Loughlin is my choreographer. She is also
the assistant manager here and she runs the cast house.
The rules are—beds made daily, personal areas kept clean.
Every Saturday morning there is a major cleanup, and
each of you will be assigned a task. The bathroom, the
kitchen, the yard, the laundry, et cetera. If you don't do
your job, I'll personally drive you to the bus. Apprentices
will do the cleanup jobs in the theater. Meals will be at

seven-thirty at the house, twelve-thirty at the theater, and
six-thirty back at the house. If you like the food, tell old
Mrs. Godshell, the cook, and she'll give you an extra
portion. If you don't, keep it to yourself. No singing in the
house, no television, no radio, and no sex.

"The first show, which will begin rehearsal tomorrow,
is *Carousel*. The cast list will be on the bulletin board as
you leave here. Today, I suggest you go down to the
beach and enjoy yourselves. You probably won't have
much time for that after we start rehearsals. Any questions?"

Silence.

"See you tomorrow."

The kids got up and made their way into the lobby to
check the cast list. Only Cee Cee, now with her feet
crossed and up on the chair in front of her, still sat,
puffing on her second cigarette. Perry folded his chair and
placed it against the wall. It bothered him that she didn't
even seem to feel the need to have the others like her. To
stay with the group so she'd be in on it. He started out
through the curtains.

"Where do *you* live?"

"What?"

"You. Where do you live?"

"I have my own house on Marion Avenue. It's on the
ocean about six blocks from the cast house." Again he
started out.

"Nice?"

"Beg your pardon?"

"Is it nice?"

"I like it."

"Good."

Jesus Christ, she was pushy. He turned to walk into
the lobby where the kids were congratulating and commis-
erating on the casting of the first show, but Cee Cee's
voice stopped him.

"I'm in the chorus. Right?" she asked coolly.

"How do you know that?"

" 'Cause the Julie part's a soprano, and the Carrie part's an ingenue and I'm not either one of those."

"Yes. You are in the chorus, Cee Cee—but it's just the first week and there's eleven other shows, and . . ." Why was he apologizing to her?

"I'm not a chorus singer."

"You are now."

Her green eyes flashed with anger and Perry steeled himself for an attack, but it passed.

"Yeah," she said softly. "I guess so."

> *This was a real nice clambake*
> *And we all had a real good time*
> *We've said it afore*
> *And we'll say it agen*
> *We all had a REAL-GOOD-TIME!*

The applause was loud, and the summer people were loving the show. They had arrived in droves, some new, some old favorites of Perry's, to buy season tickets and to stand around the bulletin board looking at the eight-by-ten glossies of the kids, wondering which of them would play what part in the list of shows Perry had posted for the season. The lucky ones who attended the opening night performance would come to the party and meet the amusing young crew of dancers and singers Perry had brought to the island this year.

Bertie White was in the third row next to Aunt Neetie. Bertie was afraid she'd never recognize Cee Cee. It had been so long. It was funny to see Cee Cee's name in the program next to the words SINGERS' CHORUS. Cee Cee's name was first, probably because her last name started with a B, and there she was on stage. In that funny puffy-sleeved dress, trying to look like she lived in New England and enjoyed clambakes. She stood out. At first, Bertie thought maybe it was because she knew Cee Cee

and not the others, but that wasn't why. Something else
about Cee Cee made Bertie unable to take her eyes away
from her. A confidence that didn't fit with the others, who
seemed to be working so hard at pretending that it showed.

The stage was very small, and the actors were so close
to the audience that once Bertie actually thought Cee Cee
looked right into her eyes during the "Mister Snow" song
when the girls sang the part that went, *What a day. What
a day*. Maybe Cee Cee recognized her. But then, Bertie
hadn't even told her when she and Neetie would arrive on
the island. Up until the last minute, Bertie hadn't even
been sure she was coming, anyway. Her mother, Rosie,
wanted her to get a job in Pittsburgh. And she tried. But
just before she took the job at Nelson's Children's Store,
Neetie convinced Rosie she needed Bertie's company.
Bertie could get a job in New Jersey and stay with Neetie
while she mulled over her divorce.

So there they were, still wearing their wrinkled clothes
from the nine-hour drive from Pittsburgh. She'd talked
Neetie into coming for a drive with her from the house in
Ship Bottom, where they'd stopped just long enough to
leave their luggage, to find the theater where Cee Cee
was working. People were lining up to go in, and just on a
whim Bertie decided to walk up to the box office and try
to get seats. There was a cancellation—two seats in the
third row. Neetie wanted a drink, to change clothes at
least, but there was no time.

"Please, Aunt Neet," Bertie had begged. And now
she was glad that Neetie had given in and was smiling as
she watched the show.

Bertie wished she could do something that somebody
would refer to as talent. But she didn't know what it could
be. Talent. It obviously meant dancing or singing or playing
a musical instrument, or even yodeling, and she couldn't
do any of those. When she talked about it with her mother,
her mother would say, "Oh, Bertie, being beautiful and
smart are talents, too." Even though Bertie knew they

weren't. "And you can sew," Rosie usually threw in when she saw Bertie's pretty face fall. And Bertie would imagine herself on *The Ted Mack Amateur Hour* with Ted Mack spinning the wheel of fortune as he said, "And now, let's give a big welcome to little Roberta White from Pittsburgh, who will show us how to hem a pleated skirt, by hand."

Talent. Cee Cee Bloom had talent. She was a great singer. And Bertie's pen pal. Boy, would she be happy to see Bertie.

> *Walk on through the wind*
> *Walk on through the rain*
> *Tho' your dreams be tossed and blown. . . .*

Some of the people in the audience were crying. This song gets everybody, Perry thought. He watched one of the young apprentices quietly sweeping the lobby with a pushbroom in preparation for the show's end. Any minute, the audience would emerge. Thrilled, filled with superlatives, they would crowd around Perry, calling this year's cast the best assembled, and then, in the traditional way, he would invite them all to Dukes Hotel for the party. The entire audience. Three hundred people at the opening night party. It was unheard of, but it was the kind of thing that brought them clamoring back every year.

Cee Cee was depressed. She sat in front of the mirror in the tiny cramped dressing room after the show in her bra and pants and looked at herself. Body make-up on her arms stopped at the place where her sleeves had started. On her chest, it went down to the place where the round neckline began on that crummy yellow dress, and the rest of her was white. Ugh, that looked bad. And she was getting fat from all the starchy crap Godshell was feeding them. Macaroni and puddings, and other cheap, filling, goyishe food Leona would have laughed at.

The others were already almost dressed when the tap on the wall and John Perry's voice interrupted Cee Cee's thoughts.

"Someone to see you, Cee Cee," Perry said.

Who the hell . . .

The curtains that separated the dressing room from the backstage area parted and a dark-haired girl walked in, her eyes scanning the others before they stopped at Cee Cee, who quickly wrapped a towel around herself.

"Cee?" the girl said tentatively.

Oh, now, wait a minute. This could not, no way, nohow, be Bertie White, the ponytailed little girl from Pittsburgh, standing here looking like maybe she was Audrey Hepburn, or I'll throw up from being jealous, Cee Cee thought.

"Bertie?"

The girl nodded and squealed and hugged the sweaty, pansticked, chubby Cee Cee. The other girls watched and smiled happily.

"My pen pal," Cee Cee told them, still in the hug, sorry immediately she'd exposed such an asshole part of her personality.

"My aunt is dying to get back to the house we rented in Ship Bottom, but I wanted to come to the party I heard they were giving for the cast at some restaurant—so if maybe someone could drive me home after the party, then I could come with you, and send Neetie back now. She'd let me do that," Bertie said.

She talks the same way she writes letters, Cee Cee thought. Just rambling. And she's so damned . . . skinny. Leona would have said too skinny—but, boy, oh, boy. Even if I starved I couldn't look like that.

"Yeah, sure. Somebody'll drive you."

Cee Cee watched Bertie run out of the dressing room to send her aunt back to Ship Bottom. She took her red cotton dress off the hook marked BLOOM. She wouldn't bother to take off the body make-up. That dress could cover the lines, and at least the make-up made her look like she had a little color. A little life. Life. Bertie White had life. And a good haircut. "A good haircut is the most important thing a woman can have, after a clean purse," Leona had told Cee Cee many times. And there was not once that Cee Cee ever remembered having had either, and certainly not both. Bertie's purse was probably clean, too.

"She's beautiful," Kaye, that skinny dancer, said to Cee Cee, looking out through the curtains where Bertie had gone.

"Thanks," Cee Cee said, pulling the red dress on. Thanks? Why had she said that? She had nothing to do with Bertie's being beautiful. She looked at herself in the mirror. Maybe she'd put on just a little more blusher.

Bertie was waiting for her in front of the theater. Most of the others had left for Dukes, and Cee Cee could hear the music from the jukebox at the old hotel, even though it was three blocks away.

"Sorry I took so long," Cee Cee said. Boy, it was funny. Here was this person standing in front of her who looked like a stranger, a girl who was so pretty that if she had— Cee Cee tried to stop herself from thinking the rest of that thought, which was that if Bertie had gone to high school with her in the Bronx, she would have been too popular to be Cee Cee's friend, but she thought it, anyway. And instead of ignoring her, this girl was smiling at her and taking her arm so they could walk closer together.

"It's okay," Bertie said. "I guess you probably need lots of time after a show to kind of unwind, huh?" she asked.

"Uh . . . yeah. Sure," Cee Cee said, noticing that for someone who hadn't changed clothes in a whole day, Bertie looked real fresh, as if she had just had a shower.

They walked in silence for about half a block.

"Cee Cee," Bertie said finally, "I'm really glad to be seeing you after all this time. I mean, can you even believe it? I mean, didn't you think that maybe we'd never see each other again? That I was always going to be just a name on some stationery forever?"

Cee Cee nodded.

Dukes was mobbed. Every member of the cast was surrounded by groups of people from the audience. Probably, Cee Cee imagined, they were saying, "You were the best one," to one actor and then moving on to say the same thing to the next actor.

Bertie's eyes were wide. "I want to meet everybody," she said excitedly to Cee Cee. "But I have to go to the ladies' room first." She giggled and started off alone, leaving Cee Cee at the edge of the crowd watching her make her way across the room.

"She's very pretty," John Perry said, coming up beside Cee Cee.

Cee Cee was startled.

"Your friend. That girl. She *is* your friend, right?"

"Yes," Cee Cee answered. She hated herself. She was jealous.

"Actress?"

"No," Cee Cee said, maybe too harshly. I'm the one. I'm the actress. Me. Me. She's just a plain ordinary person visiting here with her aunt who was deserted by a bookie. But she didn't say that part.

"You did well tonight, Cee Cee," Perry said.

Cee Cee turned to look in his eyes. For the last ten days, he had practically ignored her, talking only to Peggy Longworth, who was playing Julie, or to cutesy Dinny Lee, who was playing Carrie. He called them "baby" or "honey" while Cee Cee, who had memorized the chorus music the first time she looked at it, stood and watched impatiently, wondering if her turn would ever come. But now, this second, looking in John Perry's eyes, it was almost as if maybe he . . .

"You'll get your chance soon," he said, as though he could read her mind. And he walked away.

Shit, Cee Cee thought. Why hadn't she said something funny, witty, even shocking to him? He had finally talked to her, and she had stood there like a blob. What could she say? That every night when the room was quiet, when she was positive the others were asleep and she moved her hand slowly into her pajama bottoms, through her wiry hair, to touch those throbbing little folds that ached to be caressed, she was thinking of him? Oh, sure.

Cee Cee watched Perry move through the crowd. The men envied him, she could tell, and the women were all over him. Even the older ones. He flirted and joked and kissed them lightly on the cheek and moved on to the next, scattering a bit of attention on each, so no one would leave unsatisfied.

A waiter with a little round tray passed out glasses of champagne. Cee Cee spotted Bertie as she emerged from the ladies' room. Bertie took a glass from the tray, and her eyes sought out Cee Cee as she made her way across the room. Cee Cee thought it was amazing what poise Bertie had, just reaching for the glass like that. I mean, after all, she was only—what? Sixteen? Holy shit. She was so . . . Cee Cee took a deep breath, and just as Bertie was about halfway back, John Perry, on his way through the crowd, caught her arm.

Bertie looked at him and flushed. Perry said something with a smile. Bertie nodded and laughed. Cee Cee was straining to hear, but the fucking jukebox was blaring The Supremes and she couldn't hear anything. Should she walk over there? Should she stay where she was and grit her teeth in silence? Goddamn it. Bertie didn't even belong here, and she wouldn't have even come here if Cee Cee hadn't told her she'd be doing summer stock here. She would have stayed in Pittsburgh, where Cee Cee wished she'd go back to, right now.

"Perry said he'd drive me to Ship Bottom," Bertie said breathlessly as she reached Cee Cee.

"Great."

"He's adorable. Looks so young. Offered me a job at the theater. What's an apprentice?"

"Cleans the theater, builds scenery, works props and costumes. No pay."

"He said he'd pay me."

"Great," Cee Cee said.

"I may get to be here all summer. Wouldn't that be fun?"

The waiter with the tray walked by. He had one glass of champagne left. Cee Cee reached for it. A woman in a white dress reached for it, too, and Cee Cee was left holding out an empty hand. As she lowered the hand, Bertie took it and squeezed it.

"I'm so glad to be here, Cee," Bertie said, and Cee Cee heard the exclamation points in her voice. "Now you and I will get to be real friends. You know?"

Cee Cee knew, but as much as she wanted to be real friends with somebody, especially somebody who once told her she was proud of her, she didn't know if that could ever happen.

The next day, Perry put Bertie to work on costumes because she told him sewing was her specialty. And it was. Right from the start she had good ideas about how to add a little row of sequins here or a little piece of satin there to make a frumpy dress or suit look glamorous on stage. But it was to her friend Cee Cee's costumes that she paid the most attention.

Bertie was very thoughtful. That was the word Leona used when she talked about Cee Cee's cousin Myra. Myra was thoughtful, too. She sent Cee Cee a card every year on her birthday, and every year Cee Cee would open the card and feel a pang of guilt because not only did she not know when Myra's birthday was, she didn't even know the names of Myra's three children. (Sherry, Beth, Evan? Susan, Bobbie, Kevin?)

Even when Cee Cee was only in the chorus of *My Fair Lady* ("Sorry, Cee, maybe next week," Bertie said sweetly when the cast list went up and Peggy Longworth was playing Eliza), Bertie had made sure Cee Cee had the prettiest dress in the "Ascot Gavotte" number. And she always gave Cee Cee a little gift on opening night. Even if it was just a flower with a "break a leg" note attached to it. And she was an expert with hair. She would meet Cee Cee early at the theater and help her work on her hair. First she'd set it with big giant rollers to straighten all the frizz, and later she would brush it out so the top was straight and help Cee Cee pin up the back so she had an elegant up-do.

Sometimes, after the shows, on nights when Cee Cee was too keyed up to sleep, the two girls would go out for coffee and talk.

"Do you ever wonder about men?" Bertie asked one night, making circles with her spoon in her coffee, stirring it again and again, even though she drank it black.

"Who?" Cee Cee asked.

"Men," Bertie said. "Like the ones you go out with on dates?"

It took a minute to sink in. Cee Cee didn't go out on many dates, and when she did, she still thought of the guys who came nervously to her door not as men, but as boys. Men were Mr. Solomon, Mr. Colfax, and Mr. Cooperman, her father's gin rummy club.

Bertie put the spoon down on the table and put her two hands around the coffee cup.

"I mean," she said, "when you look at a man, doesn't it ever go through your mind what it would be like to be—"

"Doing it with him?" Cee Cee blurted out, finishing Bertie's sentence, at the same time Bertie was finishing the sentence by saying, "married to him."

Cee Cee was embarrassed. Sex was something she wondered about all the time. Not just about how it would be with the boys she went out with on dates, but about ones she saw on television, or in the pizza place or sometimes on the subway. But marriage. No. Never. She didn't want to get married.

"I'm too busy thinkin' about my career," Cee Cee said, shaking her head. "No gettin' married for me till I'm so old and feeble I need someone to wheel me into the sun at the old folks' home. That's when I'll get married."

Bertie was serious.

"But what about all those years without a man? Won't you get—"

"Horny?" Cee Cee said.

"Lonely," Bertie said. "I mean, sometimes I think about my poor mother . . ."

Cee Cee remembered from a letter long ago that Bertie's father died when Bertie was only three.

"Now *there's* a woman who, even though she would never tell anyone, is probably desperately—"

"Lonely," Cee Cee said.

"No," Bertie said. "Horny," and they both laughed, Bertie with a close-mouthed giggle that made her face red, and Cee Cee with a guffaw so loud that the few other people in the coffee shop turned to look at her.

Bertie never ate dinner at the cast house. She always ate with Neetie before the show, and then Neetie would drive her to the theater. One night, she asked Cee Cee to join them. Neetie picked them both up in her station wagon after the afternoon rehearsal.

It was Cee Cee's first glimpse of her. She was dark-haired and skinny like Bertie, and she had a very good tan. But she was very quiet. Even though she drove with both hands on the wheel, she still managed to hold a cigarette in the right hand and a handkerchief in the left hand, and as they drove silently to Ship Bottom, she would alternate. First the right hand to her face so she could puff on the cigarette, then back to the wheel, then the left hand to her eyes so she could wipe away a tear, then back to the wheel, then the cigarette again.

Cee Cee watched her, fascinated. Jesus Christ! If she

made a mistake she would go puff on the handkerchief and put the cigarette in her eye. She giggled at the thought.

Cee Cee noticed that Bertie was thoughtful of Neetie, too. She helped get dinner on the table and wash the dishes, even though she'd been sewing all day and Neetie had only been sitting on the beach puffing and wiping. Neetie never said one word to Cee Cee until she dropped the girls back at the theater. Cee Cee said, "Nice meeting you," and Neetie said, "Yeah."

Boy, you'd think living in that house would depress anybody, but Bertie was always cheerful and a pleasure to be around, and there was no doubt about it. She and Cee Cee were becoming best friends, even though Cee Cee thought that was an asshole way to describe it.

Cee Cee woke up with a start and looked around. The first few times she'd done this in the middle of the night, it had taken her a few sleepy minutes to remember where she was. This time she knew immediately where she was and she felt fine, but she was wide awake and it was one forty-five. She could see the little travel clock her father had bought her, after she came home breathlessly that day to tell him she got the job.

"Luminous dial," he said proudly, as though he'd invented it himself. She would have to write and tell him how valuable the luminous dial was to her when she woke up in the middle of the night. Maybe not. He would worry she wasn't getting enough rest. He worried about everything. That Leona was pushing Cee Cee too much, to which Leona always said, "Butt out." That Leona was eating too much, to which Leona always said, "Too bad." That Cee Cee had no interest in college, to which Leona always said, "So what?" And then Nathan, Cee Cee's sweet father, would shrug and sit down and open the newspaper in front of his face, not so much because he was interested in the news, but to hide. She should write to him and tell him how well she was doing, finally. He would be glad.

She would tell him about Bertie and how much fun they had. And how she was making other friends, too. How every morning at breakfast Richie Day, who was very cute, would tease her by singing (badly), "Does your mu-ther know you're out—Ce-cilia? Does she know that I'm a-bout 'ta steal ya?" And how, when after all those weeks of playing crummy chorus parts, Cee Cee finally got the part of Lola in *Damn Yankees*, Peggy Longworth hugged her and said, "You deserve it." And how when Mrs. Godshell made macaroni and cheese (puke) for dinner last Friday and all the dancers decided to go out for dinner instead, they invited Cee Cee to come along. Everything was perfect.

Okay, so there was one little thing bothering her, but nothing she would tell Nathan in a letter, especially a letter Leona would open and devour before Nathan got home from work. It was Bertie and John Perry. She felt like a jerk even thinking about it. It wasn't that Bertie was doing anything, exactly. Jesus, this was stupid, but it was the way Cee Cee saw them laughing together sometimes, or the way she saw him give Bertie little pats on the ass he never gave anyone else. Maybe it wasn't Bertie's part of it so much—but, well, here she was, Cee Cee finally playing a lead, and Perry still not paying any attention to her. Christ, Bertie was a costume girl. That's all. Bertie wasn't belting out, "A little brains, a little talent," until it knocked everyone dead at rehearsals, and Perry still seemed to like her better, anyway. All he ever said to Cee Cee during rehearsals was, "Got your lines down, Cee Cee?"

Lines down? Even in the sixth-grade play, she'd had her lines down the first day.

And sometimes, when Cee Cee was trying to rehearse her song with Jay Miller at the piano, Perry would be laughing with Bertie.

Cee Cee hated herself for thinking even one crummy

thought about Bertie, who was spending every day making
a wonderful dress from scratch for Lola's dance number
where she teases Joe, "Whatever Lola wants." Bertie promised the dress would look "really spectacular" (with exclamation points).

Bertie was so sweet. And she couldn't really be involved with John Perry. How crazy. Jesus, she was only
sixteen and he was in his thirties. That would be nuts. He
could get arrested or something. Probably it looked that
way because Bertie was such a big flirt. She flirted with
everybody. She batted those long, gorgeous eyelashes at
every guy. Even that old "faygelah" (Leona's word) Moro
Rollins, who joked when Bertie fitted his pinstripe trou-
sers for Henry Higgins that it was "the best time he'd had
in weeks." Who was he trying to kid?

Cee Cee drifted off to sleep.

The beach was peaceful early in the morning. And
now, in the middle of July, it was hot enough to get a tan
by nine o'clock. Cee Cee lay on her stomach on a towel
reviewing the lyrics to her songs. Sunday was becoming
her favorite day. The theater was dark and everyone was
pretty much free to work alone on lines or routines, unless
the show was in a crisis, which *Damn Yankees* wasn't. Cee
Cee knew she should have put some oil on her back, but
she also knew if she got oil on her hands she'd end up
getting it all over the musical score, and besides, she
didn't feel like it. She felt comfortable and warm and
happy. Even the dancers had told her what a great job she
was doing. That was a real compliment because Lola was a
part a dancer could have played if only the singing wasn't
so hard. But Cee Cee could sing and dance, too. So she
got it. The show would open tomorrow night. She couldn't
wait.

"Hi."

Cee Cee looked up. It was Bertie. In a ruffled two-
piece suit. Boy, she was pretty. Even though the sun was

behind her and Cee Cee couldn't see all of her features,
she still looked pretty.

"Neetie let me have the car all day," she said, spread
ing her towel next to Cee Cee's.

"That's great," Cee Cee said.

"No, it isn't," Bertie said, plopping down and reach
ing for Cee Cee's suntan oil. "She only did it because she
feels guilty." There was a silence as Cee Cee wondered
what the tearful Neetie could feel guilty about.

"We're leaving on Tuesday morning."

Cee Cee felt a terrible pang and turned on her side to
face Bertie.

"No! Why?"

"Oh, Herbie's been calling her. He says he misses
her and loves her, and didn't mean to go with that other
girl since Neetie's the only one for him, and lots of other
stuff like that. Frankly, I think the other girl probably got
tired of him. He's a creep. Anyway, she's chomping at the
bit to get back to him. She wanted to leave this morning,
but I talked her into waiting at least until I saw your show
open."

"Can't you stay without her?"

"Nope. I called my mother this morning and asked
her. I told her the other apprentices lived in an apartment
near the theater, and I could move in there, and that I
really wanted to stay and be with you, and she didn't care.
She said, 'Roberta, you're only sixteen, and I still decide
what's best for you, and I want you to come home!' I'm
furious at her."

Cee Cee couldn't speak. She had imagined that she
and Bertie would be together all summer. Now it was all
ruined.

"My mother doesn't trust me," Bertie said, pouting.
"One minute she lets me come here to be Neetie's nurse-
maid, and the next she's making me come home like I was
a six-year-old child instead of a sixteen-year-old woman."

"What does she think you'll do?" Cee Cee asked.

Bertie took a deep breath. "Get laid," she said.

It sounded funny, like a punchline to a joke, and Cee Cee laughed. Bertie started to laugh, too, and they laughed harder when their eyes met. Finally, shrieking with laughter, the two of them rose and ran down the beach into the water, splashing and ducking each other, coming up sputtering and squealing. After they ran back up the·beach, water-logged, and dried off, Bertie held the music score from *Damn Yankees* to see if Cee Cee knew the words.

"Perfect," Bertie said when Cee Cee finished.

The sun was getting higher in the sky. Bertie scrunched sand between her toes, let it go, and scrunched it again.

She was thinking about her mother, who had raised her alone, without a man, for fourteen of her sixteen years, and never once said, "God this is hard," or, "I envy other women for having husbands." People said Rosie was "resourceful," or they would tell Bertie, "Your mother is amazingly strong." Bertie knew Rosie loved the image of being not only beautiful—which she was, a little like Katharine Hepburn—but also tough like the characters Hepburn played in movies.

And as far as family, it was almost as if her mother enjoyed not having a husband. Just being the two of them. Not having some man around to boss them or needing to be catered to. Just the two of them to "carry on," as Rosie would say. But even though her mother didn't complain to Bertie or to anyone, there were lots of times when Bertie felt sorry for her. Like the time when she was outside shoveling snow from the driveway, so she could pull the car out to get Bertie to school. And up and down the street all the other people who stood in the driveways shoveling were men.

And those times on Father's Day when, to make Bertie feel better about not having a father, Rosie would take her out to North Park for a picnic and in honor of the day tell stories about Bertie's daddy Joseph, and how they met and what a "helluva good guy" he was. God rest him.

When she told those stories, Bertie could always see the loneliness in Rosie's eyes.

There was no doubt that Bertie's mother made their lives very bright and full and kept her daughter from feeling deprived though fatherless, and probably because she didn't have a husband to worry about and fuss over, she worried about and fussed too much over Bertie. Certainly protected her too much, in Bertie's mind. Like the way Rosie hated the thought of Bertie's working at a theater.

"If I'd had any idea you'd end up being involved in show business," she said on the phone, not finishing the sentence—not having to.

"Show business," Bertie said aloud. "It's so strange. I guess my mother's right in a way. I'll be better off in Pittsburgh. I'm really a fifth wheel around here."

Cee Cee was spreading the damp towel out on the sand again. She'd put oil on now. Her shoulders were starting to sting. She wished the bookie would change his mind and leave Bertie's Aunt Neetie for good, so Neetie would have to stay in Ship Bottom all summer and cry, and then Bertie could stay around. Or she wished Bertie's mother would let Bertie stay without Neetie. But, most of all, she wished she could say things she was feeling, instead of keeping them locked inside, because then she could tell Bertie how important their friendship had become to her.

"Let's go out to dinner tonight," Bertie said. "Just the two of us. To Dukes. A celebration of the opening of your show and a good-by dinner for me."

Cee Cee smiled. It was a great idea.

Bertie couldn't believe that in Cee Cee's whole life she'd never had a shrimp cocktail. She made her have two at Dukes. Both girls wore cotton sundresses, and with her tan Cee Cee felt as if she looked almost as pretty as Bertie.

Bertie rambled on about all the odds and ends she had to pull together before she left Tuesday morning, as if she were the owner of the theater instead of just an apprentice. She talked excitedly about the opening of *Damn Yankees*, and Cee Cee felt a rush of excitement at the thought of how she was going to look in the Lola costumes. John Perry would have to love her in them. Oh, yes. John. Had Bertie told him she was leaving?

Bertie flushed. She had. He said he would be sorry to see her go, and she changed the subject to Neetie or her mother or something.

"Bertie," Cee Cee asked as she sipped her coffee, "don't you think John Perry is really sexy?"

Bertie looked at her watch. "It's late, Cee," she said, "and you need your sleep for tomorrow night."

Bertie dropped Cee Cee at the cast house, made her promise she wouldn't sit in the living room and yak because it was bad for her voice, and drove away.

Cee Cee walked through the living room. Peggy Longworth was sitting in a chair reading *An Actor Prepares* by Stanislavsky, and somebody with a pillow on her face was asleep on the sofa.

"Good night," Peggy said as Cee Cee walked upstairs.

She had fallen asleep almost immediately, even though she knew going to sleep too early was a mistake and now her eyes were open and it was, according to Nathan's luminous dial, two A.M.

John Perry. Why was he on her mind? Cee Cee turned over on her stomach. Her body ached from all the dance rehearsals. And she ached inside, too. She would miss Bertie. John Perry. Oh, yes. Him. John Perry in those tight white pants; he must own a dozen pairs. And those tight T-shirts. His arms looked so strong. If only she could fall back to sleep. Had Bertie blushed when she asked her if she thought Perry was sexy? Actually, it wasn't even an original question. It was something she'd heard one of the dancers ask Marilyn Loughlin, who had laughed and said, "I don't *think* he's sexy, honey. I *know* he is." What did that mean? Were Loughlin and John Perry lovers? Did they used to be lovers? Lovers. Aunt Neetie and her bookie husband. Bertie's desperately horny mother. Shit. She was wide awake.

Slowly and quietly she got up, dropped her pajama top to her feet and stepped out of it, and slipped a caftan on over her baby-doll pajama bottoms. No one stirred. On tiptoe, she made her way to the door at the top of the stairs and opened it. Down the long wooden staircase that led to the living room. It looked odd in the darkness. The old wicker furniture was tattered, and everything smelled of mildew. Above the sofa hung a needlepoint legend. "You ought to go to Hollywood. The walk will do you good."

"A walk will do me good," Cee Cee said to herself, as if she didn't know where she was going. As if this was just some insomniac's way of tiring herself out so she could fall asleep after a nice walk on the beach. Marion Avenue. Was it north or south? North. She had passed it one night when she went with Richie Day to the bus to pick up his mother who was coming to visit.

"Perry's house," Richie had said, pointing.

Cee Cee had turned to look and couldn't believe what she saw. It was a palace. A mansion maybe. Big and white and colonial. And Perry's black Lincoln convertible parked right out in front made the house look even more elegant.

Now the whole place was dark. Totally. Cee Cee had walked the six blocks rehearsing the words, "I hope I didn't wake you," and now they seemed silly. Of course she would be waking him. There wasn't a light on anywhere. Maybe she should go back. Then why did she keep walking toward the house? She held her breath as she passed the black convertible and walked to the front door. The door knocker was heavy in her hand—but she lifted it and then let go. Just once. The sound was loud and Cee

Cee closed her eyes. Her heart was pounding. Now was the time to go. To run. To get back to the cast house before she said or did something really schmucky. This was a good stock job, and she shouldn't fuck it up with her crazy big mouth that Leona was always telling her about. "Steppin' all over yourself," she called it. Leona should talk.

The door opened about three inches, and a sleepy-faced John Perry looked out.

Cee Cee was too nervous to talk.

"Cee Cee? Is that you? Come on in, kiddo."

Kiddo. Not even dear. Just goddamned-no-sweet-talk-for-you, Bloom-Kiddo! Well, fuck you, John Perry. Oh, yes. Fuck you.

She followed Perry into the warmth of a beautifully furnished living room.

"Y'okay?"

"N'huh!"

"Sure?"

"Yeah."

"Wine?"

"No."

"Sit down?"

"Okay."

Oh, God. Now she'd done it. He was waiting for her to speak. To tell him what it was that got her to walk here at two in the morning in her caftan and wake him up, for God's sake. How long could she stall?

"Cee Cee. What is it?" Perry said, stifling a yawn.

Now he was bored, Cee Cee thought miserably. What was she doing here? Her foot hurt. Maybe she'd gotten glass in it walking barefoot. Why didn't she run? Not to the cast house. To the bus station.

"Cee Cee darling." There, he said it. "What in God's name do you want from my life at this hour? Hmmm?"

Cee Cee took a deep breath. This was it.

"I want to get laid," she said.

Why didn't it sound funny like the other day when Bertie said it, and they laughed so much? Why did it sound like begging? Why had she blurted it out so quickly when she meant to be really seductive and mysterious and just tell him at first she wanted a little nightcap, like people said in movies. And would he want her? Want to go to bed with a virgin who at nineteen was finally giving up "the golden crotch"? (That's what Marsha Edelman, a girl in Cee Cee's high school, had called hers, which she finally gave to her doctor fiancé.) Cee Cee realized she was crying.

Perry still hadn't said a word, and Cee Cee wished he would speak because the only sound in the room was the sound of her sobs. Outside, the ocean pounded against the beach; she had a subliminal flash of *A Star Is Born*, where Norman Maine walked out into the water, leaving his robe on the shore while Esther Blodgett/Vicki Lester sang. Maybe Cee Cee would keep her caftan on when she walked into the water instead of leaving it. At night that water probably felt very, very cold.

Perry moved toward the sofa where Cee Cee had seated herself and sat down beside her.

"Cee Cee," he said. "Cee Cee, please stop crying. For now and forever more, if there is one person who doesn't have to cry, it's you. Do you hear me?"

Oh, yes, she heard him and she saw him and she felt him in that white (Norman Maine) terry-cloth robe next to her, with those adorable furry legs and . . .

"Yes," she said. "I hear you."

"Cee Cee," he said. "Cee Cee. If I have stopped myself once from telling you what I am about to tell you, I have stopped myself ten thousand times. I swear to you on everything that is holy. But you've pushed me, forced me, and now I will do it—prudence, caution, and good sense be damned."

Oh, my God. He loves me, Cee Cee thought. She steeled herself. Could it be? Oh, my God. Of course. Of course. That's why he ignored me. Afraid he'd be exposed in front of the others. They won't understand, and we—

"Cee Cee. You don't want to go to bed with me. You want my attention, that's all. And I've known it from the first day you got here. But frankly, baby" (oh, yes) "I'm a little afraid of you, and that's why I've held back."

"Huh?"

"Cee Cee. You're a star. You have the voice of an angel. The timing of Jack Benny. Confidence that any other actor would kill for. Cee Cee, you are it. I knew it the day I saw you. I told Jay Miller and Marilyn. They knew it, too. You see, my love, although I hate to admit it, you're wasting time in my stinking little theater. You're major stuff. Virtuoso. And you're right. I have ignored you. Deliberately. I haven't directed you because you don't need me. You are beyond me. You know intuitively what I could spend years studying and still wouldn't learn. Do you hear me, Cee Cee? Do you know what I'm saying? I mean, by all means, stay out the season with us . . . but, sweetheart, you will be, I predict, on Broadway next year. One good vehicle and good-by. Straight to the top."

Cee Cee was shocked. Confused. Yes. Yes. She knew that everything he was saying was true. She knew he meant it, too.

"Straight to the top in the most competitive cutthroat business in the world. Because everyone wants it and dreams about having it—and you're one of the few who will."

"John . . . I . . . don't . . ."

"I know you don't. You don't know how to deal with it. It's heady. It's big. And you're scared. Well, you should be. Now go back to the cast house and get some rest. You'll be fine in the morning, and tomorrow night the show will open and you'll knock 'em dead. Now go on."

Cee Cee got up slowly. Her eyes were puffy, but she'd use some Murine and they'd look fine tomorrow. Perry put his arm around her and walked her to the door.

"Will you be okay getting back?" he asked.

"Sure."

He kissed her on the cheek and gave the caftan a little pat where he guessed her ass would be, and she was out in the night walking back to the cast house.

Virtuoso, she thought. Baby, she thought. I'm a star. And he's afraid of me. That's why he's steered away from me. She felt warm and sleepy and happy. He's probably been in love with me since my audition, she thought. Afraid to approach me. She could see the cast house in the distance and was tempted not to go there and crawl back into her little bed but to run out onto the beach instead and scream at the top of her lungs: John Perry thinks I'm a star! We love each other!

After all the years when the only boys who really wanted her were "shlubs," as Leona dubbed them. After all the years when she watched all the top guys going for the other girls. Girls who—what? Were pretty. That's what. This time, Cee Cee had finally won out. This man, this fabulous man, John Perry, was different. Because he saw past things like looks. He was deep. And that's why he appreciated Cee Cee. Loved her.

Cream rises to the top. That was an expression her singing teacher had used when he had promised Cee Cee that her talent as a singer couldn't possibly go unnoticed. So, too bad, Stanley Berger, the schmuck who was supposed to be her date for the senior prom two years ago. The only reason he'd asked her to the prom was that he'd been out of school sick for a month, and when he came back, every other girl had already been asked. But then Cee Cee actually overheard Barry Rubin say, "Hey, Berger, you're not takin' B.P. Bloom to the prom, are you?"

"What's B.P.?" Stanley Berger asked.

Cee held tight to her locker door, braced to hear the answer, but Barry Rubin said it so fast that she couldn't make it out. All she heard was Stanley Berger laughing really loud. And she was afraid to ask anybody what B.P.

was. Couldn't ask any of the other girls. And certainly not the boys. She sat for hours at home that night writing a "B" on a piece of notebook paper and a "P" a few inches away, and filling in words. Bad Person, Boring Pushover, Big Prostitute. At eleven o'clock that night, in tears of fury, she finally grabbed the phone and called Stanley Berger to break the date.

"I don't want to go *anywhere* with you, Berger, you turd," she said. "So forget I said yes to the prom, okay?"

He wasn't one bit disappointed.

"Okay. I'll take my cousin Joanne," he said. "See you."

But before he could hang up Cee Cee shrieked, "Hey, wait a minute, Berger. Just tell me one thing. What in hell does B.P. mean?"

"B.P.? Huh? Oh, yeah . . ." and Stanley Berger laughed. "It means Brillo Pad, Cee Cee. You know? Like your hair." He laughed again and hung up.

She didn't go to the prom. In fact, the night of the prom she made Leona process her hair with some foul-smelling lotion that was supposed to do the opposite of what permanents do. By the next day, she no longer had Brillo Pad hair or straight hair either, which had been the hoped-for result. It was more matted and wiry than straight, but it didn't look like a Brillo Pad. Shit, Cee Cee thought. Now it looks like the bristles of a clothes brush. She welcomed her frizzy hair as it began to grow back in, but it didn't matter anymore. She was a graduate now and who cared what any of those high-school boys thought. Someday she'd go back to the Bronx and take John Perry with her and every one of those boys and their jerky girlfriends would shit from the shock. Hah.

Now as she walked, wild fantasies of Broadway marquees danced in her head. She'd better get some sleep. Tomorrow her show was opening, and she needed all of her strength to knock 'em dead!

* * *

Cee Cee's heart was pounding wildly. Maybe it was the third glass of champagne. No, it was the memory of her curtain call. The applause had risen audibly when she stepped on the stage to take her bow. She had glanced briefly into the wings, where Bertie stood clapping more than anyone else, even though she held under her arm one of the dancers' skirts that had ripped during the first act. Cee Cee noticed Bertie had tears in her eyes. Christ, she was a good friend. She was proud. Proud of Cee Cee's applause. Maybe almost as proud as Cee Cee herself.

And now, at the opening night party, the tiki torches on the beach outside of John Perry's house looked to Cee Cee like birthday candles on a huge sandy cake. Probably because the only other times she'd ever felt nearly as good were her birthdays when Leona would help her open the inevitable box of new tap shoes, and then the box containing a pretty new outfit that Cee Cee would want to wear to school, but Leona would say, "Sure, sure," and then make her save it to wear to auditions.

Cee Cee was elated. My God, how she deserved this. Perry hugged her after the show. A little reserved, but then the others were around, and whispered so only she could hear, "I told you so."

She laughed, too loud, hoping the others would know, could tell her secret. He was hers.

"Cee." It was Bertie. The two friends embraced. The party had been going on for at least an hour, but Bertie had just arrived. She was so thorough. She would stay at the theater after every performance, darning little holes in the costumes, ironing for the next night so she wouldn't have to do it during the day, when she was working on the clothes for next week. Even now, the night before she was leaving, she still finished her work. She was a wonderful person.

"How do you feel?"

"Great," Cee Cee said.

"Want to go for a walk?" Bertie asked.

"Sure."

The water looked like a huge black monster advancing on the beach, then creeping away, then advancing again. The moon was not quite full, but very bright. The girls carried their shoes and walked slowly and silently. The tide was high and they stayed close to the houses, sometimes catching sight of a plastic bucket or shovel left by a child who had played there during the day.

"I'll miss you, Cee," Bertie said.

"Yeah," Cee Cee said. Too choked to respond.

They walked silently again for a long time until Bertie broke the silence again.

"Cee Cee," she said. "I did it."

Later, when she thought about the conversation, Cee Cee remembered that the minute Bertie said those words, she knew exactly what Bertie had done and with whom, but she was hoping (God, are you listening?) she was wrong.

"Did what?" Cee Cee asked, and she stopped walking.

"Got laid. By John."

Cee Cee couldn't speak. It was a joke. Now Bertie would say, it's a joke, Cee. You didn't believe me, did you?

"Oh, boy, I didn't mean to blurt it out like that," she said instead. "To say I got laid—which is really an awful way to put it, because it wasn't like that. We made love. I mean, we really made love, and it was so neat, Cee Cee, not like it probably would be with someone my own age. He was so gentle and sweet. And you want to know the funny thing?"

"Yes," Cee Cee managed to say. Oh, God, yes, she wanted to know the funny thing. Let the funny thing be that this was a lie, and that everything she was picturing now that was making her feel weak wasn't true.

"The funny thing is that I don't feel guilty, and I don't feel dirty, and I'm not the least bit in love with him. You know the old myth about the man you give your virginity to being the first man you fall in love with. Well, I'm not. And I think that's really great."

But I am! Cee Cee screamed inside. Outside, she just stood there, looking at the ocean, unable to look at Bertie. Beautiful Bertie. With John Perry.

"I'd never tell another soul, Cee," Bertie said hastily. "I mean, I'm not embarrassed or ashamed, because he's a wonderful person and everything, and I'm glad it could be with him my first time, but I had to tell you."

A chill came over Cee Cee, and she wished she'd brought a shawl.

"When was it?" she asked quietly.

"Last night," Bertie said. "After I dropped you off, I went to his house to go over a list of the stuff I needed to tell him before I left tomorrow, and one thing led to another, and . . . well . . . I wanted him, Cee Cee. That's why I was so tired all day today. I didn't get back to Aunt Neetie's house until one-thirty."

One-thirty. A half-hour before Cee Cee arrived at John's. Maybe if she'd gotten there earlier. No.

"I knew you wouldn't be shocked," Bertie said, hugging her. "You're so sophisticated. You probably think I'm a baby, making such a big deal about all this."

Cee Cee forced a smile and shook her head to show that she didn't think Bertie was a baby, and the two walked back up the beach to the party.

That night was the first time since Cee Cee arrived in Beach Haven that she slept without waking in the middle of the night. She dreamt about Leona. In the dream, Cee Cee was lying in the bathtub and Leona came into the bathroom, put the seat down on the toilet and sat on the lid watching Cee Cee wash herself. As Cee Cee moved the soapy washcloth slowly over her body, Leona got angry and shouted, "How many times have I told you not to touch yourself? Don't touch yourself, and don't let any boys touch you, either. Don't touch yourself. Cee Cee. Cee Cee. Cee Cee."

"Cee Cee." It was Bertie's voice. "Cee Cee?"

Cee Cee turned over. She opened her eyes, then squinted from the glare of the early morning sun. Bertie stood beside the bed, dressed for travel in red linen slacks and a pink T-shirt. When she saw Cee Cee was awake, she sat on the bed next to her. Her eyes were filled with tears.

Why was she here? Hadn't they said their good-bys last night because Bertie and Neetie were leaving early this morning to avoid the traffic on the Pennsylvania Turnpike? Hadn't they exchanged promises to write more often, more newsy, and try to plan more visits together? And hugged? And promised unending loyalty? Well, Bertie had promised that. Cee Cee had nodded. Then why was Bertie sitting here with tears in her eyes?

"Cee," Bertie said softly. "John just got a phone call from your father. Leona's dead. It was a heart attack. I'm so sorry, Cee Cee." Bertie began to cry. Cee Cee didn't.

"I'll help you pack. Neetie and I will get you to the bus, and then she and I will go on. John had to go into Newark to get some stuff for the theater, so he's gone— but he said to tell you you can come back as soon as you feel like it. He says you can do Annie in *Annie Get Your Gun* at the end of the summer if you want to."

Cee Cee turned and put her feet on the floor. There was sand under them. There was always sand everywhere in this fucking place.

She was glad to be leaving. Glad to be going . . . home? What was at home if there wasn't Leona? Nathan, behind his newspaper? Now he'd have to talk to her. Be close to her. Maybe he'd want to take her bowling again like when she was a little girl. She remembered hearing him ask Leona if he could take Cee Cee bowling; when Leona laughed at the idea, he said he thought he should take Cee Cee more places and be close to her. After that one time bowling, the closeness campaign ended, but Cee Cee was never sure why. Maybe she would ask Nathan about that today.

Bertie had already finished putting Cee Cee's things in the suitcase when Cee Cee came out of the bathroom. Bertie led her downstairs. Neetie sat in her car, smoking. She no longer had a handkerchief in her left hand. No one said a word all the way to the bus station. When they got there, Bertie said, "I'll go," to her aunt, as if Neetie were dying to walk Cee Cee into the bus station. Neetie turned off the motor and lit another cigarette.

The bus station was empty, but the eight A.M. bus stood outside with its doors open. Cee Cee would be the only passenger this morning. Bertie looked at the bus, then at Cee Cee.

"Cee," she said. "I promised you last night I'd be your friend forever and I meant it. If you get to New York and it's too, awful, call me and I'll figure out a way to get there and be with you. Okay?"

"Okay," Cee Cee said hoarsely.

" 'By," Bertie said. A quick kiss on the cheek and she turned and started for the front door of the station.

Cee Cee watched her. Bertie. Roberta White. The little girl she'd met on the beach in Atlantic City so long ago. Her pen pal. And now her best friend. Yes. She had to admit it. In spite of John Perry. In spite of the fact that she was so beautiful it was sometimes hard even to stand next to her.

Cee Cee Bloom had a best friend for the first time in her whole life.

"Bertie," she cried out. "Bertie, wait." Her voice was filled with so much need and so many years of holding it all inside, and with a shrillness that meant, maybe I will never have this moment again, that Bertie turned and ran back to where Cee Cee was standing.

"Bertie," Cee Cee said, with tears in her eyes and her throat, "I love you. I love you a lot."

Bertie put her arms around Cee Cee, and the two girls stood in the tiny bus station, crying and holding one another tightly.

Dear Mr. Perry:

    This is to thank you for the six weeks you allowed me to work in your summer theater in Beach Haven and to ask you if it would be all right if I used your name as a reference in the future to obtain employment in my home town. Awaiting your reply, I remain

                              Sincerely yours,

                              Roberta White

John,

    For God's sake, I hope you get this before you get that typed-up formal note my mother made me send to you about references. Yipes, it was awful. She stood over me like a police guard. Please send a formal answer. Thinking of you.

                              Bertie

Berta love,

The funeral was a bore. I'm back in Beach Haven for the last few weeks . . . and, are you ready??? Sit down. I am no longer Cecilia Bloom. I am Cecilia Perry. Leona would die to think I married a goy (a gentile person) if she wasn't already dead but she is, so tough shit on her.

Oh, I know you think I'm awful, but John and I have discussed Leona every night and day and we know that she did terrible stuff to me, so how bad can I feel just saying tough shit on her? We will stay in Beach Haven till the theater is all locked up tight, and then, heaven knows what. Maybe the Big Apple and singing lessons for me. John really believes in me, says I am a big big talent and has oodles of contacts. Hope you'll be at the opening night of my Broadway hit.

Sincerely,

Mrs. Cecilia B. Perry

(Can you believe it,

Bert???)

Dear Miss White:

The Board of Regents of Pennsylvania State University wish to congratulate you on your acceptance to our School of Liberal Arts.

VARIETY, June 1962
Hallie's Club, Newark. Cee Cee Bloom, a dazzling young thrush, performs a set worthy of bigger and better rooms. The voice is tops, the patter funny. Expect more from Cee Cee Bloom.

My dear daughter Roberta,

Naturally, your warm reception into the sisterhood of Chi Omega did not come as a surprise to me. You carry the legacy of your mother's membership with you, and I am proud that you have chosen to join the same sorority I did.

Your relationship with the other gals will be priceless, Bert, and they can do important things for you, the most important being to help you to maintain your respectability and a sense of your womanhood so you can make the biggest step of your life—finding the right man who will eventually become your husband.

Your father and I met in college, and we were happy until his death, even though people said he mustn't have been happy if he had a heart attack so young. Nevertheless, I hold my head up high and don't need to date or to remarry to prove anything to anyone. That is all a part of what it means to be a real woman, not a cheap person without values. Men are different from women. Their needs for certain things are needs we don't have and will never understand. If you remember this, you won't get hurt.

I am sending you some money, which I hope you will use to buy some cute outfits to wear on dates, etc.

Please call me once in a while.

Love,

Your mother

Mrs. Joseph White
requests the honour of your presence
at the marriage of her daughter
Roberta
to
Mr. Michael D. Barron
On Saturday, the twelfth of January
at two o'clock
The Webster Hall Hotel
Pittsburgh, Pennsylvania

Dear Cee and John,

   Knew you wouldn't be able to attend but thought I'd send this.
   As you know, Michael is a law student graduating from the University of Pittsburgh Law School. I will drop out of college and maybe finish someday in the future. He's going to be a very successful lawyer, so maybe I'll just retire and be Mrs. Michael D. Barron.

Love,

Bertie

Dear Cee,

I probably won't ever mail this, and if I do, afterwards I'll be sorry because I really shouldn't say what I'm about to say here, but there is no one else in the world I can say it to, so I'm writing it to you.

I don't want to marry Michael. Ugh. When I look at those words on the paper, they look really official, and I feel terrible, but they're true. Now I'm crying so I have to get a Kleenex before I run the ink!!! Wait a second.

Now I'm not crying anymore, but I still don't want to marry him, Cee, and I'm afraid to tell my mother who thinks that I've been blessed beyond words to have this fabulous boy in love with me. Cee Cee, maybe this is dumb, but I always thought that when you married someone it was because you couldn't wait until he got home from work, so you could hug and kiss and be alone and romantic and sexy all the time. Well, Michael and I aren't, and what if we never are? We could spend our whole lives just being polite to one another.

The real secret in this letter is that there's somebody else I like a lot, and maybe that's the real reason I'm thinking I don't want to marry Michael or anyone. This other guy is named Joel and we went to high school together, only I never noticed him in high school, and I guess he sort of liked me from a distance but never asked me out. Well, the other night at a party, we were talking and then he called me and, Cee Cee, I met him for a drink. (I borrowed my mother's car and said I was going to the library.) My mother would have a stroke if she knew. He's very cute, but more than that, he's sexy and funny and, even though he's not going to go to law school, as Michael is, or med school, I still think he'll make something of himself, but I guess you never know about those things.

Cee, you're so lucky to have such an exciting life. I'll probably always be the wife of someone, and I'm afraid.

Right after I wrote that very last line, Michael called. He really loves me. Tonight we're having dinner at his parents'. I think I'd better burn this, or mail it fast while I still have the nerve.

Love,

Bert

Monterey, California, 1983

The Monterey airport was small and quiet. Right after the airplane landed, a man in a gray business suit who had been sitting across the aisle from Cee Cee helped her get her bag out of the compartment above her seat. He said, "I can't wait to tell my kids I met Cee Cee Bloom," and then blushed. A skycap smiled a huge smile when she passed him and said, "Now I can die happy, 'cause I seen you," and the Hertz girl asked her for her autograph. But after that she was on her own. Driving this piece of tin, pain-in-the-ass rent-a-car.

The sign said Highway 1 South. Was that right or was it supposed to be north? Shit, she was lucky she'd even started this car, but now she had to find the goddamned place, too. Without a driver. That would be a miracle. Jesus, it was starting to rain. Where the fuck were the windshield wipers? There. Okay, now just take it slow, she told herself. You'll get there.

Everyone back in L.A. would scream bloody murder when she called to tell them she wouldn't be back for a few days. Well, fuck 'em.

The rain was falling so hard now she could hardly see the road, and she wasn't sure how to put the windshield wipers on a higher speed. She was afraid to take her eyes away from what she could see of the road to try and figure it out, so she slapped around madly at the dashboard. No. *That* button was the lights. Maybe she'd turn them on just to be safe. No. That was the turn signal. Aha! There. Windshield wipers always sounded like drumbeats to Cee Cee, so when she twisted the end of the turn signal and the tempo of the wipers changed from "Way down upon the Swanee River" to "Everybody Loves My Baby," she sighed with relief.

There it was. Ocean Avenue. Hoo-fuckin'-ray!

Cee Cee fumbled with her purse with her right hand while her left hand clutched the wheel. She was searching for the piece of paper with the directions. DOWN OCEAN AVENUE. LEFT ON CARMELO.

Carmelo. Carmelo. Come on, Carmelo. Left. Why weren't there any addresses on the houses? Bertie said it would be easy to find. Third house on the right. An old Spanish one. The Frank House. There. A sign. The Frank House. The Franks were the people Bertie was renting from. That's what she'd explained on the phone. Cee Cee pulled the car over to the curb and turned off the engine. She sat for a minute just looking at the house, then she sighed a relieved sigh.

She pushed open the door of the Chevy and decided she would leave her suitcase in the trunk for now. Every house as far as she could see in either direction looked perfect. Surrounded by a hedge or rosebushes or a white picket fence. Cee Cee crossed the street and walked up to the little tile porch of the Frank House. There was a note taped to the door.

Jan
Door open.

Who was Jan? This had to be the place. But where
was Bertie?

Cee Cee opened the door and had to smile as she
walked into the house. Bertie had great taste, even in
rentals. The little house was beautiful. Hardwood floors,
beamed ceilings, and lots of windows so the sunlight could
come pouring in. Cee Cee walked to the coffee table.
There were some magazines, a few ashtrays, and a small
framed picture of a little girl of about six or maybe seven,
surrounded by sand piles she'd made with the bucket she
was holding. She was sitting on a beach. It was Bertie.
Her mother must have taken it the summer Cee Cee and
Bertie met in Atlantic City. Cee Cee looked more closely
at the picture. It looked like a color Polaroid shot. But
then, of course, it couldn't be Bertie. Cee Cee grinned
and put the picture back on the table.

"Bert," she called out. There was no response.

There was a phone on a little table next to the sofa.
Cee Cee picked up the receiver and dialed. First the area
code, then the number she wanted.

"William Morris Agency," a voice answered.

"Larry Gold," Cee Cee said.

A moment later, Larry Gold's secretary picked up.

"Larry Gold's office."

"Yeah. It's Cee Cee Bloom."

"Oh, good!" the secretary said hastily. "He's been
looking for you."

I'll bet, Cee Cee thought.

A click. Another click.

"Where the fuck are you?" Larry Gold's angry voice
asked.

"None of your goddamned business," Cee Cee replied. A cigarette. She looked around the room for one.

"Cee Cee," Gold said. "Don't give me that shit. My

ass is on the line. At three o'clock this afternoon, when it
became apparent you were taking a very long lunch, I was
with a director, a producer, two guest stars, eight dancers,
and three network executives who were sitting in the
fucking rehearsal hall, waiting for you to come back. To
your own goddamned show. And you didn't. By four, I
was sweating blood, you self-indulgent cunt. Where the
fuck are you?"

"Gold, you little prick," Cee Cee said, slowly and
carefully. "Don't you ever talk to me like that again.
'Cause if you do, you can take your ten percent and shove
it up your greedy ass. I had something to do. Someone I
had to see, and I don't care if Jesus Christ Himself was
there waiting for me."

"Now wait a minute," Gold began, but Cee Cee went
on.

"No, you listen to me, you sawed-off little bastard,"
she said, amazed by how calm she was feeling despite her
words. "You postpone the rehearsals until I call you and
let you know that I'm ready to come back."

"Cee Cee, you can't just—"

"I can, Larry," she said. "I can. Because I'm hot shit
and you know it. I'll be there when I get there."

Cee Cee hung up the phone and sat down on the
sofa. There. She'd handled it. Now she'd sit, read a magazine, and wait for Bertie to come and tell her what was
going on.

Hawaii, 1967

Bertie closed the metal clasps on the front of her suitcase. Thank God they were leaving for Hawaii. Thank God they were getting out of Pittsburgh, even for a measly week. Maybe in Hawaii she could look at Michael across a dinner table without seeing a furrowed brow, and without having to hear his preoccupied voice give her perfunctory answers to questions he'd only half-heard.

"No time," he'd said when she told him she needed— they needed—to get away. For four solid years, Michael had worked every day at the big law firm. And for two of those years he had moonlighted every evening from a rented desk at an insurance office in Whitehall, as a way to build his own practice. The schedule exhausted him and made him finally say, as he sat on the bed one night in his bathrobe, staring at something he wasn't watching on television, "You know what? I think you ought to book a vacation for us."

Hawaii was Bertie's first choice; it was the place they had gone on their two-week honeymoon, four years ago.

Island hopping. This time they would only have a few days. Time enough for one island, Oahu, where they would stay at the Kahala Hilton. That had been Bertie's favorite spot during the last trip.

The timing was perfect. It was February, never a great time to be in Pittsburgh, but worse this year, because the gray, slushy, leftover snow lined the riser of every curb and stayed lodged between the cobblestones and inside the streetcar tracks as a chilling reminder that the freezing temperatures might last for months.

"The only way to get through a Pittsburgh winter is to be somewhere else," was what Mrs. Ellis said. Mrs. Ellis was the owner of the Ellis Art Gallery, where Bertie had worked for two years in a job she loved. She loved learning about art, meeting the artists, and learning about the tastes of the collectors, but that was before Michael opened the night practice in Whitehall.

"Tell her you have to be home at five, Bert. You have to have dinner on the table for me by six-fifteen, otherwise I can't be in Whitehall by seven-thirty."

"Michael, the reason Sylvia Ellis hired me was so that I could close up the gallery every night and she could be home at five to serve Jules dinner."

Michael shrugged. It was a shrug that meant Jules Ellis's dinner was not his problem, and that day Bertie told Sylvia she'd have to quit the job at the gallery. Michael came first.

After that she went looking for other jobs. Flair, the lingerie shop in Shadyside, needed someone three weekdays and Saturdays, but Michael was home on Saturdays, at least in the mornings, and he wanted Bertie to be home on Saturdays, too. The Pittsburgh Playhouse had a job opening in their box office but the hours were four P.M. to ten P.M. No matter how she tried, she couldn't find a job that was convenient for him.

"Get a goddamned volunteer job," he told her. "The little bit of cash you bring in doesn't matter." Bertie felt as if she'd been slapped. She'd been so proud of her checks from the Ellis Gallery.

"Ahh, come on, Bert," Michael said, noticing her look. "For God's sake, you *knew* that."

Bertie had driven past the Home for Crippled Children many times, and just the name of the place made her sad. One morning at the corner of Northumberland Street, instead of taking a right to go to the market, she took a left into the parking lot of the Home. Something made her. A voice that said, Go on. You like children. Want to have dozens of your own. That's what you always say about yourself. And you would, too, if you could only conceive. She hadn't used her diaphragm in two years, and yet her period appeared every twenty-eight days like clockwork. And she was developing what she called a "niggling fear" that maybe she would never be pregnant. Oh, go on, Bert, the voice said. This is just what you're looking for.

The heels of her sandals tapped along the linoleum floor of the lobby, and she followed the sign with the arrow that said RECEPTION into a tiny office, where an older gray-haired woman wearing a nurse's uniform looked up from her typing and over the eyeglasses which had slipped almost to the tip of her nose.

"Yes?"

"I'm Roberta Barron, and I live in the . . . I live down the . . ."

Bertie was very nervous. It was as if she were about to ask the woman to give her something she needed badly, but didn't deserve.

"Do you, I mean, do you have a volunteer program here?"

"Not officially," the woman said, "but we can always use help."

On the following Monday, Bertie started work at the Home for Crippled Children. She went every Monday and Friday morning and stayed for a few hours. She had various duties, but her favorite job was reading stories to

the younger children. She would push them in their wheel-
chairs into a semicircle in the recreation room. Sometimes
there would be five or six children, sometimes more,
depending on how they were feeling that day. She would
read to them from little Golden Books—*Scuffy The Tug-
boat, The Little Engine That Could*—and hold up the
books so the children could see the pictures. Not one of
the children looked the way Bertie thought a child was
supposed to look, probably because their faces were so
weary. She tried hard to read with a lot of expression,
hoping that if she made the story exciting or funny she
could elicit a childlike reaction from them. But rarely did
they do anything other than listen quietly and nod when
she asked if she was talking loud enough, or when she
asked if they could see the pictures from where they were
sitting.

Carla was six years old, and she liked to stroke Bertie's
long brown hair. At first, it had made Bertie nervous, but
when she saw that letting the child touch her hair made a
tiny smile appear on Carla's face, Bertie let her continue.
One day she gave Carla a brush and let her happily run
the bristles through her hair again and again.

Just before she fell asleep one night, Bertie remembered a doll that Rosie had given her when she was Carla's
age. It was called a Toni doll, and it had hair that could be
washed and curled and combed. Bertie remembered playing
"beauty parlor" every day for weeks with the doll. Little
girls like pretty hair.

The next morning, Bertie telephoned every toy store
that was listed in the Yellow Pages, looking for a doll with
hair that could be washed, combed, and set. Not one of
the stores had anything like that. Chatty Cathy, Betsy
Wetsy, Tiny Tears, "but nothin' with no hair, lady."

Bertie got into her car and drove to Rosie's house.

"Hi, darling."

"Hi," Bertie answered distractedly. "Looking for something." She raced past her mother and down into the cold, damp cellar that smelled of detergent and ammonia.

She pulled boxes from shelves and out of storage bins. Clothes, dishes, photo albums, holiday items, all carefully labeled in Rosie's neat hand. Ah! A large cardboard box with the word Clorox printed on all four sides, and underneath the word Clorox, also on all four sides, and on the top and bottom just to be sure, Rosie had labeled the box BW's TOYS.

Bertie ripped off the packing tape and opened the box. One look at the contents filled her with memories of her childhood.

Blackie, the furry little stuffed scotty, a baby toy that had sat on her night table even when she was in high school. Lula, oh, sweet Lula, the faded Kewpie doll her father had won for her at Kennywood Park right after her third birthday. Just before he died. Jake or Joco or JoJo, a teddy bear with no face; she couldn't remember what she'd called him. Mr. Muggs, a stuffed monkey wearing tennis shoes. Four storybook dolls in their native costumes of Ireland, Scotland, Holland, Spain. And Lisa, the beautiful Toni doll. Bertie had given the doll the name she'd wished her mother had given her. Instead of Roberta. Ick. A girl version of Robert.

Lisa. The doll was smaller than Bertie remembered. She was dressed in the red and white ruffled dress Rosie had made in order to teach Bertie how to use the Singer sewing machine that later replaced all of the toys in Bertie's affection. Lisa had peach skin and yellow blond hair and green eyes. Bertie used to wish she looked like Lisa.

On Monday morning, Bertie took Lisa from the top shelf of her closet where she'd put her; she had waited until Michael left for work so she wouldn't have to discuss this with him. Then she gently wrapped Lisa in tissue paper and put her in a large cardboard box. She wrapped the box in more tissue paper and sat it on the passenger seat of her car as she drove to the Home.

Carla was gone. Her parents had picked her up to take her on a weekend outing, and on Sunday when things were going well they decided that they didn't want their little girl to live at the Home for Crippled Children anymore. That maybe they were capable of caring for her after all.

"Isn't that great for Carla!" Bertie said to the nurse who gave her the news.

But she felt cheated, as if something had been stolen from her. She felt like crying. It was a feeling she had a lot lately. Wanting to cry from frustration.

"I'd like to have Carla Berns's address," she said to the receptionist at the front office. She was trying to sound calm. "I have something I'd like to send to her."

Dr. Esther Shaw, the child psychologist at the Home, was in the office when Bertie asked for the address. Dr. Shaw was tall and thin and had blue-black hair with square-cut bangs. She was always very serious. Bertie told Dr. Shaw how Carla liked brushing her hair and how she'd gone and looked for the doll and . . . She wasn't sure why, but suddenly she felt herself talking very fast. Maybe it was because of the look on Dr. Shaw's face.

"I'm very sorry, Roberta," the doctor said when Bertie finished, "I'm afraid we can't give you the girl's address. Sending Carla the doll now would be entirely too intrusive."

"Pardon?"

"Intrusive. You see, Carla's parents couldn't afford to buy her the kind of toy you're thinking of sending. If she gets a toy like that in the mail from someone who works *here*, those parents could think we're trying to seduce Carla into being happier here than she is at home, and the truth is, Carla's already ambivalent about living in the care of her parents because they've been known to be extremely negligent. So, even though I'm delighted that you became so attached to one of our children, I feel that at this time—Roberta?"

Bertie was crying. Hard. Intrusive? She wanted to

help Carla. Make a little girl smile. Not be intrusive. For God's sake. What was the problem? "I'm sorry," she said, embarrassed at her own outburst. "I'm so sorry."

"Is it possible, Roberta," Dr. Shaw said gently, "that maybe you're not able to detach yourself enough emotionally from these children to be doing this kind of work? What do you think?"

Bertie didn't answer. She tried, but she couldn't answer. Not without crying. She turned and walked out of the building, still carrying the box with Lisa inside. Then she got into her car and drove home.

Later that week, she wrote a note to the Home thanking them for the time during which she had worked there, apologizing for her error in judgment and telling them that she wouldn't be back. When she put the note into the mailbox at the corner she felt awful.

Why had she behaved like that? Maybe it was because she hadn't felt really useful to anyone since her summer at the Sunshine Theater. The Sunshine. She still wasn't sure what she felt about her summer there. After she'd left Beach Haven, there was no doubt in her mind that she and Cee Cee were going to be lifelong friends, even if they did live far apart. But then she got the news of Cee Cee and John's marriage. No, she thought. This has to be a joke. Out of nowhere. John and Cee Cee. Impossible. She felt left out and deserted. By both of them. She stayed alone in her room for days. Rosie begged her to talk about it. Finally, when Bertie wouldn't acknowledge her mother's presence in the room, Rosie announced in a hurt voice, "I know this has something to do with sex, Roberta, and I certainly hope you're not in trouble."

Bertie had needed a few months to get over her sadness, even though she knew she'd never been in love with John Perry. Could John have already been in love with Cee Cee and planning to ask her to marry him when he went to bed with Bertie? Was Cee Cee already in love

with John when Bertie told her that she and John had
been lovers?

A long time went by before Bertie answered any of
Cee Cee's many letters. Cee Cee never, in any of them,
mentioned Bertie's brief moment with John. Maybe when
people got married they liked to act as though all the
previous sex partners either of them ever had were somehow magically canceled out. Bertie had been sure that the
man *she* would marry would be a man of so much sensitivity that she would easily be able to tell him everything
about herself, including the story of that summer in Beach
Haven when she lost her virginity.

After a few months passed, Bertie started feeling
better about everything. She was glad Cee Cee was still
writing to her, and she wrote back. Long, newsy letters.
Sometimes she used her letters to Cee Cee as a kind of
diary, jotting down random thoughts, leaving one letter on
her night table for a few weeks and adding to it late at
night when she couldn't sleep. In fact, it was better than a
diary because Cee Cee always answered her.

The summer after her freshman year in college, Bertie
met Michael. Michael Barron was first in his class at Pitt
Law School. He was very refined. That's what Bertie
loved about him. He was nothing like most of the grubby,
beer-swilling college boys she had been meeting. He was
very well groomed, almost elegant. Set in his ways, in a
grown-up, reasonable, fatherly way. He gave advice to the
other law students, advice to Bertie's friends who had
problems, in a calm, even tone of voice that made Bertie
feel as though nothing could go wrong that Michael couldn't
fix. She loved that.

She also loved that when they were together they
called themselves Mickey and Minnie Mouse. And that he
sent her flowers and didn't make awkward sexual advances
like every other boy did. In fact, he made no advances at
all most of the time, and that was because he respected
her enormously. She decided never to tell him about her

meaningless time with John Perry. Not that he wouldn't understand, but she didn't want to make him feel in any way that he wasn't the most important man who'd ever been in her life. She felt good about her decision. It wasn't a lie. It was simply a discreet choice she'd made, and she'd never thought much more about it until two days after she'd sent off a letter telling Cee Cee how excited she was to be finally getting away to Hawaii alone with Michael, and the phone rang.

"Bert?" It was Cee Cee. The voice was unmistakable.

"Cee?"

"We're coming to Hawaii. With you. I mean, at the same time. Could you drop dead? We need a vacation so bad, so when I got your letter, I begged John and swore I'd do filthy things to his body if he'd take me there, and you *know* how he can't resist that."

Bertie was silent. Did Cee Cee mean literally that she *knew* or . . . no. That was a joke.

"Great," Bertie said, a little unnerved. Michael knew she wasn't a virgin when they met, but he didn't know . . . "At the Kahala?"

"Yep. We can't get there on Sunday, though. It's my last day of the show. I'm so exhausted I could cry."

Cee Cee was always promising to visit Bertie. Usually, the promise came in the form of a dashed-off postcard from some town where she was playing a club she hated, and the visit was her idea of a way to hide from show business, but this time she was serious.

Bertie wanted to be able to say Cee Cee, not now. Go to the Bahamas or the Virgin Islands, they're closer to New York. I need to have Michael's undivided attention. I need to be alone with my thoughts, so I can figure out why when a crippled little girl goes home to her parents, I take it personally.

"Well, Cee Cee," she began. "Isn't it awfully far for you, just for a few—"

"Hey, I don't care *where* it is," Cee Cee said. "I'm comin' to see *you*."

"That's very sweet," Bertie answered.

Michael took the news in his usual stoic fashion.

"Yeah. Okay," he said. "Does her husband play tennis?"

"Don't know."

He seemed bored by the stories of Bertie's and Cee Cee's childhood meeting and of their reunion in Beach Haven, but listened politely the same way he always listened when Bertie described the stoneware she'd just seen in Kaufman's, or the store she'd discovered on Murray Avenue called Ratner's where they had every single houseware item in the world.

Bertie snuggled up to Michael as they approached the Kahala district. Something sultry and sensual in the tropical climate made even Michael feel sexy.

It wasn't that he didn't like sex. When he did it, he seemed to be enjoying it. He just didn't want to do it that often. But now that they were on vacation he would relax. Bertie knew that what seemed to be coldness was simply his having so much on his mind.

The taxi stopped outside the hotel and Bertie sighed happily. Bright pink bougainvillea hung from the balcony of each room. Michael helped her out as the driver gave their bags to the bell captain. Michael walked to the reservations desk, and Bertie continued walking through the lobby. She loved looking in the window of Pex, the jewelry store near the front desk, at the jade and the emerald pins and rings and earrings. She never went into the store, just looked in the window.

Bertie remembered that when they were here on their honeymoon, she had looked in the window and seen a little turtle pin made of gold, with a shell covered with tiny pearls. Every day after breakfast, she would walk through the lobby so that she could see if that turtle pin was still there. On the fifth day, it was gone and she was disappointed and mad at herself. She knew if she'd just mentioned it to Michael he would have bought it for her. That night at the buffet she stood in line next to a very feeble old woman who shook so much that her daughter had to carry her plate for her. The old woman was wearing the turtle pin. As Bertie and Michael ate their dinner, Bertie saw the waitress bring the old woman a piece of cake with a candle on it. The old woman's daughter didn't sing "Happy Birthday" to her, but she had bought her Bertie's turtle pin. Bertie was glad then she hadn't asked Michael for it.

Michael tipped the bellhop and closed the door to their room. God, his rear was cute.

"I love you, Mickey Mouse," Bertie said.

"You too, Min," he said, kissing her lightly. Then he walked to the louvered shutters to look outside.

Bertie felt sexy. She wanted him. Maybe if she started getting into her bikini, her naked body would . . .

"Let's unpack," Michael said, lifting his suitcase onto the bed. He was so organized. Sometimes they laughed about it. Repeated that joke about the man who was so compulsive that after he took off his clothes, he had to put shoe trees in his shoes before he could make love to a woman.

Bertie felt like being held, kissed, lusted after.

"After we unpack, we can run on the beach," he said, carrying a pile of T-shirts to a drawer.

"Michael," Bertie said. "Michael." She walked over to him and put her arms around his neck. "Let's make love, honey."

Michael sighed. "I'm tired, Bert. You know. Jet lag."

"But you just said you wanted to run on the beach."

He looked caught. "Yeah . . . well, that's different."

Bertie's arms felt awkward around his neck, heavy. As if this man were a stranger, and her arms shouldn't be there. She walked over to her suitcase.

"Bert," Michael said. "Why do you do that?"

"Do what?"

"Set up situations like that where you know you'll be rejected. Why do you always decide you want to make love at weird times?"

"Why is being alone with my husband in an ocean-front hotel room in Hawaii a weird time to make love?" Bertie asked, not looking at him so he couldn't see the hurt in her eyes.

"It's broad daylight. We just got here. I've been breaking my ass in town to be able to get away. I want to unwind and relax."

"Some people think that sex is very relaxing."

"Then why don't you give those people a call," he said, walking to the door.

Bertie knew she should stop him. She knew if she just said, Michael, wait, I'm sorry, he'd come back into the room, and they'd hug and kiss sweetly, and maybe if they kissed for a long enough time, the kisses would get passionate, and then he would touch her and get hot and finally close the shutters and get into bed with her. But she didn't say anything and he left the room with the angry sound of a door slam. Michael would take a walk and be back within an hour. It was familiar.

Bertie looked inside her purse for a cigarette. At least with Michael out of the room she could have a cigarette. Then she'd open the doors and air the room out and wash her hands and face with soap and hot water and use a little mouthwash and he'd never know.

Where were the cigarettes? Damn, she'd left them in her winter purse at home. She lifted her suitcase onto the bed and opened it, trying not to think about what had just happened with Michael. It wasn't rejection. He just didn't feel like it.

She took her pink cotton robe from the top of the suitcase, hung it on the hook in the bathroom and walked back to the suitcase. Her nightgowns were folded neatly side by side. Maybe she'd buy some new ones. Most of

these were from her trousseau. The white one was looking
a little gray. The white one Rosie bought her for her first
night, begging her not to get one with little yellow flowers
on it because a bride should wear pure white. What a
joke. She and Michael had been to bed maybe a dozen
times before. . . . Michael in bed.

There it was again. She remembered their first night.
When they got to the hotel. Bertie was a giggling bride.
Of course, she was not a virgin, but this was different. It
would be her first time as a married woman. That was
new, exciting, dramatic. At least she wanted it to be. She
had gone into the bathroom and put on the white nightgown. Then she brushed her hair and thought about everything that happened at her wedding. Michael was so adorable. He was beaming all day, holding her closely as they
danced, and everyone applauded, and Dr. Barron's friends
kept coming over to them as if they were cutting in on the
dance and handing Michael envelopes that he would slip
into the pockets of his tux. She'd come out of the bathroom that night in the white nightgown, certain that Michael would be under the covers waiting for her. But he
wasn't. He was sitting at the tiny desk across from the
bed, still dressed in his tux, with a pen in his hand, and all
of the open envelopes were in a neat pile.

"Jeez, Bert," he said. "We got six thousand dollars."

"Michael."

"Aren't you glad you didn't register for a lot of china
and stuff? I mean, I *think* it's six. Maybe it's more. Let's
see. The Kleins gave us five hundred. Old Doc Klein.
Isn't he a hell of a—"

"Michael."

Then he looked up. "Pretty nightgown."

"Thanks."

Oh, yes, later that night he'd held her, called her
Mrs. Barron, his own wife, and made love to her. But it
wasn't the same. She decided then that it was okay. That
loving someone in a grown-up way didn't include panting

and pawing the way it did when you felt sexy about someone in college. But every now and then she wished that Michael would want to leave someone's dinner party early because he couldn't wait to get his hands on her, or decide to be late for work because he had to have her in the morning.

The key rattled in the door. Bertie grinned to herself. It was Michael. Maybe he changed his mind. Maybe he'd come back to make love.

"Maid service," a woman's voice said. "Need any towels?"

Bertie sighed. "No, thank you."

When she finished unpacking, Bertie opened the doors and walked out onto the balcony. It was windy and it looked like it might rain. Down below at the lagoon next to the pool where the dolphins lived, a Hawaiian man in shorts was feeding fish to the dolphins. Some little children were helping him. The dolphins came up for the fish and the children threw them a ball. The dolphins batted the ball with their noses, and the children squealed with delight.

Bertie looked out at the ocean. The water was choppy and there were no swimmers. On the big wood raft several yards out where the sunbathers usually gathered, she could see a young couple who were oblivious to the gray clouds. The woman was lying on her stomach, the top of her bikini undone. The man was on his side, pressed closely against her, stroking her bare back. Bertie felt a rush through her whole body and she closed her eyes. She'd go inside and take her clothes off. Get between the sheets and make herself come. Make this aching disappear. She opened her eyes and looked at the couple again. Now the woman was facing the man. Her breasts pressed against him, her whole body close to his.

Bertie opened the glass door and walked into the chill of the air-conditioned room.

"Hi." Michael looked at her almost shyly. "Want to go downstairs and have dinner?"

"Sure," Bertie said. "I'll change."

The music from the hotel's nightly luau on the beach kept Bertie awake long after Michael's first snores told her he was asleep for the night. She thought about looking for something to read, even considered putting some clothes on and going downstairs to join the party. Michael thought luaus were stupid. When Cee Cee and John arrived, Bertie hoped that they would want to go to one, and then maybe Michael would be too embarrassed to say no and he'd try it.

This was a real nice clambake
And we all had a real good time.

The funny little Sunshine Theater in Beach Haven. She'd loved her days there so much. John had sold the theater last year. He wanted to spend all of his time with Cee Cee. That's what Cee Cee wrote to Bertie in one letter. Was that romantic, or was it business? Cee Cee's star was beginning to rise, she wrote. "I'm closing in *Bring It Home,* that off-Broadway show that's been running for several months." She didn't have the lead, but all the reviews she mailed copies of to Bertie singled her out. "Exciting." "Memorable." John was her manager. It must be nice to have a husband whose life revolved around you, whose income and success depended on how you looked, felt, performed. He would have to pay a lot of attention to you.

Bertie remembered reading an article once about Ann-Margret and Roger Smith. She was sure Roger Smith looked at Ann-Margret before they went out for dinner and said, "Why don't you change, baby? You look much better in the black dress." Bertie sometimes asked Michael how she looked because he never told her on his own, and every time she asked him, he said the same thing.

"Ah, Bertie. You always look great. Why do you have to ask?"

Bertie sat up and looked at Michael. He was lying on his back, snoring loudly. She lay back down, put a pillow over her head and fell asleep.

The phone rang five times before Bertie realized where she was. The water in the shower was running.

"Hello?"

"How 'bout some macadamia nut pancakes, honey?" It was Cee Cee.

Bertie laughed. "Where are you?"

"Downstairs in the open-air dining room. My dear, the fucking birds fly right in here and land on your pancakes. I think one just shit in my coffee. I will try to fend them off till you get here."

"What time is it?" Bertie asked.

"It's six hours earlier than it is in New York," Cee Cee said. "And I'm punchy, so put on your muumuu and get your ass down here. Oh, and bring the husband with you. We want to have a look at him. 'By."

Bertie hung up the phone and rolled over. Michael was out of the shower.

"Hi," she called in.

"Hi."

"Cee Cee and John are here. They're having breakfast downstairs."

"Great," he said. "I'm starved."

Bertie's eyes scanned the Lanai Room for Cee Cee and John. Oh, God, she thought, as Cee Cee stood up and waved. Her hair was flaming red now and long and frizzed out in every direction. Her strapless sundress was red too, but it was a shade that clashed with her hair. And her long nails were bright pink. John would have to have a talk with Roger Smith. Bertie craned her neck to see John.

From that distance it looked as if he was wearing white pants and a tight T-shirt. Just like in Beach Haven. Bertie glanced at Michael to check his reaction. His brow was a little wrinkled when Cee Cee came bounding toward them. Probably he was thinking "freak city," which is what he said sometimes when they drove past unusual-looking people on the streets of Pittsburgh.

"Well, fancy meeting you here," Cee Cee said, throwing her arms around Bertie. "Four schmucks from the East come all the way to Aloha-land to see each other." She smelled like Jungle Gardenia.

Bertie hugged her warmly. Michael shifted uncomfortably. Several people having breakfast in the Lanai Room were watching the two women embrace.

"I'll get to you in a minute, toots," Cee Cee said to Michael, and then planted a big kiss on Bertie's cheek.

Cee Cee extended her hand to Michael. "Hiya, Mike. I'm Cee Cee."

"It's Michael," Bertie said.

Cee Cee ignored that. She already had each of them by the hand and was dragging them to her table, talking nonstop.

"Well, our trip was just the worst from beginning to end. They lost the goddamned bags in L.A., and we thought we'd have to stay in that ratty airport hotel, and . . ."

Bertie was face to face with John Perry. She hadn't seen him since the morning she left Beach Haven, two days after she'd given him her virginity. How often she'd replayed that day in her mind, wondering what would have happened if she had handled it differently, behaved some other way. Would it have changed her life? Bertie remembered being startled that morning when she saw John's big black Lincoln pull up outside Aunt Neetie's rented beach house. She'd been awake for hours, packing her things while Neetie slept, making some coffee for Neetie in preparation for the long drive back to Pittsburgh. She hated the thought of leaving, and she hated her mother for insisting she come home. Maybe if she stayed, she and John could have a real love affair. Maybe she would move into the house on Marion Avenue. And suddenly she looked outside and there he was. Bertie had the fleeting hope that he was here to say, "Bertie, oh, God, Bertie, I . . . for two days I haven't thought of anything but you. Loving you, holding you, having you."

Instead, he tapped quietly on the door, and when Bertie opened it, hoping she looked grown-up and pretty and just the way he wanted a woman to look, he said, "Boy, I'm glad you're up. I just got a really bad phone call. Cee Cee's mother died." He was all business, and as soon as he was sure she could handle Cee Cee, he drove off with a little wave and, "Oh, have a nice trip home."

That was the last time she saw him.

"Hello, John," Bertie said. "This is my husband, Michael Barron. John Perry."

"You little fucker, get out of here!" Cee Cee screamed. They all turned. A tiny bird had landed on the back of her chair.

Bertie looked at Michael. He was steel-jawed. "Buzz off, cocksucker," Cee Cee said to the bird. Bertie lowered her eyes. There was a long silence. "Shoo," Cee Cee said. The bird flew away.

"How do you like that?" Cee Cee asked. "I wasted all that filthy talk on him, and he wouldn't leave till I said shoo!"

Bertie held her breath and was surprised when Michael started to laugh. Then Cee Cee, John, and Bertie laughed, too.

One day when it rained, the four of them sat in a corner of the lobby together and played word games. Cee Cee shrieked with open-mouthed laughter when she won a round, which she usually did by changing the rules or cheating. Once, when Michael won, she actually jumped up on the pretty pastel sofa in her bare feet, digging her red painted toenails into the pillow, and shouted, "I hate him, Bert. Divorce the bastard. He's too fuckin' smart."

John laughed. Bertie smiled nervously. Michael acted as if he didn't notice.

But at least Bertie didn't have to be alone when Michael went over to the Kahala Country Club to take a tennis lesson. She sat on the beach with Cee Cee and listened to stories about New York. Cee Cee and John had a tiny apartment in the East Sixties. They were living on the profits he'd made from selling the theater. Off-Broadway paid "shit money," but that was just a stepping-stone.

Sometimes John would join them on the beach. Bertie watched him carefully oil himself. His legs, his chest, those arms. She wanted to ask him if he worked out in a gym to get his arms to look like that, but she didn't. She was afraid he'd think she meant something by it. Sometimes she wondered if he ever thought about that night. Maybe he didn't even remember. She knew she looked good in her black bikini. She saw it in the eyes of some of the men on the beach as she walked by their blankets. Better than Cee Cee, although Cee Cee looked marvelous. She wasn't the least bit chunky anymore.

"Water diet," she told Bertie. "No food. You drink and piss and drink and piss for two weeks and presto—you're skinny."

"God, she's crass," Michael said to Bertie later when they were alone. "She talks like a man."

Bertie wondered to herself why certain language was considered the property of men, but she didn't say anything, especially when Michael added, "You're such a lady, honey. It seems crazy to me that you two are friends."

A lady. That was a good thing to be. It made her feel better than Cee Cee. But Cee Cee was such an exciting person. She was so funny and interesting and had so many stories to tell that Bertie felt unimportant when the four of them were together. All of Bertie's stories were about Michael. As if Michael's life was their mutual life, and her own life had some meaning only as it related to his success, his future.

"He's adorable," Cee Cee told her.

"Huh?" Bertie turned over. Too much sun was bad for her skin. She'd better put a hat on.

"Your hubby," Cee Cee said. "He's got a great ass. And he's so classy, Bert. Does he wear a tie when he goes down on you?"

Bertie didn't answer. She looked out at the waves. A group of children were riding on brightly colored motorized surfboards near the shore.

"Do you love him to pieces?" Cee Cee asked.

"Of course," Bertie said. "He's my husband."

"You think loving and husbands have to go together?" Cee Cee asked. "Boy, are you wrong. That's not the way I've seen it where *I've* been."

Bertie looked to see if John was listening. He wasn't. He was lying on his stomach reading what looked like a script, and he turned the page.

"Does he like me?" Cee Cee asked.

"Michael?" Bertie asked, stalling until she could think of a way to answer.

Michael had told Bertie to figure out a way to get out of having dinner with Cee Cee and John that night because he wanted to go to Nick's Fishmarket for dinner and was afraid "that mouth" would embarrass him in that nice quiet restaurant.

"He, uh . . . well, he doesn't ever really say too much about people," Bertie offered. "He probably thinks you're nice, though. Otherwise he would have said something about not spending time together . . . or, I don't know." She was afraid Cee Cee knew she was lying.

"Well, I think he's great. I've always had a thing for hotshot lawyers," she said, "and he can handle me anytime."

Bertie looked at her.

"Be my lawyer," Cee Cee added.

Bertie nodded.

That night, when Bertie was in the room wondering how to tell Cee Cee that Michael wanted them to have dinner alone at Nick's, the phone rang.

"Bert. Cee. Me and my honey are sapped," she said. "The goddamn sun wasted us. So we can't have dinner with you tonight. Okay?"

"Sure, Cee Cee."

"We're gonna stay in our room, order some food, fuck our brains out a few more times, and pass out. See you at breakfast."

"God, they are so straight," John said to Cee Cee as she got out of the shower.

"Well *he* is," she answered, reaching for a towel. "But she seems the same as before, don't you think?"

John didn't answer. He was putting a toilet paper patch on a tiny bloody spot where he'd nicked his cheek shaving.

"Anyway," Cee Cee said, "we could use a dose of straight around here, pal," she said, and smacked him on his naked ass. "Hang around with a nice solid couple outta Middle America and maybe that settled shit can rub off."

John took a small towel and wrapped it around Cee Cee's head and rubbed her red orange mass of wet curls.

"You wouldn't know what to do with settled," he said. "You'd die of boredom."

When he stopped rubbing she looked up. Her eyes were as bright as a child's.

"I wouldn't die of boredom." She dropped her towel and pressed her damp body against his. "I'd cook and sew and get preggie and be straight."

"Oh, really? And what would I do?" he asked, pulling her close against him. "What's my part in this barbecue fantasy? This portrait of domestic bliss? Huh, Mrs. Perry, my spouse?" He nuzzled his nose in her hair.

"You wear a tie and have a job in the city," she said.

God, she loved this gorgeous yummy man. She kissed his chin and kissed his neck.

"Doing what?" he asked.

"Anything you want." She nibbled his ear.

"Anything I want? Well, in that case, I pick directing big stars in shows on Broadway." He kissed her, and she started to kiss back, but stopped as she thought about what he'd just said.

"Like *what* big stars?" she asked.

"Like Barbra Streisand or Angela Lansbury or Carol Channing. Big stars!"

"Hey, what about Cee Cee Bloom?" she asked, pouting a mock pout. "Who's, without a doubt, going to be the biggest star of them all."

"You mean that gal that retired to go straight just before her career took off?" John teased. "She's living in the suburbs with a couple of kids."

"John."

"Oh, she had a chance to be big, but she gave it up to cook and sew." His hands moved slowly up and down her sides, until she moved her body away, freeing her breasts so he could caress them.

"Well, maybe I'm too young to settle down," she said, only half-kidding.

John was excited and exciting her.

"That was *my* line when you asked me to marry you," John said, kneeling and pulling her down to the floor with him.

"Hey, you asked *me*."

"I did not."

"You lie like the trade papers, Perry, you did ask me. You said you couldn't live without me. Swore you'd take care of me forever. Would you get your hand outta there? Isn't that what you said? Mmmm, J.P., you get me too crazy and then I can't remember what you did that pissed me off so the next thing you know I'm . . . J.P., oooh."

*   *   *

The next day the weather was great. John broke down
and rented a racket, and he and Michael went over to the
Country Club to play tennis. The girls took the shuttle
into Waikiki to shop.

The International Marketplace was bustling, and Bertie
and Cee Cee watched the tourists clamor for overpriced
souvenirs. They bought pineapples on a stick and ate them
while they walked in and out of the stands.

"Hey, how is it workin' at that place?" Cee Cee asked
as she wiped the pineapple juice dribbling onto her chin.
"The one you wrote me about where you read to those
kids?"

Bertie felt a rush of sadness. She was too embarrassed
to tell Cee Cee the truth.

"Oh, it's okay, I guess," she said.

At one of the stands Bertie bought a pair of Japanese
thongs and a straw mat for the beach and a hat made out
of palm leaves. Cee Cee bought an imitation grass skirt
made out of cellophane, a T-shirt with a picture of a beer
mug on it that said "Suck 'Em Up," and a little plastic box
called a concert kit that contained a roach holder and some
papers for rolling joints.

"You smoke?" Cee Cee asked.

Bertie hesitated.

"I mean dope," Cee Cee said.

"Uh . . . well, we have." There. *We* again. Even
alone with Cee Cee she referred to herself as Bertie and
Michael. "Once. Tried it once. At a party at one of the
lawyers' house."

"Great, huh?"

"Well . . ."

"We'll do it tonight. Hawaiian's the best. From Maui.
Let's get some ice cream."

They could pick up the shuttle back to the hotel at
five after two. It was one forty-five. While they were
eating their ice cream they wandered into a jewelry store.
Cee Cee looked in the case at some watches.

"Can I try that one?" she asked the clerk, pointing to a beautiful gold watch with a diamond face.

She held it around the wrist of the hand that was holding the macadamia nut ice cream cone and looked at the diamond face closely.

"How much?" she asked.

"Fifteen hundred dollars," the clerk replied.

"Hmmm. Well, thanks," Cee Cee said, handing it back. "I'll tell my husband." The clerk put the watch back in the case and Bertie and Cee walked outside.

"Fifteen hundred dollars for a watch," Bertie said, chomping on her ice cream cone. "My God."

"That's nothin'," Cee Cee replied.

A Hare Krishna group was playing an eerie tune outside the Liberty House department store. Four sailors walked by and gave Bertie the once-over.

"I'm gonna have a watch like that and five more," Cee Cee said.

"You are?"

They were walking toward the crosswalk to get to the Outrigger Hotel where they would catch the shuttle, when Cee Cee stopped Bertie suddenly by grabbing her arm.

"Bertie," she said, "I mean it."

"Mean what, Cee?" she asked. The urgency in Cee Cee's words told Bertie what she was about to say was something so important they couldn't be walking while she said it.

"About having it all."

Bertie was silent. She still wasn't sure what Cee Cee was talking about.

"It's not just bullshit, Bert," she said. "I'm gonna be big. A star. A real true superstar. I'm sure of it. More sure of it than anything in the world. I'm great, Bertie. And everyone who sees me perform and hears me sing knows it, too."

"Cee Cee, I know that. I saw you—"

"No," Cee Cee interrupted. "Not like in Beach Haven. That was nothing. It was kid stuff. I am going to be the biggest name ever. Bigger than Barbra Streisand, bigger than all of them. No shit. And it'll be soon, too. I swear to God, it'll be very soon."

Cee Cee was practically trembling with emotion. Bertie didn't know how to respond. Before she could think of something to say, Cee Cee took her arm again and turned her toward the crosswalk.

They rode in the shuttle back to the hotel, deposited their purchases, and met out on the beach in their suits. They were both very tanned.

"The guys must be having a good tennis game," Cee Cee said, stretching lazily.

"Mmm." Bertie pictured Michael and John on the tennis court. She imagined they were playing for her. To win her. To have her. In the fantasy she was lying on a chaise longue next to the tennis court, nude. The men were sweating, running back and forth, each desperate to win.

"Deuce."

"Ad In."

"Deuce."

"Ad Out."

"Deuce."

Finally, one of them would win that particular game and walk to the outside of the court to make love to her while the other one waited. Then they would begin again. Each time the winner would run to her and, sweaty and hot, take her. First Michael, then John, then Michael again, and again John. Someone was blocking the sun. Bertie looked up.

It was Michael. "Hi."

"Who won?" Bertie asked, trying to extend the fantasy.

"I killed him," Michael said, deadpan.

Bertie was disappointed.

"Hiya, cutie," Cee Cee said to Michael. "Where's my old man?"

"Changing into his bathing suit, and feeling even older," Michael boasted. "He's not bad, but my game is a killer. That pro over there taught me some really good stuff. Goin' in the water."

Michael ran down the beach. Bertie watched Cee Cee watching him.

A Hawaiian waitress wearing a T-shirt and shorts came by. "Drink?"

Bertie started to say no, but Cee Cee interrupted.

"Bring four mai-tais," she said.

The girl nodded and walked away.

"Why not?" Cee Cee looked at Bertie and shrugged. "We're on vacation. Right?"

Michael emerged from the water and John from the hotel just as the mai-tais arrived. Bertie was going to apologize to Michael. She figured he'd object to the drinks, but when Cee Cee signed for them and handed him the mai-tai, he grinned.

"Great idea," he said.

The cold drinks were perfect, and the four of them sat quietly looking out at the water.

"In order to redeem myself," John said suddenly, "that is, to prove I am not such an old man as I looked on the tennis court, I made a rather heavy investment at the hotel gift shop on my way down here, and I hope all of you will participate in its use." He reached for a white paper bag and pulled out a bright orange Frisbee.

"Hey," Michael said happily. Bertie was reminded of when she first knew Michael in Pittsburgh, when a Frisbee or a whiffle-ball and bat could make his eyes shine. She was feeling very light-headed, maybe even a little dizzy.

"Well, all right," Cee Cee said, jumping up. "Let's do it!"

"C'mon, Bert," John said.

"I'll watch," Bertie managed to get out. The idea of

even standing up was rough. Chasing after a Frisbee would be impossible.

The others ran down to the shore looking like the cast of a Pepsi commercial. It seemed to Bertie as though all of them were trying just a little too hard to have fun. John was carrying the Frisbee, and as they got to the waterline he threw it with great expertise.

"Great shot," Michael shouted, leaping for it like a playful puppy.

"Great catch, Mike," Cee Cee yelled.

No one ever called him Mike.

Michael ran back several yards and threw the Frisbee at an angle. It headed out into the water and both Cee Cee and John ran into the surf after it, screaming. Cee Cee was fast, but John snatched it as Cee Cee reached for it, and she went facedown into a wave. When she came up the red frizzy hair was tight around her head and her white one-piece suit clung tightly to her body. Even from where Bertie was sitting she could see Cee Cee's dark nipples through the wet suit.

"Y'okay?" John asked her.

"Bet your ass," Cee Cee said.

John threw the Frisbee to Michael as Cee Cee ran back to her position in the middle. Michael threw the Frisbee back to John.

"Hey, what is this?" Cee Cee yelled, pretending to pout. "Give the Jewish kid a chance here."

John tauntingly faked a throw to Cee Cee then threw it back to Michael.

"You bastards," Cee Cee said. "Let me play."

All of them were laughing and Bertie smiled to herself. She was glad they were getting along. She'd been worried about that.

John had the Frisbee and Cee Cee was jumping up and down in mock anger.

"Give it to me. Come on."

John took a few steps back and flung the Frisbee in Michael's direction. Cee Cee started to run for it.

"No, you don't," Michael shouted, running backwards. "Oh, no."

"Oh, yes," Cee Cee screamed, and as they both jumped in the air to reach for it, they collided and fell to the ground in a heap.

For an instant nobody moved. Bertie looked at the two of them. They were all entangled. Arms and legs everywhere. Then they started to laugh. But they still didn't move. They just stayed there in that position laughing, until slowly, very slowly they began to get up. Helping one another, brushing the sand from one another.

Bertie looked at John. He hadn't taken a step. He was still standing where he had been when he threw the Frisbee.

"I'm suing for whiplash," Cee Cee said, and everyone laughed. "And I'm also quitting the game to go take a nap."

"I'll come with you, babe," John said.

Cee Cee started back to the blanket to get her purse, then turned back to Michael.

"Say, Mike, old boy. No hard feelings, huh?"

Michael looked at her for what Bertie thought was a long time.

"No," Michael said, grinning. "Nothing like that."

"Let's all have dinner in town tonight," Cee Cee said.

Bertie looked at Michael for an answer.

"Great," he said.

"Later," John said, nodding to them as he and Cee Cee turned and walked up the beach toward the hotel.

The Marketplace at night reminded Bertie of Kenny-wood Park. Kennywood was an old amusement park in Pittsburgh where her mother took her every year of her childhood. They packed a picnic and met Aunt Neetie and Uncle Herbie there, and the grownups took Bertie on rides all day and into the night. Every year, Bertie cried when it was time to leave Kennywood, and every year Rosie promised to bring her back for another day before the summer was over; but when other summer activities started, Bertie forgot about Kennywood until the next year.

Later, when Bertie was a teenager, she asked her dates to take her to Kennywood and they obliged. The bright lights and the carousel music and the smell of greasy food frying made her heart race. She'd taken Michael there once and afterwards had been sorry she did. He thought it was tacky. Just like now. He thought the Marketplace was tacky. But Bertie was in heaven.

There was a little Japanese restaurant right around the corner. Someone in New York had told John about it, so they tried it. The place was very tiny. A piano player sat at a beat-up upright piano in a corner playing pop tunes.

Michael ordered tempura because it was "nothing more exotic than fried shrimp." Bertie ordered teriyaki steak, and Cee Cee and John ordered sashimi. Michael winced when the waitress brought their dinners. "Raw fish? You like it that way?"

"I like it every way, honey," Cee Cee said.

Everyone laughed but Bertie. She was a little bit high from the sake, and she'd had only one. The others had had at least three. Michael hardly ever drank at home. It was strange to see him like this. He was acting . . . how could she describe it? Cute. Boyish. In a way she'd never seen him act before. Wasn't this what she wanted? For him to unwind? For him to be able to be the real Michael? But if this was the real Michael, it bothered her. She liked him better the other way. Maybe. Maybe not. Maybe she could get used to him like this.

"Piano player's not bad," John said. "Wanna get up, honey?"

There were several other tables filled with people.

Bertie looked expectantly at Cee Cee. She hadn't heard her friend sing in years and after that speech Cee Cee made in Waikiki this morning, she must really be singing better than ever.

"Sure." Cee Cee got up casually and walked toward the piano. She was wearing white pants and a blue print Hawaiian shirt tied up, so her newly-thin-from-the-water-diet midriff showed.

Bertie watched her with awe. Bertie couldn't stand up in a strange restaurant and have everyone look at her, even to tell them the place was on fire, and now Cee Cee was going to stand there and sing with some piano player she'd never met before. After only a minute of conversation, Cee Cee and the piano player were laughing together. What had she said to him? Bertie wondered. There must be some kind of show business language that only people in show business understood that helped them to connect that fast. There wasn't a microphone up there. If Bertie remembered correctly, Cee Cee didn't need one. Arpeggio.

Cee Cee sang "I Wish You Love." After the first two bars, all of the people who were eating stopped to listen. She was wonderful. To put such feeling into a soapy ballad. Now Bertie understood what Cee Cee meant that afternoon. It wouldn't be long before she'd have at least five watches. Bertie looked at John. There was something familiar about the way he watched Cee Cee, nodding at every phrase. Leona, Bertie thought. That's the way Leona used to watch her.

Bertie looked at Michael. He was stunned, really surprised. It was as though he'd never really listened when Bertie told him about Cee Cee's singing, and now he was saying to himself, "My God, what a singer."

When the song was over, the audience burst into applause, stomping and yelling for more.

Cee Cee had a look on her face Bertie could only describe as regal. She turned briefly to the piano player and said something. He nodded and she turned back. This time she sang "God Bless the Child." In the middle of the song some man in the back was so turned on he yelled out, "Ooh, sing it, mama!" And she did. It was better than anyone Bertie had ever heard. This time the applause was even louder. Again Cee Cee didn't acknowledge it. She walked slowly back to the table with her head high, and when some people shouted "More! More!" she finally smiled a little smile, shook her head no and sat down. The people went back to their food.

John gave Cee Cee a peck on the cheek. Michael said, "Nice voice," kind of shyly, and Bertie said, "You were great, Cee." Cee Cee, deadpan, downed the rest of her sake.

The waitress brought green tea ice cream, compliments of the management. It tasted like perfume. Bertie ate a spoonful and hated the taste so much she tried not to wince.

"Isn't this yummy?" Cee Cee said, suddenly animated again. "It's delicious."

"It's great," Michael said.

Bertie shifted in her seat.

"I'll bet it would be better if we were high." John giggled.

John giggled, Bertie thought. John Perry giggled.

"Let's try it," Cee Cee said. "We'll ask them for a doggie bag."

Michael, Cee Cee, and John thought that was hilarious, and they summoned the waitress and asked her to pack up a carton of green tea ice cream to take out. Bertie was getting depressed. This was certainly not what she thought was going to happen on this vacation. She'd been worried for days before they got here, even after they'd all met, that poor Michael would feel left out because Bertie and Cee Cee and John knew one another from before. She was sure that the three of them would discuss Beach Haven and recall all the fun they'd had there and wonder whatever happened to this one or that one from the cast of the Sunshine Theater, but those things never came up. And now here Bertie was, sitting with Cee Cee, Michael, and John as if *she* was the outsider.

John paid the check after Michael promised he'd get the next one, and Michael hailed a cab on the street. "Kahala," he said, and the cab driver took off with a start. John held the bag with the ice cream in it on his lap. No one said a word all the way back to the hotel, but Michael hummed. He couldn't carry a tune very well, but Bertie was sure he was humming "I Wish You Love." She felt nauseated from the sake and the bumpy cab ride, and she could still taste that perfumy green tea ice cream in her mouth. She wanted to tell Michael to stop the goddamned humming and ask the driver to slow down, but she didn't.

The hotel lobby was quiet and Bertie realized it was pretty late. They hadn't left for Waikiki until nine. Cee Cee had napped all afternoon and wasn't ready to leave till then. Then they had wandered around in the Marketplace and, after that, had that very long dinner. Bertie wished now that she'd had an afternoon nap because she was really ready to go to sleep. In fact, she'd tell them that.

"Well," Cee Cee said, taking Michael's arm. "Your place or ours?"

"Ours," Michael said, before Bertie could object.

Bertie and Michael had a suite with a beautiful spacious living room and Cee Cee and John just had a room. It had given Bertie a slight feeling of importance these past few days to know that she and Michael had their room service breakfast in a fancy living room while Cee Cee and John had theirs in their bedroom. Now she wished it wasn't that way. If the four of them were in Cee Cee and John's room, Bertie could excuse herself and leave if she got uncomfortable or too tired. With them in her suite she would have to entertain and politely stay awake.

The four of them took the elevator to the eighth floor

and walked down the silent hallway to eight fourteen-eight
sixteen. Michael turned the key in the lock. This was one
of those times Bertie was grateful for Michael's neatness.
The room was in perfect order.

"Wow," Cee Cee said, looking around. "Would you
look at this! Next year we get a suite, too. Right, Perry?"

"Right," John said, not listening. He was already at
the wet bar, rolling a joint.

Michael opened the glass doors and the sound of the
pounding surf filled the room. The luau group was long
gone. It was very late.

Cee Cee rummaged around in the wet bar looking for
spoons.

"Oooh," she said after she opened the refrigerator.
"You still have your pineapple." The management sent
one to every room. "We ate ours the first day. Right after
we ate each other." She laughed and took the precut
pineapple out of the refrigerator.

John had the joint lighted, and as he inhaled deeply,
he walked out onto the balcony where Michael was standing at the railing and handed him the joint. Bertie watched.

Some of their friends in Pittsburgh smoked pot, and
Michael always criticized them. He told Bertie he didn't
need that stuff. He said he was "high on life," an expression she knew he must have heard someone else use.
They had tried it at one party, and Michael said it had no
effect on him. The smoke had burned Bertie's throat.
Everyone else at that party got very giggly, and Bertie
remembered that she and Michael left early. Michael was
irritable, and he made some speech in the car about moral
decay.

Now Michael took the joint from John and inhaled
deeply. Then again.

"Save some for me," Cee Cee yelled, running out to
the balcony, holding a piece of pineapple in her hand.

Bertie felt left out again.

"Bert," John said, turning back to her. "Want a hit?"

She didn't. She was feeling queasy and sad, and for some reason, suddenly those three people out there looked like strangers. She wished she could just say no and walk into the bedroom and fall onto the bed and sleep. She'd had too much sun today and her face was hot and the cold pillow would feel so good.

"Sure," she said, joining the others.

John was holding the joint, which was only half a joint now, and Bertie put it to her lips. She remembered the instructions. Inhale. Hold it in your lungs for as long as you can. Exhale. She took another hit. The sound of the surf pounded inside her head. No one spoke. It was as though they'd been standing there for hours.

"Ice cream," Cee Cee said.

They went back inside. John had forgotten to put the ice cream in the refrigerator. It was runny and soft. Cee Cee gave them spoons, and they stood around the container digging in. Bertie thought maybe if she tried it again, maybe after smoking the pot . . . but she hated it. It tasted like . . . which perfume was it? Shalimar? No. Jungle Gardenia. No. Cee Cee was wearing Jungle Gardenia. Maybe she should sit down. She walked to the sofa. The surf was so loud. The others were laughing about something.

"Bert? You all right?"

"Huh? Yes. Fine."

She was sleepy. John was standing next to the sofa. He had rolled another joint. He handed it to her. She took it and inhaled again. Then again. John took the joint from her and went back to the bar. Bertie heard Michael say something about macadamia nuts, and then Cee Cee made a joke, but Bertie only heard the last word, which was nuts, and the three of them laughed. Maybe being polite wasn't so important. Maybe it didn't count on vacations. Maybe Bertie would take a little nap and come back and join the others later. She stood up slowly and started for the bedroom.

"Something we said?" John joked.

"I'm sleepy," Bertie told him. She wasn't even sure if he heard. She didn't care. The pillow. Where was the pillow? Ah, there. Bertie fell asleep.

The dream she had was about Cee Cee. She was standing on a corner about a block away from where Bertie was, and Bertie could barely make her out, but she knew it was Cee Cee. She was wearing a funny little flat hat that was smashed down on her head, and a big giant raincoat. Bertie wanted to get to her to ask her why she was just standing there on the corner like that and she started to walk toward her, but there were people. Other people. So many people.

Every time she tried to get near Cee Cee the other people got in her way, pushed past her, stepped on her toes. Finally she got there, and Cee Cee looked sad like Buster Keaton and didn't say a word, and Bertie said to her:

"Cee Cee, what are you doing here looking like that?"

Then Cee Cee ripped off the hat and threw it to the ground and underneath, mounted on her frizzy red hair, was a diamond tiara. And then slowly she opened the raincoat and underneath she was wearing a marvelous beaded gown. Then suddenly the people, who were just ordinary people before, became fancy, elegant people wearing fur coats and tuxedos and they rushed toward Cee Cee, grabbed her, lifted her over their heads, and carried her away.

"Howsa boutta swim?" Cee Cee asked Michael and John. The three of them sat silently on the sofa staring out toward the ocean, even though the blinking light of a small boat was all they could see.

"Not for me," John said. "I'm hitting the sack."

"I'm game," Michael said.

"I'll go get a suit," Cee Cee told him. "Meet you at the pool."

The lights in the Kahala pool were off, and Cee Cee and Michael silently swam laps, passing one another in the warm water, and then Cee Cee suggested they race and Michael won every time. Once they started a race by diving in from the side, and as he dove, Michael's foot caught on Cee Cee's robe that was sitting on the edge by the deep end and he accidentally pulled it into the water.

"Schmucko," Cee Cee yelled when she swam back and saw her robe sinking to the bottom. "I'm gonna freeze my ass off," and she dove for it, and came up laughing.

Michael was laughing, too, apologetically. He wrapped himself in a towel, carried the wet robe upstairs, and Cee Cee wore his robe.

"Why am I getting off the elevator here?" Cee Cee asked as the shivering pair stepped off the elevator into the hallway of the eighth floor. It was five-thirty in the morning.

"So you can give me my robe, and I can give you some clean dry towels to wrap around you and your wet robe to take to your room," Michael said.

When he opened the door to the living room of the suite, it was very dark. Cee Cee stepped inside after him, and when he turned back and reached out his arm, she thought he was reaching for the light switch.

Bertie woke up. Her face was still throbbing. That dream. It was so strange. Lying there now, thinking about it, she realized that throughout the dream she had hated Cee Cee. Wanted to have the beaded gown and the diamond tiara for herself. Wanted the fancy people to take *her* along as well. Hated her friend Cee Cee.

Bertie had spent every minute of the vacation watching Cee Cee closely. The outrageous style she had, the sexy way she talked, the way she casually said things that Bertie could never bring herself to say out loud in front of a man. Someone else's man. Michael. Did it arouse Michael? The thought that it might made Bertie's stomach hurt. Bertie turned her pillow over so she could put her hot face against the cool side of it. That was when she realized that Michael's side of the bed hadn't been slept in.

She sat up quickly and could see the living room light coming in under the door. What time was it? She clicked on the bedside lamp and looked at the clock. Five thirty-five A.M. She put her feet on the floor. She felt shaky and feverish. It must be because she'd had too much sun. She stood up slowly and was going to walk into the bathroom, but instead she walked to the door that led to the living room. She turned the knob, but then when she heard Michael talking, some instinct told her not to push the door open.

"I've wanted to fuck you since I saw you. And you've wanted it, too, so what are we waiting for? She's asleep, he's asleep, nobody's gonna know. C'mon, Cee Cee, you know you want it. If your bathing suit wasn't wet before, it is now," he said softly.

Then Bertie heard him say, "Come here."

There was a moment of silence, and then . . .

"Michael," Cee Cee said. "Michael."

Bertie's eyes opened wide. She was filled with disgust and rage. She put her hands to her hot face, and then rushed into the bathroom and closed the door. She looked at herself in the mirror. Red skinny face, squashed with pillow marks. Hair flying everywhere. Ugly. Horrible. No wonder Michael hated her. No wonder he didn't want to make love to her and wanted to make love with Cee Cee. Wanted to fuck you since I saw you. Oh, God. She felt sick. Bathing suit wet. My God.

"Michael," Cee Cee said, her eyes closed. "You are the lowest, most pitiful slime on the whole fuckin' face of this earth, and you know what, you shitpile, if my loud dirty mouth made you think I was trashy enough to fuck with my friend's husband, I'd like to cut my fuckin' tongue out, because I'd die on the rack before I'd dream of it. And you know what else? You're not fit to be in the same world as Bertie," Cee Cee said, and she walked out the door and closed it quickly behind her. She was still wearing Michael's bathrobe. She couldn't wait for the elevator. She found the exit to the stairs. She opened the door and stood on the landing, leaned against the wall, and cried.

"Bimbo," Michael said to the closed door, and looked at the clock. Eleven forty-five in Pittsburgh. Perfect, he thought. He could make a few business calls before Bertie woke up.

Bertie splashed cold water in her eyes again and again, scrubbed her teeth and pulled a brush through her hair. She found some Noxema in the bottom of her cosmetics bag, unscrewed the lid and dipped her finger into the thick minty cream, pulled out a glob and spread it on her face. Now she had a cooler face, but her eyes were still stinging from her tears.

Michael dialed the long distance Oahu operator to put him through to Pennsylvania.

"Jeffrey," Michael said when his law partner took the call.

"Barron, you bum. How's Hawaii?"

"Not bad," Michael said.

"Wait till I tell you who we're about to sign as a new client," Jeffrey told him. "Boy, oh, boy—you go away, pal, and big things happen here. Well, you're gonna shit when you hear. Now sit down."

"Who?" Michael asked.

"A major friggin' star," Jeffrey said. "And maybe he'll throw in season tickets."

Bertie came out of the bathroom. She was weak with shame and rage. What could she do to him? To them? She couldn't go out into the living room now and confront them. Cee Cee and Michael. Probably hot and writhing on the sofa. On the floor. She walked again to the door of the living room, her hand on the knob.

"Oh, my God," she heard Michael say. "Cut it out and don't tease me anymore. Come on."

"Maury Wills," Jeffrey said.

Michael was ecstatic.

"Oh, no. Oh, God. Is that great. Oh, yes," he whispered, realizing that the sun was coming up and if he was too loud he might wake Bertie.

Bertie froze to the spot. Michael and Cee Cee were out there. Making love. Fucking their brains out, Cee Cee would call it. Good God. Somehow she managed to turn herself toward the bed, lie down, pull the covers and the pillow up, and sob so long and so hard that in exhaustion and pain she finally fell asleep.

Michael hung up the phone and danced a happy little dance all around the room. Maury Wills. That name would bring the firm up a peg. Yes, it would. Maury Wills. God, he was hungry. He'd call room service and order himself breakfast. Maybe he'd order Bertie breakfast, too, and he'd ask them to send up a warmer, to keep it for her. That way when she woke up it would be right there. That would make her happy. So would the news about Maury Wills. Maybe to celebrate he'd buy Bertie a little bauble in the jewelry store. Well, not really to celebrate—to soften the blow when he told her that instead of waiting until Sunday, he really wanted to get back to the office right away, and he knew she wouldn't mind if they had to leave today instead.

He took the room-service breakfast menu out of the drawer. Just reading the names of all the delicious breakfast possibilities made his stomach growl. He'd order French toast and pancakes and fresh papaya, and some crisp bacon, and blueberry muffins with lots of butter, and he'd have them send up a newspaper, and then he'd sit on the lanai and watch the day begin at the Kahala pool.

*   *   *

Cee Cee sat on the balcony of her room smoking a cigarette. Shit, she said to herself. Shit. Fuck. Shit. Am I that bad? Do I come on that whorey that he could think I'd do it? Maybe Bertie thought that too, and hated her now. And maybe if Bertie thought that too, she would go back to Pittsburgh and never want to write to her again. She ran her fingers through her wet tangled mass of red hair and pulled at it, furious at herself. Why was she always opening her big fat mouth? When it was a decent hour, she'd call up Bertie and go get her and take her for a walk on the beach. She'd explain. She'd say, listen, Bert, sometimes I open my dumb asshole mouth and get raunchy. John says it's 'cause I need attention so bad, I'll take it even if it's not *good* attention, you know? Like a little kid who wants a spanking—because it's better than nothing at all. So you're probably gettin' the wrong impression of me. That was a good beginning. What else could she say? Nothing. She wouldn't say anything about how Michael had come on to her last night. She wouldn't breathe a word about the scuzzy mongrel tryin' to rub up against her, and grabbin' her at the door of the hotel room. She'd just talk about herself and Bertie. She had to square things with Bertie.

"What're you doing up so early, hon?" John Perry stood sleepily in the open arch of the sliding glass door, wearing a white robe.

"Nothin'," Cee Cee said.

"Thought you promised you were quitting smoking," John said.

"Go back to sleep, J.P. I'm okay," Cee Cee told him.

"As you would say, my love, bullshit. What's up?"

Cee Cee was quiet for a minute. She looked out at the calm Pacific, the morning light making it look alternately orange and gray. Then at the pool where the beach boys had already begun putting up umbrellas.

"Am I a whore?" Cee Cee asked her husband. "Am I really the piece of crap low-life I feel like now?"

John didn't answer. He pulled a chair up next to his wife's chair, sat on it, then pulled Cee Cee out of her chair and onto his lap.

"Cee Cee," John said, beginning a speech he'd made to her many times in many forms. "You're a woman who needs to be loved so badly that the need seems to be never-ending. Bottomless. So you work for love, beg for it, demand it, seduce for it. In every way. With your voice when you're singing on the stage, you seduce the whole audience. And with people you meet individually, you seduce them, too. You tap into them and somehow figure out what they want from Cee Cee Bloom. What will make them fall for her. And then you put *that* part of you out there for the person to take."

Cee Cee buried her face in the shoulder of John's robe. She loved the way he smelled in the morning and the way he felt so warm.

"You're not a whore," he said, "because it isn't sex you're after, even though you make it seem that way. What you really want is for the whole world to do this." As John put his arms around his wife, he felt her tears on his neck.

Bertie was awake. She knew Michael was still out there, and the clinking of glass told her that he must have ordered room service. Of course. She remembered him saying many times that there was nothing like a good breakfast, afterwards. God, she hated him. But it didn't matter anymore. She would leave him. Go back to Pittsburgh and divorce him. Rosie would want her to come back and live at home, but she wouldn't do that.

Michael, you're a very sick man, she would say to him. Michael, I'm taking the next flight out, and you'll be hearing from my lawyers, she would scream at him. No, saying it calmly would be better. Michael, I'll tell every

one of your partners what a pig you are. I'll tell all your
clients, too. I'll ruin you. I'll—I'll—Bertie almost made
herself laugh. One of her thoughts of vengeance came
directly from her childhood. I'll tell your mother, she
thought. But the smile from that fleeting thought was
gone, and she was filled with the heart-pounding energy
of her anger. The phone rang and she grabbed it.

"Hello."

"Bert?"

Bertie closed her eyes. The last time she'd heard Cee
Cee's voice it was saying, "Michael . . . Michael," obviously caught up in the passion of the moment. Probably
touching him. Wet bathing suit. "Come here," he'd said.

"What do you want?" Bertie asked.

"You okay?" Cee Cee wanted to know. That fake
concern in her voice. Well, she was an actress. Actresses
faked emotions for a living.

"I'm perfectly fine," Bertie said.

"Well, if you didn't eat yet, why don't we go for a
walk and maybe get some breakfast, 'cause I've got some
stuff I want to tell you and—"

"Cee Cee," Bertie said. Now she would tell her. She
would shock her when she said, I heard every word you
and Michael said, you whore—and I know what went on
here. "Cee Cee, I don't want to go anywhere with you or
hear anything from you, or see you again as long as I live,"
she said, wanting to say more, wanting to tell her why,
but she couldn't, so she hung up the phone. Then she got
out of bed, went into the bathroom, washed the Noxzema
from her face, brushed her teeth and put on some make-up,
all the while reciting what she would say to Michael.
You're a very sick man. The color from her sunburn looked
great with her pink robe. She felt better than she had
earlier. Pretty and strong; that would make it easier.

The bright light from the living room was too bright
for her eyes for a moment, but when they adjusted, she
saw him on the balcony reading the newspaper and pick-

ing at some food from the table. As she got closer to the window, she could see the pool area below. A few early sun-worshipers were spreading towels on the chaise longues and oil on themselves.

Michael turned and saw her and smiled the sweetest smile she'd ever seen.

"Hi, Minnie, honey," he said, and stood. "Got your favorite breakfast here. Did you have a good sleep?"

Bertie couldn't believe it. Did he actually think he could stand there casually like that after what he'd done? No. He had no idea that she knew. Had heard him. Bertie took a breath, clenched her fists, and spoke.

"Michael, what did you and Cee Cee do last night?" she asked, wanting to sound tough like a lawyer in a movie questioning a witness, but it came out sounding a little whiny.

Michael raised his eyes heavenward. "Bert," he said. "She is such a bimbo. Why you keep that friendship going is—"

"What did you do with her?"

"I went swimming with her," Michael said.

"And then?"

"Then she came up here because while we were out there I pulled her robe into the water by accident, so I gave her mine, and then she went back to her room." Michael's eyes narrowed. "What's with you?" he asked.

Bertie said nothing.

"Bert, you can't possibly think anything could or would ever happen between me and . . ." Michael laughed and came toward her. "Ah, baby, you're jealous. And I think it's cute. She's a trashy little would-be star. And you're jealous." He put his arms around her, but she pushed him away.

"Michael, did you touch her?" Of course he touched her. "Did you—"

"Bert, if this wasn't so funny, I'd be getting really mad. It just so happened that I stayed up all night and so did she. That's all. I don't want other women. Why would I? Look at you. You're the best-lookin' broad on the face of the earth. Think I'd leave you for that skag? You need your head examined. I'm calling the airlines. I don't want to be here with you anymore. With your crazy paranoid stuff about some low-life show business hopeful and her sleazy old nobody husband. And you can stay here with them if you want, but I'm packing and heading home."

He walked into the bedroom. Bertie stood in the doorway between the two rooms. "Michael, you can't—"

"I can do whatever I want," he said, shouting at her. Now he was really angry. "You're a goddamned whining pain in the ass. I don't give you enough sex. I don't like your friends, after I extend myself to the ruination of my one vacation in years to be with those two losers and go to their lousy restaurant choices. I played tennis with him and acted charming to her and listened to her get up and embarrass herself with that phony voice. And now I have to take this shit from you? Let's get a divorce, Bertie, we don't work."

Bertie forgot her anger as panic took her over. *She* was supposed to say that, and *he* was supposed to fall apart when she did. Confess, and beg her to forgive him and to understand so they could go on. And he'd be true to her forever more. The way her Uncle Herbie had come back to Aunt Neetie. And their friends all admired the way Neetie had gritted her teeth, as if to say knowingly, "Men will be boys," and took Herbie back.

No, Michael. I'm divorcing you for adultery. Of the worst kind. With my friend. You can't divorce me for whining, she thought.

"Michael, you're not divorcing me," she began.

He had pulled his suitcase out of the closet and was pulling clothes out of various drawers and throwing them into it.

"Well, then," he said, "if you're coming home with

me, I suggest you pack. I'm not going to feed into this insecurity of yours."

A tropical breeze swept across the outside balcony, rustling the tablecloth, and moved through the door in the living room. Bertie felt it on her back. Even though it was warm, it made her shiver. Almost all of Michael's clothes were in the suitcase now, and he stopped packing and looked at her, then spoke softly.

"Bert," he said. "Nothing happened. Nothing."

Bertie felt unsure and afraid and confused.

"I love you," Michael said. "So much that I couldn't wait for you to wake up so I could tell you I called Jeff early this morning, and he told me the firm is signing Maury Wills."

"Really?" Bertie asked numbly.

"That's such good news, I was crazed," Michael said, smiling a smile Bertie knew was put on. "I was sure he was teasing me."

Teasing.

"That's great," Bertie said.

"Ah, c'mon, Minnie Mouse," he said, coming toward her again. "I love my princess too much to see her upset like this," and he pulled her close to him and she let him hold her tightly. "Let's go home to Pittsburgh, honey," he said into her hair. "What do you say?"

Bertie just stood and felt him holding her. She needed him to hold her. She wanted him to make it better, to make it not hurt. She had to decide what to say to him now. He was her husband. He took care of her, and she loved him, but he was with Cee Cee last night. This morning. She was sure of that.

"Won't it be nice to get back home?" he asked softly, sweetly, lovingly. "To our pretty apartment. Why don't we have your mother over for dinner when we get back? We can tell her all about our trip and what a good time we had. C'mon, sweetheart. I'll even help you pack. Okay? Bertie, c'mon."

Now Michael moved her an arm's length away from him, his hands still on her shoulders, and he looked at her confused face and waited for her answer.

Bertie looked into his eyes. Then she put her hands over his and removed them from her shoulders. She walked slowly over to the bed, sat on it, and thought for a while about what would be the best thing to do. Michael didn't say a word while she did. Finally, she spoke.

"Yes," she said, "let's go home." Then she stood, walked to the closet, removed her clothes from their hangers, and began to pack.

Bertie felt as if they'd been away from Pittsburgh for a much longer time than six days. Being back in her little home felt comforting to her. There was her same room, and her same bed, and her same bathroom with her same tub. But when she looked at herself in the bathroom mirror, she saw someone there who seemed different from the Bertie who'd left Hawaii less than a week before.

"Back to the old grind," Michael said as he took a last sip of coffee, gave her a peck on the cheek, and was out the door to work.

As soon as he was gone Bertie dressed quickly. She knew what she wanted to do today, and she knew that she had to do it right now. She'd thought about nothing else on the long flight home. Within minutes of Michael's leaving, she was out the door and in her car.

The visitors' lot was full, so she parked on a nearby side street and made her way slowly around the building. When she opened the door, the familiar feel of the place convinced her that she was doing the right thing. Down the hall past the reception office, through the doors and . . .

"Is Dr. Shaw in?" Bertie asked.

"Well, Roberta. How nice to see you," the gray-haired receptionist Madeline said.

"It's nice to see you, too, Madeline."

"She's in a staff meeting," Madeline said. "Want a cup of coffee?"

There was one moment when a heavy feeling in her chest made Bertie unsure that this was smart. Made her want to say something light. Something like, "Well, I just stopped by to say hello—so give everyone my best, but I have to go now," and then she could leave. But instead, she sat on one of the hard metal folding chairs in the reception area.

"No coffee," she said. "Thank you, but I'd like to wait for her if I may."

A half-hour later, when Dr. Shaw emerged from her meeting, she seemed genuinely glad to see Bertie. And yes, she did have a few minutes to talk.

"Come into my office," she said.

Bertie held tightly to the arm of the chair she sat in across from Dr. Shaw's desk.

"I'd like to come back here," she said the way she'd rehearsed it silently to herself so often. "Only I'd like to volunteer for five full days a week instead of two half-days. And I think I can promise you there won't be another incident. It was unfortunate, and it won't happen again."

Dr. Shaw nodded.

"You're a hard worker, Roberta," she said. "I suspect you were going through some personal crisis, but if you feel you can keep that separate—"

"I will," Bertie said. "I mean, I know I can. And . . . I'd like to be here. Very much."

Dr. Shaw nodded again.

"Let's try," she said, standing to let Bertie know that their few minutes' talk was at an end.

"Thank you," Bertie said. She wanted to throw her arms around the serious lady shrink and kiss her all over her face.

"I'm so glad." My God, she thought, if there's anything I mustn't do now it's cry. "So glad."

"I'm sure," Dr. Shaw said, moving around the desk, guiding Bertie toward the door, "that Carla will be glad, too."

Bertie looked surprised.

"She came back last night," Dr. Shaw said, taking Bertie's arm.

The two women walked together into the corridor.

Dear Bertie,

This is at least the tenth or eleventh letter I have written you and you aren't opening them and you are sending them back and I don't know why. Well—I think I do—but I'm not sure. I think you've got some crazy idea about me and your husband—only I swear it isn't true. That's what I wrote in the last ten or eleven letters, too, and I'll keep sending them till you give up and answer me one day.

Did Michael say something happened? Bert, I swear on everything it's not true.

I am opening in my first Broadway show next week. It's a small part but I have a solo that's really good.

I have been fighting a lot with John and wish I could talk to you or write to you about it. I need your advice a lot.

PLEASE, BERTIE, I'M BEGGING YOU. DON'T THROW THIS AWAY. READ IT AND WRITE TO ME.

Cee Cee

Dear Roberta,

Well, here I am in Neetie's beautiful new home in Miami Beach. I wish you had come with me, but I understand that Michael likes to have you at home instead of traveling without him.

The weather here is as usual very warm and compared to the temperature it was in Pittsburgh when you took me to the airport, this is paradise.

Neetie and Herb have a friend they want me to go on a date with, but I don't know. It seems silly when I know I'll be back in Pittsburgh in a few weeks, for me to date a man in Miami. Neetie says, for God's sake, Rose, it's only to go out to dinner, you don't have to think about marrying the man.

They are happy to have made the move here. Herb's business is thriving, even though your aunt lives in the fear every day that he'll get thrown in jail.

Neetie thinks I should move here, too, so at least I can be near her, but then it would mean I couldn't be near you and Michael and someday, this is not a hint, a grandchild. Neetie says you'll bring the grandchild to visit.

I guess I'm feeling lonely today, and maybe I'll try to call you tonight, because you always cheer me up.

Give my best to Michael.

Love,

Mother

WHATSERFACE
FIRST NIGHTERS
ONE MAN'S OPINION BY DAVID BALLARD

Whatserface is the story of the rise to stardom and power of a woman who falls into it all by accident. If by some accident you should fall into the Brookhurst Theater while it's playing, I hope you stay awake longer than I did.

Cami Dunnet, who was the only breath of spring in John Campbell's *Honey Bear* off-Broadway last year, has fallen prey to Marc Rothfeld's stodgy directorial hand, and the result is deadly. Dunnet's transition to star model from cleaning lady is so devoid of transformation, you wonder why she even bothered to change for her last number into the bugle beads (overdone by designer Celia Fenwick).

Hal Collins's lyrics and David Gelman's music are just a shade less childlike than Helen Newsome's book, which received (not an exaggeration) actual hoots in several places from members of the audience who were brave enough to remain for the second act. Particularly when Bob Foxdale, in a mercifully small role, tells Dunnet how the modeling world will take girls like her and "chew them up and spit them out."

Can this show be saved? Absolutely not. And yet, magnificently cast in the role of Miss Dunnet's associate on the night shift is a young actress-singer named Cee Cee Bloom, who has such presence, such a dazzling voice, such extraordinary sparkle that when she performed her song, "This Is Who I Am," a few people who were on their way up the aisle were compelled to turn back and stay. (P.S. After she made her exit, so did they.)

Ergo, Virginia, every cloud seems indeed to have a silver lining. So, rest assured that just as the sun rises and sets, you can count on *Whatserface* to close real soon. But . . . keep an eye out for Cee Cee Bloom.

My dear daughter Cecilia,

I must admit when you called me on the telephone to ask if I would come and see you in a play on the Broadway stage, I had my worries and my doubts as to if I should do it or if I shouldn't do it, even though you are my only child.

After all, since your mother died, may she rest in peace, I go out very little. I am not complaining because I like it that way. I have a nice person who comes once a week to clean, and she also makes a trip to the supermarket so I wouldn't have to. Once in a while I go to your cousin Myra, who is a thoughtful girl to include an old man, and she makes a nice brisket and gives me leftovers to take home in an "uncle bag." (That is a joke between me and Myra that I find funny.)

Anyhow, when I told Myra you invited me to Broadway, she told Herman and they wanted to come also, so that is why I asked you to leave three tickets. Myra said, Uncle Nate, how bad could it be? Right? Even though I always used to worry when your mother, may she rest in peace, would try to make you go every week to dancing lessons and singing lessons, and sometimes you would cry bitterly and I would say let her sleep late, Leona, darling, and she would get mad at me and tell me to shut up.

Cecilia, to make a long story short, I didn't like for you to be in show business, and I can't lie about it.

So Saturday night when you came on the

stage and you sang a song with a voice like a bird, I am ashamed to admit that my eyes were so full of tears Myra gave me her hankie.

After the play, I came backstage to see you and give you a kiss and see your nice husband, but I couldn't say too much because everyone was there, and if I bragged too much they would think it's because I'm your father, and maybe that's why I thought it was so good, because I'm related. But it's not. I would think you were the best one even if you were a total stranger. Myra said so also. As did Herman on the way home.

Even though I hope your mother, may she rest in peace, is resting in peace, I wish she, over anybody, would have seen our daughter Cee Cee (why can't you use Cecilia? It's much better in my opinion and also in Myra's opinion) Bloom?

> *Your loving father,*
>
> *Nathan Bloom*

BILLBOARD HOT 100®
FOR WEEK ENDING JAN 3 1970

THIS WEEK	1 week ago	2 weeks ago	3 weeks ago	TITLE, Performer, Producer Record Company	weeks on chart
1	3	5	9	**RAINDROPS KEEP FALLING ON MY HEAD** B. J. Thomas (Burt Bacharach–Hal David) Scepter	10
2	2	1	2	**LEAVING ON A JET PLANE** Peter, Paul & Mary (Albert B. Grossman & Milt Okum) Warner Bros.–Seven Arts	11
3	1	2	3	**SOMEDAY WE'LL BE TOGETHER** Diana Ross & The Supremes (Johnny Bristol) Motown	9
4	4	3	5	**DOWN ON THE CORNER/ FORTUNATE SON** Creedence Clearwater Revival (John Fogerty) Fantasy	10
5	5	4	1	**NA NA HEY HEY KISS HIM GOODBYE** Steam (Paul Lake) Fontana	12
6	9	12	–	**THIS IS WHO I AM** Cee Cee Bloom (Hal Collins–David Gelman) Athena	3
7	8	17	19	**I WANT YOU BACK** The Jackson 5 (The Corporation) Motown	8
8	19	31	77	**VENUS** Shocking Blue (Robert van Leeuwen) Colossus	4
9	6	9	13	**HOLLY HOLY** Neil Diamond (Tom Catalone & Tom Cogbill) UNI	10
10	14	14	34	**LA LA LA (If I Had You)** Bobby Sherman (Jackie Mills) Metromedia	7

T.V. GUIDE

ED SULLIVAN
VARIETY—SUNDAY, JANUARY 21ST

ED'S GUESTS INCLUDE IMPRESSIONIST DAVID FRYE, CONNIE STEVENS, COMIC JOHN BYNER, AND SINGER CEE CEE BLOOM SINGING HER HIT SONG "THIS IS WHO I AM."

Miami Beach, Florida, 1970

Bertie was too numb to look out the window of the taxi, and Miami Beach, at least from what she'd seen as she stood at the airport taxi stand, didn't look at all the way it had in that James Bond movie.

"It's like what Patricia Neal had," Neetie had told her on the phone, giving Bertie hope that her mother, like Patricia Neal, would somehow bravely retrain whatever parts of her body had been damaged and pull through. Not her mother. Bertie thought of the children at the Home for Crippled Children where she worked. About the hours of physical therapy they struggled through every day and how slow their progress was, in spite of all their zeal to be stronger. Rosie could never make it through that kind of struggle.

The taxi was on Collins Avenue heading downtown. The paper with Michael's directions was still clutched in her hand. ST. JOSEPH'S HOSPITAL. MIAMI BEACH. I.C.U. INTENSIVE CARE UNIT. COME RIGHT IN THROUGH EMERGENCY.

Michael had spoken to Neetie after Bertie heard the news. Bertie had handed him the phone because she was sobbing so violently that Neetie could only say, "Please, Bertie. Please."

Michael had written down the directions to the hospital. Michael had packed Bertie's clothes. Michael had driven Bertie to the airport, taken her to the VIP Lounge because the plane's departure was delayed an hour, and made her have a Coke to drink. "It's free," he said. Twenty-five dollars to belong to the VIP Lounge, which they never used. This was a twenty-five-dollar Coke. She had laughed at that to herself and then felt guilty. She was laughing. Rosie, on the other hand, was . . . don't say it. Say it or not, she was sure this was it.

Oh, my God. Oh, my God. If only she could stop her thoughts.

"Take a Valium," Michael said.

Those were his last words. Not, good-by. Not, I love you. Not, I hope she gets well. "Take a Valium."

Maybe if she cried she'd feel better. She tried to cry, then decided there was no such thing as trying to cry. You either cried or you didn't. How did actresses do it in the movies?

Without looking, Bertie could feel the Miami Beach buildings the taxi was passing. Pink and white and glitter-filled stucco-fronted hotels. The ones that had been the most beautiful were now the poor cousins to the modern high-rise condominiums. Maybe she wasn't looking because it was festive and she was going to a hospital where . . . Bertie forced her head to turn, then closed her eyes immediately. Her first glimpse out the window had taken her breath away like a blow to the stomach. CARILLON HOTEL. FEB. 14–28. CEE CEE BLOOM.

Cee Cee was here. In Miami Beach. Performing at the Carillon, which, Bertie realized, as the taxi pulled up and stopped outside a large pink Spanish building, was right around the corner from the hospital. February 14–28. Today was, what—the twentieth or twenty-first?

Cee Cee again. Only a few weeks ago, Bertie and Michael had been at a dinner party at the home of Marshall, one of Michael's law partners, and Marshall's wife, Sheila.

"Eat a lot of hors d'oeuvres," Sheila said, " 'cause we can't have dinner until after Ed Sullivan."

"My wife has a lot of class," Marshall said, grabbing Sheila around the waist and pulling her close to him. Sheila giggled and kissed her husband on the cheek with a big MWAH sound. Bertie envied their playfulness.

"She'd serve us dinner in front of the television every night if I let her," Marshall said.

"That's not true. Only for Ed Sullivan. I love Ed Sullivan. Tonight he's having David Frye. I love David Frye."

They were sitting in Marshall and Sheila's rumpus room. There were two other couples. When Ed Sullivan said, "And now, a really wonderful . . . really, really wonderful singer," Bertie tapped her foot on the linoleum floor. She was hungry. God, Bertie thought, wouldn't it be crazy if the really wonderful singer was Cee Cee? No. That would be impossible because Cee Cee wasn't famous enough to be on *The Ed Sullivan Show*. You had to be a big star to be on *The Ed Sullivan Show*. So it wouldn't be Cee Cee.

"Direct from the Broadway show *Whatserface*," Ed said.

Good heavens, Bertie thought. I think that's the name of the show that she's in. Rosie had clipped a review from *The New York Times*.

"Let's welcome . . ." Ed Sullivan put his hand out and said, "Cee Cee," and he put his hand up to his face, paused a minute, and said, "Bloom."

Then there was some music and there she was. Cee Cee. Singing. Belting out a wonderful song. Bertie's face was flushed and her heart was pounding. She looked out of the corner of her eye at Michael for some reaction. There was none. He sat at the end of the sofa watching, his left hand toying with an ashtray on the end table next to the sofa. Lifting the ashtray and gently placing it back on the table, again and again.

"This girl's fabulous," Sheila said after Cee Cee had sung about half the song.

"Yeah, Bertie knows her," Michael said. No one heard him but Bertie.

When the song finished, the applause was peppered with people in the audience shouting bravo. Bertie excused herself, went to Sheila and Marshall's powder room and splashed cold water on her face. Cee Cee again.

And now she was here, in Miami.

Bertie paid the taxi fare and carried her suitcase into the corridor. The smell and the feeling of the hospital filled her senses, and her head began to pound. It's only a hospital, she told herself. The Home for Crippled Children is kind of a hospital. You should be used to the way a place like this feels. But she wasn't.

"Excuse me." She heard her voice sounding very tiny. "My mother is in I.C.U. and I don't want to take my suitcase there . . . and I don't know where exactly to . . ."

"Just put the suitcase in there," a busy nurse said.

Bertie dragged the case a few more feet and put it in a closet. What if someone took it? So what? Have to get to Mother before she . . . oh, God.

"Elevator to the third floor," the nurse said coldly. Why not? It wasn't *her* mother.

I.C.U. and an arrow. Bertie rounded the corner and entered the room. Neetie was there. Neetie was a younger version of her mother, and for a split second when Bertie saw her, she thought it was her mother. Yes, maybe it had been, please, dear God, a joke they were playing just to get Bertie to come to Miami. Neetie looked at Bertie for what seemed like a long time before she real-

ized it was Bertie. Her eyes were half-closed and she got
up slowly and put her arms around her sister's child.
That's what she always called Bertie. "My sister's child. I
love you as if you were my own."

Bertie didn't move. Neetie's smell engulfed her. Jean
Naté. It was the way Neetie always smelled. The way her
house in Pittsburgh had smelled all the time. There were
giant bottles of it all over her funny little house. The
house that Bertie used to think was magical because it had
three telephone lines, with three different telephone numbers, all unlisted. Only later, when Bertie found out that
Uncle Herbie was a bookie and what a bookie did, did the
three telephones with the three different telephone numbers lose their magic.

"Come," Neetie said, taking Bertie's arm.

Bertie's heart raced. She knew Neetie was taking her
to see her mother, and she wasn't ready. Ready? More
make-up? Her mother was in a coma. Patricia Neal, remember? Coronary Care Unit. Doesn't that mean heart
attack? Swinging doors. Little cubicles. Nurses. Someone's in an oxygen tent. Which one is . . . Neetie moved
her. Guided her. Take a deep breath. Not too many.
Don't hyperventilate. Cubicle seven and . . . oh, my God,
no, please, God, don't let it be. Mother. Mommy. Oh,
God.

Tubes. In every part of her. Tubes. The ominous one
was in her nose. There was a computer connected to her
with numbers that got higher and lower.

Bertie was afraid to look at Neetie. Neetie was used
to it. She had seen it before. Since yesterday.

Yesterday in Pumpernicks. Rosie had to go to the
ladies' room. She was fine. Neetie had finished her corned
beef sandwich, a little more coffee, please, when she
heard the screams. In Pumpernicks there had been screams
before.

"Some *alta kocker* croaks in here once a week," a lady from New York with too much eye make-up said.

Neetie finished her coffee. A crowd was gathering by the ladies' room. Neetie looked at her watch.

Maybe we'll take a little walk on Collins, then we'll go back to my place and see how Herbie's doing, she thought. Then later, if Herbie's busy, Rosie and I will go see a movie. Rosie. Where the hell was . . . Neetie heard the ambulance and stood up to see where it was headed.

No, it couldn't be. She walked toward the ladies' room. The door was open. A few people were inside. A heavy man wearing a flower print shirt was sitting on the floor beside the woman who had collapsed. Next to him a waitress was holding a pair of sandals. They were the sandals Neetie had picked for Rosie in Burdines.

"Rosie," Neetie said. "Oh, not my Rosie."

"Mom," Bertie said.

"She can't hear you. She doesn't know it's you. The doctor told me."

"I don't believe it. Mom."

The numbers got higher. Heartbeat increases.

"I'm here, Mom," Bertie said.

The tubes were moving liquids in and out. Intravenous. Catheter. There were slurping sounds with each labored breath.

"Look at her eyes," Bertie said.

Rosie's head was way back, probably to help the tubes to stay in, and her eyes looked as if they were half-open.

"Sometimes they flutter," Neetie said. "Sometimes, I swear she wants to open them and look at me."

A nurse entered briskly. For a second Bertie thought she was about to throw them out of the room. There had been a sign on the way in that said something about visiting I.C.U. rooms only on the hour, but it must have been the pained look on Bertie's face, or maybe her resemblance to Rosie that told the nurse she was the daughter and damn the rules.

Bertie felt Neetie's hand on her arm, trying to direct her out of the room, but she didn't move. There was something telling her that maybe, if she stayed there, stood there, sang songs to Rosie, talked to her, read to her, tirelessly, constantly, that Rosie might wake up and respond.

"Mom," she said. She was too embarrassed by the nurse's presence to sing. If only she had the nerve, she would lean over the bed and sing "Poor Butterfly." It was the song Rosie used to sing to her when she was a child to get her to feel better.

"Mom." Bertie said it a little louder. She wanted to scream it out, but she was afraid the nurse would be shocked and tell her she had to leave because screaming was against hospital policy.

Bertie saw a nun walk through the corridor and enter one of the cubicles. That's right. This was a Catholic hospital. This was probably a good time to be a Catholic, Bertie thought. To have a lot of faith.

She remembered reading some article about the Lennon Sisters while she was waiting at the beauty salon to get her hair cut one day. The Lennon Sisters' father had been shot and killed by a man who was such a crazed fan of theirs that he wrote letters to them, saying he believed he was the real husband of Peggy. Or was it Kathy, the prettiest one? Then one day, so the article said, the man approached the Lennon Sisters' father, who was on the golf course at the time, and demanded to know where to find Peggy, or Kathy, or whichever one he thought he was married to. The Lennon Sisters' father wouldn't tell the man, so the man killed the Lennon Sisters' father. Shot him. The horrible part came when the police finally found the murderer. He was dead. He had shot himself, at least that's what they said. But somehow, his body was in the trunk of his own car, surrounded by piles of fan magazines.

The Lennon Sisters were Catholic, and Bertie couldn't remember now exactly what the article said, but mostly it was about how the Lennon Sisters believed it was "God's will," and they accepted it with peace in their hearts. And even in the photographs where they were coming out of the church from the funeral, they looked peaceful and serene and accepting.

Neetie edged her to the door, and Bertie took another look back at Rosie. There was no polish on her mother's fingernails now. Bertie couldn't remember ever seeing her mother's nails without polish. And her hair. It looked like straw. She'd been bleaching it some yellowy color; now the roots were showing. If Rosie were awake and could see herself she would say, "Oh, my God. Don't I look like hell?"

"Mom," Bertie said.

"Come." Neetie moved her out of the cubicle and through the big swinging doors through the corridor to the waiting room.

A woman of about forty was sleeping on one of the plastic couches. She was using a raincoat as a blanket.

"Mrs. Koven," Neetie said, seeing Bertie look at the woman. "Her husband had a very serious heart attack. A young man, too. Forty-one."

Bertie sat on a hard chair and tried to think what to do next.

Neetie went on. "She told me last night she's been here for eleven days and nights straight. Doesn't leave the waiting room except to go and sit by his bed and cry. Her daughter brings her food and clothes. She eats in here and changes in there." Neetie pointed to a door that must obviously be a rest room. She seemed very interested in the woman's case. She lit a cigarette and offered one to Bertie, who took it gratefully.

They sat and smoked. Bertie felt drained. She wanted to curl up on one of the plastic couches and cover herself with a raincoat, like the wife of the man with the heart

attack, but she knew there was too much to do. Things to
take care of. Like what? she thought. Doctors. Yes.

"Where's my mother's doctor? Who's her doctor?"

"A little guy," Neetie said. "He was the one who was
here when they admitted her. Spatz? Spitz? Something
like that."

"Where is he?"

"He'll be here later."

"When?"

Neetie shrugged. "Last night he said he'd be here
tomorrow. That's today. So I guess later."

Bertie put her cigarette out and stood up. "I have to
talk to him."

She walked out into the hall. Bertie had just seen a
look in Neetie's eyes that she recognized. It was a look she
herself sometimes gave Michael when she felt grateful to
him for taking over some difficult situation. A situation she
had tried to handle herself, but couldn't. A look of relief
that said, now that you're here, and you're going to be in
charge, I can become helpless again. Bertie knew from the
look that Neetie expected her to take over, believed that
Bertie, who hadn't even been able to pack her own suitcase to make the trip here, would now do it all. She would
force the doctors to pay attention, she would make sure
they got the information they needed. Yes. She would
somehow put it all together to make Rosie well. Bertie
looked at the big black doors of the coronary care unit.
There was a nurses' station in there. She could go in and
find out from one of the nurses how to reach Rosie's
doctor.

And then what? What would she say once she reached
him? Make my mother well? She took a few steps toward
the big doors. Her heart was pounding. She knew the
nurses' station was right outside of Rosie's room, and she
would have to look at Rosie again. Look at her and see
those terrible tubes and the computer, and Rosie's eyes,
wanting to open and to see Bertie, see how she looked.

Wanting to ask her the question she asked her nearly once a week: "Well? When are you going to make me a grand-mother?" It always made Bertie feel guilty when she said that. "Make me a grandmother." It wasn't as if Bertie and Michael weren't trying. Had been to specialist after spe-cialist. And Bertie *told* Rosie that. But still she said it in person or on the phone at least once a week. "Make me a grandmother," as if Bertie were deliberately holding out on her.

Bertie pushed the doors open and walked toward the nurses' station. She decided not to look at Rosie, but she couldn't help it. The nurse who had been in there must have moved Rosie's arm to make it easier for the intrave-nous tube to get into her system, because now her right arm was kind of lifted over the metal railing that flanked the side of the bed, and Rosie's index finger, with an unpolished nail, looked as if it was pointing toward the door of the room. Pointing at Bertie.

You didn't make me a grandmother, the frozen ges-ture said to Bertie. And now look at me. I'm in a coma, and probably I'm going to die . . . without a grandchild.

"Yes," the nurse said, looking up.

"Uh, I'm Mrs. White's daughter, Roberta Barron," Bertie heard herself say.

"Yes?"

"Uh, well, I wanted to know. Um. Would it be possi-ble for you to tell me . . ." Bertie hated herself. Good God. She was a twenty-six-year-old woman and she sounded like a child.

"Could I speak to . . . I mean, who is my mother's doctor?"

The nurse looked irritated.

"Which one is your mother?"

"Rose. White. Mrs. Rosie White."

"Which room number?" the woman said impatiently.

"Room number?" Bertie looked anxiously at Rosie's door. She didn't see a number.

"That one," she said, pointing.

"Seven," the nurse said. Bertie looked all around the door of the room. She didn't see a number seven anywhere. Her eyes caught Rosie's pointing finger again, and she looked back at the nurse who was studying a chart.

"Myron Spatz," the nurse said. "He was the admitting doctor." She put the chart down and went back to her work. Bertie was nervous. "Can I speak to him?" she asked softly.

"Of course."

"When?"

"When he gets here," the nurse answered, as if to a child.

"When will that be?"

"I don't know, dear," the nurse said.

Bertie was feeling angry, and her stomach hurt. She remembered an ad she once saw. Maybe it was for the American Cancer Society. In the big letters of the ad it said something like AUNT MARTHA or AUNT MAGGY or some name like that, DIED OF SHAME. There was a picture of an old-fashioned-looking woman, and then in the smaller letters it said something about how this old-fashioned woman had been too embarrassed to examine her own breasts or to let a doctor examine them, so she never knew that she had breast cancer, and then she died. The moral was, don't let this happen to you. Don't be intimidated. Speak up and save your life. Rosie's life. Bertie took a deep breath.

"I want to talk to him now," she said.

The nurse didn't even look up.

"Can I reach him at home?"

The nurse shuffled some papers. Bertie's heart was pounding. She could turn and walk back out to the waiting room. She could tell Neetie the doctor wasn't available just yet. She turned her eyes for a glance back at Rosie's room. The finger was still pointing. She had to speak up or

Rosie would die of shame like Aunt Martha or whatever her name was from the ad.

"I said," she announced, surprising herself with the sound of this big new voice, "I want to talk to him now." She paused for a moment as the next thought came to her. "Even if it means calling him at home."

The nurse was silent for a long time. She didn't look at Bertie.

Bertie's mind raced. How did other people do this? Maybe if she was a man it would be different. Maybe then the nurse would be sweet, nice, even flirtatious. Saying, yes, sir, of course, sir. I'll reach your mother's doctor right away, but how about if I fix you some coffee first? Maybe this nurse didn't like Bertie because she was pretty, and the nurse wasn't, although she knew she couldn't look too pretty, filled with Valium, and after that five-hour flight.

How could she get to her? She studied the woman for a moment when her eye caught the little plastic pin. Susan Byers, R.N. Susan Byers. Didn't Susan Byers love a mother? Couldn't she imagine what it was like for Bertie to see Rosie, who had fed Bertie, clothed her, hugged her, taught her to walk, to talk, sang "Poor Butterfly" to her when she was sick, called her "Puss" and "Mommy's precious," lying there helpless and dying? Unless somebody did something. Soon. Fast. Oh, God. Bertie felt the tears welling. There was a sob moving in her throat. No. She choked it back and leaned forward. She took a deep breath and leaned forward.

"Susan," she said quietly.

The woman, surprised, looked up and into Bertie's eyes.

"Susan, I know that you have an enormous amount of responsibility working in this unit, and I appreciate that and respect it. I'm grateful that my mother was brought to this hospital and am sure that she's in good hands. But, I'm a stranger here, Susan." The woman flinched a little every time Bertie said her name. "The last time I saw my mother she was very healthy, and now she's in a coma, and I'm upset." The tears were fighting to come, but Bertie fought them right back. "I know you'll understand my need to see Dr. Spatz right away. So please tell me how we can arrange that. Okay, Susan?" No tears. Not yet. Control.

Suddenly the woman who looked back at Bertie was totally changed. She reached out and touched Bertie's hand. Susan Byers, R.N. Bertie had been wrong. She was pretty. Maybe even prettier than Bertie. "I understand," she said. "The reason I can't call Dr. Spatz is because he's en route. He'll be here any minute."

Now the tears could come.

"I'm sorry about your mom," Susan Byers said. Bertie knew she meant it. She also noticed now that Susan Byers was only about twenty-three years old.

Bertie walked into cubicle seven. The seven was very prominent over the door. She gently touched Rosie's pointing finger.

"I love you, Mom," she whispered, getting closer. And one of her tears fell on Rosie's arm. Maybe it would be the way things happened in a fairy tale, and the fallen tear would awaken Rosie. And her awakening would awaken everyone else in the hospital who was unconscious. And they would all jump to their feet and sing, "There's gonna be a great day," as they danced through the hospital corridors. But Rosie didn't move, and Bertie turned and walked toward the swinging doors. She looked back at Susan Byers, who was on the phone now, and Susan Byers smiled at her and waved a warm little wave. Bertie had handled it. So far. Maybe Rosie wasn't going to die after all.

Bertie's stomach was churning. She was hungry. Maybe Neetie would go and get sandwiches for them. No. Not if the doctor was due. Neetie would want to hear what he had to say. What did other people do about food around here? The lady whose husband had the heart attack had a daughter who brought her clothes and food. Maybe they could call Uncle Herb, or . . .

Cee Cee. How had Bertie forgotten that Cee Cee was appearing nightly right across the street? There had been so many other feelings bombarding her since her arrival that Cee Cee had slipped from her mind, but now she was back, lodged there. Cee Cee and Michael making love in Hawaii. All of those letters that came later. Letters Bertie couldn't read, couldn't look at. Hated even to touch as she marked them RETURN UNOPENED and put them back in her mailbox for the mailman to take. Only a few months ago, she had come upon the recognizable handwriting again in her pile of mail. This time the envelope was very large, as if purposely to get her attention, and underneath the place where it was addressed to Bertie, a note was printed in large letters: PLEASE BERT, I'M BEGGING YOU TO READ THIS.

Bertie had looked at the sealed envelope for a long time. She could just hear Cee Cee saying those words, I'M BEGGING YOU. It was so dramatic. Cee Cee was dramatic. That's probably why she was such a good actress. And a successful one, too. In a play on Broadway. Rosie had seen a review of a play in which Cee Cee had appeared. She cut it out and gave it to Bertie one day at lunch. Later Bertie had heard her mother bragging about Cee Cee on the phone to a friend.

"Listen, my daughter's pen pal, her very close girlfriend in New York, is in a play on Broadway," she said, as if it had anything to do with her. And Bertie had fought the urge to pick up the extension phone and shout into it, "She's so close she slept with my husband," and slam it down.

That last envelope had taken on a life of its own. The large letters danced before Bertie's eyes. Instead of sending it back immediately, she'd kept this one unopened in her drawer for nearly two weeks, trying to decide what to do. Once Bertie even held the envelope up to the light just to see if she could see a word or two. That's when she really felt ridiculous. What did it matter? Cee Cee had done a terrible thing to her and it was over between them. Back to the mailbox the letter went, finally, and she wished Cee Cee would stop sending the damned letters. Every time one came she relived that scene in her mind. Waking to hear Michael and Cee Cee out there in the living room of the suite.

"Mrs. Barron?"

A short, round-faced, balding man emerged from the swinging doors of I.C.U.

"I'm Dr. Spatz."

Neetie must have heard him because she came bounding out of the waiting room like a shot and stood very close to Bertie.

"This is my aunt, Mrs. Burton," Bertie told Spatz.

He nodded at Neetie. Bertie saw that Neetie was trembling.

"My mother," Bertie said.

"Yes. Mrs. White," Spatz said. "I admitted her yesterday."

Through the door of the waiting room, Bertie could see the woman whose husband had a heart attack, Mrs. Koven. She was eating a sandwich and French fries. A teenaged girl was sitting next to her eating a brownie. Bertie's stomach growled.

"Mrs. Barron, your mother has suffered a subarachnoid hemorrhage from a ruptured berry aneurism. That means she's had bleeding in the layers around her brain from the blood vessels at the base of her brain."

The doctor stopped talking. That was it. That was the whole thing.

Bertie felt weak. She was tired and very hungry. She wanted to ask the girl in the waiting room for some of her brownie, but the girl put the last bite in her mouth and wiped her face with a napkin. Now what?

Yes, Rosie. The doctor was waiting for Bertie to ask him something about Rosie.

"What do we do now?" Neetie asked.

"Will she live?" Bertie asked. Bertie was amazed how numb she'd become in the short time since she cried hysterically on the phone last night. Was it only last night?

"I'm afraid you'll have to call in a neurosurgeon," Spatz said. Bertie noticed that while he talked he rolled forward and rose onto his toes. Maybe he did that because he was short and if he spent part of the time on his toes he would seem taller.

"They will want to do a brain scan and an angiogram to find precisely where the berry aneurism is located. After that, they'll probably want to operate."

Neetie was chewing on her fingers. "Do you think my sister can live through an operation like that?" she asked softly.

The doctor merely gave Neetie a patronizing look. It was the look a waitress gave you when you called her over and asked if you could order now. Only when the waitress gave that look, she also said, "Sorry, that's not my table."

Whether Rosie would live or not wasn't Spatz's table.

"Which neurosurgeon?" Bertie asked.

"There are several on the staff here."

"How do I find one?"

"They'll give you a list."

"How do I know who the best one is?"

That wasn't Spatz's table, either. He only told you what to do. Not how, with whom, or what the outcome might be. Bertie wanted to kick him.

"I'm sure you'll find someone," he said politely. "I'll be by again tomorrow." With one last rise onto his toes, he nodded, then turned and walked down the corridor.

Cee Cee's throat hurt. And the goddamned sequined dress weighed a ton. Jesus, it was a good thing there were only five more days to this gig, otherwise Miami Beach was gonna do her in. With the heat, and the old people, and nothing to do all day. She couldn't stay in the god-damned hotel room anymore or she'd go stir crazy. She couldn't stay at the pool oiled up like a French fry, either. Because all those people kept coming up to her and saying "Oh, honey, you're just like my grandchild, with that big mouth of yours. So come and let's have our picture taken together."

Well, sure. That was great for the first few days. It was *better* than great. It was what she'd waited for, for her whole life, and she played it to the hilt. Hugging the nice people. Clowning for their pictures. Thanking them over and over again when they said how sensational she was on *The Ed Sullivan Show* a few weeks ago, and how she was even better in the show last night. In fact, they were coming again to see her tonight. And she loved it most of all when she overheard them say to one another, "She's such a nice person. So real."

But now it was starting to get to her. Maybe it was because she was fighting with John about dumb little things every day and *that* was getting to her, too. When things were okay with John, everything else seemed good, but the minute the two of them got out of whack, everything turned to shit.

Like last week when all of a sudden, out of nowhere, John decided to try and get the hotel to give them a bigger suite. Cee Cee told him that was silly because she was perfectly happy in the suite they had now, but he had some kinda bug up his ass.

"Hey," he said, "business in this place is better than ever, and it's because *you're* bringing the audience in. So why should *you* be staying in anything less than a pent-house suite?"

And he was so serious and redfaced when he said it that she shrugged and told him, "Fine. Let's ask." But when he called the management to ask, they told him they were sorry, but there wasn't a penthouse suite available.

Well, that made him *really* pissed, in a way Cee Cee
hadn't seen before. And he wouldn't give up, either. He
told the guy on the phone that the hotel ought to pay to
move him and Cee Cee to another hotel where there was
a penthouse suite available. The guy on the phone thought
about it for a minute and then said he'd get back to John.
But he never did.

After that John was more edgy than ever. He'd go
down to the pool for a quick swim in the mornings, then
he'd come back up to the hotel room and sit in the
bathtub for hours. He'd start drinking wine around four
o'clock. Then at eight o'clock he'd come down and sit at a
table by the entrance to the showroom, and while Cee
Cee was singing she could make him out back there,
throwing down a few more drinks. And even though he
told her every day that he loved her, she was scared.

Tonight he seemed better, she thought, pulling the
heavy dress up to take it off. She was relieved when he'd
begged off to stay in the suite and watch some old movie
on TV. He said they could call room service after the show
when she got upstairs, and he seemed more relaxed. Five
more friggin' days of Miami Beach. Then they'd go back to
New York. They needed that. To be in the city in their
own dumpy little apartment where they were comfortable.

Cee Cee hung the sequined dress on the rack, slipped
a muumuu over her head, put some sandals on her feet,
turned off the light in the dressing room, closed the door,
and walked down the hall toward the service elevator.

She was hungry. Always after a show she got those
hunger pangs like she could eat a friggin' horse, and now
she couldn't think of one goddamned thing on the room
service menu that appealed to her. Club sandwich. Blah.
Salade Fruits de Mer. Yech. Meat. She needed a sandwich. Double decker. Maybe triple. What Nathan, her
father, used to call a Dagwood sandwich. He'd pile the
cheese on there, and then the cole slaw, and three different kinds of meat, with mustard and mayonnaise and then

call out, "Hey, Cecilia, c'mere and take a bite out of this," and Cee Cee would come into the kitchen and they'd both start laughing at how funny the sandwich was, until Leona came in, and said something shitty like, "Even Cee Cee's mouth ain't big enough for *that* thing," or, "Nate, you pig. Eat like a person. Not an animal, fa chrissake," and ruin their laugh.

That deli across the street was open all night. Maybe they had something good. Maybe she'd walk in there and pick up a couple of sandwiches and take them back to the room and have a little picnic with John. That would cheer him up. She took her dark glasses out of her purse and put them on, just as the doors of the service elevator opened.

The lobby was dead. Old people go to bed early. The man at the front desk was reading a magazine and didn't look up as Cee Cee walked by. She knew she must look a little weird with her stage make-up still on, dressed in her muumuu and wearing sunglasses at two in the morning. Maybe not. Maybe in Miami Beach that was the right way to look.

The warm night felt soothing, and even on a busy street like Collins Avenue, with bus fumes and odors wafting from the restaurants, Cee Cee could still smell the salty ocean air mixed with the perfume of the tropical growth that was planted in stucco planters around the outside of the hotel.

There were only four full tables in Pumpernicks, and nobody at any of them seemed to notice Cee Cee.

"Help you, hon?" a short waitress with blond hair and black roots asked. Cee Cee improvised the ingredients of two different sandwiches, and the waitress made them while she waited.

A couple who had to be at least in their eighties came through the door. They both walked very slowly. The man carried a cane. The woman had her arm through his, and they walked toward a booth not far from where Cee Cee was standing. Just as the woman was about to sit down on one side of the booth, the man lifted her wrinkled old hand to his lips and kissed it. The woman smiled a girlish smile at him and then she sat as he went to the other side of the booth and sat, too.

Cee Cee grinned. She wondered if the couple was on a date. No. These two had been married for at least fifty, maybe even sixty years. Christ. Would she have that kind of marriage with John? It had only been ten years, and the bickering was so bitter, sometimes she didn't think she could stand it.

"Anything else, hon?" the waitress asked, handing Cee Cee the bag with the sandwiches. "I threw in a couple of pickles for you."

"Thanks a lot," Cee Cee said.

"And you pay the cashier up front."

Cee Cee twisted the key hard to the right and then pressed against the door to the suite with her shoulder, but the door didn't budge. The dogs inside began yapping when they heard her out there. Shit. Maybe the key was supposed to go to the left. She'd better put the bag with the sandwiches down till she figured this out. Besides, her muumuu was starting to smell of the garlic that was seeping through the bag with the pickles. Every goddamned hotel door was different, to the right, to the left, pull first *then* push. Ah, the left and a little nudge from the hip did the trick. The suite was completely dark. The two poodles ran around her feet sniffing out the corned beef. John must have fallen asleep. Well, maybe she wouldn't wake him, Cee Cee thought as she bent to pick up the bag of sandwiches. Maybe he needed this rest and she'd just nibble her sandwich, down a beer from the refrigerator, and then crawl in beside him.

Nah. He'd love it if she woke him. She'd bring in a couple of beers, rip open the deli bag and tell him how great the show had gone, and which songs worked the best and . . .

"Cee?"

It was John's sleepy voice calling from the bedroom. Great. He was awake. He was gonna *loove* these sandwiches.

"Baby, guess what I brought," she said. The only light in the bedroom came from the orange end of the cigarette John was smoking. He had quit smoking years before, and just started again a few weeks ago. Right about the time Cee Cee was on *The Ed Sullivan Show*.

"Ayy," she said. "I got something that's gonna knock your socks off, Perry, so I hope you're hungry."

"Great," he said. "But sit down first, okay?"

"Yeah, I will," she said. "Soon as I unwrap these, and get us a couple of beers and feed the dogs and—"

"Sit down *now*, Cee," John said. He sounded really serious. So serious she wished it wasn't dark so she could see his face. Then maybe she could tell by his expression that he was kidding.

"Cee Cee," he said. Her eyes were getting used to the dark, and she could see he was putting out what had become a cigarette butt. And then he reached for another cigarette.

"We both know that you're a big talent," he said. "The biggest. And I told you from the beginning that when you finally made it, no one was going to be bigger. Didn't I say that?"

Cee Cee heard her heart in her ears. She tore a tiny piece of paper from the bag she was still holding and rolled it between her thumb and forefinger. Both dogs jumped in her lap.

"Yeah, you said that. And the reason I'm so good is on account of *you*. You made me this good. I mean, because you're always pushing me to do better and stuff."

Now Cee Cee blessed the dark because she was biting her lip knowing that she had stretched the truth more than a little. Not that John didn't push her. Because he did, but . . . For a long time neither of them said a word.

Now and then John's cigarette would glow as he puffed it.
Cee Cee was more scared than before. It felt like something bad was going to happen any second, and she didn't
know how to stop it. She wanted to drop the sandwich bag
and jump on him and say, Please, don't leave me, J.P.,
you're the only man who ever even liked me a lot, let
alone loved me—so please don't leave me. Only she didn't.
She just sat there in the dark room praying to God that he
wouldn't. That that wasn't what this was all about. Just sat
there listening to the lousy air conditioner drip. And then
John said, in a really quiet voice, "Cee Cee, I think what I
need is a woman who will bask in *my* glory."

She knew it. He was saying what she had always been
afraid he'd say eventually. That he couldn't live like this
anymore. That he'd given away his balls when he sold the
Sunshine Theater. That he'd spent thirty-some years being
hot shit, and now his big job in life was to carry her fuckin'
hair dryer. She was afraid he'd say that one day, and now
there he was, saying it. But it wasn't her fault. She didn't
make him do that. It was all *his* idea. Anyway, it didn't
matter whose fault it was. Or whose idea it was. What
mattered was she had to make him change his mind. Now.

"Well, what're you gonna do about it?" she asked
him, her voice filled with fear.

And after a moment he said, "I'm going to try and
find another little theater. There's one in Ohio I heard
about."

Then there was no sound but the air conditioner for a
long time, and finally John said, "And I'm going to let you
go ahead without me."

"No," Cee Cee said. "No. You're not. Now just stop
it," she said, and she dropped the bag that she'd been
hugging to herself, and lay on the bed next to him. She
was crying. "You know if you're going to Ohio, I'm going
to go with you. I mean, I don't want any success if you're
not there." She could feel him crying, too. Felt his tears
on her face.

After a minute he sat up and reached over to the night table and turned on the light. Then he looked at her face, and she was sure she must look horrible with tears smeared all over her goopy stage makeup.

"Now, baby," John said. "We both know that isn't true."

"It is, it is," she said, kissing his face. "J.P., take it back. Say you won't go, honey. Say it." She loved him. She was sure she loved him more than anyone had ever loved anyone in the world. Without another word, John made love to her. And then they slept tangled in one another's arms and legs, and the next morning when she opened her eyes, barely awake yet, she saw him standing, showered and dressed, at the foot of the bed. He was holding his packed suitcase. He was so beautiful. No, she thought. Please. Don't, John.

"I love you, Cee," he said. "A whole lot."

And he was gone.

For four days Bertie's life was a cycle of sitting first on the plastic couch in the waiting room, sometimes awake, often asleep, while Neetie sat right next to Rosie's bed; then Bertie would go to the plastic chair next to Rosie's bed while Neetie moved out into the waiting room and had a cigarette, and finally Bertie would be in the stark white neon-lit ladies' room, even if she didn't have any need to use the bathroom. She thought that maybe she was going in there (and this made her laugh as it passed through her mind) for a change of scene.

The neurosurgeon was Dr. Metcalfe. He was slim and tall, with very short salt-and-pepper hair, and they had chosen him after Bertie called Michael. Michael called his father, Dr. Barron telephoned a Dr. Fishmann, with whom he'd gone to the University of Pittsburgh and who now practiced in Miami, and Fishmann called Metcalfe, who was on the staff of St. Joseph's. Bertie had been terrified she would make the wrong choice. Certain that because

Michael's father was a doctor, he could come up with the name of some miracle worker to save Rosie.

Metcalfe was not a miracle worker.

They took Rosie's inert body down for an angiogram one night while Bertie slept. The damage was too great for any surgery.

"Then what do we . . ." Neetie said, unable to ask the question.

"We wait," Metcalfe said, answering the unfinished question.

At each mealtime one of the "cast members," which was the way Bertie had come to think about the other people who were sitting similar vigils for their own parents or husbands or wives, would walk over to Pumpernicks and get sandwiches for the rest, so that it seemed to Bertie she now had eaten at least seventeen corned beef sandwiches with cole slaw and Russian dressing—one of the sandwiches at every meal. Bertie and Neetie hadn't been asked to take a turn going for the food yet. Maybe it was because Neetie said very loudly one day in front of everyone that she'd die first "before I'd ever go back to that lousy Pumpernicks whose food probably did this to my sister."

On the fifth day, when Mr. Heft offered to go over and pick up some deli for "a little nibble for everyone," Bertie volunteered to go along to help carry. Mr. Heft's wife was in Intensive Care after an operation. She was not doing well, it seemed, because on several occasions Bertie saw Mr. Heft sitting with a dark-haired woman who must be his daughter, and they were both crying. Mr. Heft had decided to leave just as Bertie emerged from Rosie's cubicle, and it was Neetie's turn to sit by the bed. Bertie said, "Back in a few minutes, Neet," but when Neetie heard that Bertie was going to leave the hospital building, Bertie saw panic in her aunt's eyes.

"It's okay," Bertie promised. "I just need a breath of air."

As Bertie and Mr. Heft silently walked the few blocks
from the hospital to Pumpernicks, Bertie realized how full
her lungs had been, not just her lungs, but her clothes,
her unwashed hair, her mouth, with the smell and the
taste of the hospital. No, she couldn't let Rosie die. Not
even in her mind. She mustn't put that negative energy
out in the atmosphere. When Mr. Heft took Bertie's elbow gently as they crossed the street, she realized she
hadn't even looked at him since they left I.C.U., her eyes
had been so busy taking in the parts of the hospital she
hadn't seen or noticed on her way in.

Old people. Mostly old people in every room. Maybe
because in this neighborhood there were mostly old people. Bertie remembered Uncle Herbie saying one time
that Miami Beach was "God's waiting room."

"Your mom any better?" Mr. Heft asked her.

Bertie smiled and shook her head. She was starting to
feel close to Mr. Heft. This morning he had shown her
pictures of his married daughter Ruthie and her husband
Max and their four kids. "Boy, do these kids love their
grandma," he said, pointing to the I.C.U. doors. "They
couldn't live without her," he said, his lip trembling.

She also felt close to Mrs. Devlin, the tiny red-haired
lady of about fifty who regaled them all, including some of
the nuns the night before, over corned beef sandwiches,
with the story of the mastectomy she herself had had two
years before, which, when *she* told it, seemed like the
funniest comedy routine anyone had ever done. Now,
Mrs. Devlin was waiting for news of her husband, who
had had brain surgery yesterday; but this morning she'd
said to Mr. Heft, "Don't worry, Heft honey, she'll dance
at the grandchildren's weddings. I'm telling ya!"

A support system. That's what they were for one
another. Even Peter Gaché, the young man. He was very
handsome. He looked like Hugh Hefner. But he didn't
sleep there with the rest of them. Instead, he came every
day to visit his father, who'd had his third coronary. Gaché

wore a suit and brought a fresh package of cookies from a bakery which he left in the waiting room for the others. The first day he had looked longingly at Bertie, who was certain the longing looks decreased in direct proportion to how dirty her hair became over the next four days, during which she did not dare leave the hospital.

Well, she was glad to be outside now. At last. To walk on Collins Avenue. Just to breathe. Just to—

CEE CEE BLOOM. FEB. 14–28. There it was again. That marquee. Cee Cee. Bertie thought about Cee Cee every day. Everything made her think about Cee Cee's being in Miami Beach. Mrs. Devlin's story. Bertie kept thinking that as funny as the story was, Cee Cee would have, could have, told it better. Late that night, while Bertie and Neetie sat on the plastic sofa in the waiting room, whispering because Mr. Heft was asleep, and munching leftover chocolate brownies from Pumpernicks, Neetie asked, "How is your girlfriend, that girl from Beach Haven? The singer. I saw her picture in some magazine. And then we watched her on *Ed Sullivan*."

Bertie nodded.

"She's here," Bertie said.

"Where?"

"Miami Beach."

"No kidding? So why haven't you seen her?" Neetie asked loudly, loudly enough to make Mrs. Koven, who was sleeping as usual, covered with her raincoat, on one of the plastic sofas, turn over. "Is she staying near here?" Neetie asked.

"Neetie, should I go be with Cee Cee before I sit in I.C.U., or when I come out?" she snapped, and was instantly sorry.

"You're right," Neetie said. "Sometimes I forget for a minute."

Of course, the real reason Bertie wasn't looking up Cee Cee was one that Bertie could never tell Neetie or anyone else in the world.

The anger rose in Bertie again. Cee Cee Bloom. Bertie had to force her eyes away from the marquee. Cee Cee was a star. Just like she said she would be that time in Hawaii. Hawaii. Cee Cee and Michael.

Mr. Heft was pushing open the glass door of Pumpernicks, and holding it open for Bertie, and as they approached the deli counter, he pulled a small folded piece of paper from his shirt pocket. The paper was a little limp from being against his perspiring body, and he peeled it open.

"What'll it be, pop?" the clerk asked.

Mr. Heft read his deli order from the piece of paper to the clerk.

"Three corned beefs, two roast beefs, and a chopped liver with onion," he said, and then looked apologetically at Bertie. "That chopped liver's for me. I'm getting sick of corned beef."

Bertie smiled and looked out the window toward the driveway of the Carillon Hotel directly across the street. A white Cadillac pulled up and stopped. What if the door of the Cadillac opened and out stepped Cee Cee?

A white-haired woman of about sixty got out of the Cadillac, and Bertie sighed and realized she'd stopped breathing, waiting to see who would emerge.

"Maybe you should try the chopped liver, too," Mr. Heft said to Bertie. "With a red Bermuda onion. I'm tellin' you, there's nothin' like it."

Bertie smiled. "No thanks." She had to go to the bathroom. Why hadn't she gone before they left the hospital? "Always make a stop to be safe," Rosie had taught her. "Even if you think you don't have to." Now Bertie would have to use Pumpernicks' ladies' room, which was where Rosie had . . . no. She'd wait until she got back to the hospital. She watched the man in the white apron behind the counter gingerly slice the corned beef. He was singing a song along with the movement of the slicing machine. It sounded like "What the World Needs Now Is Love Sweet

Love." She looked around the restaurant, trying not to
think about what it must have been like a few days ago
when they found Rosie, and the ambulance came and . . .

Mr. Heft took the paper bag filled with sandwiches to
the cashier and paid for them. Bertie looked out the
window again, and across the street at the marquee of the
Carillon Hotel. FEB. 14–28. When she looked back at
Mr. Heft, he was motioning to her to come along with
him. Yes, back to the hospital. To eat a sandwich and sit
with Rosie and eat another sandwich and sit some more.
Mr. Heft opened the door of Pumpernicks, and the two of
them were outside again in the hot, salty-smelling Miami
Beach day.

As they turned the corner and began walking toward
the hospital, Bertie stopped. "Mr. Heft," she said, "would
you mind going on ahead? Tell my aunt I had something
to do. Tell her I'll be back in a few minutes. Could you do
that for me, please?"

Mr. Heft patted Bertie on the arm and turned to go.
Bertie stopped and watched him, and as he walked toward
the hospital, he took his chopped liver sandwich out of the
bag, unwrapped it with the hand that wasn't holding the
bag, and took a bite out of it as he walked along. It must
have tasted good because he shook his head the way
people do when they can't believe something is as good as
they'd hoped.

Bertie walked back to the corner, waited for the light
to turn green, and crossed the street toward the Carillon
Hotel. She kept telling herself that she was just going to
find the ladies' room in the lobby, use it, and leave.

It was a busy day. Several cars, three of them new
Cadillacs, stood in line waiting to drop people off. Bertie
caught sight of her reflection in the glass front door of the
hotel. God. She looked like Rosie's favorite expression,
"the wreck of the Hesperus." For years, she'd meant to
look that up in the encyclopedia or somewhere, but hadn't
done it yet, and now here she was again, still not sure

what the wreck of the Hesperus was, but certain she looked like it.

The lobby of the Carillon was bustling with people. Laughing people. People who didn't care that Rosie was in a coma or that Bertie's hair was dirty, or that she was standing there now, shivering, wondering if it was because the air conditioning was too high, or in fear of running into Cee Cee.

What was she doing here? Why hadn't she gone back to the hospital with Mr. Heft? It must be her turn to sit by the bed again. Suppose Rosie woke up? Came out of the coma, even for a moment, and she wasn't there? "Sorry," Neetie would have to tell Rosie, "she told me she was going out for a breath of fresh air and to help the old man carry the corned beef, but he came back with the sandwiches and said she went off somewhere, probably to have a good time." And Rosie, disappointed in her again, would go back into the coma.

To have a good time. That was not why Bertie was here, now, in the lobby of the hotel. In fact, it was as if she couldn't help coming here. But why? To be in the vicinity of Cee Cee? Why would she want to do that? Curiosity? Maybe. Rage? Was she coming here to unleash all the years of her pent-up anger?

The dark-haired girl at the desk directed Bertie to the ladies' room. It was pink and gold and what Rosie would have called "fancy." When Bertie came out of the cubicle to wash her hands, she tried not to look at herself in the mirror, but as she turned on the spigot, the hush it made at the moment before the water came, sounded as if it said, "Hesperus."

Bertie walked back into the lobby. She would leave now. Stop playing this dumb game with herself. Go back to the hospital, and the safety of . . . The blond woman with the frizzy hair who was just walking in the door was back-lit, so Bertie couldn't make out her face, but she had two poodles on leashes, so it couldn't be Cee Cee. Cee

Cee had once told Bertie she thought dogs were revolting little creatures who panted all over you and breathed their disgusting breath in your face. Like most of the men I've dated, she added, and then she'd laughed.

"Sure, outside you wouldn't do nothin'," said the loud familiar voice to the dogs. "And now you'll probably take a big crap right here in the lobby and make *me* look bad."

She was heading for the desk now. Bertie watched her. That walk. That great slinky walk.

"Any messages for five-thirty-one?" Bertie heard Cee Cee ask in a voice so loud that everyone in the State of Florida could have heard her say it. The woman at the desk looked in a pigeonhole and pulled out what must be a big stack of messages and handed them to Cee Cee. Cee Cee didn't look at her messages, just stuffed them in the multicolored basket that hung on her arm and started walking. Even though the poodles were each trying to pull her in different directions, she was definitely heading for the elevators.

Bertie's heart was pounding. She didn't move. Cee Cee was in front of the bank of elevators now. Some people who were waiting for the elevator had recognized her and they were asking her some questions, and all of them were laughing. Cee Cee picked up one of the poodles, and held it as if it were a baby. An elderly woman patted the little dog on the head.

The elevator doors opened, and a few people got off. When the elevator was empty, the elderly woman, still laughing and chatting with Cee Cee, got on. Cee Cee took a step toward the elevator.

That was when Bertie screamed as loud as she could.

"Cee Cee! Wait. Cee Cee," and ran toward the elevator with such a burst that the poodle Cee Cee was holding leapt out of her arms, and both dogs barked furiously.

Cee Cee looked worried for a second, as if she thought this crazy person running toward her was some overwrought fan, but when she realized who it was, the look in her eyes changed. Bertie couldn't tell to what. Was it surprise? Maybe concern? Or pain?

Bertie didn't wait to figure it out. Her arms went around Cee Cee's neck.

"Oh, God, Cee Cee, this is crazy. I feel crazy for saying this, and crazier for coming here—but I'm so glad to see you, and I feel awful for sending your letters back all those times. Never opening them, but I was so hurt, so threatened.

"And now . . . and then . . . I mean, I was surprised to see you were here because *I'm* here. I mean I'm here because my mother is in the hospital, at St. Joseph's in I.C.U., and I've been sitting there for days with all these people I don't know . . . and sleeping on the sofa . . . afraid she's going to die—and . . . eating sandwiches and . . ."

As she clung to Cee Cee, she could tell by the stiffness in Cee Cee's body that Cee Cee didn't care what she had to say, or how long she'd been sitting anywhere, or how badly she felt. Bertie moved away from Cee Cee and looked into her face. "Cee Cee, I couldn't forgive you. I had to blame you for what happened. Not Michael. Because I needed Michael so much that if I . . . Cee Cee, maybe if we talked about it, worked it out, I could forgive you now."

Cee Cee smiled. Thank God. There it was. Her knock-out smile. Bertie sighed, and then she smiled, too. Thank God. Thank God. It was going to be okay. Bertie was relieved. So glad she'd made the effort to come here. To say all those things. Of course, the two of them would probably never be best friends again, but at least—

"Fuck you," Cee Cee said, with the same smile that Bertie realized now was forced, because Cee Cee's eyes were filled with anger. "Now go back to the hospital," she said, and she turned and walked back toward the eleva-tors, but after she'd gone halfway across the lobby she turned back, and now without the smile, she shouted,

red-faced and furious, at Bertie, who stood still and numb.
Shouted from her guts across the distance that separated
them. "Fuck you, because every time I opened one of
your goddamned letters I was smiling and happy before I
even read it. Just to get it. It made me glad. Made me feel
alive. Made me feel important. I would close the door
wherever I was so I could be alone and read it a couple of
times. And then I'd put it away, and then I'd take it out
and read it again later and then another time that night. I
needed those letters. I got used to seeing them in my
mailbox, tearing them open and devouring every line like
dessert, like whipped cream. Every fucking exclamation
point. All the way back to your stories about which asshole
was tryin' to feel you up in high school, or about how sad
you were when they passed you over for senior queen.
And all your theories about getting married, being married, staying married. And about what you were gonna do.
Remember that, Bert?"

She was still shouting. So loud that two women who
were walking by looked over and clucked to one another
in disapproval. When Cee Cee noticed they were two
women she had talked to at the pool, she seemed to get
control of herself for a moment, then strode toward where
Bertie stood frozen, unblinking. But the fury still burned
feverishly in Cee Cee's eyes. Only now the angry words
were forced out in a hoarse whisper.

"Well, what about me? What about what *I* was gonna
do? For the last couple of years, when my marriage was
falling apart? Who was *I* supposed to talk to about that?
When I was dying inside, and needed to know you were
out there? Needed you to tell me it will be okay, Cee,
you're great, Cee, you're the best, there's no one better,
you wouldn't even open my fuckin' letters because you
had some craziness in your mind about me.

"Well, maybe you coulda helped me, Bertie. Maybe
if I would have had you out there, I would have been able
to figure out how to make it easier for John that it was *me*

who was living out the big show business dream instead of
him. Not just working in some goddamned airplane hangar with a bunch of amateurs. Me who was up there with
the big-time showbiz guys, where John never was or never
will be.

"Maybe you coulda told me how to act girlish through
it all, or how I should have made him feel more important
at home so it didn't hurt him too bad. And then maybe—"
Cee Cee stopped talking for a minute, and it looked to
Bertie as if she was biting the inside of her lower lip, and
when she stopped she said, "Then, maybe he wouldn't
have walked out on me."

Bertie wanted to touch her. Just touch Cee Cee's
arm, but she didn't dare.

"Bertie," Cee Cee said, "don't you get it? You took
yourself away from me without askin' if you were right to
do it or not. And you weren't. I didn't do anything with
your husband. Ever. Never touched him. Maybe I said
some suggestive things, which I do, and sometimes at the
wrong times, but that's all. That's what it said in all the
letters I sent you that you were too tight-assed to open.
And you know why I didn't do anything? Because I didn't
want to. Because I knew something about my friendship
with you that you *didn't* know. That it was more important
to me than some guy's dick and where he wanted to put it.
That it was more important than anything, because I trusted
it, I believed in it. But you didn't, and your husband
didn't. So you can take your dirty little suspicious mind
and find yourself a friend who doesn't care that you don't
know how to trust her, or about your smarmy husband's
idea of how to be a man."

Cee Cee's fists were clenched as if she wanted to
pommel Bertie, who stood speechlessly by.

"So thanks a lot for forgiving me, thanks a whole
fuckin' lot, but I *don't* forgive you, and I never will."

And Cee Cee turned to go again, but after a few steps

she turned back and said, in a very soft voice, "I'm real sorry about your mother."

The elevator door opened as Cee Cee got to it, and she was gone. Bertie stood still for a long time, oblivious to the stares of the people in the lobby, finally forcing herself to put one foot in front of the other and make it to the door of the hotel.

The bright sun made Bertie squint. Her eyes were already sore from crying. Slowly she made her way back toward the hospital, her head pounding. John had walked out on Cee Cee. Something about my friendship with you that you didn't know. Nothing happened. That's what Michael had said. But she heard him out there in the other room that night. Making love to Cee Cee. Imagined them to be writhing, hot, wild for one another. Imagined.

The piercing siren of an ambulance on its way to the hospital emergency entrance startled her for a moment, and she was relieved to enter the hospital, as if she needed the security of the medicinal and bodily smells.

Neetie was still in with Rosie when Bertie arrived. Metcalfe had been by, Neetie said, had looked at Rosie, marked something on a chart and said nothing. Bertie wished she could think of something positive she could say to Neetie. Something about Patricia Neal. She'll come back. Like Patricia Neal. But they both looked at Rosie with her finger still pointing and they both knew.

Even though there were no windows in the intensive care waiting room, it was easy for Bertie to feel when the night fell. The new shift of nurses came on, the evening shift of nuns came in and straightened things, and that dinnertime hunger gnawed at her. She thought, as she washed her face and changed her blouse, how perfect it would be to sit down at a table somewhere, anywhere, and eat a hot meal. Not even anything fancy. Just something on a plate instead of a sandwich again. Selfish, terrible thought. But all evening, while the others chatted, she ached to say to Neetie, Let's go out. Let's go sit with napkins on our laps and knives and forks in our hands. But when somebody brought sandwiches she ate part of one, turkey this time. She played gin rummy with Mr. Heft, read some of Mrs. Koven's magazines. Peter Gaché stopped by on his visit to his father and left cupcakes this time. Bertie tried dozing for a while. Every time she drifted off to sleep, she could see Cee Cee's angry face—"Maybe he wouldn't have walked out on me."

Finally, at midnight she went to a phone booth in the corridor and called Michael. She hadn't called him in two days. He'd be eager to hear how everything was going, even though it was late and she'd probably be waking him. She heard the phone ringing twice.

" 'Lo?"

"Michael?"

"Bert. Hey. How's it going?" He asked as if she was calling from a football game, and he was asking her the score.

"No change," Bertie said.

"Sorry, babe," Michael said. "Probably be the best thing for her to just check out, I guess, huh?"

People always said things like that about someone who was in a condition like Rosie's, and Bertie could never understand it.

"Probably," she said, wishing she could shriek at him, "If it was someone you loved as much as I love my mother, you'd want them to do everything. You'd pray every second. You'd talk to her and—" She couldn't say that.

"Michael, Cee Cee's here," she said, wishing she could see his expression. "She's working here in the club at the Carillon Hotel."

Michael said nothing. Bertie was tired. So tired. And she ached from all the nights of sleeping on the I.C.U. sofa.

"I saw her," she said.

"You went to a club?"

"I went to the hotel. To use the ladies' room. It's nearby and she—we bumped into one another."

Michael was silent.

"She hates me, Michael. I tried to work things out with her, but she wouldn't."

Silence.

"Michael, when I get home, you and I have a lot to discuss."

"About what?" Michael asked, with almost a smirk in his voice.

Terrible weeping in the corridor. Wracking sobs.

"Michael, I don't know if I—" The sobs were long and loud and filled with terrible anguish, and Bertie leaned out of the phone booth to see where they were coming from.

Old Mr. Heft and Mrs. Devlin were locked in each other's arms, heads on each other's shoulders, weeping, keening, moaning. It was so terribly sad that one of the nurses who was standing by sobbed, too. The nurse held a small tray with a tiny plastic cup on it. The cup was filled with blue liquid.

"Please, take this," she said, but no one was listening to her. "It'll relax you, dear," she said.

Bertie wondered what had happened. Was it Mrs. Devlin's husband? Mr. Heft's wife?

"Bertie, are you there? You don't know if you *what*?"

Michael sounded angry, but Bertie didn't care what he was saying, or how he felt.

"I have to go," she said.

"Bertie, the best thing that ever happened was when you gave up that friendship," Michael said hastily.

Bertie heard something in his voice she'd never heard there before. It sounded like fear.

"She's a scumbag," Michael said.

Bertie hated that expression. Michael only used it to refer to prophylactics and women.

"Don't start getting impressed by her big star act. I

pegged her the first day. You remember I did. I said . . . Bert?"

Bertie didn't even hang the phone in its cradle. She was down the hall trying to help Mrs. Devlin and the nurse get old Mr. Heft off the floor, where he lay sobbing. A male orderly and one of the nuns came up the hall.

"Can't live without her," Mr. Heft said. His face was red and swollen with tears. "Can't live without her."

"His daughter's down in the lobby to take him home," someone said, and an orderly helped Mr. Heft gently while the nurse placed the little plastic cup to his lips and he closed his eyes and drank the liquid. Then one of the nuns brought a wheelchair and Mr. Heft sat in it. The elevator doors at the end of the hall opened, and a pretty, dark-haired woman got off. Bertie remembered the woman being there a few times with Mr. Heft. When the woman saw Mr. Heft, she ran to him and bent over him in the wheelchair. They were both sobbing. They patted one another and cried more, and then with the help of one of the nuns the woman wheeled Mr. Heft down the hall toward the elevator, and everyone else dispersed. Except for Bertie. She continued to stand there, watching as the dark-haired woman and the nun carefully lifted the front wheels of the wheelchair onto the elevator. That was it. The end of Mrs. Heft. And good-by, Mr. Heft. Only Mr. Heft hadn't even said good-by to Bertie or Mrs. Devlin or Mrs. Koven. He was simply wheeled away in his anguish.

Bertie continued to look down the corridor long after Mr. Heft was gone. Mrs. Heft had just checked out. Probably the best thing. Michael. Oh, God. She'd left him hanging on the phone. He must be furious. She walked to the phone booth, picked up the dangling receiver and put it to her ear. Dial tone. As she was hanging up the phone, two nurses who had just emerged from the elevator walked by, and Bertie heard part of their conversation.

"She was on *The Ed Sullivan Show* a few weeks ago, and now there she was coming in the door downstairs. I

couldn't believe it." The two nurses stopped right near the
phone booth. One was taking something out of her purse.

"She went over to the patient information desk," the
other nurse said. "So I figure she must be coming to see a
friend or something. . . ."

But now the nurse stopped talking, because she could
see what Bertie could see. Cee Cee, still wearing what
must be the dress that wowed them all in the eight o'clock
show, had emerged from the elevator and was walking
down the hall carrying a huge cardboard box that had
aluminum-foil-wrapped containers piled inside it. Her high
heels scuffed noisily along the linoleum floor. The sequined low-cut dress looked out of place and silly in the
hospital. Almost disrespectful. But Cee Cee didn't care.
She was as jaunty as if she was on her way to the circus.
When Cee Cee saw Bertie, she spoke as if everything had
always been okay between them.

"They only serve chicken and prime rib at the dinner
show, so I had 'em pack a few of 'em up for you."

"Cee Cee," Bertie began, but couldn't finish because
Cee Cee was surrounded. Every nurse on the floor was in
the corridor gathered around her, a few interns, Mrs.
Koven and her daughter, two orderlies, Mrs. Devlin, and
some nuns.

"Sign this." "Saw you on TV." "I have your albums at
home." The whole group moved into the I.C.U. waiting
room, which was now filled with smiling excited faces, all
wanting Cee Cee's attention. Cee Cee put the box of food
on the plastic sofa. Bertie sat next to it and picked at the
aluminum foil. The food smelled great. But she wasn't
hungry. Cee Cee was there. Forgiving her for forgiving
her. Making everyone laugh. Using one of the nun's backs
to lean on while she signed an autograph for the other
nun. And everyone adoring her.

"I coulda become a nun," she said, as if she was doing
a stand-up comedy routine. "But there is one thing, just

one little thing that a girl like me cannot live without that is a no-no for nuns."

"And what is that, Cee?" Mrs. Devlin asked, as if she were the straight man for the comic.

"Sequins," Cee Cee answered, and everyone laughed.

When Bertie walked her into the waiting room, Neetie smiled a little smile through her tears and said, "We watched you together on *Ed Sullivan*, and I remembered when you were in those shows in Beach Haven, and I was tellin' Rosie how you sang so good, even then, and how you used to come over just like any other friend of Bertie's, only Bertie always was saying how you were the best of all. I told that to my sister, and now look. . . ."

Cee Cee put her arms around Neetie and Neetie cried some more, and then Bertie said, "There's some food here, Aunt Neet. Cee Cee brought food."

"No, thank you," Neetie said almost shyly, as if she was afraid to offend Cee Cee. "I gotta go back and sit with my sister. Somebody should be there."

"I'll go, dear," one of the nuns said. "You stay a while and have a little visit."

Neetie sat with relief on the plastic sofa.

"Hey, have the chicken," Mrs. Devlin said to Neetie as she poked around among the remaining foil-covered plates.

Cee Cee seemed to be surveying the scene now as if to determine that everything was all right, then she took a deep breath and looked at Bertie. "Hey, listen, I gotta run," she said. "Got another show to do tonight. So I'll be toddling off," and she stood.

There was so much Bertie wanted to say, but everyone was sitting there. Maybe she should walk Cee Cee to the elevator and on the way ask her what this visit meant. Were they friends again? Or was this just a burst of charity? (That's the way Cee Cee used to describe it in her letters when she sang at fund raisers.) Was there anything Bertie could do or say to make up for not being there for her for so long? Bertie wondered if maybe she should ask Cee Cee if she wanted to see Rosie. Then she remembered Cee Cee's letters about how after Leona died, Nathan, her father, got sick, and how being near him when he was in the hospital gave her "the creeps." Bertie remembered now what she said in that letter. "The sick and the dying are not my territory, kiddo." She would never want to go into cubicle seven and see the corpselike Rosie. The I.C.U. was no place for Cee Cee.

"I'll walk you to the elevator," Bertie said.

"Nah," Cee Cee insisted, gave Bertie a little tap on the arm, and then a smile, and without even a good-by to anyone, she was gone out the door of the waiting room.

"The chicken is very juicy," Neetie said, with a mouthful of chicken, and Mrs. Devlin agreed. Mrs. Koven and her daughter were having the prime rib. The daughter was trying to cut it with a plastic knife the hotel had sent.

"My sister Rose loves chicken," Neetie said.

"I'm going in, Aunt Neet," Bertie said.

Neetie waved a chicken leg in approval.

As soon as Bertie pushed open the big black doors of the I.C.U. and saw the nuns standing, their heads bowed, their hands held as if in prayer, outside of cubicle seven, the tears rushed to her eyes. Gone. Rosie was gone. That was for certain. Had to be. And they were praying for the safe journey of her soul to heaven. Bertie moved closer, pushed the nuns apart, and forced herself to look into the room.

Standing a few feet from the bed, her face filled with emotion, was Cee Cee. She was singing to Rosie, the monitors clicking away in an eerie accompaniment, as the nuns and Bertie listened:

> *The moments pass into hours*
> *The hours pass into years*
> *And as she smiles through her tears*
> *She murmurs low. . . .*

The song Rosie had sung to Bertie as a lullaby all through her childhood. She must have told that to Cee Cee once. Maybe more than once. The young nun who was standing near Bertie put her arm around Bertie's waist, and Bertie was grateful for the strength in the woman's arm.

> *The moon and I*
> *Know that he'll be faithful*
> *I'm sure he'll come to me by and by . . .*

The I.C.U. nurses were gathering now; Bertie felt other people breathing near her, behind her, all around her in the doorway, but she couldn't take her eyes from Cee Cee.

> *But if he don't come back*
> *Then I'll never sigh or cry. . . .*

Cee Cee's voice cracked with tears, but she grabbed a breath and went on.

> *I just must die*
> *Poor butterfly.*

The last notes were in full voice. That beautiful voice that sent a chill through Bertie and everyone in the doorway. They all stood quietly. Too moved to utter a sound. Cee Cee continued to look at Rosie, but finally she sighed, moved toward the door, walked over to Bertie and hugged her. A warm, holding-very-tight hug. Then they walked together toward the black doors of the I.C.U.

"I thought you didn't do the sick and the dying," Bertie said.

"It was okay," Cee Cee said. "I didn't look at her."

Bertie shook her head, looked at Cee Cee, and they both smiled.

"Anyway, I got a late show and then I'm hittin' the road right afterwards. I'm already packed. So I should be gettin' a letter from you at my New York address any day now. Right?"

Bertie smiled. "Right," she said, and the two friends hugged again, and Cee Cee was off, down the hall, sequins flashing, moving in that unmistakable gait that said, here I am, so if you're lookin' anyplace else, you're wastin' your time. Waving good-by to this one and that, and when she reached the elevator, she turned back to look at Bertie, who she was certain had been watching her the entire time, and blew her that special Cee Cee kiss.

Rosie died that night. Bertie called Michael, who showed up right away. It was clear that he wasn't happy about having to miss the time away from work. He dealt with the hospital and shipping the body to Pittsburgh and funeral directors, and Bertie didn't have to do a thing but wash her hair and sit in the bathtub for hours crying, and to sleep, at last, at home in Pittsburgh, in her own bed.

Within a few days, life seemed nearly back to normal. In another week, Bertie would go back to work at the Home. Tonight she and Michael sat silently at the dinner table.

"Cee Cee and John have split up," Bertie said. She knew she shouldn't have said that. She knew she should leave it alone. What was she doing? Why did she have to open that up? Maybe just to get him to react to her. Michael cut into his veal, speared a piece with his fork, put it into his mouth, chewed, and swallowed. Then he picked up his glass of white wine, took a sip, looked long into the glass, and then put it down on the table.

"Guess he finally found out about her," he said.

"What does that mean?" Bertie asked. She should have never started this. It was provocative. And she didn't want to know what Michael meant by that.

"What that means is that she's garbage, Bert, believe me. You don't even know how bad she is. You don't want

to get me going on what I think of her, because it's just
going to stir up a lot of stuff. Okay?"

"Michael, she's not garbage. She's just different. And
not the kind of person you understand."

Now she should ask him what happened. To stir up
what stuff? About what *really* happened that night? She
wanted to. But what if . . .

Michael was smiling a smile that she'd seen on his
face before. It was the smile of a wise father to an innocent
child who he hoped would someday see the light. And
along with the smile went a pat on her hand, and a little
burst of air from his nose that signified his amusement.

"You're such a good person that you sometimes just
don't even see what's real. If you're truly smart you'll keep
doing the same thing you've been doing all along with her
letters—send them back. Don't write to her. Don't call
her and don't see her. She's the lowest, Bert, and she'll
drag you down. Change your address. Honestly, your fatal
attraction to her is the one thing about you I've never
been able to see. Or respect, for that matter."

"Michael."

"Besides, I've got a great way for you to change your
address for at least six months out of every year," he said,
as he continued to pat her hand.

"Michael, let's finish this."

"I think we have," he told her. "Let's just say you
think one thing about it and I think another. I'm not going
to change my opinion, but I hope *you'll* change yours.
Okay? Now let me tell you about the deal I'm making in
Sarasota, Florida. We can get a winter place down there
for practically nothing. And maybe even live there half the
year."

The next morning, after Michael left for work, Bertie
did the breakfast dishes, prepared herself a second cup of
coffee, and reached for the telephone. But then a wave of
sadness stopped her. She had been about to call Rosie. In

Miami Beach. Some early mornings in the past when she felt like having company for morning coffee she had done that. And they would chat and have "girl talk" about this or that, and when things weren't going so well they would tell one another, "Hang in there, old chum." Never again. She would go to the market this morning, make a shopping list to fill the empty refrigerator. And then this evening maybe she'd make a big dinner for Michael. Something special. She took her paper and pen and her coffee tray into the dining room.

She sighed and sat alone for a long time at the dining-room table. The only sound in the silent house was the clink of her spoon in the coffee cup as she stirred it and watched the whirlpool she made in the cup.

Groceries in the house. Dinner for Michael. That's what she had to get to. She put down her spoon, picked up her pen and began to make the list. Rice, lettuce, tomatoes, chicken breasts. . . . Her mind wandered from the list, and after a while she stopped, tore that page from the tablet and wrote on the next page instead.

Dear Cee Cee, she wrote, and then she smiled to herself and continued writing. It was her first letter to Cee Cee in a long time.

Dear Cee Cee,

Just the act of sitting down to write to you always makes my day brighter. I guess because I feel less lonely—knowing you're there. I honestly miss my mother terribly. Even though she could sometimes be too demanding and even though she had values that I'm certain fouled me up in many ways, she was a dear lady and a close friend. Someone I could really count on.

I wish so much that I could have given her the grandchild she wanted so badly. I am still trying. I mean, we are—but to no avail, I'm afraid, and our lack of success is difficult for us both. Michael is pretty nice about it, sympathetic when I get my period, etc., but I think he'd just as soon keep our life the way it is.

The winter home we bought in Florida is gorgeous, but it seems to be a kind of consolation prize for me, so that while I'm busy decorating it, maybe I'll forget about pregnancy. Instead, of course, I think about it more, as I fill a big empty house with furniture. And I miss my work at the Home, too. I send one letter to all my friends there, and get back fourteen letters from the children. Instead of cheering me up it makes me wish I was in snowy slushy Pittsburgh and I fall apart.

Help! I re-read this and realized I sound like I'm complaining!!! I don't mean to. Guess when I sit down to write to you I make a beeline for my most important feelings and put those down first. I am aching to know how this play you are rehearsing is going. After you told me you'd be playing Sarah Bernhardt, I got a book out of the library on her life. I think that's the perfect part for you. When does it open? I'll ask Michael if we can come. Or maybe if he doesn't mind, I can come alone. I know you'll be a big hit.

Write or call.

Love,

Bertie

Dear Cee,

  Break a leg tonight. I wish I was there. You'll be a better Sarah Bernhardt than Sarah herself.

All my love,

Bertie

THE NEW YORK POST—SARAH!

Bloom Blooms on Broadway. One spectacular talent playing another is a sure-fire formula for success. And Cee Cee Bloom as the fiery Sarah Bernhardt is an utter joy. With spontaneity, a big bold voice, and a presence that makes everyone else onstage disappear into Arthur Rachman's impressively lavish sets, La Bloom makes it clear to anyone who doesn't already know why La Bernhardt was so loved by so many.

THE HERALD TRIBUNE—SARAH!

When you have the extraordinary good fortune to see "Sarah!," and I urge you to run there, and not walk, you will not only get to see the glorious Cee Cee Bloom play the spectacular Sarah Bernhardt, you will also get to see Bloom playing Bernhardt playing Hamlet. And Bloom playing Bernhardt playing Marguerite Gautier. Each performance within a performance is so unique, so special, they could have easily charged me for three tickets. The show is dazzling and magnificent. And so is Cee Cee Bloom.

HOLLYWOOD REPORTER

Visiting Tinseltown for biopic "Sarah!" actress-songstress Cee Cee Bloom skedded to recreate role she played on Broadway. Cameras will roll in January at Columbia.

Dear Bert,

Well, here I am in hooray for Hollywood and if you want to know what I think of the place I'd have to tell you the truth and say it eats it. Everyone is sooo full of shit their eyes are brown. (I used to say that in grade school, did you? Of course not, Cee Cee you a--h---. See how polite I'm getting?)

I'm supposed to be grateful that they're letting me play Sarah, the part I won a Tony for, instead of them giving it to Julie Andrews or somebody like that. The movie is going to be real different from the play. They're cutting a lot of the songs, and they're adding some other songs which I don't like very much. But maybe it'll turn out okay.

I haven't met one decent man here yet. But I want to. Just so I don't have to go home every night to this house I rented that you wouldn't believe in the Hollywood Hills. And be alone.

The second night after I got here I was invited to this party, and I didn't want to go. I felt real out of it, because I figured I wouldn't know anybody, right? Then I thought of that pep talk you gave me about how I'll be a big hit here because I'm so funny—the funniest person I know, you said. So I look at myself in the mirror and I say, Hey, Cee, you're funny. People at the party are going to like you 'cause you're funny. So I get to the party and I'm pretty early and there's very few people there yet. And I'm saying over and over to myself, Cee, you'll be the funniest person at the party, and the doorbell rings and the next three guests who come in are Neil Simon, Billy Wilder, and Mel Brooks. I didn't say one word all night.

Anyhow, Sarah as a movie is what my life's about now. I'm trying to be on a diet because if the camera adds ten pounds to me like they say it does, I'll be playing Kate Smith instead. Maybe you could sneak away and visit me here sometime, Bert. We would really have laughs if you did. I'll try and call you next week.

Love C.

Big Barn Theatre
Steubenville, Ohio

Dear Cee Cee,

Thought of you today as this year's cast rehearsed Damn Yankees. *No Lola will ever equal yours. I got married in June to a gal who teaches fourth grade here. She's a sweetheart. You would like her, Cee. She sure as hell is tired of hearing about you, though.*

Best,

J.P.

Carmel, California, 1983

It was beginning to get dark outside. Cee Cee switched on the table lamp next to the sofa and sat. She'd already read a copy of *People* magazine that she found on the coffee table, and leafed through a copy of *Vogue*.

She was cold and getting hungry. She didn't even know what bedroom Bertie meant for her to sleep in. Maybe if she went upstairs and looked around she could figure it out. Then she could at least go get her suitcase out of the car and unpack.

The wooden steps creaked as she walked slowly upstairs, wondering where the light switch was mounted. She couldn't see anything beyond the top of the steps. When she reached the upstairs hallway, she saw that one of the doors was open a few inches, and that the room was illuminated by the moving light of a television, so she walked toward the door. The television sound was off.

"Bert," she said as she looked into the bedroom. The light from the television was a pinkish purple. Sometimes it was bright and then it would get dark. When the bright pink light was cast, Cee Cee could make out someone who was asleep on the bed, with the covers pulled far up, covering part of her face. But that wasn't Bertie in the bed. It was a much older person. Cee Cee could see that. Maybe it was Aunt Neetie. That nice old aunt of Bertie's from Florida must be here visiting. But why wasn't Bertie here? Probably she didn't figure Cee Cee would come running up this fast. Just because she said it was an emergency or urgency or some Bertie word like that. Always with those exclamation points.

Cee Cee decided to go back downstairs. If she started schlepping her suitcase up here and unpacking in one of the bedrooms, she might disturb poor Aunt Neetie. As she got to the landing, she heard the front door burst open. Bertie. Boy, was she gonna be excited to see her.

"Bert?" Cee Cee said, running down the rest of the stairs.

But the woman who looked at her with huge dark eyes wasn't Bertie. "You're Cee Cee Bloom," the woman said with a smile and a look of recognition.

Cee Cee nodded. Even as she stood on the bottom step, the woman was taller than she was, and very pretty. Cee Cee's mind raced trying to guess who she could be. Her name didn't help.

"I'm Janice Carnes," the woman said, putting a hand out for Cee Cee to shake. "I'm very glad to meet you. Roberta talks about you all the time."

"Yeah?" Cee Cee asked. "Well, she called me this morning, said she needed to see me this second. So I busted my ass getting up here. I mean there weren't any flights I could get on, and I was even tryin' to borrow a goddamned plane. But then when I couldn't, and this'll kill her when she hears it . . . *I* flew standby. Bertie knows me so she's gonna die when she hears that. I mean this better be good," Cee Cee said. She was getting a little headache.

Janice Carnes smiled, a bigger smile this time, and said, "I'm sure she'll be grateful."

Cee Cee was annoyed. "If she's so friggin' grateful, then *where* is she?"

"What do you mean?" Janice Carnes, whoever the fuck she was, asked.

"Maybe she thought I wasn't gonna get here this fast, but she tells me it's important, so I kill myself for her. I walk out on my own show. I try to bum some movie producer's airplane and . . ."

But Janice Carnes wasn't listening. She had already moved quickly past Cee Cee and was taking the stairs two at a time. Cee Cee followed behind her for a few steps, still talking, but stopped when she saw her push open the door to the bedroom where the television was and then close it behind her.

There was no sound at all for a couple of minutes and then Cee Cee heard a muffled conversation between Janice Carnes and someone else. For a second Cee Cee even thought it might be Bertie. Jeez, it sounded like her.

And then, when the thought that the person she'd seen in that bed in the room, the strangely gaunt person whose face she had looked at by the light of the television, might be Bertie, when that thought first hit her, Cee Cee was filled with an eerie feeling that started in her ears, and moved into the back of her neck, and then spread through her body, until finally she couldn't move. Not that person in the room. That person had a pain-filled face, and was breathing with effort, and the hair . . . the hair wasn't Bertie's. Couldn't have been. Nothing about that person was like Bertie. It had to be someone else. Please, Cee Cee thought, please, God.

Sarasota, Florida, 1975

Bertie sat on the deck looking out at the water. The ocean was brown closest to the shore, then yellow-green, then darker, almost emerald green near the skyline. A catamaran with a rainbow sail moved slowly along what looked like the edge of the world.

If only it was, Bertie thought. I could swim out there and fall off. A unique suicide. That's what I need. If I'm going to do it, I might as well do it in an original way. Ways to die. Cee Cee had made that a category when they played Facts in Five in Hawaii. The day it rained. They came inside and Cee Cee suggested they play it. Each of them wrote a mutually-agreed-on five-letter word across the top of a piece of paper. This time the word was C-A-N-D-Y. They had to come up with ways to die that began with the five letters of the word candy.

"C, carcinoma," Michael said.

"Cancer," Bertie said.

"That's what I had for C," John said. "What do you have, Cee?"

"Cunt falls off from overuse."

Everyone, even Michael, had screamed with laughter.

"That is *not* a way to die," Bertie said, remembering now that she couldn't believe how much Michael laughed at that.

"Oh, no? Well, it's how *I'm* planning to go, baby. I get fifteen points!" Cee Cee, who was keeping score, wrote a bold number fifteen under her own name.

Last week on the phone Cee Cee had said, "That asshole left you? Thank God. Now you can start to live a little, kid. He was a low-life, a putz, a schmuck, a no-good dog, and a louse. Other than that, a great guy."

Bertie could hear the tour guide's voice coming over the megaphone of Le Barge, as the sightseeing tour boat approached. Every day at one-thirty it came by. Today the guide was a woman with a very nasal voice. "This is the Long Boat Key," the nasal voice said. "High-priced residential area."

Bertie pulled her towel around her shoulders and looked down at her lap, hoping none of the people in the boat could see her sitting there. Certain that they all could, and were craning their necks to try and find out who could afford such a house. What kind of person lived there, and was she really happy?

"No," Bertie said aloud. Not loud enough for the people in the boat to hear, but loud enough to be considered talking to herself, which she did a lot of the time, and which Michael had told her was a crackpot symptom. Michael—she missed him, actually missed him. Insane, how insane. Just because he'd walked out on her, left her. That must be why. Otherwise, there was no earthly reason. He hadn't been loving to her, or even nice for nearly a year. They had only made love once in the last six months, a few weeks before he walked out, and then it was grudgingly.

A pelican dove for and missed a fish that swam just beneath the surface of the water.

Bertie had made a dinner on that particular night that she knew Michael loved—liked—used to love—said he did, anyway. She had been so eager to try to stop the coldness between them that she had spent the whole morning shopping for the dinner ingredients, spent two hours in the afternoon at the hairdresser's, and then ages setting the table and dressing, trying to look casual and unstudied, but sensual. She felt like one of those women in an article from *Cosmopolitan*, "How to Make Your Man Sizzle with Lust."

But when she had greeted him at the door and he looked at her, and then past her at the elaborately set table, she saw in his eyes that it hadn't worked. He didn't care what she did anymore. It was over. They sat silently at dinner, Bertie drinking three glasses of wine instead of her usual one, not even tasting the chicken she'd nurtured so carefully to just the right state of tenderness, Michael looking out the window rather than at her.

Finally, mercifully, it was bedtime, and Bertie was under the covers, as far on her side of the bed as she could go, beginning to sink into the safety of sleep, when she felt the bed move and Michael edging slowly toward her. Soundlessly, he moved his arm under her back and pulled her to him . . . and for a moment she felt a rush of hope that this was an apology for the coldness, the months of disregard, and that the words would spill from him into her ear—"Love you. Sorry. Need you. Never again."

It wasn't. His thighs covered hers and instantly he was inside her, pushing, insisting. This was getting off, not an apology. Nothing would be different afterwards.

Four weeks. Four weeks after that, maybe to the day (she would have to count backwards to be sure), she watched him pack, wondered if she shouldn't have some lines to say, like: "Are you sure you want to do this?" or "Can't we just try again?" All of a sudden, in her mind, she could hear Neil Sedaka singing "Breaking Up Is Hard To Do," and that made her smile, so she had to leave the

room because, after all, when your husband was leaving,
you probably weren't supposed to smile. He would move
to a hotel or apartment and she could have the house, or
she could go to Sarasota to the winter house there, until
she felt ready to make a decision about where she wanted
to live.

Sarasota. It was warm there and innocent, and Bertie
loved the house. It was filled with wicker and canvas
furniture she'd thought was beach-housy and bought much
too much of, so that it was what Rosie would have called
"too match-matchy."

If Bertie went there instead of staying in Pittsburgh,
she would miss her work at the Home. But she could be
far away from Michael and the prying questions of their
mutual friends. It was cold and snowing in Pittsburgh, and
the Sarasota house opened onto the beautiful, sifted-flour
sandy beach. She could walk up and down the warm
beach for hours, if she wanted to, and never have to think
about Michael. So she went to Sarasota right away, and
walked up and down the beach. And all she thought about
was Michael.

How could he leave her? Where would he go? Find
somebody else? Love somebody else? He didn't even give
her a reason. Well, okay, he did give her a reason, but
that couldn't really be the reason. Nothing there anymore.
There was just nothing there anymore and out the door.
He was right, of course, there was nothing. No fun. No
joy. Nothing even to talk about. The empty words repeated themselves month after month. Pat questions with
pat answers.

How was your day? Fine. Yours? Great. Dinner ready?
Yes, hungry? Mmmmm, busy today? Yep, you? Not much.
Like a drink? Sure. Wine okay? Mmm. For you? Sure.

Didn't that happen to everyone after a while? Or did
some marriages, the ones that lasted fifty years, have
surprises in them every night? What did it matter how
other people worked? The point was she and Michael

didn't anymore. And he'd left her. And people were calling and tsk-ing and saying terrible things about Michael
that started with, "You know, I never wanted to tell you
this when you two were together, but . . ." And at least
five people had said, "Look at it this way. It could have
been worse. What if you'd had children?"

Worse? Imagine. How could anyone think that would
be worse? Little loving darlings around to climb on her lap
and whisper, "Don't worry, Mommy, *I* still love you."
Isn't that what they would certainly do? But as hard as
Bertie and Michael had tried, and no matter how many
doctors they'd consulted, there were no children. Mrs.
Barron is barren. The words rang through Bertie's mind
every time she went to see another doctor, certain that
one of them would say that. But each one gave her hope
and a chart with which to use her basal thermometer and
determine her time of ovulation, and Michael would oblig-
ingly try to be romantic on cue.

After a while, it had become a joke. They would
lower the lights and play old Frank Sinatra albums each
time, and month after month, her period would come and
Bertie would tell Michael, and he would tell her Ol' Blue
Eyes was slipping because it certainly couldn't be *them*.

Bertie heard the neighbor's German shepherd bark-
ing loudly. At two in the afternoon, there was probably a
delivery truck out front. Maybe it was at *her* door and not
the neighbor's. Maybe she should go and see.

The air conditioning in the house chilled her, and the
tile felt icy on her feet when she came inside and walked
through the silent house. The doorbell rang a few impa-
tient times. It *was* for her. It was probably the parcel man
with the blouse she ordered from Burdine's.

When she pulled open the door, the person who
stood there looked so bizarre, Bertie almost closed the
door again in shock. Pudgy. Dark glasses. Strange hat.

"So yer gettin' a divorce," the weird person said. "Big

fuckin' deal. You'll be fine. *I* got one and look at me, for chrissake."

"Well, I hope I don't turn out looking like that!" Bertie said as the two women embraced, a huge grasping hug, that made the beads on Cee Cee's dress catch on Bertie's pink terry-cloth robe.

"Didn't expect to see *me* here, did you, bitch?" Cee Cee asked, as the two friends moved apart to get a look at one another. And the beads pulled threads of the pink terry-cloth robe with them.

"Cee," Bertie said, walking her into the living room, "what are you doing here? Is everything okay? I mean, you look weird." Cee Cee's earrings hung down to her shoulders. She wore a flowing beaded top over a black leather miniskirt, and knee-high snakeskin boots.

"That's because it's two o'clock in Sarasota. At midnight in Hollywood I looked perfect. Now, where's my room? I'll get the taxi driver to bring my bags in."

A rush of joy swept over Bertie.

"You're staying? Really?"

"No, you dipshit. I always make it a habit to pass through Sarasota no matter where I'm goin'. I'm here, thank your lucky stars, to get you outta the doldrums. Hey, what the hell is a fuckin' doldrum anyway? And why are *you* in it? You're tall and thin and gorgeous."

Cee Cee. There was nobody like her. It was like turning on your favorite television show when she walked in the door. You knew before the story even started that you'd be laughing any minute. She was out the door to the taxi and then she was back, being followed by the driver, a black man who was wearing a Hawaiian shirt and carrying two Vuitton suitcases and a hanging bag.

"Percy, this is Bertie," Cee Cee said to the man. Bertie nodded at the man who flashed her a smile filled with huge white teeth. As Bertie led Percy toward the guest bedroom, Cee Cee, who was trailing behind, kept on talking.

"Bertie's single now, Percy, so she's open to all offers."

Percy laughed, then spoke with a Jamaican accent.

"My wife won't let me make no offers to nobody, Miss Cee Cee," he said. The suitcases were placed on the bright yellow carpet next to the yellow chintz-covered chair that matched the yellow chintz ruffled bedspread and the yellow chintz ruffled curtains.

"Your loss, Perc," Cee Cee said, handing him five dollars. "But it could be worse. You *could* have to stay in a room that looked like Big Bird exploded all over it."

"Thank you, Miss Cee Cee," Percy said, and he nodded to Bertie. "I'll go see your next movie soon as you make one." A little nod of the head and Percy was gone.

"A fan," Cee Cee said. "Recognized me at the airport."

Probably because not too many people wear snakeskin and sequins around here, Bertie thought.

Cee Cee pulled a cigarette out of her purse and lit it. "Ya know, I used to have this shrink," she said as exhaled smoke came pouring out of her mouth. "Lou Tabachnick was his name—in Manhattan. He was a little old Jewish daddy, and I'd walk in and sit in a chair a few feet away from him and he'd always start off my sessions the same way by saying: 'So? How *are* you?' And then I would say, 'Well, Lou, since I last saw you, this happened and that happened and I went here and I was there,' and I'd blab for about twenty minutes, and finally when I ran out of things to blab about, I'd stop and be quiet and then Lou would say, 'All right, now that we got that out of the way, how are you *really*?' "

Bertie smiled. "What I'm sayin' is, let's skip the opening bullshit," Cee Cee said, "and get right to it. So how are you really?"

Bertie smiled. "I'm great," she said. And then her eyes filled with tears.

"That's what I did when Lou asked me," Cee Cee said.

"I'm okay. I'm fine," Bertie said. "I mean I *should* be

fine because Michael and I weren't even happy together,"
and she smiled a forced smile.

"A detail," Cee Cee said. "You break up, it's tough,
no matter what."

"Cee Cee," Bertie said, "I have to find a career, or at
least a job. Isn't it a good thing that I don't have a child to
worry about?" Her jaw was tightly clenched. She closed
her eyes to stop any more tears and pulled herself together. "I'm sorry," she said.

A moment later she took a deep breath and tried to
talk again. "I sit here alone every day. The only time I
leave the house is to go to the market, which I do once a
week. Sometimes I wait ten days or two weeks, and . . ."
Cee Cee took a Kleenex from the yellow box on the
bedside table and handed it to Bertie. Bertie wiped her
eyes. "Thank you. Anyway, I know it's psychosomatic, but
I can't stop sleeping. I'm always sleeping. And sometimes
I'm kind of queasy. But I'm embarrassed to call the doctor
because I know it's nothing physical. It's just my terror of
being alone. Aren't you sorry you asked?" she said. And
the two women smiled at one another.

"Well, now I'm here," Cee Cee said, and blew a
smoke ring, "so you'll be better."

But she wasn't. The nausea awakened her every day.
Cee Cee would hear her in the bathroom and put the
pillow over her head to close out the ugly sound. At noon,
when Cee Cee woke up and emerged from the yellow
bedroom, she'd find Bertie sitting pale at the kitchen table
trying to eat "just one little piece of toast," which is what
Rosie used to say to her when she wasn't hungry.

And by the third day, Cee Cee was getting on Bertie's
nerves. She would stand in the kitchen in her flimsy little
robe, half open, her now-chunky body sticking out here
and there, and she'd make herself a huge breakfast with
food she bought the day she'd arrived (she had taken
Bertie's car and come back three hours later with what she
announced was "a shitload of food"). So there was always

sausage and bacon cooking, or cheddar-cheese omelettes and onions, and every whiff of the food made Bertie worse.

But the food was the least of it. Cee Cee dropped her clothes everywhere. Bathing suit in the lanai, shoes in the living room, jacket on the floor. The floor! Near the front door! If Rosie were alive, she'd die just hearing that, Bertie thought, picking up the jacket and putting it in the closet. And picking up the shoes on the morning of the third, or was it the fourth day, when she took the shoes to Cee Cee's room? And after a quick tap on the door, which she was sure would suffice, since it was late in the afternoon, Bertie pushed the door open and a startled Cee Cee, who had her finger on one side of her nose, and was leaning over the mirror and the white line of powder, said, "Shit . . . I guess I shoulda locked the fuckin' door."

"Cee Cee," Bertie said, "why are you doing that?" She was shocked and she didn't hide it. She'd never seen anyone do anything like that.

"To kill my appetite," Cee Cee said without looking up. She inhaled the cocaine. "I do it every day."

Cocaine. Bertie had read enough articles to know what it looked like. Cee Cee using cocaine. In her house.

"Well, it doesn't work," Bertie blurted out. "You've been eating like a pig." She was sorry she said it, but Cee Cee wasn't fazed.

"I know," Cee Cee said, "and with the calories in the booze . . . shit, I'm gonna be the fuckin' Goodyear blimp by next week." She opened a little case she'd been holding in her hand and scooped out some more of the cocaine and lined it up on the mirror.

"Cee Cee," Bertie said quietly, "why are you *doing* that?"

Cee Cee inhaled the line through a rolled-up piece of paper, and when she had, she scrunched up her face for a minute and looked long at Bertie, who stood there, appalled.

"I'm doing it," she said, her voice sounding unlike

Bertie had ever heard it before, "because I'm a very lonely semisuperstar who has everything there is except the one thing that I want, which is a man who will place his naked body on top of my naked body and say to me and mean it, 'Cee Cee, you are the only woman in the world I ever care to touch, hold, kiss, caress, and love, and I will never leave you. So, have my babies, won't you please, and if you never want to sing another note, that's okay, too, 'cause I'll take care of you forever.' "

"And you think sniffing white stuff is going to get you that?"

"You sniff glue, you snort cocaine," Cee Cee, obviously annoyed by the intrusion, said in that same shrill, panicky, weird voice. "And no, it may not get me that, but it does dull the pain of knowing I'm probably not ever going to get it. At least I think it dulls it. A little. Sometimes." Cee Cee chewed on her lower lip while she thought about it. "No, it doesn't," she said after a moment. "Anyway, don't judge me, you skinny bitch. You could have any man you wanted. Anytime. You'll get over Michael in a week or two, and you'll be beating them away from your door. All of 'em wanting to jump all over your gorgeous bod. Not one of 'em wanting this little porker," Cee Cee said.

Cee Cee's eyes were very sad and angry as she threw her robe open so Bertie could see her nakedness. A mass of bulges and flab. A wave of nausea passed over Bertie, but the anger she was feeling was more powerful than the sickness, and as Cee Cee closed her robe and was about to sit down on the bed, Bertie grabbed her by the shoulders.

"Cee, Cee," she said, "why are you doing this? Do you want to be Judy Garland? And die some dramatic show business death? Be a legend? Have stories about your neuroses passed around Hollywood for years after you die? Or make yourself fat and pitiful and hooked on drugs till you take too much?"

"Bertie, this isn't heroin. I know what I'm doing."

Cee Cee looked annoyed now. Pestered. The way Bertie had seen her look at Leona when she tried to boss her.

"Then tell me why you're *doing* this." Bertie's eyes were flashing. She took her hands from Cee Cee's shoulders. And put her arms around herself. Hugging herself, trying to stop herself from shaking with anger.

Cee Cee sat on the unmade bed, which Bertie realized hadn't been made in the four days since Cee Cee's arrival. In fact, the whole room was a mess, clothes everywhere, full ashtrays. It was as if the room had taken on Cee Cee's frazzled, uncombed personality. Bertie remembered how the room had looked when Rosie had visited. Meticulous Mommy, Michael had called her. "I hope your mother doesn't get out of bed to go to the bathroom at night—knowing her, she'll make the bed each time she goes."

Cee Cee didn't look at Bertie. She looked out the window at the ocean softly playing on the white sand. "I thought maybe I wouldn't do it here," she said.

"Do what?"

"Coke. I guess you should know now that I didn't come here for you. I came because I've been going with a guy for six months and just found out he fucks twelve-year-old boys, and last month a studio gave me this great new part in a movie, only when I got there for my first meeting they said I was too fat and they took it away from me. So I figured I'd come here and clean up my act. I figured being with you would make you rub off on me—only I'm not doing so great, am I?"

Bertie looked into the oval mirror over the chest of drawers at the picture she saw. The two of them. They looked to her like two gray-faced harridans with furrowed brows. One too fat, the other too thin, in the slovenly bedroom, and no one outside the bedroom caring about either of them. Certainly not Michael, who hadn't called Bertie once since he left, and Cee Cee's bisexual boyfriend wasn't exactly beating the door down, either. Cee

Cee's father was the only remaining parent either of them had, and he was in a convalescent home somewhere. The loneliness of it all filled her with an aching sadness.

"Cee, let's help each other," Bertie said softly. "We can. You'll stop the drugs, and I won't let you eat and you make me eat. We'll take long walks any time you want to have cocaine. I'll go to the health-food store and we'll get some good food and we'll take care of one another and . . ." Bertie couldn't finish the sentence. The color drained from her face and she quietly left the guest room so she could throw up in her own bathroom.

The crowd of women that had been sitting in the doctor's waiting room when Bertie and Cee Cee arrived was nearly all gone. It would be Bertie's turn any minute.

"You want me to come in with you?" Cee Cee asked. "I only want to 'cause I got an idea this doctor keeps the good magazines in there. Like *Vogue* and stuff. I mean this *Highlights For Children* is fuckin' boring bullshit."

An elegant blond woman in her late thirties who was sitting in a far corner of the waiting room looked up huffily from her copy of *Parents* magazine. Cee Cee nodded. "See," she said to Bertie, "*she* agrees with me." Bertie closed her eyes. Cee Cee! Why did she even talk to her? The woman started to read the magazine again, then changed her mind, decided to speak her piece, and looked right at Cee Cee.

"You know, a woman like you who's in the public eye ought to have a responsibility and watch her filthy mouth. Otherwise, you should go back to Hollywood, because this is the wrong place for trash like you."

"Well, this is certainly the right place for *you*," Cee Cee said to the woman, then turned to Bertie for affirmation. "I mean, isn't this the office of the cunt doctor?"

The door from the doctor's office opened and a nurse emerged. "Mrs. Barron?"

Bertie stood and took Cee Cee by the arm. "You'd

better come in with me," she said, and despite a raised
eyebrow she was getting from the nurse, she pulled Cee
Cee into the examining room with her.

"I feel like a voyeur," Cee Cee said as Dr. Wechsler
moved the speculum inside of Bertie. "Contrary to Hollywood rumor, I've never seen one of these from this angle."

Bertie and Arthur Wechsler both laughed.

"But I'll bet yours is cuter than most, Bert," she said.
"What do *you* think, Doc?"

Cee Cee wasn't sure, but she thought maybe the
young doctor blushed.

When he first walked into the room to examine Bertie,
he'd looked at Cee Cee, then away, then quickly back
again and said, 'My God, you *are* you. Oh, my God. Am I
dreaming?" Arthur Wechsler, Bertie's cute bachelor gynecologist, was behaving like a child meeting Santa Claus.

"I've seen every movie you've made," he said to Cee
Cee while he checked Bertie's breast for lumps.

"Ouch," Bertie said. "Tender. They're very tender,
Arthur."

"I saw you on Broadway in *Sarah!* At the Alvin Theatre, and I cried real tears. . . . Breathe." He was tapping
Bertie's abdomen. "I was so in love with you." Cee Cee
grinned. He was cute. She wished she wasn't looking so
fat, but Arthur Wechsler didn't seem to notice. He was
obviously thrilled to meet *the* Cee Cee Bloom. He had
blue eyes and black hair, what there was of it. He was
bald on top and he had a black beard with flecks of gray in
it. Sweet looking. Very sweet, and he wasn't wearing a
wedding ring.

"Get dressed and come into my office," he said to
Bertie. "You did a urine specimen, right?"

Bertie nodded.

When the doctor closed the door, Cee Cee grinned.
"Cute," she said. "Real cute. I'd never let anyone *that*
cute check *my* parts. Unless he was doing it unofficially."

Both friends laughed.

There were no pictures of wives or kids on Dr. Wechsler's desk or his wall. Cee Cee noticed that right off.

"You're pregnant," he said to Bertie.

Bertie thought she'd heard him wrong. "Pregnant—that's crazy," she said. "I *can't* be pregnant. I mean, I never was before," and then she realized what a silly thing that was to say.

Arthur Wechsler shrugged. "You are now."

"Sweet heaven," Bertie said. "One time. Do you know we had sex *one* time in six months?"

"That's all it takes," Cee Cee said, and chuckled.

"Not happy with the father?"

"Getting a divorce," Bertie said. "We tried for ten years to make me pregnant."

Cee Cee fidgeted in her chair. "I think the son of a bitch did this on purpose."

Bertie sighed. "Well, look, let's not go on about it. Let's just set up a time when I can check into the hospital and get—"

"No." Cee Cee jumped to her feet. "You're not getting anything. We're having it. We are gonna have this baby."

"Cee Cee," Bertie said, wishing Cee Cee would just mind her own business, "I can't have a baby alone."

"Hey, who said alone? I'll stick around for a while. Or come back and forth. And Artie here is gonna be there—not to mention little Cecilia, my godchild. So whaddya mean, alone?"

"No," Bertie said.

Cee Cee looked very serious, but she had to be joking.

"Then have her and give her to me." Cee Cee was pacing.

Arthur Wechsler was smiling. Bertie could tell he

couldn't wait to call somebody, his girlfriend, somebody, and tell them he'd just met Cee Cee Bloom in his office.

"Bert," Cee Cee said, "you've wanted a baby all your life. You can't *not* do it 'cause Michael's gone. Don't you get it? That's the good news. Now at least the kid won't have to grow up being influenced by Michael's schmucky personality."

Arthur Wechsler laughed, one of those laughs where the person who's laughing can't help himself.

"Oh, you *know* Michael?" Cee Cee asked Wechsler, who laughed again.

Bertie looked at the doctor, wishing that he'd stop laughing and say, "Cee Cee's right. Have the baby." Or even that he'd say, "Your friend may be great in the movies, but she's wrong about babies. You shouldn't have one unless the father's in residence." But Dr. Wechsler wasn't even looking at Bertie. He was looking at Cee Cee, smiling a smile that looked like the smile of a sixth-grade boy as he asked her, "You married?"

"No more," Cee Cee said. "You?"

"Never."

Now Cee Cee was smiling.

Bertie couldn't believe this. A courtship was taking place in front of her, between her little bald gynecologist and her overweight movie-star friend in the middle of the worst crisis of her life, and neither one of them cared about her.

"I want to know how come no one grabbed *you* yet, Doc," Cee Cee said. "I thought a Jewish doctor was every girl's dream."

"I am definitely every girl's dream," answered Wechsler with an expression on his face Bertie could only describe as cute. "That's *why*—I'm so picky."

Bertie was really feeling sick now. She swallowed hard, hoping the nausea would go away. The banter between the doctor and Cee Cee was moving along at a clip. Bertie focused her eyes on and tried to read every word

on every framed diploma on the doctor's wall, hoping to
shut out the conversation, wanting to tell them both to
shut up, when finally the intercom buzz from Wechsler's
desk jarred him back to reality.

The doctor grabbed the receiver. "Yes? Uh . . . okay.
Tell her I'll be right there." He hung up the phone and
turned to Bertie, serious again.

"You don't have to decide now," he said, "as long as
you decide within a few weeks."

"Nah," Cee Cee said, taking Bertie's arm and standing her up. "She's decided already. *We're* having it."

Arthur Wechsler took Cee Cee's hand and shook it
heartily. His eyes never left hers, even when he patted
Bertie on the arm and said, "Let me know."

In the parking lot, Cee Cee did a little dance of
celebration and insisted they go and have a champagne
lunch at the Colony Tennis Club, and after a few sips of
champagne, Bertie was starting to think that maybe having a cuddly little person to take care of would be healing,
strengthening, give her a reason not to want to swim out
to the edge of the world and fall off. Then Cee Cee
dragged her into Baby Makes Three, a baby-clothing store,
and they looked at lacy dresses and tiny patent leather
Maryjanes and baby blue jeans and fringed vests in a size
zero, and little stuffed lambs, and then they stopped at
Pompano Pete's overlooking the water and had a few
Bloody Marys and laughed about the idea of Cee Cee's
never going back to Hollywood.

"I'll be the kid's father," Cee Cee said. "I mean, shit,
I'll be here with you when it comes out, so it'll think I'm
the father." And when they got back to the house, laughing like loons, Bertie was nearly convinced that having the
baby was the thing to do, and she was about to call Arthur
Wechsler when the phone rang, and he was calling her.

"How do you feel?" he asked. How about this service? Bertie thought. He's worried about me. Never knew
a doctor to do anything like that until Wechsler said,

"Listen, how long is Cee Cee Bloom staying in town? Because I'd like to take her out."

Bertie sobered. "I don't know," she said. "I'll put her on. . . . Cee, it's Arthur Wechsler."

Cee Cee looked surprised, but only for a second. Once she got the phone in her hand she was the confident Cee Cee, playing one of her roles.

"Hey, Doc, whaddya say?"

Bertie watched Cee Cee. Charming Cee Cee. Maybe Arthur Wechsler would be the naked man. That's what Cee Cee said: A naked man to place his body on top of her body. Naked bodies. Michael's baby. Imagine. Maybe she should call Michael tonight. Yes. She'd call him and tell him. Michael, guess what. I'm calling to tell you that the best and strangest and most wonderful thing has happened. I'm pregnant. I'm going to have our baby, darling. After all these years of waiting. And Michael would say, Sweetheart, don't budge. Don't move a muscle. I'll be right there. And he would come to Sarasota, and he and Bertie would embrace and kiss and drive Cee Cee to the airport because Michael was moving back in, and he would tell Bertie, in front of Cee Cee at the airport, that he would be a changed man now. Now that he was going to be a father he'd be loving and passionate and adoring to his wife and child, his family—I have a family now, he'd say, and Cee Cee would hug them both, and wave goodbye as she walked up the steps to the plane.

Cee Cee was sitting on the tile floor talking to Arthur Wechsler, giggling like a teenaged girl talking to a boyfriend.

"Seven-thirty," she said, and looked at her watch. Bertie looked at her own watch. It was six-thirty.

"You got it," Cee Cee said. "See you then." She hung up the phone and leapt to her feet.

"Bert, he's crazy about me. And I've never looked worse. This guy has seen every snatch in Sarasota, and he wants *me* . . . to take me to dinner. He's obviously into great personalities. I've gotta look through my clothes. We're going out in an hour. Jesus."

Cee Cee ran to her room. Bertie stood alone. She'd be alone for dinner. On the night she found out, after waiting her whole life, that she finally was pregnant, she'd be alone. Never mind—it would be a relief.

At seven-thirty, the neighbor's German shepherd barked and then the doorbell rang. Cee Cee screamed, "Oh, shit, fuck, shit . . . I'm not ready for this asshole. Who ever comes exactly on time, anyway? He's already proving to me before we even have dinner that he's a class-A putz."

Bertie, who had fallen asleep on the living room couch, could still taste the celery salt from the afternoon's Bloody Marys in her mouth as she walked to the door and opened it.

Arthur Wechsler looked adorable. In a navy blazer and blue shirt and tie. His face looked scrubbed, the little bald spot on the front of his head was shiny, and he smelled delicious. Wearing some divine cologne. Michael had never worn cologne, and Bertie had always wanted him to. Arthur Wechsler, her gynecologist—Bertie had only seen him in his white coat in the office where he never wore cologne, and now here he was in her doorway, smelling delicious and looking cute, waiting to take out Cee Cee, fat Cee Cee, which Bertie was certain he *wouldn't* want to do if he'd seen her messy room. The clothes all over the—Bertie stopped the thought and chastised herself for being jealous. She loved Cee Cee. She didn't care about the messy room. She only cared that maybe Arthur Wechsler would be Cee Cee's naked man, even for a few nights.

"Hiya," the doctor said, smiling. He was carrying something in his hand. Bertie squinted to see what it was. She was so surprised when she realized that she said it aloud.

"A corsage?" Bertie said, and then she laughed. But

she felt a pang. A corsage. No one had given *her* a corsage in years. Michael, for some college party, a million years ago.

"Come on in, Arthur," Bertie said, and for a minute had the strangest feeling that Cee Cee was her teenaged daughter. The feeling nearly made her laugh because she realized that she was afraid Cee Cee would emerge from the bedroom now, wearing something outrageous, and the boy with the corsage wouldn't like her, and would be ashamed to introduce her to his friends.

Cee Cee didn't disappoint her.

She wore jeans that she was bursting out of, with red sequins up the side of each leg, red boots, a red sequined long-sleeved low-cut top and long red dangling earrings, all of which not only looked bizarre and ridiculous, but also clashed with her curly orange hair. After Bertie took a glimpse of her, she turned quickly to see Arthur Wechsler's reaction.

But the doctor's eyes were wide with admiration. "Gee," Wechsler said to Cee Cee, "you look great. Didn't you wear that in *The Long Walk?*" he asked. "In the bar scene?"

Cee Cee lit up. "Yeah," she said. "Shit, *I* didn't even remember that." She looked at Bertie. "Go figure, he'd know that. I kept all the clothes from the picture."

Bertie looked at the two of them. They would make a strange-looking couple tonight in some restaurant. As she watched the gynecologist (was it timidly?) hand the corsage to the movie star, who grabbed it and ripped the lid off the box, Bertie realized that Arthur Wechsler, her gynecologist who had graduated from Harvard, traveled all over the world, and was a sought-after bachelor, didn't notice that the orange hair clashed with the red sequins, or that the lavender orchid looked absurd on the outfit where it was now being clumsily pinned by Cee Cee. He only saw Sarah Bernhardt and Polly from *The Long Walk* and all the other sexy, witty characters Cee Cee had played, and he was smitten.

Cee Cee took Arthur's arm and gave it a squeeze. "This is a real date, honey," she said. "Just like high school. Except for one thing. In high school nobody wanted to date me."

Oh, God, Bertie thought, not those I-was-so-unpopular stories. Arthur Wechsler turned to Cee Cee and said, "Really? Me neither. I was too short, and I started going bald when I was a teenager."

"Well, I was pudgy and my hair was frizzy, and . . ."

A match made in heaven, Bertie thought, and the two of them waved a little good-by to her and were out the door. The sound of Arthur Wechsler's Porsche starting in the driveway made the neighbor's German shepherd bark. Bertie sat down on the living room sofa.

The house was very quiet. No more quiet than before Cee Cee had appeared, but it seemed quieter because of the racket Cee Cee was usually making about something. And now Cee Cee was on a date. Bertie felt lonelier than ever. She looked at her watch. It was seven forty-five. Michael probably had plans. A date? No. He wouldn't. She should call him. She really owed it to him, after all, to tell him about the baby, especially since she was planning to—probably would—no, not probably, damn it. She was going to have this baby, and maybe he'd say . . . she was dialing, maybe he'd say, baby, I'll be there. One ring. Two. Three. Her heart was pounding.

"Hello."

"Michael," Bertie said, and burst into tears.

"Hello?" Michael said on the other end.

"It's me," Bertie managed to get out.

"Bert?"

"Yeah."

"Oh, hi."

Oh, hi. Maybe that was a good sign. He wasn't hanging up on her. Or saying, "What do *you* want?" Oh, hi, was pretty good. She sniffled. She couldn't ask him to hold on while she looked for a Kleenex. "Listen, Michael," she said, "I went to see Arthur Wechsler today with—" No, she'd better not tell him Cee Cee was there. "I went to see Arthur Wechsler," she said again. Her voice sounded tiny and thin, and she wished that it didn't. "And he—"

"Who?" Michael said gruffly.

"Arthur Wechsler, remember? The gynecologist in Sarasota who—"

"Yeah, what about him, Bert? You sick or something?"

"No." She laughed a funny little forced laugh. "Not sick, Michael. Pregnant. I'm pregnant."

There was a long silence. Then, finally, Michael spoke. "So, what do you want, Bert? Money? I told you when I left you'll get all the money you'll ever need."

Money. How could he think it was money she was calling for? The lump in her throat was so thick she couldn't talk. She had to talk, to say to him, Michael, maybe we can work this out. Maybe a baby would help us. They'd always thought children would bring them—what? Closer. They hadn't ever been close. This was a cold man on the other end of this call. Why had she imagined he'd say anything to make her feel better?

"You're not thinking about *having* it?" Michael said. "Please don't tell me that."

"I—"

"Bert, you're a crackpot. A lunatic. I don't want a goddamned baby. Not with you. We're finished, and if you really *are* pregnant, you'd better dispose of it, pronto. I'm not going to support some accidental child for the rest of my life."

"Michael," Bertie said. But Michael had hung up.

Bertie put the phone down and walked into the kitchen. Through the window she could see a moonlight cruise boat going slowly by, and just make out strains of the music the band was playing—"I Could Have Danced All Night." She opened the refrigerator and looked at the contents. It hadn't ever been this full when she lived with Michael. Michael. Cold. An accidental baby. He was right about that.

One night in six months. After ten years of trying. Bertie closed the refrigerator. Maybe she'd just—oh, God, she was hungry and tired and pregnant and queasy and deserted by Michael and even Cee Cee was off somewhere and she . . . Bertie sat down in a heap on her kitchen floor. She was glad to be alone so she could just sit for a while and sob.

It was morning and some part of Bertie knew it, but she couldn't seem to awaken from a dream about two tiny babies, twins. They were her babies, and one looked exactly like Cee Cee and one looked exactly like Michael and, even though they were infant-sized babies, they were talking to one another in the crib they shared while Bertie stood near enough to hear, but not for them to see her. They were arguing.

"She should dispose of it, pronto," said the Michael baby, "because I don't want it."

"Go shit in your hat, you putz," said the Cee Cee baby. "We're havin' the fuckin' baby 'cause I *do* want it."

"No money."

"Aunt Cee Cee."

"No father."

"You asshole."

Bertie opened her eyes when she heard a key in the front door. Who had a key? Michael. Maybe he'd . . .

A moment later, Bertie's bedroom door opened, and Cee Cee stood smiling, still in her red sequins, her makeup askew. The orchid was gone from where it had been pinned to her chest, but the pin was still there.

"Did I make curfew?" she asked, grinning.

"Did you *just* come in?" Bertie asked.

"This is a man," Cee Cee said, the grin never leaving her face, "who knows his way around a pussy." And then she laughed, stopped in the middle of the laugh to cough a cigarette cough, and then laughed some more.

"I'm kidding," she said, "I mean I'm sure he *does*, 'cause that's all he sees all day, but I wouldn't let him lay a glove on me. Bert, this guy is normal, straight, smart. He went to Harvard, Bert, graduated from Harvard, and he's Jewish . . . and . . . cute. I mean, he ain't Cary Grant, but cute. Don't you think so? I mean, I *like* the fact that he's balding. I think it's . . . sexy. I really like him, a lot. I mean, go figure. A doctor in Sarasota, Florida. It seems crazy, but we laughed a lot and he, well, he said he hopes I stay around for a while. And I could, Bert, I mean you notice the phone hasn't been ringing for me? That's 'cause I told everyone in L.A. that I was serious about getting away from it all. So, ya see, I could help you with the pregnancy and stuff at least for a few weeks, and then keep goin' out with Arthur. So, can I for a while, Bert?"

Bertie was quiet. Cee Cee in the house every day. For how long? Weeks? Months? But maybe it would be a blessing. It took so much energy to be with her, but worth it. She was cheerful. Up. Made Bertie laugh.

"Look, I'm going to sleep for a while," Cee Cee said. "We stayed up talking all night, anyway. . . . Think about me staying for a while, will ya?"

Bertie nodded.

It took Arthur Wechsler three days after his first date with Cee Cee to call her again. Cee Cee, who decided after the first day passed without a word not to call *him* no matter what, decided on the second day that maybe it wouldn't be so bad if she called him. But Bertie said no, it was wrong, and managed to keep her away from the phone. On the third day, Cee Cee decided the guy was a putz, a low-life, and a no-good dog like all men, but when the phone rang while both of them were sitting outside on the deck, Cee Cee ran inside to get it so fast she twisted her ankle.

He said he'd been busy with his parents, and deliveries of babies, and had wanted to call sooner.

Cee Cee had barely eaten for the entire three days. Not because she wasn't hungry, but because she had vowed that the next time she went out with him she would look perfect. Yet, she'd been preparing food for Bertie, keeping up her end of the deal, making Bertie eat as she had promised. Making appetizing healthy sandwiches for her and then sitting across the table sipping an iced tea and yakking while Bertie, who was beginning to feel better, devoured them. Bertie didn't ask her if she was still using cocaine to curb her appetite, but there was something about the way Cee Cee was behaving that made her think not. Now and then Cee Cee would telephone some agent or producer in Los Angeles, but she didn't scream and yell and carry on at them the way she usually did. She seemed calm, calmer than Bertie had ever seen her.

And when Arthur Wechsler not only asked her out for dinner that night, but lined up a few other dates with her—one of which was to meet his mother—she was filled with some strange new hope. The hope was unverbalized for a while, but finally, after she'd gone on three or four more dates with him, she asked Bertie to take her shopping and "dress me like a real person."

"What?" Bertie asked.

"I mean a straight person," Cee Cee said. "A person Arthur's mother would like. Bert, I almost choked on those words. I don't believe they came out of *my* mouth." And they both laughed.

"Cee Cee, you're not—"

"Wondering if I could become an ordinary person? You bet I am. Wondering if I could be Mrs. Arthur Wechsler? Bertie, last night we did it for the first time. It was fantastic, and Arthur said . . . he loves me, Bertie. Even though I'm fat and divorced, and I used to snort a lot of coke, which I told him, and had lots of men, and some of 'em were major dopers, and we both know I won't exactly fit in with his friends who I haven't met yet, but he told me they've all seen my movies. . . . He loves me."

Bertie wasn't sure, but it looked like Cee Cee was going to cry. "He *should* love you, Cee Cee," Bertie said, "because you're great."

The two friends hugged, and while they were hugging, they each said the same words at the same time:

"Let's go shopping."

Bertie knew every shop in town, and it was fun to go into them with Cee Cee and Cee Cee's unlimited budget. Bertie had never really thought much about how recognizable Cee Cee was, even after Arthur Wechsler's starstruck reaction, until they were walking through the shopping area and people stopped to stare and nudge their friends and point at Cee Cee, who with the weight loss was starting to look more like she did in her movies.

"I'm fainting because it's you," the saleswoman in John Baldwin said as Cee Cee modeled a white wool suit.

Cee Cee smiled at the saleswoman, then looked at herself in the three-way mirror. "This one makes me look like a nurse in a very fancy hospital," she said.

"I think it's perfect for mother-meeting," Bertie told her.

Cee Cee bought the white suit, the same suit in navy and in black, and silk shirts in brown and white and black, a black crew-neck sweater and a white lace blouse, and cashmere sweaters in burgundy and red. Black loafers and plain black pumps, plain gray pumps, and burgundy pumps with a bow.

Except for the orange hair, she was almost unrecognizable in the clothes. Each time she emerged from the dressing room to model an outfit for Bertie, she looked to Bertie like Cee Cee playing some strange role. As she paid for the clothes with her charge card, she said to Bertie, "If his mother hates me on the first meeting, I'll bring everything back." Bertie laughed. The salesgirl looked nervous and said to Cee Cee, "What was that, dear?" Before they left the store Cee Cee gave her autograph to one of the saleswomen, who had asked by saying, "It's for my granddaughter who idolizes you. Could you please write, 'To Stacey Bruckner.' " Cee Cee did, smiling and all the while trying to discuss with Bertie if the white was better for Arthur's mother or the black.

"I'm scared, Bert," Cee Cee said as they put the packages in the trunk of Bertie's Cadillac. "Isn't it nuts? I've sung in front of trillions of people all over the world, sometimes I had the flu, once even pneumonia, when I had to go on and my heart pounded and I felt clammy and afraid, but I did it, and wowed em! And now on Wednesday I'm meeting a little sixty-year-old Jewish lady, and I'm a basket case from thinkin' about how to act like a real person with her. You know? That's what it is. Acting. Like if I had some part where I had to play a real together person? That's what I'm doin', Bert. I'm doin' it with Artie, too. Acting. I don't say fuck or shit or cunt in front of him. Never. Or even call him an asshole. I mean he's *not* one. But that's not why I don't do it, I mean even as a joke like I sometimes do, because he's a gentleman and he makes me want to not be some flashy show-business type, some star, because you know why?"

The two women got into the car, and Bertie pulled out and headed down toward the shore.

"Because I don't trust what I have. What I am in the world. This famous-person shit. Because it fucks you over. It gives you fake highs and makes you think you're so hot no one can get anywhere near you. And for a few minutes you're sure no one is prettier than you, no one is smarter, no one is sexier, and no one sings better, and you carry that with you like it's some possession, some precious stone in your pocket. Then, as the days go by, you know what happens? You start feelin' for it. Checking your pocket to see if it's still there or if you let it fall out through a hole, or maybe it got stolen, or you left it somewhere, and lots of times you're panicked because it makes you think you can't live without the high, and if you lose it you'll be nobody. Nowhere. A bag lady. Sometimes I see those ladies, the ones who live in between buildings, and I think, if I don't make a good movie soon—no, a great movie, where people in the audience go home crying about how heroic I was, or how funny I was—I'm gonna end up living in between buildings, too."

Cee Cee rolled her window down, and took a deep breath of the salty air. The breeze blew her red curls away from her face, and as Bertie glanced at her, she looked cherubic and happy suddenly as she spoke.

"I know what counts is being married to someone solid, Bert. Someone who loves you every day. Because *that's* worth somethin'. *That* doesn't fuck you over."

"Cee Cee, you're crazy. *John* loved you every day. I don't want to put a damper on this fantasy you're having, but I'm afraid you're thinking that marriage is going to save you, and it doesn't. And I don't know why you think it will, because you thought that last time, and it didn't. Cee, I know you're unhappy in Hollywood now, and you're looking for some fast solution to feel better, so you think it should be Arthur Wechsler, and maybe it *is*. But you need to take your time."

"Bert, John loved me, but he couldn't take my success in show business. Arthur doesn't care if I'm Cee Cee Bloom or the cleaning lady."

Bertie had stopped the car for a red light just then, and when she looked into Cee Cee's eyes, they both knew what Cee Cee had just said was a lie. The cleaning lady would not be invited to meet Arthur Wechsler's mother.

The mother-meeting went wonderfully well. Cee Cee bought a bouquet of flowers and took them with her to present to Ethel Wechsler, who had spent the entire day over a brisket: "Even though my son offered to take me to the Colony Tennis Club for a nice piece of fish, I said, listen, a girl like that probably would like a nice Jewish meal sometimes. . . . So aren't you glad?" Cee Cee said she was very glad, and then she looked at Arthur's baby pictures, and also his teenaged pictures.

It wasn't a lie that he was balding when he was a teen, but he was also gorgeous and smart, Ethel Wechsler said, several times. A Harvard graduate. And when the phone rang, and Ethel Wechsler answered it and had spoken to the party on the other end of the line for a while, she came out of the kitchen where she had taken the call and asked Cee Cee if she'd mind saying hello to her sister, Arthur's favorite aunt, who loved her in *Sarah!*, which she'd seen six times. Cee Cee said, of course, she'd say hello. So Ethel dragged the telephone out of the kitchen and brought it to her.

Arthur was all smiles. He held Cee Cee's hand and looked lovingly into her eyes. Then the aunt, whose name was Fanny, said, "Don't try and kid me, I know it's not Cee Cee Bloom on the phone because if you are, you'll sing something from *Sarah!*"

Cee Cee laughed. Arthur put his head next to hers and she held out the earpiece of the receiver so Arthur could listen to Aunt Fanny with her cute little Yiddish accent say, "So nu. So sing."

Cee Cee was uncomfortable. She looked at Arthur and he nodded as if she should go ahead. This *was* his favorite aunt. Cee Cee took a breath and sang in full voice:

> *Needing so much love,*
> *I stand before you.*
> *Needing so much love,*
> *How I adore you.*

Aunt Fanny screamed, "Oy, my God, Cee Cee Bloom. Oy, my God."

And as the proud Ethel Wechsler took the phone out

of Cee Cee's hand and walked a few feet and said into the receiver, "Would I *lie* to you? . . . She's crazy about my Arthur," her Arthur was kissing Cee Cee a thank-you kiss for pleasing his mother and also Aunt Fanny. A very grateful kiss.

"He was even more grateful later," Cee Cee told Bertie happily. "Mmmmm, I'm crazy about him. And the mother, Ethel—she likes me. When we went back to his place, she called there. She calls him every night. Of course, she doesn't know *I'm* there, but she called and said I'm much more attractive in person and that so long as he was happy she was happy, too. And, Bert, early this morning, when the sun was coming up, he told me she has a ring that his father, who's dead now, gave to her when they got engaged, and when he finally gets married it's going to go to the woman he marries. Isn't that sweet, Bert? They're sweet people."

"Sweet," Bertie said, still convinced the bubble was a bubble.

Bertie's nausea was gone, and she was beginning to feel stronger, healthy and hungry and eager to start showing so she could believe in her pregnancy. So far the only thing that was different was the size of her breasts, and the fact that she was no longer menstruating. But she was frequently sad and depressed and lonely.

Cee Cee was completely involved in her romance. It was all she talked about when she wasn't having lunch with the wife of one of his friends, who told her over an avocado stuffed with crabmeat: "I never thought you'd be so real like this and talk to people who are just Sarasota people," or going to open houses of the most expensive waterfront homes. "Just taking a peek," she said to Bertie when she brought home the fact sheets on all the houses. It was a long time before she took a good look at Bertie one afternoon and saw the sadness that filled her eyes.

"Bert," she said one day, "I'd be the last one to say

this to you, but maybe you ought to call Michael. Tell him you're—"

"Did that already. He told me to get rid of it," Bertie said.

"Oh." And that was all. No more discussion. Cee Cee didn't want to discuss Bertie's problems. She was flying. She didn't need Bertie. She didn't need anyone.

Until after the phone call that night. When Bertie answered it, she heard the hushed sound of the long-distance line and when the man asked for Cee Cee, Bertie asked his name, and when Bertie told Cee Cee it was "someone named Allan," Cee Cee, who had been putting on her make-up because Arthur was picking her up in one hour, turned pale under all the blusher.

She took the phone in the kitchen and closed the door.

"Hello," Bertie heard her say, but then went quickly back into her bedroom because even though she would have loved to know who could make Cee Cee look that afraid, it wasn't right to listen to someone else's calls.

After about fifteen minutes, Bertie heard Cee Cee in the living room, and then back in the guest room; she wanted to go in and ask her who that was and if she was okay, but . . . this was dumb. Allan was probably her agent. It was probably about a job, and Cee Cee was afraid to get offered a job, because if she did, she'd have to choose between taking the job and going away, or turning it down and staying here with Arthur. Of course that was it. A job.

But when Cee Cee opened the door and Bertie looked at her eyes, she knew the call hadn't been about a job. She also knew Cee Cee had probably just used cocaine.

"Where're my suitcases?" she asked.

"Your what?"

"Suitcases," Cee Cee said. "I'm leaving."

"For—"

"Home," Cee Cee said.

"Cee, you can't. Arthur's due here in—"

"Bert," Cee Cee said, "there's a real big difference between wanting someone and wanting to want someone. Arthur Wechsler is the right man for me, so I want to want him. But the honest-to-God truth is I love Allan Jackson. He's an unemployed guitar player who fucks boys when he's not fucking me. He says he'll lay off the boys for a while and give me a shot—and I'm leavin', Bert. I have to be with him. Have to. I heard his voice on the phone and I said to myself, he owns you. You asshole. Face up to it. For whatever reason, he owns you. More than John did. Light-years more than this nice Jewish boy I wanted to love so I could go straight. Sometimes one person taps into another in some real deep place where no one else has been or can get to—and once you've been touched there, no other kind of love works for you. I had that with Allan, and I don't want to live without it."

She didn't even try to call Arthur Wechsler, just called a taxi, dressed quickly, packed without a word. All the new clothes looked odd next to the sequined clothes, as though the bag was being packed for two different people.

"Cee, are you sure you—"

"Positive," she said. Her voice sounded shaky and shrill again, and Bertie noticed the small mirror was sitting on the dresser again.

When she looked away from the mirror and back at Cee Cee, their eyes met and Cee Cee's were filled with pain.

"I tried," she said, "and I almost . . ." She shook her head. "It was a lie," she said.

The taxi horn honked. She hugged Bertie a fast hug, then picked up one of her suitcases and the hanging bag. Bertie picked up the other suitcase, and they walked toward the door. When Bertie opened it, Percy the black cabdriver in the Hawaiian shirt stood smiling in the doorway.

"Miss Cee Cee going home?" he said.

"Yes," Bertie answered, and she burst into tears.

Percy took the bags, and Cee Cee and Bertie hugged again.

"I love you and I already love the baby," Cee Cee said, "and I'll come back soon. I promise I will—for her, because she needs me." And then she was out the door.

Bertie closed the front door. Numb. She leaned against the door and thought about it all, from the phone call when Bertie first told Cee Cee about Michael's leaving, through her arrival—and the days filled with stories and fantasies of how Cee Cee could change and be more "Bertie-ish," as she said.

Bertie must have been very deep in thought because when the doorbell rang it made her jump. She turned quickly to open the door and Arthur Wechsler stood, one foot on the step, the other on the path. He was carrying a small bouquet and looked more dapper than ever; it even seemed as if he had more hair.

"Hello, Arthur," Bertie said.

"Hi there," he said, and the smell of his wonderful cologne came wafting into the room. "Where's my girl?"

"She's . . . gone," Bertie said, and her face must have given it all away. Because Arthur Wechsler knew she didn't mean that Cee Cee had driven to the drugstore for a pack of cigarettes.

He paled. "To L.A.?" he asked. Bertie nodded. "To be with the guitar player?" he asked, and Bertie nodded. "When did he call?" the doctor asked quietly.

"Tonight," Bertie said, looking down at her feet because she couldn't stand to look at his hurt face. There was silence for a long time, and when Bertie did look up at last, she saw tears streaming down the nice gynecologist's face. Many tears before he finally took a handkerchief out of his pocket and wiped his eyes and blew his nose. Bertie realized they were still standing in the open doorway.

"Arthur," she said, "forgive me for being so rude.

Won't you come in? Sit down. I'll make a drink and we'll talk and—"

"No," he said, handing her the flowers he'd bought for Cee Cee. Then, for a moment he stood, closing and opening the palms of his hands as if he were exercising his fingers. "No, thanks, Bertie, I think I'll go."

He turned, Bertie closed the door and, in a minute, the neighbor's German shepherd barked as the doctor started his Porsche and drove away.

The next day, Bertie became a member of the Selby Botanical Gardens and volunteered to work in their book-store three days a week, and after a few months, she met a woman at the Arts and Cultural Center who noticed she was pregnant and invited her to join a prenatal exercise class. At the exercise class, she met two or three women who lunched together once a week after class. At the first lunch, each of the women told her story to Bertie, and when Bertie told them she was having the baby alone, they all oohed and aahed in admiration and offered to help, and took turns calling her and inviting her to their homes for dinner, and when she went, even though their houses were small, and they were hard-working, and their husbands weren't attractive or interesting to Bertie, she ached with envy of them.

The only time she saw Arthur Wechsler was when she went for her monthly checkups, and from the first time he acted as though nothing had ever happened. Nothing. He checked her, asked her all the routine ques-tions, and dismissed her. The only note of warmth was on the first visit when he put his hand on her arm, promising if she needed him, he would pick her up and take her to the hospital. My God. She hadn't even thought about that. Never even considered that while she was in labor she wouldn't be able to drive herself to the hospital. Some women must do that. Or call taxis.

"Thank you, Arthur," she said. "I guess I'll have to take you up on that."

Cee Cee called once every few weeks. She sounded weary when she did, even though she seemed to have lots of exciting things happening in her life. A movie, a great one, Bert, in preproduction, with a really hot new director—she mentioned some name Bertie never heard. He's great. We really see this thing the same way. How ya feelin'?

"Great," Bertie told her, and it wasn't a lie. She was proud of her independence, and although she was a little frightened about the baby, she was excited, too. She'd hired a nurse to stay for the first month, and she'd bought lots of nursery furniture and baby things. Wechsler had told her to do that to cheer herself and it worked. The baby seemed real to her now.

Cee Cee never breathed one word about Arthur Wechsler. Had never, in any of her phone calls, asked how he took the news. Nothing. Occasionally, she'd mention Allan Jackson, but only in passing, as in Allan and I went here or there together, but that was all. Not how the romance was going, and Bertie was too polite to ask. Too polite. That's exactly what she was. Maybe, she thought, she was even having this baby out of politeness. To whom? Cee Cee, because she'd insisted? Her mother's memory? Rosie would have loved to have seen this baby. Just one time. To see Bertie pregnant would have thrilled her. Not like this, of course, with no husband around.

That was the last thing Rosie would want for Bertie. For Bertie to have to raise a child the way she had been raised by Rosie. With no father. No sense of family. Always an outcast little twosome. Arriving on Parents' Night at school with one parent. When they had the Father-Daughter dinner at Girl Scouts, Bertie just stayed home, but once Rosie convinced her to go and to take her Uncle Herbie with her. Herbie left the dinner table six times to make phone calls. He was booking numbers from the Girl Scout dinner.

"Well it could be worse," Rosie said to her on the rare times that Bertie mentioned how she wished she had a father. "At least he's dead. We could have been divorced."

Yes, Bertie remembered thinking divorce would be worse. Death was just pitiful. Divorce would be scandalous. It was good Rosie wasn't seeing any of this.

By the time the divorce papers arrived in the mail, Bertie hadn't even found herself a lawyer yet. Michael was more than generous in his support of her. And there, just to prove he believed she wasn't making it up, were the words "child support," and again a generous amount.

The lawyer in Sarasota Bertie was using for the divorce had been referred to her by one of the women in the Botanical Garden bookstore. He was young, aggressive, and wanted to fuss over every point in the papers, but Bertie said no, please, let's dispose of this marriage pronto, in a tone of voice that sounded unlike her own, but oddly familiar.

The baby was due on November ninth. On Halloween, Bertie passed out trick-or-treat candy to the neighbors' children, wondering what her little baby would wear someday to dress up for Halloween. Little Nina. Or would it be a boy? She hadn't even picked out a *name* for a boy. After she had passed out chocolate bars to three pirates, one witch, a ballerina, two skeletons, a Spiderman, and a robot, and the doorbell was silent for a while, she went into the baby's room and stood next to the crib for a long time without turning on the musical duck lamp, stood and talked to the yet unborn child.

"I love you, little person I've waited for all my life. And I'm sorry that your grandma won't be here to see you, or your father, but I promise to supply you with enough love to make up for all the grandmas and daddies in the world, so you won't even notice. And we'll have a wonderful life. I swear we will, baby, because—"

The doorbell rang. "Excuse me," Bertie said as she left the dark room and headed for the front door. She picked up a few Snickers bars and opened the door. Four trick-or-treaters held out their bags. They were so cute Bertie wanted to grab them and hug them all for lighting up her evening.

"Ooh, Snickers is my favorite," said the little hobo. "How did you *know?*"

" 'Cause they're *my* favorite, too," Bertie said, smiling, and dropped one in the hobo's bag. The hobo moved out of the way to leave room for the robot.

"Are you pretending to be a pregnant lady for Halloween?" the robot asked, showing a mouthful of braces under the silver painted cardboard box, "or are you *really* a pregnant lady?"

"I *really* am," Bertie said, grinning, and tossed another Snickers.

The green thing with a top hat grabbed the Snickers out of her hand and ran, and the tallest one with the bushy fur coat and the Frankenstein mask didn't have a trick-or-treat bag. It just stood there.

"Do you want a Snickers?" Bertie asked.

"Shit, no," said Frankenstein. "But I wouldn't mind a fuckin' Scotch on the rocks."

Cee Cee. She pulled off the Frankenstein mask. "Just like Barbara Bain and Martin Landau," she said. "I take off one weird face and here's another one underneath."

Bertie couldn't believe it. "Where did you get that costume?" she asked.

"What costume? All I got was the mask. This is my regular everyday coat. The real question is where'd you get that belly? I gotta hug you sideways," she said, hugging Bertie sideways. With the coat Cee Cee was bulkier than her pregnant friend. "Meanwhile, believe it or not, I only brought one small suitcase," she said, and ran out to the curb where she'd left it. "I had my mask with me and I couldn't resist being one of the kids. Maybe I ought to put the mask back on and see how I do down the block."

Bertie laughed.

"Don't laugh," Cee Cee hollered. "Some people give cash," and she was in the living room. Not a word about the fact that she was just popping in unannounced. Just Cee Cee unpacking again, back in the yellow bedroom. Dropping her things here and there. Smoking cigarette after cigarette; opening the refrigerator, looking disgusted, and yelling out the word "Goornisht," which she explained was the Yiddish word for nothing, meaning how could Bertie, a woman who was carrying a child inside her, have a refrigerator so empty of food?

They sat on the bed for hours, Bertie telling Cee Cee about the people she'd met over the last months, and how she was enjoying Sarasota even though she felt it was retirement- rather than youth-oriented—and Cee Cee telling Bertie about three months of working in a one-woman show, and how rehearsals every day forced her to take off weight, and Bertie told her she looked great even though she was wearing those multicolored striped stockings, and the diaper-wrapped skirt and the purple suede blouse and the gold dangling earrings and her hair in that pompadour, and they laughed, and no one mentioned Arthur Wechsler. Finally, in exhaustion, maybe even because the sun was coming up, Bertie said good night and went to her room.

The first pain woke her at six-fifteen. The second one was at six-nineteen.

"Cee," she said, knocking at Cee Cee's door. "I think it's—" Another pain. "Cee Cee, I think we should hurry."

Cee Cee was panicked.

"Where?" she said, blinking, looking around to figure out where she was. "Time for . . . oh, my God, oh, my God, I don't know what to do. What do I wear? Do *I* drive or do *you*? You're not going to bleed or anything, are you? I mean . . . do I have time for a shower? We never even made a plan about this."

Bertie was in the middle of a labor pain. "No shower,

wear anything, keys to the Cadillac are on the coffee table. Oooh, Cee, let's hurry up. I'll call Wechsler."

A look of panic passed across Cee Cee's face that looked like she was thinking, Wechsler, my God, I forgot about him, but what she said was, "Even a *fast* shower?"

Bertie shook her head. She was dialing the phone and looking at her watch. The pains were only three minutes apart now.

"Dr. Wechsler's service? This is Mrs. Barron. I think I'm in hard labor. My pains are close to—" This one felt like a truck was running over her abdomen. "Going to Memorial Hospital. You'll contact him? Thank you. Cee? Cee Cee?"

Cee Cee emerged from the guest room. By some miracle she was fully made up and dressed in a darling powder blue pants outfit, much more Sarasota-style than Hollywood.

"Ready?" she asked, grabbing the keys from the coffee table.

Bertie wanted to lie down in the back seat of the Cadillac but she couldn't, because she had to direct Cee Cee to the hospital. Cee Cee blabbed endlessly, said she felt like Butterfly McQueen in *Gone With The Wind* because she didn't know nothin' about birthin' no babies, and laughed, and said that maybe someday she'd have a baby herself, so she wanted to observe very carefully how all this maternity ward shit looked, and then she started to cry and told Bertie that Allan Jackson had left her again— but it didn't matter—that she was dating some very nice new men, and one of them was a successful movie producer and they had a lot in common.

As they drove up to the hospital's emergency entrance, Bertie saw Arthur Wechsler's black Porsche pull into a space marked Doctors Only, and when he got out of the car and saw it was Cee Cee helping Bertie out of the Cadillac, Bertie noticed that he opened and closed his hands in that nervous way of his, and took a deep breath before he walked over to help.

After that, everything was a blur to Bertie. The two hours in the labor room were hazy, Cee Cee's face, Wechsler's face, a pink-cheeked nurse, a young black nurse, all of them checking her, talking to her, hovering. Even in her foggy state, though, she noticed that Cee Cee and Wechsler behaved like strangers to one another. It was so odd. Bertie couldn't help but picture in her mind the nights they'd come home from dates like two teenagers, smooching in her kitchen, giggling lovingly on the phone, and now, a few little months later, they were strangers.

Then it was time to go into the delivery room, and everyone was wearing scrub clothes, even Cee Cee, with the orange hair sticking out, and Bertie had never felt so helpless and hurting. And while she was being wheeled into the delivery room she caught a whiff of Wechsler's cologne, and Cee Cee, who was beside her must have, too, because she looked after him with misty eyes.

"Push," Wechsler said to Bertie, and Bertie could see him in the mirror over her head, and the pain was so awful that she was gagging and straining and, "Push," Bertie looked up at Cee Cee, whose brow and upper lip were covered with sweat.

"Doin' great, Bert," Bertie heard her say. And she pushed with all her might. A baby. She was (oh, my God, the pain) having a baby.

"Push harder now, Bertie," Arthur Wechsler said. Why was he wearing cologne? He never wore cologne to work. Did he know that Cee Cee was coming last night? Did he figure she'd be here for the birth of the baby, which was two weeks early, as if to oblige Auntie Cee Cee's busy schedule? Push. Aah. Again. Oh, God.

Bertie looked at Cee Cee again, who was white as a sheet, and who reached out her arm for anything. Anyone!

One of the nurses saw Cee Cee start to go and grabbed for her just before she hit the floor.

"Is she okay?" Bertie said, and then she realized that her baby was in the doctor's hands. A girl. It's a girl. And then they placed the tiny creature on her belly and forgot all about Cee Cee.

"Nina Rose Barron," Bertie said.

Later in recovery, Bertie slept, and when she opened her eyes Cee Cee was there.

"Sorry I checked out," Cee Cee said. "But I told you I didn't know nothin' about birthin' no babies. She's gorgeous, Bert. Looks like you from head to toe. I talked to her through the window of the nursery. Promised if she came to Hollywood to visit me I'd introduce her to Robert Redford."

"How come you never promised *me* that?" Bertie asked, smiling. She couldn't feel her body. She must have had some anesthetic or pain reliever, but she couldn't remember.

Cee Cee smiled—a smile Bertie recognized as a forced one she sometimes gave when strangers were trying to her, or when she was about to say something that was difficult for her.

"Arthur's getting married," she said. "Right after the delivery, he came out to see if I was okay, and of course, once I got out of there away from all the gooey blood and placenta and stuff I was great, and—we told each other how wonderful we looked and all. I mean, Bert, I lost thirty pounds since I saw him, and he had, you're not going to believe this"—and then Cee Cee looked over her shoulder to see if anyone was listening, looked back at Bertie and confided—"he had a hair transplant. More hair, Bert. I know he thinks that's why I left. Because he was bald or short or whatever he's unsure about, but that wasn't why."

Cee Cee was too much to take at a time like this. Bertie wanted to go back to sleep or go up to her room to see Nina. Little Nina Rose Barron.

"And Allan Jackson wasn't why either, Bert. It was because I . . . you don't want to hear this, do you?"

"Go on, Cee," Bertie said. Poor Cee Cee.

"It was because it was possible, Bert, too possible, you know? Too much of a chance at realness. And I don't do realness. When you get down to the blood and placenta, I'm gone. Only I didn't tell *him* that. I just said congratulations. His mother really likes her, Bert. The girl he's marrying. His mother likes her a lot. That's what he said. Only I guarantee you that Aunt Fanny wishes it was me. Remember how crazy she was about me, Bert?"

Bertie was asleep.

Cee Cee stayed for a few more days. She slept a lot and came to Bertie's room and sat at the bottom of the bed and watched Bertie nurse the baby. She helped Bertie compose a note to Michael about Nina's birth.

Bertie thought Nina looked just like her grandmother Rosie. This made Bertie cry, and she said it was awful that her mother would never hold the baby in her arms. And that the baby would never have a grandmother to love her as only a grandmother can.

When the baby was one week old, Bertie and Cee Cee took a walk on the beach "to show Nina the water," Cee Cee said. They moved slowly, Cee Cee carrying the baby and Bertie holding on to Cee Cee as they walked.

The beach was empty. Cee Cee stopped at a spot where three big jagged rocks stood on the sand near the shoreline. Then she straightened the little bonnet Bertie had put on Nina's tiny head to protect her from the sun and sat. Bertie sat, too. Two sea gulls shrieked and flew in circles just a few yards out to sea. Cee Cee pulled the baby close to her chest, and then she sang:

Poor Butterfly,
'Neath the blossoms waiting,
Poor Butterfly,
For she loved him so
The moments pass into hours . . .
The hours pass into years
And as she smiles through her tears
She murmurs low . . .

Then she stopped singing and smiled and said, "Hey, Bert, I think maybe I just became a grandmother."

Bertie held more tightly on to Cee Cee's arm and then, smiling, she tilted her face up so the warm sun could shine on it.

Dear Cee,

It's two A.M. and I just got Nina back down to sleep. She must have had a terrible nightmare, because she awakened with such a shriek that I was terrified. I ran into her room and she was trembling!! Poor baby.

Cee, sometimes when I sit alone (which is almost always), I think about some of the terrible choices I made for myself, and I worry about the wrong choices I could make for Nina, and that scares me.

How did I ever fall for the lie that mothers pass on to their daughters about marriage? The fantasy that makes us believe that somehow it will save us. That one man will be able to be ever-constant, ever-loving, ever-sexual (I would have been grateful for once a month).

One person can't save another. We can only save ourselves. I made the mistake of expecting Michael to tend to me and to make me feel important, and when he didn't, couldn't, was having enough trouble with his own life, I resented him for trying to make me be "only a wife" for all those years. But he didn't make me, Cee. I could have insisted on being something else. It was just easier not to try, just to shut up and be Mrs. Barron.

Sorry about all the self-pity. I've been reading a lot of feminist literature lately and feeling as if the world wronged me, when the truth is I wronged myself.

Boy, do I envy you your fabulous career. Nina and I will come to visit you and stay in the pad you described in Hollywood as soon as she is more easily carted from place to place. (You can't believe the paraphernalia required just to take a baby out for the day.)

Ooh, I knew I had gossip. Ran into Artie Wechsler and his new wife in the drugstore when I went to get Pampers a day or so ago.

She is ordinary. A kind of washed-out-looking blonde. I think she must have known the story because when Artie said to her, "You remember, Marsha" or Marcy or whatever her name is, "I told you about Bertie," a look of realization crossed her face, and after that she was very cold to me while we waited in line (they were behind me getting charcoal and paper plates!!), so I guess I shouldn't count on the new Mrs. Wechsler inviting me for dinner in the near future. Should I? Oh, Cee, the tribulations of being your friend!!!

I miss you. Call or write to me soon, old girl.

I took new pictures of Nina to the drugstore to be developed the same day I saw Wechsler there. As soon as I get them back I'll send some.

And so to sleep.

Bert

Dear Bert,

Whatever you do, cross your heart you won't go to see Jilted. It comes out tomorrow and honest to God it is trashola from the first shot. I look like a tank, and I act like one, too, but I swear it wasn't my fault. (That's what they all say, right?) To begin with I wasn't even fat when we shot it, I was at my low weight, and they dressed me in those tents so I look huge.

The director was a maniac, and after the first day of shooting when he tried to jump on me in my dressing room one night and I called him the usual (putz, schmuck, low-life and no-good dog), I was not, to say the least, his favorite persona.

Last week when you called you sounded so happy with little Nina-poo. I'm glad to hear she's "almost talking," whatever the fuck that means. No wait. I know what it means. It's what I did in Jilted. Don't see it, Bert.

Love,

C.B.

THE NEW YORK TIMES
Jilted

One hopes that Cee Cee Bloom, so brilliant in every past endeavor, will forgive director Jack Arquette for allowing her to be so badly dressed, abysmally lit, and insensitively photographed in *Jilted*. In the first moments of the film, it seemed as if some semblance of a performance by Bloom seemed to be struggling to emerge, but alas, never made it.

VARIETY
Jilted

Based on a recent news story about a man who married thirty-two women in fifteen years, *Jilted* optimistically bills itself as a comedy, but is completely devoid of same. Mostly due to the shrill, unpalatable, charmless performance of Cee Cee Bloom as the wife who catches on to the flim-flam and brings the cad (Mel Blanchard) to justice.

it was better than having fathers who didn't care. Guilty
men who made strained, insincere visits to their children.
Of course, the children felt the hypocrisy in their little
bones.

Her whole marriage with Michael had been strained
and insincere. Then why did she still think about him?
Thrill to the expressions in Nina's face that were like his
expressions? The pout that Nina assumed when she felt
hurt. The eyebrow she raised when she felt insecure. And
the shape of her tiny thumb. That sweet thumb that was
exactly the same, a miniature version of Michael's thumb.
Bertie remembered Sunday mornings at brunch in Pittsburgh with Michael, when the two of them were still
newlyweds. How she'd held Michael's hands and touched
his fingers, one by one, memorizing them. Even now, she
thought, if Michael exploded and all that was left of him
was his hands she could identify him by them. That was
such an insane thought, it made her laugh out loud.

If Michael exploded . . . the sound of her own giggle
brought her back to reality. She was sitting in the bathtub
trying to relax while Nina took an afternoon nap, and was
so lost in her thoughts she hadn't even noticed that the
once steaming water had cooled. God, she loved sitting in
the bathtub. It had become her favorite thing to do.

Realizing that made her smile again. You know you're
aging when . . . She remembered those articles from the
Mad Magazines one of her college roommates had read
endlessly. That would be a perfect article for *Mad Magazine*. You know you're aging when your favorite place to
be is in your bathtub. Alone. At noon. Noon? Bertie
looked at her watch. Twelve-fifteen. No, she'd better not
add more hot water. She'd better get out, dry off, dress,
get Nina dressed, and hurry over to the Seaside Tennis
Club. She'd promised Libby Collins that she'd come there,
dressed in tennis clothes. And maybe if there was a teenager available to take care of Nina for an hour or so, she
would hit a few tennis balls with Libby. Libby Collins was

about fifty, blond, bubbly, and what Bertie's mother would have called "a pistol."

Libby barraged Bertie with questions one day when they were both volunteers in the bookstore. She seemed sincerely interested in Bertie's welfare, and Bertie answered her frank questions, thinking later she owed Cee Cee a debt of gratitude for teaching her that people could be like that. Could just say anything. After her own upbringing, in which one's buttocks were referred to as a "bum," female sex organs as "girl parts," and real feelings seldom if ever confronted.

"Being single," Libby said, and tsked, "who in the hell loves you up, honey?" Bertie blushed. "I mean, if I didn't have Wally's fuzzy legs next to me every night, I'd never fall asleep. Take my word for it, a girl needs fur. And I don't mean the kind you put in cold storage every summer."

Bertie allowed a smile.

"Hey. I know you don't want all kinds of creeps traipsing through your bedroom. Hell, no. Giving your daughter the wrong idea about how a woman's supposed to conduct herself. But find yourself one good, strong, healthy, sexy man and get him to come by your bedroom on a steady basis."

One good, strong, healthy, sexy man. For nearly a year after Nina was born, Bertie had barely thought about men. Except, of course, for Michael. And even though she hated herself for wanting it, and knew in her heart it was impossible, she fantasized a great deal about a reunion. Sometimes late at night in a half-asleep state, she would think she heard a car pull up outside, and imagine that it was Michael coming home. He'd say, what a fool I've been, or some other bad movie line like that, only he wouldn't be the cold, indifferent Michael; he would have undergone some enormous transformation and he'd be funny and warm. But then the car outside was only passing by, and eventually she would fall asleep, sometimes with the thoughts of Michael moving into her dreams. Dreams where he ran and played with Nina on the beach, and when the blazing morning sun pried her eyes open, she would be overcome with the grief that they would never be a family and at the same time the relief that she was free of those tension-filled years she'd spent with him.

One good, strong, healthy, sexy man. She hadn't met one. Not the first year. When Nina was a year old, Bertie met Donald Solow in the waiting room of the pediatrician's office. Donald was with his son Jason, five, who was coughing so much Bertie was terrified that the germs were filling the room and spraying on baby Nina.

"The cough is my fault," Donald said apologetically. "I mean my fault that he has it. That's why I had to bring him here, 'cause it's my fault."

Bertie nodded and looked into the reception window, hoping she could catch the nurse's eye and tell her they just had to hurry Nina, who was only there for a routine checkup, in to see the doctor. But the nurse was on the phone and too busy, and Nina was shifting around uncomfortably in Bertie's lap. Bertie picked up Nina's bottle of apple juice from the side table where Nina had pushed it, to give the baby a drink. Just as she did, Jason Solow let out another belt of a cough. Bertie put the bottle back down. It must be covered with Jason's germs now, too.

"He was playing outside in the rain, naked, at my house," Donald said to Bertie. "His mother would never let him do things like that, which is why she and I aren't together anymore. You see, I'm a free spirit, and she isn't. Right, Jase? Don't you have more fun with Daddy?"

Jason responded with a simultaneous nod and a cough so powerful it made his little face bright red.

"See," his father said to Bertie. As if she cared.

"Does your little boy have a divorce?" Jason asked Bertie, moving closer to look at Nina. Bertie wanted to push him away.

"She's a girl," Bertie said, "and yes, she does."

The next day, Patty, the nurse who worked for the pediatrician, called her.

"Mrs. Barron?" she said. "One of the fathers who brings his little boy here asked for your number."

"Really?" Bertie said, surprised, having completely forgotten Jason, his terrible cough, and his nondescript father.

"So since I said I wouldn't give it to him, he asked if I'd give you his."

"No. Thanks anyway, Patty," Bertie said, and put the phone down.

"He thinks you're stunning," Patty told her the next day, when she called again. "He says, please. Just talk to him. Just have a cup of coffee. I told him you said no. He was in here again today. Doctor had to put the little boy Jason in the hospital," Patty said sadly. "He's got pneumonia."

"Poor Jason," Bertie said, feeling a protective rush for the same little boy who only two days ago she could have cheerfully strangled.

"Do you want Don Solow's number or not?"

"Well . . ." A hesitation. After all, the poor man's son was in the hospital. Was that really why she was weakening, she wondered, or was it those nights, those aching nights when she'd made herself come and wept afterwards with loneliness? What did those nights have to do with some drippy man in the pediatrician's office, anyway? He wasn't going to fill her nights or her longings or her . . . girl parts—what would Cee Cee call them? "Snatch, cunt, box, pussy, hole, wazoo, slit." And Bertie would laugh and say, "Cee Cee. Enough." And Cee Cee would say, "Bert, you dumb S.C.B.P.H.W.S., why don't you get it through your thick head that the fucking word isn't the fucking thing? Words don't mean shit, you asshole."

"Why, you know," Bertie would say, "I do believe you're right, Countess," and the two of them would shriek with laughter. After all, how bad could it be to let the nurse give Donald Solow her number? After he called and they talked, if she didn't like the way he sounded, she could say no.

"Have him call."

She didn't like the way he sounded. He sounded arrogant and kind of childish, and he complained and whined and asked questions that Bertie felt were too personal. And he certainly didn't sound like a free spirit, which is what Bertie remembered he'd said about himself. He told Bertie on the phone that as soon as Jason was out of the hospital, he would take her out for a nice steak dinner. Ick. She didn't like him. And she never ate steak.

A week later they had dinner. By the time cocktails were over, he had told her she was not his type, and that he'd already decided that the woman he would make his second wife couldn't have a child of her own, because he'd want her to focus completely on Jason. He also said that if he and Bertie ever decided to move in together he'd never live in that house, where he'd picked her up, because he had a really *great* house that was on the bay not the ocean, but much larger than hers.

Bertie laughed a polite laugh and, as she'd been taught to do by Rosie so many years ago, instead of yawning in Donald Solow's face or even behind her hand, she yawned, as Rosie had described it "through her ears," with her mouth completely closed; the only tell-tale sign was her flared nostrils, which Donald happily didn't notice. And when she yawned through her ears for the third time, she vowed to herself that she would not only never go out with him again, but she never wanted to hear the sound of his name or look at his creepy green-eyed face again. And that was that.

On their fifth date, after the baby sitter left and she was certain Nina was asleep, Bertie locked the bedroom door and went to bed with Donald Solow. And when he crept out at six in the morning to go home to be with

Jason, she sat in the kitchen, drank a glass of milk, chewed on a baby's teething biscuit, and sobbed.

She couldn't stand him, or herself for doing it, but she was lonely. Very lonely. No, that wasn't a good enough reason. The next time he called, she would tell him she didn't want to see him again. Say it nicely. Sweetly. Want to be friends. Think highly of you. You're a sweet man, but it just isn't . . . doesn't . . . can't work. That's what she wanted to say. To end it. But he never called her again. One good, strong, healthy, sexy man. No, it wasn't Donald Solow.

And it wasn't the real-estate magnate she met at a party, who, after one quiet dinner of fun conversation, went back to New York and sent her a bracelet from Tiffany's with a note saying that he couldn't stop thinking about her. And in the weeks that followed sent dozens of flowers and then called and said he'd send the company plane to fly her to him in Bermuda, and when she asked for a telephone number so she could call him back after she'd decided about Bermuda, he said he couldn't give her his home phone number because his wife wouldn't understand.

And it wasn't Frederick the handsome psychiatrist friend of a woman she'd met at an art opening. A practicing successful Jungian shrink who lived his own life by astrology. Rosie would have loved that irony.

"When's your birthday?" Frederick asked Bertie over drinks.

"September twenty-second," Bertie answered. Maybe he was going to make a note of it so he could send her flowers.

"Oh, God," he said, genuinely perplexed, "you're opposing my Venus."

"Pardon?"

"Well, so much for that. It'll never work with us."

Frederick didn't even walk her to her door.

And it wasn't Martin, her married hairdresser, who

told her about every other time he'd fooled around on his wife. Or Minos, the Greek restaurateur, who hovered over her cafe table, and when the place cleared out, and Bertie still sat reading a paperback while Nina napped in her stroller, came by and said, "Excuse me, but can I take you home?"

Bertie looked up, confused.

"No, thanks. I have my car."

"I meant to *my* home," he said with a straight face.

Bertie tried to laugh it off.

"Oh. That's funny. A joke, eh?"

"No joke," Minos said, moving closer. "One of my bus boys, he'll watch the sleeping baby for an hour."

Bertie stood.

"Check, please," she said.

"No!" Cee Cee had screamed. "You said, 'Check, please'?" And then laughed endlessly on the phone when Bertie told her about the incident.

"Oh, Bert," she said through her giggles, "that's where we're different. I woulda given him a little cooz-oh for the ouzo."

"Cee Cee," Bertie said. The story had been a serious one for her about the terrible behavior of men to single women.

"Yeah. Yeah. Yeah." Cee Cee had laughed. "Check, please. You kill me. Gimme a break. So what happened?"

"He wouldn't give me the check. He refused. Finally, I just wheeled the stroller out and left."

"Well, Bert, if I were you, you know what? I wouldn't go back there again. At least not by yourself. You have to wait until Cee Cee comes back to town."

No, it wouldn't be Minos.

Nina looked darling in her white shorts and blue and white striped top, and everyone at the tennis club oohed and aahed as Bertie walked and Nina held on to her hand around court four, which was where the girl at the desk had told her she could find Libby Collins.

Court two, court three. Bertie spotted Libby on court four.

"Must have a hole in my damn racket," she heard Libby say. A pistol. She was playing with three men. When she spotted Bertie and Nina, she stopped.

"Bertie Barron," she said, "and that little doll daughter." One of the men must be Wally Collins, Libby's husband. Collins Contracting. And another man, "Bart Higgins. Nice to know you." And the young guy with the red hair. Freckles. Lots of freckles. Flushed from too much sun. Probably the pro.

"David Malcolm, Bertie Barron," Libby said. "And what's the little doll's name?"

Before Bertie could answer, Nina piped up. "I'm Nina," she said. Everyone laughed.

"Why don't we have lunch?" Libby asked Bertie.

Bertie was relieved. She hadn't played tennis since camp, and she was sure if she tried in front of all these strangers she'd be terrible at it.

"Have to go to the bathroom," Nina whispered, tugging at Bertie's tennis skirt.

"Take her right over there to the ladies', hon, and I'll see you over at the dining room."

"Nice meeting you all," Bertie said, giving a general nod. The three men nodded back.

When Bertie and Libby and Nina were seated near the window in the dining room, Nina perched in her booster chair spooning an orange freeze into her mouth, Libby gave Bertie a tap on the arm and a little smile and said, "Well. He likes you."

"Who?" Bertie asked, even though she knew as sure as she was sitting there Libby was going to tell her that Wally's friend, that Higgins guy, wanted to ask her out. Men that age always sparked to her.

"He's here from California making a deal. Malcolm. Wanted to know all about you. Malcolm Industries. Father's Rand Malcolm." Rand Malcolm, industrialist. In-

volved in politics. Bertie tried to remember the face of
David Malcolm. Handsome. That's all she remembered.
Red hair.

"Wants to call you," Libby said as if it was the best
news she had ever delivered to anyone.

"No, Lib," Bertie said. Some good-looking guy from
California. Here for a day or two. Needs company for
dinner. Exactly what she didn't want.

"He's rich," Libby said, downing her own glass of
water in a gulp, then Bertie's.

"I have all the money I need," Bertie said. No. No.
No more fix-ups.

Libby must have known by the look on Bertie's face
that she wasn't being coy so Libby would convince her.

"I'm hungry!" Nina announced. Libby gestured for a
waiter.

"You sure?" Libby asked Bertie, making one more
try.

"You bet," Bertie said.

David Malcolm called her that night. Goddamn it,
she thought.

"Bertie," he said, "please forgive Libby Collins for
giving me your number. I assure you it was under the
duress of my telling her that if she didn't, when I renovate
my buildings in Sarasota I won't use Collins Contracting
on the job." Bertie wasn't amused.

Fuck off, Cee Cee would say to somebody who didn't
interest her. Just plain fuck off. "Oh," Bertie said. Somehow David Malcolm braved her cold response. In fact, as
the conversation went on, he seemed to have a pleasant
personality.

"The kiss of death," Cee Cee would say about that.
"That's when you should have known to run for the hills,
Bert," Cee Cee would tell her. "That's the first tip-off that
they're no good—if they sound good on the phone." Now
he was telling Bertie about how he'd never married, but
that he was crazy about children.

"They'll lie," Cee Cee would say. "They'll lie through their fuckin' teeth to get in your goddamn Christian Dior panties. They'll do any goddamned thing they can. And afterwards, kid, forget it. I mean, forget it. After that they do what they want."

". . . for a drink," he was saying. Something about coming over or meeting for a drink.

"I don't drink," Bertie said. God, she sounded snotty. Nasty, maybe. She didn't want to sound nasty or mean. But really, another evening with a guy in *what* business? She didn't know anything about industry. Real estate. Whatever it was. She was certain that if he'd never married, he didn't know a thing about children. They had nothing in common. Handsome. He was very attractive. She remembered that. Red hair and freckles. Lots of freckles.

"When?" she asked, sure she shouldn't ask.

"Tomorrow night," he said. "My last night here."

God, Bertie thought. Exactly what she didn't want. Why bother?

"Just for a quick drink or coffee or something," he said. "I've got a dinner meeting later that I can't break. So why don't we get together for an iced tea?" he asked. "Before my dinner meeting and before your dinner plans."

How polite, she thought, not volunteering that she hadn't had a dinner plan in months, and now—"Why not just say hello?" he asked.

Why? Bertie thought. It's absurd. He's leaving. I'm not going to do this to myself.

"Fine," she said.

David Malcolm was handsomer than Bertie remembered, but his handsomeness was an unimportant feature compared to the rest of him. He was sweet and gracious and bright and worldly and funny, and Bertie hated how much she hoped he'd excuse himself and go find a phone and come back to say he'd canceled his dinner meeting and wanted to take her to dinner. Just to be prepared, she'd warned the babysitter to be flexible, that she could be home in one hour or several.

"I'll get back to Florida again," he told her, "in a few weeks," and then he took her hand. All right, Bertie thought. Here comes the seduction. Make me think there's a future.

"Great," she said. Any minute he'd make a move. Now he was looking at her fingers thoughtfully, the way she used to look at Michael's. First he turned her hand palm up, then palm down. His hands were pale and freckled, and at his wrist below the cuff of his light blue shirt, she could see silky golden red hair like the hair on his head. When she imagined what the rest of the golden red hair on his body must look like, she was embarrassed by the thought.

"We'd better go," he said. "I'm sorry. I wish I'd planned this a little better."

When they got to Bertie's house, he walked her to the door, squeezed her hand, said, "Call you," and left.

Sure.

Cee Cee called that night and Bertie didn't even mention her date with David Malcolm. It was as if there was something fragile about it, and if she did talk about it, maybe it would go away, and he wouldn't call or wouldn't come back to Sarasota. As if something bad would happen if she mentioned his name, especially to the irreverent Cee Cee.

But Cee Cee didn't want to know anything about Bertie that night, anyway. She was rambling on about a house she wanted to buy, and an actor named Zack she was dating who had been discovered in some show off-Broadway and "some studio people saw him, Bert, and he's gonna be huge-o-major, maybe even as big as me." She laughed. But Bertie knew she was serious when she asked, "Whaddya think, Bert, two humungous egos in one house? Me and Zack. We'd kill each other inside a year, isn't that right?"

"Maybe not," Bertie said distractedly.

"Hey, maybe you're right," Cee Cee said, grasping
or straws. "Maybe not. I mean, two people if they really
want to can—Christ, Bert, wouldya listen to me? Why do
I always think it's gonna work? I oughtta know better. I
oughtta be like you and just say there's no way some
magical guy is gonna drop in outta the sky and save me,
and the sooner I quit expecting that one of 'em will, the
better off I'll be. That's old Bertie's philosophy, right?"

"Mmm," Bertie said, thinking about David Malcolm,
of the way he had held her hand earlier.

"Well," Cee Cee said, "I gotta go get dressed. Zack's
comin' over and we're going to a screening."

"Night, Cee."

A screening? So late? That's right, it was three hours
earlier in Los Angeles. Here it was ten o'clock. Nina long
asleep. Maybe she would read herself to sleep.

The phone rang. Her heart was pounding. No. She
wasn't going to hurt herself this way—want it to be David
and be disappointed when it wasn't.

"Hello."

"Bertie?"

"David," she said, certain her voice gave away entirely too much. More than she wanted to. More than she
should.

"God," he said. "I was really a jerk. When I think
that I could have been sitting somewhere with you, looking at your pretty face, instead of listening to some boring
bankers drone on endlessly about business. Anyway, I
wanted to tell you that I think you're a terrific woman and
that if it would be all right with you I'd like to call you
from Los Angeles tomorrow. Just to chat and to get to
know you better."

"Of course," Bertie said, but she was worried. This
was feeling too good. And the next day, when she looked
at the clock and subtracted three hours from the time, ten
forty-five here, seven forty-five there, too early, one-fifteen

here, ten-fifteen there, probably hasn't arrived yet, three-thirty here, twelve-thirty there—won't call now, probably at lunch. At five, the phone rang just as she got back from picking Nina up from dancing school. She heard it as they were coming up the walk. Nina was gabbing about how Robin, her friend, had pushed her at nursery school and how Mrs. Weingarten saw it and moved Robin to the back of the line on the way to recess.

Bertie was in the door and at the phone, but by the time she'd grabbed the receiver and held it to her ear, whoever was trying to reach her was no longer there. Damn.

She sat at the dinner table only half-listening to Nina. Excited in a way she couldn't remember being in years, maybe ever. *Who* had made her feel this way? Made her mind refuse to think of anything else?

She picked at her dinner. This is dumb, she thought again. Schmucky is what Cee Cee would call it. Who was this man? Son of a rich father, Libby Collins had said, Malcolm Industries. So what? That's all she knew. That, and a one-hour date during which he told her how much he loved Libby and Wally Collins, how he grew up in Los Angeles, how he spent a lot of time in northern California and bought land and developed property and . . . something like that. She should have listened more carefully instead of looking. Counting the freckles on his handsome face.

"Time for your bath, Neen," she said.

"Oh, Mom, I don't want a bath. Please, no bath."

"Nina, come on, why do we have to have a discussion? Let's take our plates and clean up in here and—"

The phone. Seven o'clock here is four o'clock there. Another ring. That would be perfect. Day winding down. Figured I'd be here. Another ring. "Okay," she told Nina, "no bath." She picked up the phone.

"Hello?"

"Hi, Bertie? David Malcolm."

He still used his last name. Of course, because they were strangers. Nina skipped off to her room, and Bertie sat at the table, the plate containing her barely touched dinner in front of her, and took a deep breath. Take a moment. Not to sound too glad.

"Hello, David," she said. "How was your trip?"

After that he called constantly. Sometimes in the morning. Sometimes very late at night, with apologies for the hour, but saying that his day had been full and he had thought about her all day, but just couldn't find a moment when there wasn't some reason why he couldn't get near a phone. And she would tell him it was just as well because she had been running all over with errands and her daughter. But she was only telling half the truth since she deliberately had every one of her errands done by noon here, nine o'clock there, so she would be home by the time he'd even dream of calling.

There were three weeks of endless conversations. Bertie usually sitting, melted, in a chair or flopped across her bed like a teenager. At the end of the third week, David mentioned something about his education at Stanford. He had gone to school there during the war, she thought she heard him say. War? What war?

Young. He looked young, but not *that* young. Not too young. Bertie was thirty-five. How much younger could he be? No. She'd better . . . during the war?

"How old *are* you?" she asked him one night.

"Twenty-seven."

Oh, Jesus. That much younger. Bertie was glad he couldn't see the look of surprise on her face. Robbing the cradle.

"Do you have any idea how old *I* am?" she asked. She knew she looked younger. Maybe thirty-three, maybe thirty. But wait until she told him the truth. She had to tell him. She didn't want to, but before this thing got started, she ought to. Well, actually, it was already started, but at least

now everyone could back off before they were too involved or . . .

"To the day," David Malcolm said. "September twenty-
second, 1944."

"Oh, God," she said. "How?" Libby. It must have
been Libby. Of course, but . . .

"It doesn't matter," he said. "Not one bit."

Sweet, she thought. And funny. This is funny. He's
known all along. That I'm . . . an older woman. She was
an older woman to this boy. Guy. Man. At thirty-five.
Now that he'd said it didn't matter to him, the idea of it all
made her smile. Good heavens.

When she was twenty-two, already married to Michael, David Malcolm was fourteen and in prep school.
Hah. Imagine if he'd walked up to her then, a little
red-headed flat-topped boy and said, "How's about a kiss,
sweetie?" A kiss. Bertie grinned at the thought. They'd
never even shared a kiss—only barely touched—and she
was smitten, gone, fallen for a man she'd seen twice in her
life. She loved his gentle voice on the phone and his sweet
sense of humor. He told her all about what he called his
"overprivileged youth" and all the adventures he'd had
"by virtue of the remarkable accident of my birth." About
his extraordinarily powerful father's influence on his life,
and all of it was told without any pretense or any attempt
at seduction, but simply as an unfolding of himself.

At first, almost because she felt he was telling so
much she had to tell at least a little, Bertie began to talk
about herself. Her own childhood, how it was to be raised
by a single mother, how sometimes she heard herself
saying things to her little daughter that sounded like her
own mother.

"Bertie," David said one night. "I really want to see
you. Get to know you better. Spend some time with you.
And I've been trying, I honestly have, to schedule coming
to Sarasota, but between my own business and a lot of

business I'm doing for my family, I can't seem to get out of here. Why don't you come and visit me here?"

"Come to Los Angeles?" she asked, as if the request had been to come to the moon.

"Better yet, my parents have a wonderful place in Pebble Beach. They're in Europe. Next weekend I have a few meetings in Carmel, but in between, we could take walks, drives, have dinner in Big Sur."

A tryst in Pebble Beach. A romantic weekend. With a boy. What if she got there and looked at him and didn't want to sleep with him? All the way to Pebble Beach. She felt the way she had when she used to be invited to college weekends. "Always make certain that you have appropriate and private accommodations," Rosie would tell her, and Bertie would have to tell some panting college boy, "You see, I have to have my own room with a shower," and the boy would say, "Huh? Yeah. Oh. Sure. Yeah." And then find her a room on the first floor of a dormitory or sorority house so he could slip in the window to "visit" her at night, and try to jump all over her. Except for Michael. He had never tried anything like that. Until they were pinned. She should have known then that he was a cold fish.

"You can have the guest cottage, which is an absolute palace. My mother decorated it, and it's heaven," David offered.

Gentlemanly. This man had promise.

"Thank you, David," Bertie said. "It sounds wonderful. Let me think about it."

"Think about it? You wishy-washy bitch. Call the little prince back and tell him not only are you on your way, but you're bringing your friendly neighborhood movie star with you as a chaperone," Cee Cee said when Bertie told her. "Bertie, why are you stalling? This guy sounds great."

"Well . . . I've never left Nina with a sitter for so long before and—"

"Two lousy days, Bert. The kid's not gonna shrivel up and die if you leave her. *I'll* take her, for chrissake."

"No. She's in nursery school. And there's a nice woman who I trust here, and—"

"So when're you goin'?"

"David has meetings in New York and Chicago during the week. But he wants to meet me in Monterey on Friday evening."

"Hey!" Cee Cee said. "Make it four days and come to L.A. for two. Or wait—better yet, I'll rent a car. And when you get here I'll drive up there with you. We'll hang out on Wednesday and Thursday, and then when he shows up Friday I'll leave, and you two can shack up." Cee Cee sounded excited to see her. It had been a long time. And it sounded like a perfect plan. A few days of laughing with Cee Cee would relax her. Cee Cee was right. Nina wouldn't fall apart without her, and the time away would feel good. And David. Getting to see David—to be in the same room with him, to touch him—see how it felt to be this turned on about someone at last, at last.

"I'll do it," Bertie said.

David sounded sincerely delighted to hear that Bertie had taken him up on the offer and insisted the two women go to Pebble Beach directly to his parents' home. Stay there for the two days. Be let in by one of the servants, and stay there.

"Without you? Oh, no," Bertie said, imagining Cee Cee dropping clothes and cigarette ashes and spilling wine all over Rand Malcolm's estate. "We'll stay in Carmel."

"I insist," David said, and immediately air-expressed her a handmade map of "the forest," as he called the area where his family's obviously grand home was located, and instructions on how to get in the gate, and the names of the servants who would be waiting.

"David."

"All you have to do is pick me up at the airport on Friday night," he said. "I'll fly from Chicago to Los Angeles, then Los Angeles to Monterey. Be in at eight-thirty PSA."

"You'll just miss Cee Cee," Bertie said. "Her flight leaves for L.A. at seven-thirty."

"Love to meet her," and then he added, "some other time." He and Bertie both laughed.

Cee Cee met Bertie at LAX outside the baggage claim. She sat in a red Camaro she'd rented that morning. She was wearing her usual floppy hat and glasses. Bertie had one small bag and the trunk of the Camaro was already full and so messy that she had to put her bag on the back seat.

"Cee," she said after she had slid into the passenger seat and hugged her friend, "you're only going to be gone for two days, what do you have there?"

Cee Cee shrugged. "The usual. Pillow, hairdryer, face steamer, snacks, clothes, tape deck—stuff," she said, shrugging again.

She drove like a maniac, weaving in and out of traffic on the L.A. freeways, gabbing away about some new man she'd met (Zack was already old news). This one was a photographer, "He came to do a layout," she said, and couldn't miss the opportunity to lean on the pun, "and boy, *did he ever*." And as the Camaro hit the open road, she talked about some new songs she was going to record, and then with all the windows open, as they went blazing up the coast road, she sang one of the songs for Bertie, full voice. It was a country-and-western tune called "Gettin' Through a Day Without You." The words were heart-breakingly beautiful, and they made Bertie think about the fact that she hadn't been really in love in years, or maybe ever. Not the way they talked about it in songs. Never really loved Michael that way. And now she had a chance. A far-fetched chance with this . . . boy . . . young man, who seemed so nice on the phone, so self-assured, so . . . interested in her. Maybe these few days she was going to spend with him would begin something special between them.

Cee Cee didn't stop except for gasoline until they got to San Simeon to see the Hearst castle.

The lines to get in to see the home of William Randolph Hearst were long, and even though she wore the hat and glasses and Levi's and a shirt, several people recognized Cee Cee and pressed forward for autographs.

"I'm just lookin' the place over 'cause I'm thinking about moving out of L.A.," Cee Cee said loudly, and some people who hadn't noticed her before recognized her voice and came over.

During the tour she made loud jokes about Hearst and Marion Davies's sex life and the tacky taste of some people, for the amusement of the crowd. Bertie burrowed her chin into the turtleneck sweater she was wearing, as if she were trying to disappear. But soon even she had to giggle, because the jokes were funny, and she was always amazed at the way Cee Cee could make any location a backdrop for her own special act.

By four o'clock, the two of them sat outside by the fire at Nepenthe in Big Sur nibbling cheese, drinking Cabernet Sauvignon, and watching the fog roll in over the water below. Cee Cee was tired from the drive. Bertie had called Nina from a pay phone and was musing about how when the babysitter told Nina it was "Mommy calling from California," Nina wasn't all that interested. And then her mind wandered to David, and she remembered how he'd said on the phone, "I like kids. I haven't been around too many of them, but when I am I always like their honesty."

David. Tomorrow evening they'd be together.

"I'm excited for you, Bert," Cee Cee said, as if she were reading Bertie's thoughts.

"Me, too," Bertie said, afraid to say anything more, to feel too hopeful, for fear of the pain and disappointment.

The gate to the house on the Seventeen Mile Drive moved open slowly.

"Drive down long driveway to the left," Bertie read from the paper bearing David's directions. Cee Cee turned left, and as they had their first glimpse of the view from the Malcolms' estate, both women spoke at the same time.

"Good heavens."

"Holy shit."

The Mediterranean-style villa sat out on a cliff. Below it, the frothy white California waves crashed against the rocks. Close by the shore on the jagged rocks, lazy harbor seals were sprawled, watching the orange sun slip inch by inch toward the horizon.

"Hey, I think I like this guy a lot for you, Bert," Cee Cee said, stopping the car and rolling down all the windows so they could breathe the glorious ocean air. They sat silently until the sun was gone, then Cee Cee turned the car up the driveway toward the Malcolm mansion. The door opened, and a house man in a white coat stood there to greet them. He took Bertie's bag from the back seat and didn't flinch when Cee Cee opened the trunk piled with all her things. Just asked, "All of this inside?" When Cee Cee nodded, he proceeded to pick up their belongings and head toward the house. They followed him through a high-ceilinged foyer out through a glass door and past the pool, where Cee Cee whispered, "See how Hearst fucked up. He should have picked *this* place. It's closer to the ocean." And then they were in the guest cottage. Cozy, Mexican tiled floors, brightly colored fabrics, every touch perfect down to the tiniest detail.

By the time Bertie had thanked the man, who said his name was Victor, and he had told her that he could be reached by pressing button number four on the com line, and that, please, Mr. Malcolm wanted them to make themselves at home, Cee Cee's side of the bedroom was already a mess. Clothes on the bed and the floor. Cassette player and cassettes everywhere. Bertie took a deep breath and thought about the nicest possible way to say it, and was just about to try, "Cee, can I help you hang some of your things up?" when the phone rang.

It was David. Bertie was so thrilled at the sound of his voice that she almost couldn't hear what he said. Calling to make sure they were comfortable. Comfortable? What an understatement. "Don't hesitate to ask Victor for anything," he went on. "He'll bring breakfast whenever you call. There's a wonderful wine cellar. Please help yourselves."

"Thank you," Bertie kept saying. Was there no end, please God, to this man's graciousness?

"Bert," he said, finally, huskily, seriously, "I can't wait to be with you."

Bertie closed her eyes. "I can't wait for that either, David," she said.

Friday was a gorgeous May day, and Bertie and Cee Cee spent the morning on the Seventeen Mile Drive and went to the wharf at Monterey for lunch, had their picture taken in Victorian costumes on Cannery Row and finally, at four o'clock, went back to the Malcolm guest cottage to get Cee Cee's things so she could pick them up and return the car.

"Maybe I shouldn't leave," Cee Cee teased. "Maybe I should hide in the airport and just sneak a peek at this hot shot when he gets off the plane." Bertie grinned. She felt like a child on her way to Disneyland.

Bertie went to the magazine stand and Cee Cee went to the Hertz counter to return the car. There was a line at the Hertz counter, and Cee Cee pulled her hat down a little lower onto her face. The two men in front of her, both wearing suits, businessmen, were talking very seriously. Cee Cee wondered if David Malcolm was a serious type like these guys.

"Rolled over on its side," one of the guys said to the other.

"They say it was the worst one ever," the other one

answered. Cee Cee hated lines, and this one wasn't even moving. The holdup seemed to be a man at the counter who couldn't find his credit cards.

"They say takeoffs and landings are when you have to worry most," the first one said. "Once you're up there, I guess there's not much you can hit." The other man laughed. They were talking about airplane crashes. Thanks, boys, Cee Cee thought. I hate goddamn flying to begin with and now I got to listen to this? Gimme a break.

"There were reporters and photographers all over LAX," one of the men said.

The man at the front of the line found his credit cards in his briefcase and was laughing with relief.

"Hey," Cee Cee said, tapping one of the men on the shoulder, "mind if I ask what you're talking about?"

Both men turned. Neither of them looked as if they recognized her.

"Big plane wreck in Chicago. American Airlines. Chicago to L.A. A DC-10. Looks like everyone in the plane bought the farm, if you get my meaning."

Cee Cee held on to the man's arm for an instant for support, then turned toward the magazine store from which the beautiful smiling Bertie had just emerged, carrying a paper bag filled with the magazines she was planning to read while she waited for David Malcolm to arrive.

Dear Mr. and Mrs. Malcolm,

I was a friend of David's and I wanted to

Dear Mr. and Mrs. Malcolm,

*Although I only recently met your son I wanted
to write and tell you how impressed I was by*

Dear Mr. and Mrs. Malcolm,

Your son was a fine man. Please accept my
deepest sympathies on his passing.

                              Roberta Barron

Carmel, California, 1983

Cee Cee stood on the steps, leaned against the wall, and stared at the door of the bedroom. Finally, it creaked open and Janice Carnes emerged. She was silent for a moment, as if she were trying to form in her mind exactly what to say.

"Cee Cee," the woman said. There was something too sweet in her voice that made Cee Cee wince inside. "I'm from the volunteer hospice program in Monterey."

The what?

"Roberta contacted us earlier this year because she's very ill, and she wanted to die here in Carmel. And not in a hospital. People from our program come here to tend to her daily needs. So this morning when she called you, it was because she . . ."

Cee Cee slowly sank and sat down on one of the steps.

"Are you all right?" Janice Carnes asked. "Cee Cee?"

All right? How could she be all right? There was a look on the woman's face that said, don't worry. I'm strong.

269

I can handle anything, so if you want to scream and yell and fall apart go right ahead, because I can handle it.

"Yeah," Cee Cee said, "I'm all right." But she felt weak and small and afraid, and she didn't want to ask the question that came next: "What does she . . . I mean, what's wrong with her?"

"She has ovarian cancer."

"And how much . . . I mean, how long?"

"Two or three months at best."

Oh, God. No. Please. Stop. Take it away, Cee Cee thought. But when Janice Carnes just stood looking long into her eyes, Cee Cee finally forced herself into a standing position, and somehow managed to place her left foot on the next step up, and then put her right foot on the next step, and when she reached the top of the stairs, she moved to the bedroom door and pushed it open.

God, help me so I don't show how scared I am. How bad she looks. Real bad. Not as bad as she did when she was asleep. But real bad.

Bertie was sitting up, wearing a blue flannel robe. Her hair looked very neat, almost too stylish, and when she saw Cee Cee, a huge smile flashed across her face.

"Thanks for coming, Cee," she said, like they were just about to sit down to tea or something.

"So big fuckin' deal," Cee Cee said. "You're dyin'. You couldn't maybe think of somethin' original to do?"

Bertie chuckled.

"I already had my friend Peter Sellers die, my pal Freddy Prinze die. Hey, I mean, Bert, you asshole, dying is really a cliché."

Bertie was laughing now.

"Tell the truth," Cee Cee went on. "Do you really want to be in the same category as Esther Garfield, Sam Weinstein, and Abie Levine?"

"I don't know," Bertie said through a giggle. "Who *are* they?"

"They're friends of my mother's who *died*. I mean,

Bert, dying is so gauche. Even *my mother* did it. Do you want to follow in Leona's footsteps? I mean, if you want to, far be it from me to try and change your mind but . . ."

The sob that was rising in Cee Cee's throat stopped her next line, and Bertie reached out her long thin arms for Cee Cee to come to her. Cee Cee couldn't speak but she sat on the edge of the bed and hugged her friend, feeling Bertie's frail bony body through the blue flannel robe. Finally Cee Cee swallowed and spoke again. This time her voice was hoarse.

"Bert," she said, "I'm rich. I got millions. I'm not gonna let you die. I'm gonna get the best doctors in the world and fly 'em all here to save you. I know people with their own airplanes, even people who know the president, Bert, and I'll spend everything I've got. You're not gonna die so fast there, kid, and I'm gonna see to it." She sat back to look at Bertie. Bertie was still smiling, but there were very dark deep circles around her eyes.

"Cee," she said, and for that fleeting second she looked to Cee Cee like the little lost girl she'd met on the beach so long ago in Atlantic City. "Here's the thing. You see, I really *want* to be like Esther Garfield and Sam Weinstein and Arnie Levine."

"Abie Levine," Cee Cee corrected her. "Arnie is Abie's brother. His smarter brother, Bert, because *he's* still alive." They both laughed, a little laugh.

Bertie continued to smile her tired smile as she went on. "I want to die, and money doesn't matter, because *I* know doctors too. Good ones. More doctors than I ever thought there were in the world. The best ones. And it doesn't matter. Because I'm ready. Even if it means following in Leona's footsteps." Her smile grew brighter.

"But why, you asshole?" Cee Cee asked.

"Well, the big reason is so I'll never ever have to hear you call me *that* again," she said, and they both laughed. "And the other reason is because I'm sure that it's my time." And then they both cried.

When the crying subsided, Cee Cee handed Bertie a Kleenex, took one for herself, and they blotted their eyes. "I needed you to be here, Cee," Bertie said, "because I knew if you *were*, at least I would die laughing." And that made them both grin, and Bertie lay back on the pillow, looking as if the laughing had exhausted her. "And I picked Carmel because I fell in love with it that time you and I came here . . . to see . . . to be with . . ."

"David," they said at the same time. And Bertie nodded and then said the only thing she ever did when David Malcolm's name came up.

"Wasn't that sad? So very sad. God, that was too bad."

Cee Cee said nothing because she knew there was more coming. The part about a lovely man. And what a loss.

"What a loss," Bertie said. "Because he was a truly lovely man."

Cee Cee said what she always did at that point in the conversation.

"Yeah. Lovely."

Bertie closed her eyes.

"Listen, maybe I could go out and get us some food and stuff," Cee Cee said. "I'm starving. You allowed to eat?"

"I don't really want anything," Bertie said, "but you go ahead. You might find some food downstairs in the fridge."

"I'll fix us both somethin'," Cee Cee said, and stood. "Now don't go dyin' or anything while I'm out of the room, okay?"

Bertie grinned. "I'm so glad you're here," she said.

Cee Cee grinned, too, and walked out of the room with the grin plastered on her face, but when she'd pulled the door shut, she closed her eyes for a minute, then went into the bathroom, pulled the door closed behind her, turned on the faucet full blast, and threw up. Bertie.

Good God. Dying. And *wanting* to die. Looking as if she were already dead. With gray skin and those dark circles under her eyes and that hair. But her hair wasn't the color Cee Cee remembered, and it was thicker and had those kind of funny finger waves like . . . oh, Christ, it was a wig—had to be. And she hadn't been wearing it when Cee Cee first peeked in and looked at her there on the bed. A wig because she must have lost her hair from those radiation treatments people had to get when they had . . .

Cee Cee flushed the toilet and washed her hands and looked at her reflection in the mirror over the sink. Her eyes were watery and bloodshot. This was more than she could take. She would make Bertie a sandwich, have a bite herself, sit and talk with her for a while, and then split for L.A. Oh, she'd make a big fuss. Leave some money for Janice, that hospice lady, to get some more help in, and head out on some night flight back home. She was in trouble with everybody down there as it was for leaving in the middle of rehearsing her own show. She couldn't hold up a whole production staff for more than a day. It could ruin her, for chrissakes. She rinsed her face with cold water, and while her face was still dripping wet, she put some toothpaste on her finger and spread it around on her teeth, rinsed out her mouth, dried her face and hands, and sighed. Poor Bertie, she thought, and felt sad. Thank God it's not me, she thought, and felt guilty.

Downstairs Janice Carnes was in the kitchen.

"How's she doing?" she asked Cee Cee. "I heard you two laughing together, and I was glad."

"Yeah," Cee Cee said, "we laughed." Jesus. This woman looked at people who were on the croak every day. How did she stand it?

"Listen," Cee Cee said, "I'm gonna fix Bert some food and some for me, and visit for a while—and then I gotta call the airlines—'cause I really should get back down to L.A. by tonight. I got a show I ran out on and all kinds of stuff."

Janice Carnes was still smiling.

"Dinner's all ready," she said. "I sometimes eat with her, just to keep her company, so I made two portions, but you're here, so I'm sure she'd prefer to have you eating with her."

"Yeah, great, but right after dinner I've got to call the airlines and—"

"If your flight doesn't leave right away, maybe you'll meet Jessica."

"Who's that?" Cee Cee asked, watching Janice take two dishes out of the oven with something in them that looked like chicken pot pie. Cee Cee's stomach growled.

"She's the nurse Roberta hired. And tomorrow she's going to hire another one as well, for her day care."

"What about you?" Cee Cee asked.

"Oh, I'm not a nurse," Janice said. "I'm what the program calls a homemaker. I'm trained to come in and take care of her personal needs. Meals, laundry, that kind of thing. But soon she'll need more than that. She can still get herself to the bathroom now. Even come down here, which she does from time to time for dinner. Or she'll sit out on the patio. You can see the ocean from there, and more than anything she loves the beach."

"Yeah," Cee Cee said, "I know."

"But that mobility is going to be diminished soon."

"How soon?"

"A month, three weeks maybe, and she can feel it. That's why Jessica is starting tonight. Roberta really needs someone twenty-four hours. Frequently, the dying patient has a family member who's a primary-care giver, and the hospice serves as a supplement to that, but because Roberta chose to die away from her family, the nurses will be the primary-care givers, and I'll be here to tend to the house and to keep her spirits up, too."

Janice put the chicken pot pies on a tray, each with a knife, fork, spoon, and napkin.

"She won't eat much," she told Cee Cee. "But sometimes if you get her talking and her mind is busy, she'll eat a little more. I'll be by in the morning. It was nice meeting you."

Janice Carnes turned to leave the kitchen, and Cee Cee looked at the tray, dreading the idea of having to make her way up those stairs and have dinner in that room with that cadaverous person who used to be Bertie.

"What time's that nurse get here?" Cee Cee asked Janice, more as a way to keep her from leaving than because she wanted to know.

Janice looked at her watch.

"Any minute," she said, and was out the door.

Cee Cee heard Janice's car start outside, and realized that the pot pies were probably getting cold. She picked up the tray and walked slowly up the wooden stairs. Why was Bertie doing this all alone? Why wasn't Nina around?

When she pushed the bedroom door open with her hip, Cee Cee saw that Bertie was asleep again, so she set the tray down on a table, took up one of the chicken pot pies and a fork, and broke through the pie's flaky crust into the creamy chicken vegetable mixture inside. God, she was hungry. Bertie would forgive her for starting.

It was good that she'd come hurrying to Bertie's side. Heroic even. Yes, heroic. That's how she felt, but she tried to stifle her next thought because it was so tacky. The thought about how it would look in *People* magazine. STAR FLIES OFF TO BE WITH DYING FRIEND, it would say, with pictures of Cee Cee sitting at Bertie's bedside. And then shots of her coming out of Bertie's funeral, wearing some great black hat with a veil, and shrieking at the fan magazine guys to leave her alone as they swarmed around her. Tacky. She hated that she even thought that.

The only sound in the room was Bertie's labored breathing.

Cee Cee looked at her watch. What was she going to do? She couldn't just leave without talking to Bertie at

least one more time. It was seven-thirty. She'd better call
the airlines and see when there was a flight out. She'd go
downstairs, put Bertie's uneaten chicken pot pie in a
warm oven, and make some phone calls. As she got to the
door, Bertie stirred.

"Cee," she said very softly.

Cee Cee turned. "Yeah," she said. "I was takin' your
dinner down to warm it up 'cause you fell asleep and I—"

"I was thinking that I'm so glad I'm going to miss the
thrill next year of turning forty," Bertie said with a funny
half-smile. "You know," she said sleepily, "one of the good
things about dying of cancer is that I'll never have to go to
another aerobics class."

Cee Cee laughed and shook her head.

"But I'm real annoyed about missing Christmas."

She was awake. That was good. If there was a late
flight out, Cee Cee could sit and chat with her now and
then run out to the airport in time to return the car and
make the flight. What could she say to that stuff about
Christmas? Nothing. Just let her talk. Let her get it out.

"Any dinner for you, Bert?" Cee Cee asked.

"Maybe just some juice," Bertie said.

"Comin' up."

Cee Cee covered the chicken pot pie with some
aluminum foil, rinsed her own dish, and put it in the
dishwasher. Then she took the apple juice from the refrigerator, poured some into a glass, put the glass down on
the counter, and dialed the kitchen phone.

"Thank you for calling PSA," the voice on the phone
said.

"Yeah. What time is your last flight to L.A. from
Monterey tonight?" Cee Cee asked softly. Why softly?
Bertie couldn't hear her from all the way upstairs. Maybe
softly because she felt guilty for leaving.

"Ten fifty-seven P.M."

"I want to make a reservation." Hey. Why should she

feel guilty? She *loved* Bertie. Walked out on her own show today to prove it.

"Round trip?" the voice asked.

"One way," Cee Cee said.

Maybe in a week or two, when she got everything settled in L.A., she'd come back up. Sure. She could do that. That's what she'd tell Bertie. I gotta go now, Bert, but I'm comin' back. Maybe she'd wait to tell Bertie that till the nurse got there.

"Your name?" asked the voice on the phone.

"Cee Cee Bloom."

"Oh yes, Miss Bloom. I love your movies," the voice said.

"Yeah? Thanks," Cee Cee said.

"That's flight forty-three leaving Monterey at ten fifty-seven P.M., arriving Los Angeles twelve oh-three A.M. We suggest you arrive at the airport at least one half-hour before flight time."

"I'll be there," Cee Cee said with relief. "Thanks."

"Thanks for calling PSA."

Perfect. Cee Cee had started up the stairs carrying the juice glass when the front door opened softly.

Jessica, the nurse, was about fifty. She had a long thin face and what looked to Cee Cee from where she was standing like a furry upper lip. She wore glasses, a white uniform with a beige cardigan cable knit sweater, and under her arm she had a paperback copy of what Cee Cee noticed was Sidney Sheldon's *Rage of Angels*.

"Hiya, hiya," she said cutely, as if to prove to anyone listening that she was jovial. "I'm Jessica."

"I'm Cee Cee Bloom," Cee Cee said. There was no recognition on Jessica's face.

"How's the gal?" the nurse asked, gesturing with her head in the direction of upstairs.

"Okay, I guess," Cee Cee said.

"You her family?"

Cee Cee nodded, then realized. "Friend," she said.

The two women walked up the steps together. Bertie was sitting up against two pillows.

"Hello, Jessica," she said.

"Hiya, hiya," Jessica said again, walked over to Bertie, gently removed the two pillows from behind Bertie's head, plumped them up, and moved Bertie forward a bit so she could replace them. "How was your day?" the woman asked.

Bertie smiled. "Cee Cee came to visit today, so it was splendid."

"Splendid," Cee Cee said. "There are only three women in the world who use that word, Bert, and the other two both have the last name Hepburn."

Bertie loved that. Jessica didn't get it.

"Did she have dinner?" Jessica asked Cee Cee.

"Yes, I did," Bertie replied. "I mean, Cee Cee brought it to me, only I didn't eat anything because I was asleep."

"Now you know you have to eat a little something or you'll lose your strength, and you don't have that much as it is," the nurse said, and laughed self-consciously.

Cee Cee offered Bertie the glass of juice, but Bertie waved it away. "Won't you try and take a little?" Jessica asked.

"Can't," Bertie said softly.

"Fluids are good," Jessica said.

Jessica took the glass from Cee Cee, and Bertie took it from Jessica reluctantly and drank it. Jessica said, "Good girl," in a way that Cee Cee remembered she'd heard the leopard trainer at the MGM Grand say the same words when he spoke to the leopard right before the show. Bertie didn't seem to notice. Jessica must have sensed Cee Cee's discomfort with her because when the juice glass was empty, she said, "Why don't I mosey on downstairs for a bit?" and left the room.

Bertie seemed to brighten right away. Cee Cee was glad. It was time for her now to talk about leaving for Los Angeles.

"Bert," she said, "maybe I can come back up here rom L.A. to visit with you next week again, but tonight I gotta hit the road. I was in the middle of rehearsin' this big TV special when you called and I just sort of waltzed out the door. I mean, you don't know how many people I pissed off today by leavin' and they're expectin' me to come back tonight and be there tomorrow, 'cause every day I miss costs the network a bloody fortune, not to mention my production company."

"I understand. I absolutely do. You're the best person in the world to come running up here," Bertie said. "But, Cee, listen, and I mean this, if you can't get back here next week, I'll understand, I only wanted us to see each other, and to be with you *now*—before—so you wouldn't suddenly get a call from somebody and be surprised or hear about it and wonder how I was. I wanted you to know I'm okay about it. More than okay. I want it to be over."

"Where's Nina?" Cee Cee said, finally asking the question she'd wanted to ask since she'd arrived.

"With my Aunt Neet and Uncle Herb," Bertie said, her eyes testing Cee Cee's for a reaction, then looking away and going on. "She adores them and they adore her, and they've never had a child to shower all their love on, so I thought . . . Cee Cee, I've had a few hospital visits in the last few years. In Florida and in New York." Cee Cee remembered fleeting references in Bertie's letters to hospital stays for what were dismissed as minor problems.

"Every time I came home, Nina would be so helpless and so uncomfortable and so unhappy while I convalesced. And every day she'd ask me, 'Are you going to be better tomorrow?' with so much hope. I just couldn't be around her the way I am now, having to tell her this time that the answer is no. This way she gets to live a normal child's life, without the worry of a sick mother in the other room." It was all so matter-of-fact. Cee Cee couldn't believe what she was hearing. Bertie continued, "And Carmel is beautiful, so I . . . Cee Cee, do you remember when I first met you that time in Atlantic City?" She said that in the same tone of voice she used when she was talking about Nina.

"Like it was yesterday," Cee Cee answered, wondering where Bertie's thoughts were going.

But Bertie's eyes closed. She didn't speak for a while, and her breathing changed. All the interaction was tiring for her. After several minutes, Cee Cee was certain she had to be asleep, and then Bertie's eyes opened again, halfway this time, and she said, "Cee, I always wanted to tell you, but I guess I never did before, that you were so much better than that other girl. The one who walked on her hands. So much better," she repeated. Then she closed her eyes and in a few minutes she was asleep.

Cee Cee stood by the bed for a long time, and when it looked as if the sleep would continue for a while, she left the bedroom and walked downstairs.

Jessica had a fire going in the fireplace and she sat on a chair with her feet on the ottoman, reading *Rage of Angels*. "Hiya, hiya," she said when she saw Cee Cee.

"I'm goin'," Cee Cee said, and she stretched and yawned. She was exhausted. Her suitcase? Yes. It was still in the trunk of the car.

Jessica stood. "Well, it was nice of you to stop by," she said. "I'm taking good care of her, and she sure is a sweet person."

Cee Cee nodded. A sweet person. No kidding. She nodded. Standing for a moment trying to remember how to get back to the airport, then she gave the nurse her best show business smile and walked out the door.

The rain had stopped long before, and the night air was chilly and filled with the sweet smell of burning eucalyptus coming from the neighborhood chimneys. Cee Cee got into the big cold Chevrolet, started it, turned on the lights, and headed out of town. She would call Jake, her driver, from the Monterey airport, and he'd come and

pick her up in L.A. Tomorrow, at work, she'd make a big
deal of apologizing to everybody and explain about her
sick friend, and then she'd get the sympathy vote, so that
would work out great.

Hiya, hiya, Cee Cee thought, shaking her head. Good
girl. Bertie. All her life she was the good girl. Living the
good-girl life. Now she was dying, and it was just like her
to die the good-girl death, far away from her family so she
wouldn't bother them. Sparing her daughter from the
sight of her. Even inviting Cee Cee up to Carmel to
reassure her that all was okay. And now, shit. She was
dying. Dying. Bertie. You were much better than that
other girl, she said. The one who walked on her hands. So
much better. Bertie. Even if she didn't think that or
believe it, she had to say it before she died to make Cee
Cee feel good.

There. Rental car return and an arrow. Cee Cee
could see the Hertz sign at the end of the long drive. She
pulled up and stopped, turned off the car, got out of it,
and opened the trunk. Her small overnight bag looked lost
in the huge trunk space, and as she reached for the case
and began pulling it toward her, watching as the black
porter for curbside check-in moved in her direction, she
stopped. To think about it all.

"Check your bags?" he asked.

Cee Cee didn't answer. She stood, instead, staring at
her suitcase.

"Lady?"

Cee Cee never spoke to him. With a sudden deter-
mined movement she slammed the trunk, got back into
the car, started it, turned the lights on, pulled away from
the curb, and put her foot down hard on the gas pedal.

Malibu, California, 1981

In July 1981, if you lived in Los Angeles, and you were Hollywood-wise, you might drive down to the public beach at Malibu and park your car. Then you would walk north on the sand, and ease around the wire fence which is supposed to keep the public out, until you were on the private beach of the Malibu Colony.

If it was really a perfect sunny day, you'd know that on that beach, there was always a chance you might be able to spot Candice Bergen or Cher or Larry Hagman or even Barbra Streisand, sunning, chatting with friends, or playing with their kids. You'd also know that the rundown Cape Cod house on the far end of the Colony, so far down it was technically on Old Malibu Road, was being rented by Cee Cee Bloom, who threw big parties there nearly every Sunday. Catered parties, sometimes with live bands. Parties that attracted so many characters and types, you might be able to slip in unnoticed no matter what character or type you were.

Cee Cee was glad that Bertie and Nina had arrived

early in the week. It would give them a chance to talk
about the plans for Sunday's party, which Cee Cee said
was in Bertie's honor.

"Birthday?" Nina asked, clapping her perfect little
hands together excitedly.

Bertie was unpacking the one suitcase she had packed
for the two of them.

"Nobody's birthday," Bertie said, hanging the clothes,
Nina's tiny ones next to her long ones, in the cupboard of
the bedroom that smelled strongly of mildew. "Just a
party for Aunt Cee Cee's friends."

"Are we coming?" Nina asked, and looked sideways
across the room at the lady with the frizzy hair, and the
four-inch-high platform shoes, and the short shorts and
the midriff blouse.

"You betcha," Cee Cee said.

Nina had a look on her face that said she wasn't so
sure that being invited to this person's party was such a
good thing. She was a sweet-looking child, but she wasn't
as delicately pretty as Bertie, because she had inherited
her father's round face and too curly hair.

"Well, Nina, you're gonna have to slip into the al-
together, or at least a bikini, if you're gonna stick around
here," Cee Cee said, wishing she had some idea how
people were supposed to talk to six-year-olds. "But I guess
since you come from Florida, you know the rules about
bein' at the beach."

Nina just stared at her, not answering.

Bertie was looking at herself in the mirror over the
unpainted chest of drawers, brushing her hair which was
long and chestnut-colored, and free and unstyled. She
looked more casual than Cee Cee had ever seen her.

"I feel lucky she's not wearing a tweed suit," Bertie
said about her daughter. "And carrying a briefcase."

Nina looked down at her Maryjanes and turned the
toes of them in and then out, and then in again.

"I mean, I realize that compared to you I'm pretty

straight," Bertie said to Cee Cee. "But how did I ever give birth to an ultraconservative?" She spoke as if the child wasn't in the room.

"Genes," Cee Cee said.

"I would never wear jeans," Nina spouted with such conviction that Cee Cee shrieked, outraged, and Bertie laughed in spite of herself.

"She doesn't," Bertie said. "Refuses to. Dresses, skirts, jumpers, an occasional culotte. No pants. And certainly not jeans. She plays in dresses, which makes it very tricky for her to hang on the monkey bars upside down by her feet," she added as she walked over to where her daughter stood and ruffled the little girl's hair.

"So I don't," Nina said, and she put her hand up to smoothe her hair where Bertie had ruffled it.

"Gonna go look at the ocean," the child said, and walked out of the bedroom. Bertie shrugged, and Cee Cee shook her head.

"The kid is strange," Bertie said. "Maybe it's a phase. Anyway, it's one reason I decided to take her traveling. So she could expand her little horizons."

"You sure brought her to the right place for that," Cee Cee said, lying back on the plaid bedspread of the headboardless twin bed. "The ramshackle Malibu house of the has-been movie star."

"Oh, stop, Cee, you're *not* a has-been," Bertie said, plopping down on the other bed like a teenager at a pajama party. "You're just . . ."

"In between projects is what I like to call it. In between my last two movies which were major disasters and my next movie—"

"Which will be what?" Bertie asked eagerly.

Cee Cee loved that best about Bertie. She was always interested.

"Don't know." She shrugged, and waited for that feeling to come over her. The feeling that had been awakening her in the middle of the night, filling her with worry about everything. That she was running out of money, that she was without a man and maybe she always would be, that she'd never had a child, and maybe she never would or could.

But the feeling didn't come. In fact, she had a strong sense of well-being. Felt good. Even great. Must be because Bertie was with her, and here they were, sitting on beds and chatting, as if they'd just seen each other yesterday. And Cee Cee could tell Bertie things that she wouldn't ever tell anyone else. Like how afraid she was that her career was over. And the proof was that people who used to fawn all over her weren't even accepting or returning her phone calls. And how sometimes when she was singing, her voice sounded ordinary to her and maybe all these young new singers were better. And . . .

"Cee," Bertie said, "you look splendid. You're the thinnest I've ever seen you, and your skin looks pretty and your hair looks shiny. I think it agrees with you."

"Malibu?" Cee Cee asked.

Bertie shook her head.

"Being a has-been," she said, and they both laughed. It was the first time Cee Cee had laughed in a while.

That night, Cee Cee took Bertie and Nina to the Baja Cantina for dinner.

"What's a taco?" Nina said from behind the menu she was holding. The menu was almost as big as she was.

Cee Cee described it. "Crunchy shell filled with meat, sauce, beans, lettuce, tomatoes . . ."

"Do you have to pick it up in your hand to eat it?"

"Yeah."

"I'll have something else."

"Hates to eat food with her hands," Bertie said, smiling uncomfortably at Cee Cee.

"But that's the best *way*," Cee Cee said as Nina's lips pursed.

"Not for me," said the child.

The waitress, who looked like a surfer girl wearing a Mexican peasant's dress, arrived at the table.

"Take your order," she said, and smiled at Nina.

"Double margarita for me," Cee Cee said, "and a number sixteen."

"Will you have a cheese enchilada, honey?" Bertie asked Nina. "You can eat that with a fork."

"Yes," Nina replied, handing her menu to the waitress. "And a Shirley Temple from the bar, please."

While Bertie gave her own order to the waitress, Cee Cee watched Nina take her napkin, unfold it and place it neatly on her lap, then fold her hands in front of her on the table.

"So, Nina," Cee Cee said, "whaddya do for fun?"

"I go to school," Nina replied. "We have arts and crafts, arithmetic, and reading groups and field trips." Then she picked up her water glass, took a sip of water, placed the glass back on the table, and looked directly into Cee Cee's eyes.

"And what do *you* do for fun?" she asked.

Cee Cee laughed in surprise, but she didn't have an answer.

When the food arrived, Nina's table manners were perfect. She didn't slurp the Shirley Temple or even stick her finger in the glass to pull out the cherry.

"Don'tcha want the cherry?" Cee Cee asked when dinner was through.

Nina shook her head.

"And you call yourself a kid?" Cee Cee joked.

Nina's soda had long been drained from the glass and the stem of the orangey-red cherry sat lodged between two ice cubes.

"Boy, *I* do," Cee Cee said with a grin. "I love maraschinos," and she put her hand into Nina's glass and tugged on the stem, released the cherry and popped it into her mouth, but before she even finished chewing, she saw the horror on Nina's face.

"She stuck her fingers in my glass," Nina said to Bertie. "In *my* glass, Mommy, did you see?"

"Nina, you were finished with the drink," Bertie said. "And I'll order another one for—"

"But it was *mine*," Nina said. "And she did that."

"Nina . . ."

Nina put her hand over her mouth, looked as if she was thinking about throwing up, and Cee Cee held her breath. Kids. They were so weird. This one looked like she was gonna get sick to her stomach over a fuckin' cherry.

"Hey, I'm sorry," Cee Cee said.

Nina glared at her.

"Dessert?" the waitress asked. Her arrival broke the moment. "And look who did such a good job cleaning her plate," she said, grinning her surfer girl grin at Nina.

Nina acknowledged the recognition of her goodness with a nod. Cee Cee looked over at Nina's empty plate. She couldn't believe it. Nina's knife and fork were lying next to one another across the right-hand side of the plate. Like one of those Amy Vanderbilt kind of ladies probably says you're supposed to do. Bertie's were the same on her plate. Cee Cee's fork sat on the table and she had no idea where her knife was. She thought maybe she had bumped it onto the floor with her elbow when she was reaching past Bertie for the guacamole.

Bertie tucked Nina in by nine, and at ten Cee Cee watched her peek one more time into the guest bedroom to make sure her daughter was asleep.

"Sometimes I feel sorry for her," Bertie said, in a kind of whisper, and Cee Cee could tell she was holding back tears.

The two friends walked down the stairs to the living room. The night was black and cloudy and there was no moon. The only light on the beach came from the spotlight on the deck of Cee Cee's house, which lit the foamy white of each wave as it came crashing onto the sand.

"Why don't we go sit outside?" Cee Cee said. "I'll get some wine and bring it out."

Bertie walked out to the deck and sat on the webbed deck chair, facing the water.

Cee Cee opened the refrigerator and was reaching inside for the bottle of wine when the phone rang. She grabbed it, hoping the sound hadn't disturbed Nina.

"Yeah?"

"Cee Cee?" It was a man.

"Who's *this*?" she asked.

"You'll be surprised," the voice said.

Vaguely familiar, but long-ago familiar.

"I'm in town at the Beverly Hills Hotel for a few meetings, and I got your number through a friend at the Morris office. I thought maybe I could see you while I'm in L.A."

Cee Cee searched her mind. Who the fuck . . .? There was something arrogant in the voice, detached, but she just couldn't place it.

"Hey, let's cut the guessing games," she said. Maybe it was some crank call. Sometimes those perverted assholes who ended up asking you to mail them your underpants started off the call by pretending they knew you. "Tell me who this is or I'm hanging up."

"Michael Barron."

Cee Cee's face filled with angry heat.

"What do *you* want?" she asked coldly. Christ. Maybe he knew that Bertie was here in L.A. with his kid. The kid that the filthy snake hadn't ever seen. Maybe that was why he was calling.

"Well, I thought we could start with dinner," he said almost mockingly. "I have a few of my associates in town with me. And they don't believe that I know a big movie star like you," he added. "Maybe they'd have a drink with us first."

No. This wasn't about Bertie or Nina. The son of a bitch had no idea they were here. He was lookin' to get laid. And to get a little mileage with his friends for knowin' a star. Putz, schmuck, low-life, no-good dog.

Cee Cee put her finger on the button and disconnected the line. When she listened and heard the dial tone, she put the receiver on the counter, opened the wine bottle, took two glasses from the cupboard and went outside.

"You're not gonna believe who just called here," she said.

"I hope it was Warren Beatty saying he's coming to the party on Sunday," Bertie joked.

"Warren's in New York," Cee Cee said, too seriously.

"Cee, I was just . . ." Bertie saw the look on Cee Cee's face. "Who was it?"

"Michael."

"Michael Barron? What did he say? Did you tell him I was—"

"He sounded a little bit drunk," Cee Cee said, realizing, as she said it, that it was true. Like somebody else who was drunk, too, was makin' him do it. "He's a bad guy," she added quickly because she saw a look in Bertie's eyes that she didn't want to see there. "Wanted to prove to his friends that he knew a star. He told me that, Bert. I mean, doesn't that prove he's the same schmuck he always was?"

"Where's he staying?" Bertie asked, taking the bottle from Cee Cee, pouring herself a glass of wine and drinking, downing nearly all of it on the first taste.

"Don't know," Cee Cee said. "Don't remember." Cee Cee saw in Bertie's eyes that Bertie didn't believe her.

"Beverly Hills Hotel," Cee Cee confessed, picking up the chilly wine bottle, pouring herself a glass of the white wine and refilling Bertie's glass. Bertie immediately drank the contents and when the glass was empty she stood.

"I've got to—" she began.

"Bert, she's fine. If she wakes up she'll come looking for you."

"Not Nina," Bertie said. "Michael. I've got to call him. Talk to him. We never talk. Except through the lawyers. I want to talk to him. I mean I just want to see if he'll . . ." She was nearly trembling.

"Bert, don't do it."

"I have to," Bertie said, and she walked into the house and closed the door behind her.

Cee Cee watched her through the glass door. She walked slowly and shakily toward the counter where the phone was, put her hand on the phone and squeezed the receiver in her palm for a few moments, while she stood and thought, obviously rehearsing what she was going to say. Cee Cee shook her head and looked away. Maybe she ought to stop Bertie right now. Make her wait until her mind was clear. The margaritas and the wine would make her vulnerable. If she had to talk to him she ought to wait until tomorrow.

Far out on the water, Cee Cee could see the light of a small fishing boat anchored there. She stood, but as she did she realized Bertie had already dialed the phone. In fact, she was already talking to someone. The ocean's noise drowned out Bertie's voice, but Cee Cee could see from Bertie's expression that the someone must be Michael. She was smiling, a big forced smile, as if she wanted the smile to sound like it was in her voice.

Cee Cee sat back down, this time on a lounge chair, and looked out at the ocean. She was glad she'd spent the money to rent this place. Every day here was like a vacation. Living on the oceanfront was like living with a twenty-four-hour-a-day show in your yard. The surfers and the planes and the helicopters and the boats and the joggers and the dogs and the lovers on picnics. Always something to see, to watch, to distract her.

The glass door opened and Bertie came out.

"He's meeting me for breakfast tomorrow," she said. "At some place in the hotel called the Polo Lounge."

Cee Cee didn't say a word, and Bertie's face was filled with confusion when she spoke again.

"Let's open another bottle of wine," she said.

Cee Cee pulled the royal blue comforter over her face to shut out the morning light and all that noise that was coming from the kitchen. Then the warm smell of fresh coffee filled the bedroom. What time was it? Bertie must be awake.

She got slowly out of bed, threw on her green terry-cloth robe, and walked downstairs.

"Hi," Bertie said as she dropped the saucepan she'd been holding while she tried to figure out where it was supposed to be stored.

"Over the stove," Cee Cee said.

Bertie picked the pot up and stood on her toes in order to reach the cabinet over the stove.

"Cee, I asked him," she said.

"Asked who?" Cee Cee said. "What?"

"Michael. To see Nina. I called him this morning, about an hour ago, and I said, 'Listen, Michael, here we all are in Los Angeles. You, me, and Nina. None of us planned it, but we're here. Doesn't it seem to you as if it was predestined? Well, it does to me. And I thought it would be the best idea in the whole round world if I brought Nina to breakfast today and you could finally be with your daughter.' "

Cee Cee felt inside the pocket of her robe for a cigarette. She walked over to the stove, put the cigarette in her mouth and lit it on the flame of the gas burner.

"What'd he say?" she asked at the same time she inhaled.

"He said no," Bertie answered. "And at first I got upset and tried to argue with him, but then I stopped, Cee. Do you know why? Because even though he said no,

I heard a little maybe in his voice. And that's a good sign, because that means when I see him this morning I can talk him into it. I know I can. He wants to meet her. How could he not want to? She's his daughter. And now she's not a little crying infant anymore. Now she's a person with ideas, and she'll be able to charm him, don't you think?"

"Bert, this guy is heartless. You keep forgetting that. You're gonna get your hopes up and he's gonna disappoint you."

"He won't, Cee. And Nina has to meet him. See that he exists. He has to let her, even if it's just this once." She looked at her watch. "I've got to shower. If Nina's still asleep when I leave, please, when she wakes up, just tell her I needed to do some shopping this morning, and that I'll be back a little after noon. Thanks, Cee."

Before Cee Cee could respond, Bertie swept up the steps carrying her coffee mug with her. Cee Cee stood in the kitchen silently until she heard the bathroom door close and the shower start. Then she said out loud, "The fucking son of a bitch," and poured herself a cup of coffee.

The smell of Bertie's perfume called Opium still hung in the air long after she'd run nervously out the front door after asking Cee Cee, "How do I look? Do you think I look okay?" Cee Cee had reassured her that as always she looked better than anyone in the world.

A few minutes later, Cee Cee was sprawled on the deck outside surrounded by the newspaper, her coffee cup, and three scripts her agent had sent over for her to read. Jeez, little kids slept late. She'd always thought they woke up real early in the morning and bugged their parents. Not Nina, though. She was obviously still out like a friggin' light.

An hour later, Cee Cee finished reading one of the scripts and hated it so much that she threw it across the deck. She was hungry. Maybe she'd wake up Nina and take her to lunch. To some place where they had forks. Hah! The kid was weird. There was no doubt about that.

Cee Cee opened the door to the guest bedroom slowly, but Nina wasn't in her bed.

"Nina," Cee Cee called out. Must be in the guest bathroom. No. The door to the guest bathroom was open and Cee Cee looked inside. Bertie's pretty flowered cosmetic bag sat on the sink.

"Nina?" No answer.

Cee Cee looked in every room upstairs, then every room downstairs, then walked out onto the deck, even though she knew the kid couldn't have gotten past her to go outside.

"Nina?" Weird.

Cee Cee walked in her bare feet down the few steps to the beach and looked both ways. To the north, the beach was empty of people as far as she could see. To the south were a few blankets of sunbathers in the distance, but none seemed to have a child with them.

Cee Cee walked back up to the house and checked the garage and the road outside. Maybe Nina had somehow gone out to the beach and started walking, then couldn't find her way back or recognize the house or . . .

"Nina?"

Cee Cee was out on the deck again. Kids. Christ. What was she doing with a kid around, anyway? Kids were nothin' but trouble, and now this pain-in-the-ass kid with her weird hung-up personality was pulling some stupid disappearin' act and Cee Cee had to find her. Had to. Shit. She was the goddamned babysitter, for chrissake. South. If the kid had any class she would have headed south. That was where the real fancy houses were. Cee Cee decided to walk south on the beach and look for her. She walked down to the water, thinking she would have a better view of the whole beach if she walked along the shoreline.

Nina. Where the fuck *was* she?

Later, when Cee Cee told Bertie how it happened, she said she wasn't sure what it was that made her look back at the house, but when she did, something pink and very still caught her eye. Something under the deck of the old wooden Cape Cod house.

"Nina," Cee Cee yelled. And then she ran toward the house.

Nina didn't move. Just sat staring out at the sea. She was wearing bright pink baby-doll pajamas. "You okay, kid?" Cee Cee asked, out of breath now as she fell to a sitting position on the sand a few feet away from the little girl. Nina didn't look at her.

"Yeah," Nina said.

"When'd you come out here? I didn't even see you," Cee Cee said.

"You were asleep," Nina said. "It was real early."

"When your mom got up?" Cee Cee asked, edging a little closer, and realizing for the first time that she was still dressed in the terry-cloth robe.

"Right after," Nina said. "But she didn't see me neither 'cause she was on the telephone."

Oh, shit, Cee Cee thought. Oh, no.

"So did you just come right out here, or did you go downstairs and have a glass of O.J.?" Cee Cee asked, and actually crossed her fingers behind her back, hoping what she knew was true might not be.

"Huh-uh," Nina answered, then reached down and started picking at the toenail on the big toe of her right foot. "I didn't want breakfast 'cause I wasn't hungry," she said. "So I sat on the floor in the hallway for a while."

"Bet you could eat a horse now though, right?" Cee Cee said. "How 'bout I make a nice big breakfast?" Cee Cee tried.

"No, thank you."

"Lunch, maybe? Great big plate of spaghetti? I like spaghetti. It doesn't like me though. Gives me thunder thighs. But I'm crazy about it. Crazy enough to take you out for some right now. Want some spaghetti?"

"No, thank you."

"You gonna stay here all day or what?"

Nina nodded.

"Forever?"

Nina nodded again.

"Well, you're gonna miss a lot of real good times if you do," Cee Cee said, pulling a cigarette out of her pocket. No matches. "Parties. Like the one we're having on Sunday."

"You shouldn't smoke," Nina said, looking at the cigarette. "My mom stopped last year."

"I know," Cee Cee said, "but I can't."

"How come?"

"Because I'm too uptight," she answered. Christ. Now she had to answer to a kid?

"You mean like toonies?" Nina asked, brightening.

"What?" Cee Cee asked her.

"Toonies uptight."

Cee Cee was getting very uncomfortable. It was hot and musty under the deck, and she wanted to go inside and take a shower, and then have some lunch, for chrissake. She was starving.

"Like in the song," Nina said.

Cee Cee had had enough. Kids could manipulate you after a while, just by pouting, and this one wanted to sit here under the goddamn deck and chat. She was just about to get up and say, Listen, you little brat, you woke up, you tiptoed around, and you probably heard your mother begging your father to meet you and you're pissed off 'cause he said no. Well, you know what? Life is tough. Real tough. But as she started to stand, the meaning came to her.

"You mean 'Ballin' the Jack'?" she asked Nina. "*That* song?"

"Uh-huh," Nina said. "I learned it in my dancing school class."

"You swing 'em to the left and you swing 'em to the

right," Cee Cee said, and Nina smiled, and then they both
sang:

> *Step around the floor kinda nice and light.*

And Cee Cee deliberately stopped as Nina's perfect
little voice sang:

> *And then you twist around and twist around*
> *with all your might.*

Nina, proud of herself, grinned a grin Cee Cee hadn't
seen on her ever before. It was Bertie's grin.

"I learned it in my dancing school class, too," Cee
Cee said. "Did you do this with your hands?" she asked,
holding her hands up to her face as if they were a frame.

"No. We did *this*," Nina said, putting her little hands
on her little hips.

"Why don't you come up to the deck," Cee Cee said,
"and I'll show you the way I learned it."

Nina got up slowly and shook the sand from her legs
and the seat of her pajamas.

"Race you," she said.

The Polo Lounge was buzzing with people talking and
laughing, and every table Bertie could see was full. She
felt queasy and shaky and afraid. It was five years since
she'd seen Michael. He sat at the bar facing away from the
door. She looked for a moment at the curly hair, now with
a lot of gray in it, and the spot on the back of his head
which had been balding a tiny bit, showed much more
scalp than she remembered. Then, as if he felt her looking
at him, Michael turned, saw her, smiled, and stood.

They walked toward one another and hugged, a for-
mal hug. His smell, and the feeling of his arms, even the
coldness of the hug felt familiar to Bertie. The maître d'
led them to a table in a far corner.

"Well, how *are* you?" Michael asked, after a moment. And for that second, it seemed to Bertie as if he honestly wanted to know.

"I'm good," Bertie said. "This meeting feels a little odd, but I'm good."

A defensive look crossed Michael's eyes. "Bert, *you* called *me*," he said.

Bertie wanted so badly to be cool. To say the right thing. To be able, without a scene, to let him know how she felt. Michael, of course it's odd. You're the absent father of our six-year-old child. She looks like you, behaves like you, reminds me every day of my life when I look at her that you're not there and haven't once seen her face or let her see yours. And every time she asks me why you don't come to see her, I want to shriek, don't ask me. Call him. Your father. Call the cold, withholding, repressed, self-important son of a bitch, and ask *him* why he won't.

But instead, Bertie put her hand over his and told him how glad she was to see him and how good she thought he looked. His eyes softened and the waitress came, and they ordered Bloody Marys. After they'd each had one and Michael ordered another round, he looked down at the table and asked Bertie, "What does she know about me?"

"That you left before she was born, so it had nothing to do with her. That you're a very busy man and that's why you've never come to see her, and that maybe someday you will." Bertie hoped he couldn't hear the pleading in her voice.

Michael didn't say anything. Just took the pink Sweet 'n' Low packs from the little green holder and made small piles of them across the table in front of his place.

"That's true, I guess. I mean, maybe someday I will."

Once when Bertie was in the third grade she saw a tough boy in her class, Daniel McNally, twist the arm of Sharon Acklin, who screamed, and then Donny Kraft took the girl's other arm and twisted it. Bertie was horrified, and she ran at both boys with such fierce anger that even though she was a tiny little girl, she frightened them away. Later, when she described the event to her mother, she said she was always so afraid of those boys herself that she wasn't sure what had made her suddenly so brave. Rosie laughed and told her that sometimes it was easier to have guts for someone else. Now she would have guts for Nina.

"How about today, Michael? How about now? This week? Please. Not for me. Not for you—but for Nina. Even if it's just so in school, when the kids make Father's Day cards, she can make one, too, and send it off to you. She needs that, Michael. Just that little bit. I promise I won't ask for more."

Michael's face reddened.

"No," he said. "I told you my answer this morning on the phone. I thought about it all night, Bert, and I'm sorry, I don't feel like she's my child. I'll support her all of her life, but I don't have any feelings about her and I don't want to."

Bertie sat for a moment, letting what he'd just said really sink in. Wanting to remember how hateful he was so she'd never in a weak moment think their divorce was a mistake. Then she stood.

"Is the visit over?" Michael asked.

Bertie didn't respond. She made her way to the door of the Polo Lounge and out through the pink and green lobby of the hotel.

"Okay, sit down. Sit down, Mom. Sit down."

"Bert, for chrissake. Sit down and get ready for this."

"You all right, Mom? Sit down. Watch me. Watch this."

"Bert . . . you okay?"

Bertie could only nod as Nina and Cee Cee pulled her to the deck chair, and then, full out, with the glorious ocean waves smashing to the shore as their backdrop, Cee Cee, in her green terry-cloth robe, a bathroom plunger for her cane, and Nina, still in her pink baby-doll pajamas, a yardstick from the local hardware store for her cane, sang:

First you put your two knees close up tight . . .

Michael. How could a man not want to see, even for a moment, a child he'd created?

> *Then you swing 'em to the left*
> *And ya swing 'em to the right . . .*

Nina sang in her little girl version of Cee Cee's soul voice. Cee Cee winked at Bertie as the two of them moved into the dance steps.

Step around the floor kinda nice and light . . .

And now they both shimmied. Nina wasn't exactly sure how, but it was a good try.

> *Twist around and twist around*
> *With all your might . . .*

That was a conversation she had waited nearly seven years to have. Always harboring the hope that there was some part of Michael that was loving or warm or tender and would reach out for Nina. The hopelessness of the situation began to depress her, but she stopped it, caught herself, shook it off, and refused to let it hurt.

Fuck him, Bertie thought. It will be all right. *We'll* be all right. It doesn't matter what he does, and she grinned to herself, and then at her daughter, and at her very best wonderful friend.

Nina was only as high as Cee Cee's waist, and the picture of the two of them doing the same steps was the

cutest thing Bertie had ever seen. Both Hollywood performers raised their arms, holding their canes above their
heads, and then they did big high kicks.

> *Spread your lovin' arms way out in space*
> *And then do the eagle rock*
> *With style and grace . . .*

A few people had gathered on the beach below and were
watching the musical number from the back.

> *You put your left foot out*
> *And bring it back . . .*

Then Cee Cee gave Nina a nudge with her elbow, and
Nina sang:

> *And that's what I call . . .*

Then Cee Cee sang:

> *And that's what I call . . .*

And then they sang together:

> *And that's what we call ballin' . . .*

And they did a spin.

> *Ballin' the jack!!!!!*

Their arms were in the air and their happy voices
rang loud and true.

The people on the beach applauded. Cee Cee and
Nina bowed and hugged one another. Bertie gave them a
standing ovation.

After the "Three Musketeerettes," as they decided to
call themselves, had a lemonade and some sun, they went

out to buy a few little things for Sunday's party. Some beer, some soft drinks, some nuts for nibbling. Next to the supermarket was the Malibu kid's store. Cee Cee saw Nina looking in the window at the clothes. While Bertie and the boy pushing the grocery cart walked out of the Market Basket and to the car where they unloaded the bags into the trunk, Cee Cee got Nina to try on, admit she looked great in, and decide maybe she'd been wrong about, jeans. And then, just so she'd have something new to wear to the party on Sunday, Cee Cee bought her a pair.

DEAR AUNT CEE CEE,

THIS IS A THANK YOU NOTE FOR ALL THE PRESENTS YOU SENT ME ON MY BIRTHDAY. I LIKE THE SWEATSHIRT THAT SAYS ROLLING STONES ON IT THE BEST. I LIKE THE EARRINGS BUT MY MOM SAYS I CAN'T WEAR THEM TILL I'M A LOT OLDER. THE GOLD TIGHTS WERE SO GOOD. AND THE FEATHER THING THAT MY MOM SAYS IS A BOA. AND I REMEMBER THAT BECAUSE IT IS LONG LIKE THE BOA THAT MRS. LIEBMAN MY TEACHER SOMETIMES CARRIES AROUND HER NECK NAMED LUMPY.

LOVE,

NINA B.
XXXXXXXXXXXXXXXXXXXXXXXXXXXXX
OOOOOOOOOOOOOOOOOOOOOOOOOOOO

Dear Bert,

I tried to call you last night and that baby-sitter there said something about your being in the hospital. Then when I asked what hospital she got all weird and wouldn't tell me anything. Hope you were just visiting a sick friend.

I'll call again tonight.

Meanwhile, watch Channel Four next Thursday because Sarah! is on, and you can sing along with Cee Cee, and if you let her stay up that late, Nina can watch me ham it up, too.

I just signed to do a new picture opposite Burt Reynolds. It's a great part and the studio says they're going to promote the shit out of it. So things are looking good for me, kiddo. My weight is down and my hopes are up. (That sentence shows you why I sing and act and don't write for a living.)

Come visit and I'll introduce you to Burt Reynolds. You two would be cute together. When you got married it would say Burt and Bertie on your cocktail napkins.

C.

SARASOTA JUNIOR DANCE GROUP
SPRING RECITAL

SLEEPY TIME GALS . . . Erin Laughlin, Maria
   Dawes, Marcia Carsey.
HUNGARIAN RHAPSODY . . . Stacey Bishop.
RAT-A-TAT-TAT . . . Bobby Lennox, Richard
   Dean, Mike Halloran.
TAPPERS ON PARADE . . . Susan Moll, Heidi
   Brotman, Nina Barron, Gail Andrews.

Dear Cee—
   She was terrific.

B.

Carmel, California, 1983

In a matter of minutes, fueled by exhilaration, Cee Cee was guiding the big Chevy down the highway, approaching the Ocean Avenue turnoff. Shit, she didn't have those written directions with her anymore. Must have left them in the house. And she wasn't sure she remembered the name of the street now, or even if she'd recognize the house. Right turn on Ocean. But what was it? Ahh. Carmelo. And left and . . . This time she didn't take her suitcase out of the car because she was rushing.

When she pushed the front door open, the fire in the fireplace was dwindling and Jessica was no longer in the living room.

"Hello," Cee Cee called out, hoping the nurse would hear her, but that she wouldn't disturb Bertie. She walked up the stairs. The bedroom door was closed. The bathroom door opened and Jessica emerged. She looked surprised to see Cee Cee.

"Why, I thought you were . . ."

"Jessica," Cee Cee said, feeling the flame of her

conviction rising in her cheeks. "Don't take this the wrong way, but you're fired."

The older woman's eyes opened wide and she looked blankly at Cee Cee.

"I mean, Bertie doesn't need you here. Won't be needing you here anymore, because I'm here, and I'm gonna do it and I'm her friend. So that way it won't be so nursey, Jessica, it'll be friendly because . . ."

Cee Cee was crying, and Jessica pulled a handkerchief out of the pocket of her white uniform and handed it to her. Cee Cee wiped her eyes and went on. "Because I love her," she said. "So you'll have to teach me to be her primary-care giver. You and Janice. About pills and bathroom detail and rubdowns and CPR, whatever that is. And I guess you'll even have to teach me what to do when she finally hits the road," she said, not believing these words were coming from her mouth. "Like the details about who I gotta call to come and get the remains." That thought made her shiver, but she went on. "You know what I'm sayin', Jessica? I mean I'm talkin' about *me* doin' the whole enchilada. On my own." Cee Cee blew her nose into Jessica's handkerchief.

"That's very lovely," the nurse said, "but are you sure you—"

"Sure?" Cee Cee said, and laughed a little laugh. "Let me put it this way, hon. Once, when I was a kid, a bird fell off a wire, and I watched it die on the sidewalk in front of my apartment building. I was twelve, and that was the only dead creature I've ever seen in my whole life before or since. I say the only one because when my mother died, by the time I got back from summer stock to the funeral, there was this closed coffin. You know? It coulda been empty for all I knew. And the other people I knew who died? I was too chicken to go to their funerals. Thought it was too spooky. Too weird. So that's my experience with the dyin'. What I'm tryin' to tell ya is, that I'm not sure one bit, and in fact I don't have a clue here. So do me a favor, okay, and lay it on me real slow and careful. And get ready to hear the dumbest questions you ever heard, and for me to make like there's no way in America I'm ever gonna get through it. And for me to make dumb mistakes, and maybe even puke 'cause I'm scared or turned off or both."

The older woman looked at Cee Cee the way she might at a mental patient, but Cee Cee went on: "But I'm *doin'* this, Jessica. I'm, excuse my language, goddamned fuckin' *doin'* this, no matter what else happens in the world."

That statement made Jessica look flustered for a second, and it seemed to Cee Cee as if she might begin to cry herself, but after a moment she gathered her forces together and looked almost pleased, and she said, "Well, then, let's go downstairs and get started."

Cee Cee and Jessica sat at the kitchen table until morning, and Cee Cee learned about titrating Bertie's medication for pain, and how she would eventually have to be able to lift and move Bertie from the bed to the wheelchair and back again, how when Bertie was no longer able to get out of the bed, she would have to make the bed with Bertie in it. How to feed her, how to wash her, how to turn and massage her, how to use and clean the portable commode. And, finally, when the millions of questions Cee Cee asked seemed to be answered, the nurse took her hand and patted it.

"I'm afraid you'll have plenty of time for hands-on application of all of this soon," she said.

It was six A.M. Jessica made some coffee. When Bertie opened her eyes a few hours later, the morning sun poured into her room so powerfully that for a moment she couldn't make out who was standing there. When she saw Cee Cee, she was sure she must still be dreaming. And when the apparition said she was staying for an unlimited amount of time, and then told her in a voice that sounded as if someone from the British stage had dubbed it in, "as your primary-care giver," Bertie's reaction, which made Cee Cee's face fall, was a peal of unreserved laughter.

"Hey, I said I'm gonna take čare of you, Bert," she said giddily. "Aren't you glad?"

Bertie couldn't stop laughing and when she finally did, she looked a little nervous.

"Cee Cee," she said. "This isn't a movie. You're not going to be Sarah Bernhardt nursing the wounded during the siege of Paris, wasting away because you gave your food to a handsome soldier. This is real death. With tubes and pain and injections and foul-smelling excretions. No offense or anything, Cee Cee, but the truth is I called you here for laughs, not nursing. I love you a lot. You've been a wonderful friend throughout my brief but boring life. Now go home. Jessica . . . send her . . ."

But Jessica had discreetly left them alone.

"I'm not leavin'," Cee Cee said.

"Oh, yes, you are," Bertie said as harshly as she could muster.

"Uh-uh."

"Cee Cee," Bertie said, "I want to die the way I want to die, and you're spoiling it. Now the discussion is over."

"Hey, Bert," Cee Cee said, pleading with her, "you gotta gimme a chance, for chrissake."

"This isn't an audition," Bertie snapped. "And if it was, you'd be wrong for the part." Then she called out, "Jessica!"

"I fired her," Cee Cee said.

Bertie laughed a shocked laugh. "You didn't. You're crazy. Jessica!"

"But don't worry," Cee Cee said. "She'll stick around for a few days to train me."

"No," Bertie said. "No, no, no." She was laughing, but outraged at the same time.

Cee Cee walked over to a chair nearby, picked up a copy of *Time* magazine, then sat and opened it in front of her face as if she were reading.

"What's going to happen to that TV show you were rehearsing?" Bertie asked. "They'll fire you or sue you. Can't they do that?"

Cee Cee didn't answer. Just kept holding up the magazine.

"What are you doing?" Bertie asked.

"I'm takin' care of you," she heard Cee Cee say from behind the magazine.

"No," Bertie said, "you aren't."

"I even know how to cook now, Bert, I learned when I was outta work for a while."

"Cee Cee, whether you can cook or not is hardly the point."

"Fuck you," came the reply.

"Cee Cee!"

"And you know what else?" Cee Cee said, flinging the magazine to the floor, "as soon as you have your breakfast, you and me are going to the beach."

During the next few weeks, Bertie was still able to get out of bed and dress herself, and sometimes after a little coaxing from Cee Cee she might even put a little blusher on her cheeks. Then, slowly, she'd make her way downstairs. Cee Cee would help her into the car and drive down Ocean Avenue to the beach area, find a parking spot and help her out of the car. Then Cee would put her right arm around Bertie's waist and almost completely support Bertie's weight. She would also carry two blankets, a backrest, her purse, and a bag of things they might need under her left arm, and walk down the sandy hill to a spot where the sand was nearly level. When they found the perfect spot, Cee Cee would spread one blanket, place the backrest on it, help Bertie down, cover her legs with the second blanket, and sit next to her.

The bag Cee Cee packed very early in the morning, before Bertie was even ready for breakfast, was loaded with goodies. Juice and yogurt and bread crumbs for the sea gulls, and magazines the drugstore had delivered after

Cee Cee called them and told them, "Send over one of each," and she would read Bertie the articles.

"Okay," Cee Cee said. "This one's from *Cosmopolitan,* it's called 'Single Men: Where to Meet Them, How to Dazzle Them.'" Bertie would laugh and Cee Cee would rewrite the article as she read it: "Single men may come on to you at the beach if you're sitting with a dying friend." Bertie gave her a weak punch on the arm. Cee Cee continued as if she were reading.

"'You two girls doing anything next week?' the man may ask. 'Well, I'm available,' you should answer, 'but my friend here may be dead.'"

"Cee Cee!" Bertie said, throwing a magazine at her and laughing.

Sometimes they would just quietly feed the sea gulls for hours.

Once, two little girls were flying a kite. Running and falling and laughing. Cee Cee watched Bertie watching them. Cee Cee weighed her words carefully before she spoke, but she had to say this:

"Bert, Nina ought to be here. To say good-by. Otherwise, she's gonna grow up thinkin' that people she loves just go off someplace, disappear, and die. That's bad for her, Bert." For an instant after she said it she was afraid, with Bertie being so weak and all, that maybe she was wrong to bring up something that was so painful. No. Fuck it. She knew she was right about this.

"No," Bertie said, "absolutely not."

Cee Cee wanted to press, to talk her into it. Convince her. But she didn't. And she hated herself for changing the subject. Rattling on and on about some Hollywood gossip. And she was relieved when Bertie laughed at the stories, a big belly laugh.

On most days, Bertie would doze or ask for her medication, and Cee Cee, who carried the packets of medication in her purse, would give her what she needed, along with some juice from the thermos in the bag.

When Bertie had had enough of the beach, Cee Cee would pack everything up, saving the blanket for after she had carefully helped Bertie to her feet. Then, slowly, they would move to the top of the slope to the waiting car. When they got back to the house, Cee Cee would help her friend into the bathroom, then back into bed, then go downstairs and make them a light dinner of eggs or pasta. After they ate, Cee Cee would lie on the cot that Janice Carnes had brought over for her and read to Bertie from the Monterey paper or the *Carmel Pine Cone*.

"Ya know what? There's no crime in this town. No wonder I don't like it here," she said one day. "They got the daily police reports written in this *Pine Cone* paper. And here's one of 'em. 'A dead squirrel was found on the corner of Fifth and Dolores. Police called to the scene, removed the animal and'—Bert . . ."

Bertie was asleep. She slept longer now, and woke up for shorter intervals. Cee Cee was exhausted and was grateful for the opportunity to grab some sleep, too. Janice Carnes still came by to help around the house, and she had found Cee Cee a young woman named Madeline, who lived in Pacific Grove, who drove in to Carmel every other day to do the heavier housecleaning, so *that* wasn't a problem. It was having to be constantly alert, and be ever-patient, and moving so slowly to help Bertie get around, and never knowing when Bertie would call out to her, so even when Cee Cee was reading or napping, her mind could never be free of Bertie's needs. The television special she'd been rehearsing was canceled indefinitely after dozens of phone calls to Los Angeles and threats from managers, agents, and lawyers about having her drummed out of show business. She could tell that they didn't believe her anyway from the yeah, sure, right, too bad kind of response they gave her when she told them the truth about why she wasn't coming back for a while.

She only had the clothes she'd brought with her in the little overnight bag on that night that now seemed centuries ago when she first arrived. And the clothes she was wearing that night. So every other day, she would change them, and Madeline would wash whichever outfit Cee Cee wasn't wearing at the time.

The clothes were getting tighter and tighter on her, because while she cooked the meals she would nibble, and while Bertie stared at her own food Cee Cee would hungrily wolf down hers, and when she took the dishes downstairs, before she washed them she would nervously nibble what Bertie had left on her plate, which most of the time was the entire meal.

The only time that Cee Cee spent away from Bertie was the few hours a week that Jessica came to check on them, or Janice stopped in for a visit. When Cee Cee was certain that Bertie was in good hands, she'd run out, hop into the car, and do errands. The shopping center on the highway had everything she needed. Market, drugstore, bakery. In fact, it was in that shopping center that she got the idea that she was sure would make Bertie think she was a maudlin schmuck. Or not. Maybe she'd actually like it. When Cee Cee walked into the store and told the owner what she wanted, it helped that he recognized her from the movies, so he knew she could afford it. She wrote him a check and somehow they managed to get a big sheet over it and fit it into the trunk of the pain-in-the-ass rental car.

When Bertie woke up at about five that afternoon, Cee Cee said, "Let's go downstairs." Bertie agreed, even though she wasn't sure she felt able to get out of bed. Cee Cee helped her to her feet, and dressed her in a warm robe and slippers, and led her down the stairs.

"Oh, God," Bertie said with a smile. "In July, Cee. It's gorgeous."

The Christmas tree was perfectly decorated from top to bottom with perfect, delicate ornaments and tinsel, and the multicolored strings of teeny-tiny lights blinked on and off warmly. The tree stood in the corner and looked almost picked-from-the-forest real.

"The Holiday Hutch," Cee Cee said. "That store in the shopping center. They sell ornaments and stuff all year round. So when I saw it I figured . . ."

"It's perfect."

"Are you sure?" Cee Cee asked. "I mean, Chanukah I know from. If the assignment was to bring a menorah, I would have been aces, but I had to take this guy's word for it."

Bertie put her arms around her friend.

"Merry Christmas, pal," she said, and hugged her as tightly as she was able.

That was the last time Bertie was downstairs. In the days that followed, it became too difficult for her to get out of bed. Twice a day Cee Cee would gently turn her on her stomach and give her back rubs, and while she was rubbing she would sing songs from her old nightclub act. And then she'd remember the patter that she'd done in between the songs. "Once, in this toilet club, I told this audience, 'We'd like to do a little medley now of songs I've recently recorded.' I didn't mention the fact that where I'd recently recorded them was into my tape recorder in my bedroom." She could feel Bertie's giggle.

Soon, getting as far as the bathroom was difficult without exhausting Bertie, and Jessica arrived with the portable commode. She taught Cee Cee how to help Bertie use it, and how to clean it.

"Cee," Bertie said. "It's too much. Too much for you to do this. We'll get Jessica to come here more often. You have to stop this."

"What?" Cee Cee said, with a look of mock alarm. "And get outta show business?" Bertie didn't know what that meant, so Cee Cee told her the story of the guy who worked in the circus, whose only job was to clean up after the elephants, just follow behind the parade and clean up after the elephants, and finally one day someone asked him why he kept such a job. Why didn't he quit? And the guy said—but Cee Cee didn't get to finish because Bertie smiled and said the punchline softly. " 'What? And get out of show business?' That's funny."

But on the first day when Cee Cee took the bowl of the toilet into the bathroom to empty and clean it, it wasn't funny. She talked to herself for strength. Now, this is the test. How can I fuckin' do this? How can I keep it together? I don't think I can do this for another day. Maybe I made a mistake. No more. I can't. But her life had become hooked into Bertie's and her thoughts so attuned to Bertie's every sigh in the night that by the next day she emptied the toilet as if she were a nurse who had done it for years. Not Cee Cee Bloom of stage, screen, and television whose maid, secretary, cleaning lady, business manager, manager, and agent had separated her from the everyday realities for years, never mind the horrible realities like terminal illness and death. Impending death. Now she could see that it was closer every day.

Cee Cee called her business manager one morning when it occurred to her that none of her bills were getting paid at home, since she wasn't there to sign the checks.

"Cee Cee," Wayne said, in a tone that she recognized as a phony glad-ta-hear-from-ya-kiddo voice, because she'd used it many times herself. After they'd discussed her financial business, he asked if he could mail her some scripts of movies people wanted her to consider, and she said yeah, what the hell. When the scripts arrived from Air Express, Cee Cee left the unopened envelope on the coffee table. After a few days she opened it, and tried to read while Bertie slept. But she couldn't concentrate. All she could hear were Bertie's breaths in and out. Were they steady? Normal? Was she comfortable? Warm enough? Medicated enough?

One afternoon, Jessica noticed Cee Cee's bloated, unmade-up, tired face.

"Why don't you get out of here for a few hours and see a movie?" the nurse asked her.

A movie. Maybe that would be a good change. Cee Cee drove to the multiplex theater in the shopping center and walked to the ticket window.

"Gimme a ticket," she said absently, putting her cash on the counter.

"Which picture?" the cashier asked, gesturing to the marquee.

Cee Cee hadn't even noticed. There were four movies playing. She had to choose one, and she looked at the titles. No. No. No. No. Forget movies. She put her money back in her purse and drove back to the house. She was overwhelmed with exhaustion, but it wasn't just the fatigue that was getting to her. Jessica had told her that she should expect this depression. That she was already mourning the loss of her friend. But it was even more than that. She was aching inside, in her stomach, the way she did when she knew something was very wrong.

The minute she realized what it was, her mind was made up, and she made the necessary phone calls. At four o'clock the next day, when Janice came to the house to visit Bertie, Cee Cee left for the airport.

The little girl stood at the top of the steps, holding the stewardess's hand. She was a foot taller than the last time Cee Cee had seen her. And slim. She had grown to look like her mother. Had Bertie's nose-in-the-air style. She was the last passenger to emerge. Cee Cee had watched all of the others, envying them their casual laughter and greetings to one another, knowing that any minute it was her job to tell a little girl that her mother was dying. After the poor kid's fuckin' father left her before she was born. Christ, Cee Cee thought, the kid could be weirded out for the rest of her life.

Nina spotted Cee Cee right away, and she let go of the hand of the stewardess and walked with great poise down the steps. Cee Cee walked toward the plane. When the child got to the bottom and saw Cee Cee waving, she stopped moving.

What do I say now? Cee Cee thought. What do I . . . She reached out for the child.

"My mother's dying," Nina said.

Cee Cee was grateful they were hugging so the child couldn't see her face.

"Aunt Neetie said she only has a short time left, so she probably looks awful and scary and doesn't feel well, so I'll have to be careful not to disturb her and—"

"Hey, Nina," Cee Cee said, moving the child away so she could look at her. Nina's eyes were almost squinting, as if she thought keeping them that way would help her not to cry.

"I want you to disturb her. I want you to do all the things you'd do at home. Crash into the room. Fall on the bed. Hug and kiss her if you feel like it. Even if she does look a little different. Skinnier, and her hair isn't great and sometimes—"

"She wears a wig," Nina said.

Thank you, God, for making this a tiny bit easier, Cee Cee thought.

"She wore it in Florida sometimes when she had radiation therapy."

"But it doesn't matter how people look," Cee Cee said, hoping the kid would buy it. "Does it? When you love them and they love you?" That was so saccharine she couldn't believe she said it. Neither, obviously, could Nina.

"If she loves me so much, how come she left and lied and said she was going on some trip?"

"So you wouldn't have to feel the way you feel now," Cee Cee said, walking the child toward the baggage claim. "Scared about how she looks or how fragile she is. To protect you. But you don't need protection from your mother, do you?"

"No," Nina said. But while they stood by the con-

eyor belt waiting for her suitcase, she held tightly on to
Cee Cee's hand.

Bertie was restless. Her sleeps were filled with dreams
of being cured and well and, sometimes, still married to
Michael. Today the dream was about being at La Mont, a
restaurant overlooking Pittsburgh, where she and Michael
used to go. At night the view of the rivers was beautiful.
And Walt Harper's band played there every weekend.
The dream was so real that Bertie could hear the music
playing, and she looked across the table lovingly at Michael and she said, "Why don't we dance, Mickey Mouse?"
And though she could tell by his expression that he didn't
want to, he said, "Sure, Minnie," and stood and took her
hand and held her. As they danced, Bertie moved her face
back and forth on the lapel of his coat, loving the way it
felt, and the song the band had been playing blended into
another song, and then that song segued into another
song, and Bertie was happy and peaceful until she felt
Michael take his arm away from her back and when she
looked to see why, she realized it was in order to look
impatiently at his watch. When his eyes caught hers, he
looked guilty and then said angrily, "Ahhh, c'mon, Bert.
How much longer is this going to go on, for God's sake?"

She woke up with Michael's voice and those words
repeating themselves, and she found herself shivering in
the dimly lit bedroom, which it took her a few moments to
place. Carmel. The rented house in Carmel.

"Cee Cee," she called out, but there was no answer.

"Cee Cee," she said, a little bit louder. Maybe Cee
Cee could bring her another blanket. But there was no
sound. Ah, now someone was coming up the stairs. Someone who stood outside the door for a second. Good. It
must be Cee Cee who had heard her and was—

"Hi, Mom," Nina said.

Dear God. Bertie closed her eyes. Maybe this was
just more dream, but Nina was on the bed, kissing her

and hugging her, warming her, and laughing. Cee Cee
stood in the hallway, holding her breath, until she hear
Bertie laughing, too, and the sound that two long-lo:
people make when they're excited to see one anothe
again. The way the pitch of their voice rises and the
words jumble together as their thoughts rush out. So sh
went downstairs to make dinner.

By the time she came back with the trays of food
Nina had her shoes and socks off and was lying next t
Bertie on the bed, leafing through a fashion magazine
showing her mother which outfits she loved and whic
ones were "too dorky." And Bertie, with her arm aroun
her daughter, was all smiles.

Nina devoured her dinner, and Cee Cee noticed tha
even though she didn't stop chattering, she never onc
forgot her perfect manners. Bertie seemed to love th
time they were having, but she didn't once look at Ce
Cee. Not when Cee Cee took the trays from the bed, o
when she asked if anybody needed anything else from
downstairs. Bertie, the soul of manners, didn't thank he
for dinner. Usually she raved over the food, even thoug
she had little or no appetite. And she didn't, even whe
Nina told a funny joke, look at Cee Cee proudly the wa
she ordinarily would to share her joy.

When the meal was over Cee Cee carried the tra
downstairs and washed the dishes, and Nina took a bath
After that, clad in her pajamas, she kissed her mother an
ran downstairs with a quick hug for Cee Cee.

"Tomorrow, can I put some more tinsel on the Christ
mas tree?" Nina asked.

"You bet," Cee Cee said. "Are you glad to be here
Neen?" Cee Cee asked her.

Nina's answer was just to hug her again. Tighter. An
then she was off to tuck herself in, in one of the gues
bedrooms.

Cee Cee made some tea for herself and for Bertie an
then walked up the wooden stairs carrying the steaming

cups. Feeling good. Feeling proud of herself. Certain that she'd done the right thing. When she got to the bedroom door she pushed it open with the side of her right arm. Bertie was sitting up, staring at the wall across the room.

"Nina asleep?" Bertie asked brusquely.

"Yeah," Cee Cee said, and put Bertie's teacup on the table next to Bertie's side of the bed.

"I want you to leave," Bertie said after a moment. "I want Jessica back here full-time, starting tomorrow. I want you out of here, Cee Cee. I knew it was a mistake to let you stay here to begin with. Because you weren't doing it for me. You were doing it for you. To prove to yourself that you weren't the crazy selfish flake you've thought you've been all your life. Well, you're going to have to find that out somewhere else, because I'm not going to be your goddamned guinea pig for one more day."

Now she looked at Cee Cee, her brow furrowed.

"How you had the nerve, after I told you how I wanted it to be for me, to fly in the face of the wish of a dying person, and to expose my child to this horrible experience just to satisfy yourself, is beyond me. Pack your goddamned things and get out of here," she said. "Right now."

This person, this furious raging person, didn't even look like Bertie.

"Bert, please," Cee Cee said, sitting on the bed. "I thought—"

"Get off my bed," Bertie said. "I don't care what you thought. Get out of this house. I don't want you here. I don't want Nina here. I want to be by myself, so it doesn't matter if I want to scream when the pain hurts, or want to cry when I look out the window at the beautiful day and realize that the next time I leave this house it'll be in a goddamned plastic bag. I want you gone, Cee Cee, and I want Nina gone, too. Now get out."

"Bert, you're wrong. Getting Nina here was right. She needed this," Cee Cee tried.

"Why don't you get that you don't decide what's right here, and I do?" Bertie said between clenched teeth. "I'm the one who's dying. ME. ME. I'm the one who's helpless and in pain. I'm the one who won't live to see her daughter grow to be a woman, or even a teenager. Who won't be able to protect her from the world. And I have to die without ever having lived with a man who loves me passionately. Really understands me. Goddamn it, I feel cheated, Cee Cee. Ripped off, as you would say, because I don't want it to be over yet. I don't want it." She angrily swept her hand across the night table next to her, knocking to the ground a glass of water, the cup of tea, a thermometer, and some bottles of pills.

Cee Cee bent to pick them up.

"Leave them!" Bertie shrieked. "Leave them and leave me."

Cee Cee stood.

"I didn't want you to call Nina. Oh, my Nina," Bertie said, sobbing. "What will happen to my Nina?" She put her face in her pillow and wept.

"Maybe you'll give her to me," Cee Cee said so softly she was certain Bertie hadn't heard her.

But she had. Her wet swollen eyes turned on Cee Cee.

"Give her to you? My God, are you insane? Place the life of my child into the hands of a woman who's used cocaine and probably worse drugs than that, who's slept with God knows who and how many, who dresses like a whore and talks like a sailor?" She was screaming. "Cee Cee, you may fool them in the movies, but I know you faint in delivery rooms, and when the going gets tough you leave, you're obsessed with yourself and your career, and I don't ever want to speak to you or see you again, let alone give you my child. Now get out of here, Cee Cee Bloom, you asshole," she yelled in what was left of her voice. Then she turned her face to the pillow and cried uncontrollably.

Cee Cee sat slowly on the bed next to her. The bed shook from Bertie's deep and prolonged sighs. After a while, Cee Cee spoke. "Bert," she said, "I just can't tell you how great it is to see *you* be the crazy one for a change."

The next day, Madeline the cleaning girl was hired to come five days a week. She would take care of the house in the morning and in the afternoon take Nina walking in Carmel or to the wharf at Monterey.

Sometimes on days when Jessica was there, Cee Cee would take Nina out. To Point Lobos or down to Big Sur. The child would come back ecstatic about the harbor seals or the carousel at Cannery Row, as she and Cee Cee sat on Bertie's bed and they all ate dinner together. Once, in a burst of excitement, Nina said, "This is the most fun vacation I've ever had." Then, realizing what she'd said, she felt guilty, but Bertie grinned and said, "Isn't that great?"

After another week, Jessica had to put a catheter into Bertie, because it became clear that now even being lifted to the portable toilet was too tiring for her. Jessica also taught Cee Cee how to change the throwaway bedpads, and one night, after Jessica left and Nina was asleep, Cee Cee had to give Bertie a morphine injection. When the pain had subsided and Bertie slept, Cee Cee went outside, coatless in the crisp northern California night. She walked around the block a few times, taking deep breaths, wishing her head would stop pounding.

As she walked along the quaint Carmel streets, she heard a dog howl from somewhere. Through several windows she could see people watching their televisions. The eleven o'clock news was on. She felt bloated and aching. Soon this would be over. Soon Bertie would die, and Nina would go back to Florida and Cee Cee to Los Angeles. She would get busy with her career again, and in a year or two it would seem as if it all hadn't happened, except that there would be no more letters, phone calls, pictures in the mail from Bertie. And Nina? Maybe Cee Cee could convince Nina to write to her. Maybe even get Bertie's aunt to let the kid come to visit her once in a while.

She went back to the house, sat on the living room sofa, and read a script where they wanted her to play a female hockey player. She didn't sleep until dawn, and just as she drifted off she heard Bertie stir. It was almost time to make breakfast, so she went into the bathroom and filled a bowl with warm water, and added a few drops of Jean Naté to it, because Bertie said it reminded her of Aunt Neetie's house, and when she got to the bedroom, Bertie was awake.

"Nina still asleep?" Bertie asked.

Cee Cee nodded. Then she took a deep breath, hoping it would give her courage, and said, "Bert, I've been havin' this fantasy that you'd say, 'Cee, I've changed my mind. I want you to have Nina.' And I'd say, 'Me? Get outta here. I can't take care of another person. I'm a fainter, a whore, a sailor, and a junkie.' And then you'd say, 'Hey, you're crazy, Cee Cee. You used to be a fainter, a whore, a sailor, and a junkie, but since you came here you've been doin' a fabulous job with a guinea pig like me.' And I'd say, 'Bert, do you really think so?' And then this music would play. Real sentimental stuff—violins or somethin' like that. And then you'd say, 'Don't ya get it, Cee, even though you've been all those things and a pushy bitch to boot, you love life and you love this world, and you're full of laughs and jokes no matter what happens, so I think that maybe givin' the kid to some old aunt and uncle, as nice as they are, is a chickenshit way out. Because if Nina was with you, she'd have a real nice life of adventure and fun and craziness."

Cee Cee stopped talking, hoping Bertie would say something, anything, but Bertie didn't say a word. Just looked at the ceiling.

"Bert," Cee Cee said. "You gotta give her to me. I'm tellin' ya. I want her and it's right. I'll help her and I'll teach her. I'll show her a world your aunt and uncle never even heard of. And don't laugh at that because I mean the good parts. I swear. And I'll love her and hug her and every day I'll tell her stories about you. About me and you together. And I'll show her your letters. Ones you wrote when you were her same age, and lots of ages after that, because I have 'em all, Bert. I saved every one. Bertie, say yes. Say you'll call your aunt and the lawyers and tell them you changed your mind and that Nina's gonna live with me after you're not here anymore. And not out of politeness, either. But because you know I'm right that she could have a great life with me."

Bertie didn't say anything, and her brow was furrowed the way it was when she was in pain.

"You need medication?" Cee Cee asked.

After a while Bertie answered.

"No, Cee Cee," she said. "No." Cee Cee's heart sank. "I mean, no, I don't need medication," she added. "I'm thinking."

Cee Cee stood very still, as if Bertie's thinking was fragile, and any movement might upset it. Bertie didn't speak for a long time, and when she was ready to give her answer she turned to Cee Cee and looked into her eyes. Cee Cee's heart pounded in her throat. Bertie nodded, faintly, and then she said, "She'll be good for you."

Cee Cee wanted to shout and dance and scream, but instead she sat on the bed and gave Bertie a sponge bath. And when she'd finished she changed her into a fresh clean nightgown, and then she brought the phone to the bed so that Bertie could call the lawyers.

Nina seemed to like the idea. At least, she told her mother, unlike Neetie and Herbie, Cee Cee was "sort of young," which Bertie smiled about and Cee Cee made jokes about for days.

But then the joking stopped. Bertie's waking moments became very rare. When she was awake, she wasn't certain where she was. She asked for her mother many

times, and once she said something about having her
appendix out. One evening, she asked Cee Cee where Dr.
Wechsler was. Nina seemed afraid now, more reluctant to
come into the room, but still she did, sometimes when her
mother was asleep, to stand and look at her.

Jessica was at the house the day Bertie died. Cee Cee
was relieved. Because even though she had learned and
memorized all of the post-mortem procedures, she just
couldn't . . . not anymore.

Downstairs with Nina, she called Aunt Neetie in Florida. Neetie had received the news from the lawyer about
Cee Cee's taking Nina, so when she heard Cee Cee's
voice she was very cold, and didn't ask to speak to Nina.
In a businesslike voice she started to tell Cee Cee how she
would be shipping Nina's clothes and toys as soon as . . .

When Cee Cee could get a word in, she told Neetie
that Bertie was dead. At first Neetie was quiet. Then she
sobbed. It sounded to Cee Cee that through her sobs she
said, "Poor kid. She had everything."

Later, Cee Cee and Nina walked down Ocean Avenue to the hillside overlooking the beach.

"Whaddya say we take off our shoes?" Cee Cee asked.

Nina sat on the ground and removed her shoes. So
did Cee Cee. Then, together, arm in arm, the two of them
took a walk on the beach.

ABOUT THE AUTHOR

IRIS RAINER DART is a television and film writer as well as the bestselling author of *The Boys in the Mail Room* and *'Til the Real Thing Comes Along*. She lives in Los Angeles with her son, Greg Wolf, her daughter, Rachel, and her husband, Stephen Dart.

BANTAM
SHOP-AT-HOME
C·A·T·A·L·O·G

Special Offer
Buy a Bantam Book
for only 50¢.

Now you can have Bantam's catalog filled with hundreds of titles plus take advantage of our unique and exciting bonus book offer. A special offer which gives you the opportunity to purchase a Bantam book for only 50¢. Here's how!

By ordering any five books at the regular price per order, you can also choose any other single book listed (up to a $5.95 value) for just 50¢. Some restrictions do apply, but for further details why not send for Bantam's catalog of titles today!

Just send us your name and address and we will send you a catalog!